JAFFA BEACH

Historical Fiction

Fedora Horowitz

ISBN-10: 1481991701
ISBN-13: 9781481991704
Library of Congress Control Number: 2013906077
CreateSpace Independent Publishing Platform
North Charleston, South Carolina

PART I:

Palestine, 1943

1

Jerusalem

Her mother's voice reached the girl, "*Shifra*, are you still sitting by the window, daydreaming?" With a sigh, Shifra turned around and took in the drabness of the room.

The family lived in a two-room apartment on the second floor of a building in a narrow street in Geula, one of the two ultra orthodox neighborhoods in Jerusalem. From the kitchen, her mother's voice admonished her again. "Shifra, didn't you hear the bell of the kerosene man? He's passing through our street. Quick! Take the ten-liter container and this money. Tell the *neft* man he'll get the remainder next time."

In the street in front of each apartment building, Shifra saw women in *shaitels*, their black stockings showing underneath their long skirts.

The sky was gray. Shifra shivered. It was cold in Jerusalem, even now in March, the month that was supposed to bring back the sun she was longing for so much. Their apartment was always cold, though the kitchen's three primus stoves and the heating *tanur* in the big room were lit all the time. Their building was built with Jerusalem stone, heavy blocks of rock, dating probably from the time of the Prophets, Shifra thought, but that thought didn't warm her up.

She had arrived just in time. The *neft* man, walked alongside his cart, ringing a bell while the smell of gas invaded the narrow street. The women waited in line, Shifra the last one.

"*Nu, Shifrale, wus machst du,* what do you do?" the bearded man asked her with a smirk. She kept her head low, but he continued. "Oy, if the Almighty had blessed me with a son, I would love to have you as my *shnur,* my daughter-in-law. Since my *weib hot gistorben,* you know that my wife died, I feel so lonely."

Shifra didn't answer. She had heard these words before. Silently she handed the man his money, "My mother said she'll give you the rest next time." He counted it then gave her back two piastres. "Go buy yourself a bow for your beautiful hair," he said with a wink.

Shifra looked around. The street was deserted. She put the change in her pocket without a word, picked up the heavy can and started to climb the steps of her apartment, while from afar she heard the *neft* man ringing his bell again. It wasn't the first time the man had given her change, a few piastres, even when he was paid the right amount. For the last few weeks she'd had to listen to the man's litany. She had hidden the money in a tin can under her bed. It wouldn't be long before she would use this money for her dream.

"Hurry," her mother called Shifra from the top of the stairs. "There is much to do. Your father is going to come from *shul* soon, and you have to clean the rooms."

After Shifra's oldest sister married, her father decided that it was time for Shifra to stop going to *Beth Yaakov,* the girls' yeshiva. She was thirteen at the time. "She has to help raise the little ones," was his decision, though her father had never spoken directly to her on the subject. Actually, she didn't care for the school, where they spoke mostly Yiddish, leaving the *Lushen Kodesh*, the holy language, for the reading of the Holy Books. But she was fond of two of her classmates, Chana and Shula, and she missed them. Their tales had opened a window to a world she never knew existed. After she left school, it was very seldom that she met them, but what they told her remained printed in her memory.

"The sea is so beautiful, blue and huge. When you look at the horizon, it seems that the sea is one with the sky," Chana gushed enthusiastically one day, when she had just returned from visiting her cousins who lived near Tel-Aviv. "The water is warm, the waves cradle you. It is so delicious. When I grow up I want to live by the sea." Shifra loved the cheerful Chana.

When Shula invited Shifra to her home, Shifra discovered a house full of books, not only in Yiddish or Lushen Kodesh, but in English and other languages, too. "My father loves to read," Shula had said with pride, "There are so many things one can learn," she added. Shula told her that her father, who was born in Germany, had studied at the yeshiva, and also at the university. "Even before the Nazis came to power, he felt that it was no good for Jews to live in Germany. He left and came to Jerusalem. *Rebono shel Olam*, the Master of the Universe, guided his way."

That evening Shifra told her mother about her visit with Shula. Her father was home and overheard her. "Shifra is not allowed to go there anymore!" he screamed. As always, he did not talk to her directly. "Those books are the books of the devil."

Shifra's mother's face became livid, "You've heard your father," she whispered, "You can't go to Shula again."

Though Shifra made excuses for not visiting Shula, that didn't end their friendship, or Shifra's desire to read the books Shula lent her. As Palestine was under the British Mandate, the English language was an obligatory part of the curriculum, in yeshivas also. Shifra would wake up at dawn and read until her eyes hurt. She especially loved Andersen's story about the orphan girl selling matches in the frosty night in Copenhagen. Like that girl's eyes marveling at the warmth and the miracle of light, so Shifra's eyes opened wide at the miracle of reading.

Her mother called her a dreamer. Shifra, sitting by the window, wove stories in her mind. Many times she sang to herself melodies she had heard her mother sing when she cradled the babies. But Shifra was cautious not to sing when her father was home. She was told that a woman's voice could attract the devil. Singing was what Shifra loved most. She listened to the birds' calls and tried to imitate their trills. That's when she felt most alive. She'd love to be a bird, to feel free to sing, to feel free to fly over Chana's wondrous sea.

"We have to go to Mahane Yehuda," Shifra's mother woke her from her reverie. "Tomorrow is *Erev Shabbos*, there is no time to be idle. Take the baskets and let's go."

Mahane Yehuda was the open market on Jaffa Street, the main thoroughfare in Jerusalem. First they went to the *Shochet*, the slaughterer, to buy the chicken they ate only on *Shabbos*. Then she helped carry the baskets with fruits and vegetables after her mother bargained with the sellers, always succeeding in saving a few piastres. While crossing the street she saw the yellow bus with the sign "Jaffa" stopping not far from the market. "Hurry," her mother said, when Shifra slowed her pace, "stop looking around. The time moves fast and there is a lot to do at home."

On Friday evening after the meal, her father seemed to be in a good mood. While Shifra washed the dishes, she heard him say to her mother, "I have something to tell you. Today Klotznik, the matchmaker, came to the study house to talk to me."

"Not now," answered her mother, putting a finger on her lips, "*Vart, shpater,* wait until later."

That night Shifra couldn't fall asleep. What did her father mean? She remembered when Klotznik came to propose the *shammas'* son for her older sister. But Brana was eighteen at the time. When the entire household was quiet, she heard her father say, "It's Shifra. The *neft* man sent Klotznik to talk to me. He wants to marry her."

"You can't be serious," her mother said. "Shifra is barely fifteen. And he is about forty, if not more." Her mother's voice grew louder.

"Sh, sh," said her father, "Klotznik says that he has fallen in love with Shifra. He has only daughters. Shifra could bear a son, a son to say *Kaddish* after him. Think what a *mitzvah* that would be."

Shifra heard her mother turning and tossing in bed. "No," her mother said after a long pause, "she's too young. Shifra is still a child." But her father was snoring already.

Shifra couldn't sleep all night. At *shul* on *Shabbos* morning, though she had to strain her eyes to see through the dividing *mehitze,* she saw the *neft* man approaching her father. She couldn't hear but she saw the two men shaking hands at the end of their short conversation. Wiping his lips after the Shabbas meal, her father addressed his wife, "Get ready. We are going to celebrate a *chasana* on Lag Baomer," (the only holiday during the seven weeks between Passover and Shavuot when weddings are permitted by the Jewish Law).

"A *chasana*! A wedding! Father what are you saying? She's still a child," exclaimed her mother. She stopped suddenly when her husband, with frowning eyebrows, raised his hand to silence her.

That night Shifra's feelings went from despair to revolt. It's not right! They can't sell me to the *neft* man! There should be a law that parents can't decide their children's future! But she knew that she couldn't confront her father. He could do with her whatever he wanted. Even her mother couldn't change his mind. Her fate was sealed. She cried, her face burrowed in the pillow, afraid she might awake her siblings.

In the morning, after her father had gone to study and her mother was busy preparing the small children for school, she took the tin can with the small change she received from the *neft* man and went to count it in the privacy of the bathroom. She didn't know if the money was enough for the plan she had thought of during her sleepless night.

She realized that it was dangerous and maybe it wouldn't work, but she knew she had to act. Just to wait for the right opportunity. Until then, she was going to make herself *nishtvisendick,* as though she was not aware of what awaits her.

The opportunity arrived earlier than she had hoped for. One evening, about two weeks before Pessach, she overheard her father whispering to her mother, *"Nu, sheinele, vein?"* to which her mother, her cheeks blushing, replied, *"Morgen in der free-* tomorrow morning."

The next morning after her father and the children left for their yeshivas her mother said, "Shifra, I am going to *Mikve.* Take this note to Itzik, the grocer. I wrote everything we need on it. Ask him to add one more bottle of Kiddush wine for your father. He likes to take a sip not only on *Shabbos.* Tell Itzik that I'll come at the end of the month to pay the account."

Shifra kept quiet, though she felt tremulous. "It's going to happen, it's going to happen," her heart sang.

At the door, her mother turned around and after fishing a coin from her pocket said, "Shifrale, lately you've been such a good girl, you deserve a reward. Buy yourself something sweet from Itzik." And she left.

Quickly Shifra added the coin to the money in her tin can. She would hurry to Itzik, after which she would still have time for her own preparations. Every month when her mother went to the Mikve she spent a couple of hours there. At the ritual bath she met women neighbors and had a little *shmus,* talking and gossiping with them, especially now, when she had news, though Shifra was sure that at least half of the neighborhood already knew that she was promised to the *neft* man.

Shifra was out of breath when she arrived home, her arms filled with groceries. She packed two apples and a slice of black bread and threw her mother's old kerchief over her head. She didn't want to take any chances. She knew that she was known in the neighborhood as the girl with the golden hair. How many times her friends had told her that she collected the sun in her braids.

There was no mirror in their home. When her sister, before getting married, had asked her father to buy a mirror, he screamed, "No mirror in my house! Mirror is the devil's instrument. A woman has to be clean and modest."

Besides the *neft* man, nobody else had told her that she was pretty. And who could believe him, who looked at her with lecherous eyes?

Shifra wore two pairs of underwear, her old shoes and a dark jacket. Still wary of being recognized, she decided to walk randomly around the narrow streets of Geula until she found a way to Jaffa Street.

When she arrived at a wide street that she recognized as R'hov Strauss, she breathed more easily. She knew where she was. At the next corner she'd turn right into Jaffa Street.

Shifra didn't wait long for the fuming yellow bus. On the top was a sign with its destination written in three languages, English, Hebrew and Arabic. Shifra had a moment of confusion when the driver asked her if she wanted a one-way ticket, or *aloch hazor*.

"Where to?" The driver asked.

"Jaffa," She mumbled, without looking at him. She handed him all her money, not knowing the cost.

"You have enough to buy a two-way ticket," the driver said kindly. With her ticket in hand, and her cheeks burning, Shifra made her way toward the back of the bus, where she saw an empty seat.

She sat down and arranged the kerchief to hide most of her face. Her heart was beating loudly in her ears. What was she doing? How could she do this to her mother? She was sure that her father's anger would fall on her mother when they found her missing from home.

"*Azoy a bishe!*" Such a shame! Shifra imagined him screaming. "I'll not be able to look in the eyes of our neighbors. We are going to be the laughingstock of the community. And what am I suppose to tell the *neft* man?" Her mother would be standing there, the person to receive all the blame.

But when the driver announced the last stop before exiting Jerusalem, Shifra, though fearful and uneasy, didn't make a move. She knew she still had time to return, to tell some lies about where she spent the last hours, but she wasn't going to do it. Not yet. Instead, she watched enchanted the lovely view of the garland of hills opening before her eyes. She'd never been outside her neighborhood, except on family visits, on Shabbat afternoons to her uncle who lived in *Mea Shearim*.

How beautiful the hills were, each one gleaming in a different color. Shifra thought that she could even hear the birds singing, but she knew that it was only her imagination.

The bus distracted her with its puffing and screeching. She didn't know that she had boarded the *ma'asef*, the bus that stops at all Arab villages and other small communities between Jerusalem and Jaffa, but she didn't mind. She absorbed the new sights; the way people were dressed, the scraps of conversation she heard in Hebrew, English and Arabic. She saw bearded Chassidim sitting in front and moving their bodies up and down, praying *Tefilas Haderech*, the travel prayer. As the bus sighed and shook, winding down the narrow highway, Shifra was sorry she hadn't brought her Tefilas Haderech, too.

She knew that when she would return home after seeing the sea, she would have to fulfill the destiny that had been decided for her, but she would remember with pleasure that she had seen her dream. Since her friend Chana had told her about the *yam*, the sea, she'd had only one wish. To see it with her own eyes! To feel as free as a bird in front of its immensity, to breathe its air! She never forgot her friend's words.

It was a long bus ride. At the beginning she tried to memorize the names of the Arab villages, Jewish settlements and the cities where the bus stopped, but there were too many to remember. By the time the bus driver announced Jaffa, she woke up from her reverie. She looked out the window. What a bustle, what a mix of people—even Mahane Yehuda market didn't look like this on its busiest days.

The bus moved slowly along a wide avenue, which the driver called Jerusalem Boulevard. There were many stops along it but she hadn't glimpsed the sea yet. She panicked. How would she know when to get off? A minute later the driver announced, "Next stop, the Clock Tower, last station." Shifra saw that everybody was getting up and making for the door. She followed the crowd.

In the street she didn't know where to look first. There were Arab men sitting in front of their stores dressed in *kafias* and smoking from long pipes, young boys, running barefoot, holding newspapers under their arms and screaming in three languages, "Latest news about the war in Europe! President Roosevelt is confident that..." But Shifra couldn't hear the end because of the noise of carts driven by donkeys, the honking of buses, and the screams of vendors.

Shifra knew there was a war. She had heard her father telling her mother after reading the *Hamelitz* newspaper, lent from one of their neighbors, "Hitler, should he burn in Hell, he killed Jews. No more Jews in Poland." Shifra's mother howled like a crazy dog, "*Oi, mamoushka*, my dear mother, where are you?" Since that day her mother lighted a remembrance candle every evening for one month.

The clock at the top of the tower rang thirteen times. Shifra looked up. It was one in the afternoon. So late already! She had left home at ten in the morning on a cloudy day in Jerusalem. Here in Jaffa she felt her clothes burn her body. But where was the sea? Shifra was ready to ask an old woman seated on a bench near the bus stop when she saw an English policeman directing the traffic. She approached and asked him, her eyes cast downward, "Please, tell me how to get to the beach."

The policeman smiled. "Follow the sun," he said, but when he saw that she didn't understand him, he pointed to a street and said, "Take this street, go to the end of it. There you'll see the beach."

Shifra forgot to thank him. She ran, her eyes blinded by the sun. When she reached the end of the street a fantastic view opened before her. The azure sea sparkled like millions of diamonds, and the foam formed by the waves' crest looked like the frost adorning the cakes at weddings. And it seemed endless.

She jumped on the rocks leading to the sea. Shifra didn't remember if there was a blessing for seeing the sea for the first time, as one says a blessing before eating a new fruit.

On the beach she saw young children playing in the sand, all naked. She couldn't look at their mothers. She had never seen women so scantily dressed. She blushed. How could women be so immodest? Farther along she saw men wearing only knee-length underwear, playing ball. *Oh, her father was right, saying the world was full of debauchery.*

She wouldn't get close to these people. She found a place under the shadow of a rock, where she could follow the dancing waves without being seen, she hoped, and far from those people who have no fear of God.

It was so hot! She took off her mother's jacket and the kerchief covering her head. She placed them on the sand. She did the same with her rubber-soled shoes, which burned her feet and were now full of sand. Shifra felt the pangs of hunger and thirst. She remembered the two apples in the pocket of her jacket. She munched on her apples, her eyes riveted on the sea. With each wave it seemed to Shifra that the sea was stretching out to her, challenging her to come and play.

Would it be a sin if she took off her stockings and soaked her feet in the water? She debated with herself, *after all, why did she come?* Shifra wanted to feel the water's cool caress, its freshness, to take the foam into her hands, to taste it.

She took her black stockings off. She'd wait. People were starting to leave the beach. After everyone left, she'd walk along the beach. She closed her tired eyes.

When she woke up, the sun, a big ball of fire was descending slowly on the horizon. Shifra didn't know how much time had passed. The beach was deserted. She got up and approached the water. The sand wasn't hot anymore and it was easy to walk on it. When her feet touched the water, a shiver went through her body. What a marvelous sensation. *Could greater pleasures exist?*

Her arms raised, she started twirling, round and round, her hair, freed by the wind, blowing in her face. At last she was alone, Shifra thought, and the sea belonged entirely to her.

How long she danced, how much time had passed, she didn't know, but gradually the feeling came to her that she was being followed. She didn't dare look back. All of a sudden she became scared. She looked toward the rock, where she thought she had left her jacket and shoes, but now all the rocks looked the same. *Where were her things?*

She began to run, searching the rocks. When she ran out of breath, she fell on the sand, her eyes full of tears. She couldn't find her things. The return ticket for Jerusalem was in her jacket. *What was she going to do now?*

She would just remain there until the night jackals came to eat her. That's what she deserved for listening to *yetzer hara*, the evil instinct. She bent her head. The bitter tears falling from her eyes prevented her from noticing the barefoot young man who stopped a few paces from her.

2

Jaffa

In the spring, returning from the early afternoon prayer at the Great Mosque, Musa liked to take a detour from his regular way home and walk along the water. Today he found a girl asleep on the beach. She looked so small and defenseless, rolled up in an old jacket, a long skirt covering her feet. Her golden braids formed a crown above her head, and her face was the color of alabaster.

An angel, Musa thought. He crouched not far from her and gazed at her steadily, hoping she'd wake up. His curiosity was aroused, but he couldn't stay long; he didn't want to attract the attention of other beachcombers. But her image followed him the entire afternoon.

After the mid-afternoon prayer, Musa decided to walk along the beach again. *Maybe she'll still be there. Or maybe he'll discover she really was an angel, that Allah, praised be Him, placed on his way in order to test him.*

Great was his surprise when he saw her from afar, alone on the deserted beach, dancing and twirling, while the late sunrays played with her hair. Musa didn't dare get closer, but he had to make sure

14

that she was real and not an apparition. He stopped when she stopped. He saw her turn abruptly and run toward the rocks. She went from rock to rock, looking for something. Her hair was loose and she was barefoot. She stood for a moment, before falling on the sand crying, her head in her hands.

With his prayer rug under his arm and his slippers in his hand Musa, undecided, stood not far from her. He felt the urge to get closer, to maybe touch that marvelous cascade of hair, but it wasn't in his nature to talk to strangers, much less strange girls. Yet, he couldn't take his eyes off her, and he felt as if his feet were buried in the sand. It began to get dark. Soon the night would slowly cover the beach. *He had to go, but how could he leave her?* She was shivering from the cool breeze. And she still hadn't seen him. Almost against his will, he approached her.

"*Salaam Aleikum,*" he started the traditional greeting. No answer.

"*Min enta wa-shoo ta'amal hnana,* who are you and what are you doing here?" he said in Arabic, but seeing her frightened look, he immediately repeated it in English.

The girl didn't answer. She looked away. Musa saw that she was quite young, fourteen or fifteen at most. Now sure she wasn't a dream, he thought that maybe she had run away from home or maybe she didn't know the way back. "Where do you live?" he asked. "Don't be afraid. I will not do you any harm. I want only to help." Then he repeated it in Hebrew "*Ani l'Ezra.*"

Still trembling, she looked at him. Even though it was almost dark, he thought she had the bluest eyes, the color of the precious lapis-lazuli earrings his mother wore with such pride.

"Come," he said, "I'll take you to my mother. She's a smart woman. She'll help you. It's dangerous to remain here overnight."

She still didn't answer, but Musa's mind was made up. He thought, "I'll take her in my arms, even against her will." Still not looking at him, the girl stood up.

"Where are your shoes?" Musa asked. Hearing that, she started crying again.

"Shush, shush, don't cry, here, take my slippers," he said. She looked undecided. "Don't worry about me. I'm used to walking barefoot on the sharpest stones."

He didn't expect her to answer. To make her feel at ease he started to walk away, and after a while he felt her following him. In the deserted street, Musa blessed the darkness of the night, which made it possible for them to walk without attracting attention.

Though he knew he was taking her to a safe place, Musa was worried what his mother's reaction would be when she saw him bringing an unknown girl to their home. He was his mother's eldest son, and Musa knew he was her favorite. She never had a harsh word for him. She always saved for him the special delicacies she had reserved only for his father.

Lately he had seen his mother's eyes lingering on him. Once she whispered "Musa, looking at you I see your father, may he joyfully rest at Allah's breast, when he first came to take me as his bride. He was as tall as you, his hair and moustache as black as the sky at midnight, and his teeth as white as the Lebanon's first snow."

But now, Musa feared his mother's anger. She was a force to be reckoned with. A widow, the mother of six children, two boys and four girls, she had taken the reins of his father's business in her hands, proving herself as shrewd as his father had been. Her flourishing marketing skills had taken their famous citrus fruits to Alexandria, Beirut and even farther cities.

Musa took a furtive look at the girl who followed him at a short distance. They were walking the rocky steps of Jaffa's narrow streets, older than the Sultans' time. The *souks* and bazaars were closed, but the smell of strong spices lingered in the air. They were still at a distance from his house on Basra Street in the select Ajami neighborhood, where the houses built with tall iron gates and grated windows, were always locked during the night. Only the hanging flowers on the iron latticed balconies were proof that there was life behind the closed shutters.

Musa turned into a narrow street and the girl followed him. They hadn't exchanged one word since they started walking. Now they were on his street, close to his home. The girl slowed her pace, observing the big, somber-looking houses. Only a lost dog was heard howling from time to time. *What can be on her mind?* But he dismissed the thought as they were already in front of the massive gate of his family home, the house his grandfather Masri had built with stones brought from as far as Ashkelon and Caesarea.

Musa worked the intricate lock, and the gate opened with a tired squeak. They were in the large courtyard common to Arab houses. The house, built in the form of a horseshoe, surrounded the paved courtyard. It was dark and quiet. Musa sighed with relief. He'd give the girl something to eat, after which he'd spread a camel blanket on the kitchen floor for her to sleep on.

This would give him time to think of a way to introduce her to his mother in the morning, hoping to avoid raising her anger. But his relief was short-lived. He heard noise from the women's quarters, saw a flickering candle moving behind the dark windows and heard quick steps. In less than a minute, his mother, the formidable Fatima Masri, faced her oldest son.

"*Kan bal,* I was worried," she whispered. "*When enta,* where were you, the muezzin's call was ages ago! You never come home so late. I even wanted to—" but she stopped her hurried words, stupefied, staring at the blond girl half hidden by Musa's body.

Suddenly his mother couldn't contain her fury. "Musa Ibn Faud, what in the name of Allah is this?" She tried to keep her voice quiet, not to awaken the household or the neighbors. "It wasn't enough that you bring home stray dogs and cats, now you bring stray girls!" And after she took another look at the girl, she said with contempt "*Bint el-Yahood, a* Jewish girl?"

While she was talking, the girl started backing away. Musa, who was silent during his mother's outburst, caught a glimpse of the girl's maneuver and quickly placed himself between her and the gate.

"You are going nowhere tonight," he said to her, softly but firmly. "My mother is a good person. I shouldn't have surprised her like that." Then addressing his mother in Arabic he said, "Honored mother, please let's go inside. I'll explain everything. Let your fury fall on my head, and not on this poor girl, probably an orphan, whom I found on the beach, all alone." Musa's lips were dry. "Have pity, Mother," he added. "That's what the Koran teaches us. And what if she's a daughter of the Yahud? You do business with them, don't you?"

While Musa talked, his mother's eyes studied the girl, who kept her head down. She sighed. "How much I miss your father. He would have known what decision to make. What will your sisters and brother say when they see this strange girl in our house?" After a long silence she added, "She'll have to leave at dawn."

Fatima Masri walked toward the house as Musa and the girl followed her. "It's late, Musa. There is food in the icebox. Eat and give her some, too. Afterward, bring her to my room. I'll put a blanket on the floor for her to sleep on."

In the large kitchen with walls covered with blue tiles, each one with an intricate design, Musa silently made Shifra a sign to sit at a small table. Shifra looked at her hands. They were full of sand. Musa followed her gaze. "Come," he said, showing her the ceramic basin and pitcher standing in a corner, "You can wash your hands there."

While she washed, he took from the icebox the remnants of the supper, a leg of lamb, goat cheese, and leben. From a shelf he took a basket filled with pita bread and placed it on the table. "Eat, eat," Musa urged, seeing her indecision, "You must be famished."

His eyes feasted on her. Here, in his house, she seemed a thousand times prettier than the girl he saw on the beach. Her cheeks were rosy from the walk, and her hair, damp at the temples, shone like a myriad of lights. He saw her pour a tablespoon of lebenia on her plate and break a pita, after she murmured something he couldn't understand. Both ate in silence. Though he insisted, he saw that she wouldn't eat any more, but looked grateful for the glass of cold water filled with nana leaves he offered her. When he got up, Shifra got up too.

"I'll show you to my mother's room," he whispered.

They walked through a dark corridor, where the moon's light was filtered through the latticed windows. Fatima's large bedroom was the first one in the women's quarters. Musa pointed his finger toward the camel blanket by the foot of the large bed. He wanted to bid her a good night's sleep, or sweet dreams, but he didn't want to wake up his mother, who, according to the neighbors, slept with one eye open to better watch over her family's fortune.

3

As usual, Fatima woke up at the first call of the rooster. She was born into an old Jerusalemite family of means, and her dowry at marriage brought her husband more golden bracelets than the wives of his brothers did. Yet she loved to work. She despised idle women. She frequently urged her daughters to be industrious, work on their embroidery, especially after she discovered they had a real gift for it. Their peacock designs were so successful that the girls could barely satisfy the orders from the bazaar shops.

She felt a shock when she saw the blond girl asleep at the foot of her bed. Slowly, she remembered the events of the previous evening. Anger and pity filled her heart, anger toward Musa, who dared bring this girl into her home, pity, as she looked at the girl's innocent face. Who was she? What was she doing alone on the deserted beach? Had she run away from home? Was she lost? Should she, Fatima alert the British police? She disliked having anything to do with the police. Yet she knew she couldn't keep this girl in her house.

Her thoughts turned toward Musa. He'd had such a sensitive soul, ever since he was a child. She remembered the wounded pigeon that fell into their courtyard and how carefully he bandaged its wing and didn't let anyone else feed it. Musa wasn't like other young men, ready for a brawl or to spend a full day smoking *nargilea* at the coffee house.

He was a good son, always respectful, and though she knew that it wasn't his inclination to be a merchant, he helped her by keeping the accounts up to date. Musa had a good head for numbers. If he had continued school, who knows? No, she chased the thought, Musa was the oldest, and should follow in his father's footsteps.

And he was so handsome! A few matchmakers had already approached her, but she drove them away. He was too young, she told them. But wasn't his father the same age, just short of nineteen, when he married her?

She looked again at the sleeping girl. Her face in the pale light of dawn had the glow of a red apple. *What in the name of Allah made him bring her home?* Musa was too shy to address a girl. Enough thinking! She had a long day in front of her. A ship intended for Alexandria was waiting in Jaffa's port to be loaded with her cases of oranges, grapefruit and bananas. It was time to get out of bed.

At the sound of Fatima's steps, Shifra opened her eyes. First, she looked around her, confused. Then she jumped up, frightened. Fatima put a finger on her lips to keep her silent. Shifra quickly bent and folded the blanket she had slept on and then smoothed her wrinkled skirt. She passed her hands over her hair, trying to smooth it, too. Her movements were watched by Fatima's scrutinizing eyes. When Fatima left the room, she motioned to Shifra to follow her.

The outhouse stood in a corner of the courtyard. Fatima pointed it out to Shifra. She waited for her outside and then pantomimed that she'd take her to wash her hands and face.

When they entered the kitchen, Musa was already there. On the iron stove, the steam from boiling water was billowing. Musa never got up so early, Fatima thought. He looked at his mother with anxious eyes, red from lack of sleep. He avoided looking at Shifra, who kept her eyes downcast.

"She has to leave this house immediately," Fatima told her son, interrupting his formal greetings, "I want her out before your sisters are up. Her place is not here."

When she saw how pale her son's face became, Fatima added, "I'm not going to turn her over to the police, if this is what you are afraid of. I will talk to one of my Jewish customers, Mr. Berkowitz maybe. He is a good man. He'll talk to her and find out who she is and help her go back where she belongs."

Musa bowed his head. All of a sudden Fatima saw him jump. He was running toward the gate where a frantic Shifra was there before him, trying to unlock it. Fatima heard him say in a gentle voice, "You can't leave before having a glass of tea and something to eat. My mother is not throwing you out." He spoke to her in English.

Reluctantly the girl returned. She went to the basin and turned toward Fatima with questioning eyes. "You can wash," Fatima nodded. The girl undid her hair. A cascade of gold suddenly lit the kitchen. On the wall above the basin was pinned a small mirror in a mother-of-pearl frame. Fatima saw her looking furtively into the mirror, while she redid her braids.

The mirror reflected something else too. It was Musa, watching the girl with the eyes of a drunkard. *A drunkard or a man in love*, Fatima's heart had recognized the look.

"Come, eat," Fatima said, while quickly placing on the table jars of tahini, humus and leben. Musa added pita and brought the tea glasses already filled with mint leaves. The girl seemed hesitant. Fatima saw Musa look at her expectantly. She knew that in her presence Musa would not address the girl directly.

"*Bo'u, Ochel,*" repeated Fatima, remembering how the Jewish neighbors from the old quarter in Jerusalem used to call their children when it was time to come home for supper.

We should get rid of her quickly. Fatima cleared her throat, "I have an idea," she said, "I'm going to take her to Nathan, the Moroccan watchmaker. He always opens his store early in the morning. I will tell him what happened. Maybe he has already gotten word of a missing girl."

As Fatima got up from the table, she was surprised to see the girl, who had eaten only pita with her tea, already standing at the sink washing and drying the dishes. "*Poor lamb,*" she thought for a second.

To Musa, she said "It's time you go. They are starting the loading early. A good boss is always the one who arrives first."

After a long glance at the girl, Musa left. He was already at the gate when he returned and shyly said, "She has no shoes, mother. Please let her have a pair of your old slippers." He sounded supplicant. Fatima nodded. *I have to get rid of the girl,* nagged her again.

"Follow me," Fatima told Shifra, when they were out on the street. She didn't want to be seen walking alongside the girl. Nathan's store wasn't far away. They had to cross a few streets. From time to time, Fatima turned her head to see if the girl was behind her.

At the main thoroughfare, on Jerusalem Boulevard, a stubborn mule, kicking and making a lot of noise, stopped traffic. People were trying to cross the street between the stopped cars and buses. The noise was deafening. Everyone screamed. Fatima looked back to see if Shifra was close by, but she couldn't see her. She turned, peering everywhere, wondering if she would have to go back to find her, but people were streaming all around.

Maybe it was better this way, Fatima thought. *What would she tell Musa, when he asked her what happened to the girl,* crossed her mind. But she dismissed it quickly. She had more pressing matters. It was time to take care of her business.

4

Her eyes were still searching for a narrow passage or a shadowed porch where she could hide from Fatima's vigilant eye when the tumult and crowd around the stubborn donkey provided her with the chance to disappear. Shifra walked through streets that seemed to be leading her in circles until she saw the clock tower at the end of one street. From there she knew the way to the beach. Nobody would look for her there.

Shifra descended the rocks, grateful to be wearing the velvet embroidered slippers the Arab woman gave her that morning. When she found a shadowy place, Shifra sat down and looked around. Few people were on the beach, and, to Shifra's relief, no one paid attention to her.

How foolish it was to leave her parents' home, she thought with bitterness. What did she think she was doing? Didn't she realize that there would be no way back? Probably by now her parents were sitting *Shiva*, mourning for her. At the thought of her mother lighting a remembrance candle for her, the way she did for her parents, tears streamed from Shifra's eyes.

Was this the way to repay her parents for almost sixteen years of care? Immediately she remembered the bulging eyes of the *neft* man looking at her in a certain way, a shameful way, a way a man shouldn't look at a girl. *But m maybe she could've persuaded her father to break his promise? What was the rush?* Still, there were more than ten days before Passover, almost two months before Lag Baomer, maybe in that time Rebono Shel Olam, Master of the Universe, would have taken pity on her. She had only to pray harder.

But she knew she wouldn't be allowed to pray now. She was a sinner. The one Commandment her father always emphasized was *Respect thy Father and thy Mother* and she had been disrespectful. If she prayed, her prayers would be in vain. The Master of the Universe would not bend His ear to hear her.

Shifra closed her eyes. She remembered how much she enjoyed helping with the preparations for Pessach. How proud she was when her father, who came with a candle in the middle of the night to search her closet for traces of *chametz,* bread crumbs, told her mother that Shifra's closet was the cleanest one. Gone was the beautiful *Seder,* where she could sing without being told that her voice was too loud. Gone were the presents, sometimes a new blouse, or a new pair of shoes, bought with money her mother had saved for an entire year.

Shifra looked at her wrinkled blouse and the tired-looking slippers. A new wave of tears filled her eyes. *What was she going to do now?*

The events of the previous evening, the young Arab man who had taken her to his house, invaded her mind. How kind he was. She remembered his eyes when their glances crossed in the mirror. The memory made her blush. His eyes were like burning coals, penetrating her very soul. Even if she wanted, she couldn't forget the look on his face.

It was a hot day and her head seemed to be on fire. Shifra got up and walked until she found a narrow space between two rocks, where she could hide from the crowds. The sand was humid, a sign that the sun never intruded there. As she sat down, she saw a piece of paper hidden in the sand. She picked it up. It was torn from a newspaper, its date missing. Shifra's first impulse was to bury it again in the sand, but the headline of one of the articles caught her eye, "Girl missing." Her heart skipped a beat.

No, it wasn't possible. Her parents wouldn't advertise in a newspaper, much less in the Palestine Post. Besides, she had left home only yesterday and this was an old, faded paper. She felt relieved. But her curiosity was aroused. She mouthed the words as she read:

Alyat Hanoar, the agency for young immigrants, is asking people who know the whereabouts of Rivka Mendel to call the Tel-Aviv center immediately. It was not the first time the girl had disappeared from the youth camp. The fifteen-year-old Rivka had been one of the Teheran Train Children smuggled out of war-torn Europe. Their six months ordeal, walking or by train from Siberia to Samarkand, then by ship to Teheran ended when helped by representatives of the Jewish Agency, the surviving 1,200 reached Palestine. At the time of her disappearance Rivka was dressed in khaki pants, a short-sleeved white blouse and sandals.

Clutching the paper in her hand, Shifra closed her eyes. She had seen one of those orphan children, a girl who was taken in by her uncle. Shifra remembered her parents' comments about the lucky girl who had been able to find her uncle living in Palestine. But Shifra had seen the girl's eyes. They were not the eyes of a happy child. Shifra sighed. What was Rivka Mendel looking for? If she had been happy, would she have run away?

High in the sky a flock of birds flew in circles, some of them diving into the water to look for insects and flying up again. Shifra felt a tremor in her heart. *What a great feeling it must be to be free like a bird.* But she couldn't watch the birds for long. The sun blinded her eyes and she felt the unbearable midday heat again.

An Arab man, wearing a kafia and a long white robe, appeared on the beach. "Tamarind! Tamarind!" the juice seller screamed, ringing a bell.

Shifra remembered the day she went with her friend Shula to the Old City. On the way to the Wailing Wall, they encountered a tamarind seller. His juice box was strapped to his back and had long tubes, which Shula told her resembled an Irish pipe, a picture of which she had seen in one of her father's books. Shifra didn't know what an Irish pipe was. "It's a musical instrument," Shula explained to her.

"Let's see how he pours the juice from a musical instrument." Shula added jokingly, while buying one drink for the two of them to share. The seller poured the juice through its tube into a small metal can and then into a paper cup. It tasted as sweet as honey. Seeing the tamarind seller now, Shifra felt how dry her throat was. And the heat! She longed to plunge in the sea and feel the splash of the water on her face. The dazzling sun on the surface of the sea made her eyelids heavy.

All of a sudden she saw the shadows of a man and a woman. The man wore a black hat with *tzitzis* hanging out of his coat. The woman wore a kerchief on her head. Though she could see only their backs, she recognized them. Her parents! "Mama," she cried "look at me, I'm here." Shifra felt paralyzed, she couldn't move, her anxiety was mixed with joy.

Her parents were looking for her! Almighty, blessed be He, had shown them the way. "Mama," she cried again.

The man and the woman stopped. "Don't turn," Shifra heard her father say. "Don't look at her. She's not clean. She brought dirt and shame upon our family."

Shifra stretched her arms toward them, "*Rachmunes*, pity, have pity," but the two shadows disappeared.

She woke up shaking. Sweat poured over her face. Had it been a dream? And if it had, what was its meaning? All of a sudden she remembered her father's words, "She's not clean. Don't look at her."

Shifra shuddered, "I'm not clean." Her father was right. Feverishly she looked around. The beach was empty, though the sun was still high. She had only one thought: she had to clean herself. What better way to cleanse than the blue sea, as pure as the cloudless sky?

The waves seemed to call her, "Come, come." Shifra got up. Fearfully, she approached the water. After baking in the sun, her feet were delighted by the fresh encounter. "Come, don't be afraid," she thought she heard a song. Was that the song of a mermaid, like the one she read about in a story? She started to follow the voice.

The water came up to her knees. The long wet skirt, heavy with water, stuck to her body. A wave knocked her down. Shifra got up, only to be pulled down by another wave. The salt water made her eyes tear, but she didn't stop. Her heart was singing a glorious song, "I'm going to be clean. I am going to be pure. Mama, Papa, I'm going to be clean, I promise."

The water was up to her chest. A group of youngsters walked along the beach. They saw her, but Shifra never heard their urgent calls.

On the docks of Jaffa's port, Musa watched the loading of boxes of oranges, lemons and grapefruit. His thoughts and feelings were mixed. On one hand, he was grateful to his mother for wanting to help the girl, but he felt despondent at the thought of not seeing her again. After a few hours, his head was on fire. He had to find out what had happened at home. The slow loading looked as if it might take the entire day, and his anxiety grew with every hour that passed. The girl's image and the memory of the moment their eyes met in the mirror burned his heart.

"*Yala, yala,* faster," he screamed at the workers, as he had heard his father say. When his screams didn't help he ran to the closest grocery store and bought two bottles of *arrack.*

"Here," Musa said to the shore man, "one bottle for you, the other for the men. Try to get them to work faster. As for me, I can't stay any longer."

He heard the muezzin call for the third prayer of the day but decided to forgo going to the mosque. Anyway, he would arrive too late for the prayer, he rationalized. He was in a hurry, he had to go home. His mother would be upset that he left work early, but he had no time to worry about his mother's reaction.

When he arrived home, his family was seated around the table eating their midday meal. The aroma of the *zaatar,* spiced lamb, filled his nostrils.

"So early," Fatima wondered, "have you already finished loading?" The doubts creased his mother's forehead. Instead of answering, Musa asked, "Eumi what happened this morning? Where is she? What did you do with her?" His voice sounded strained, rising with each question until it became shrill.

"Follow me!" Fatima ordered. In the silence of her bedroom, she burst out, "Have you lost your mind? You questioned me in front of your brother and sisters who know nothing of what happened last night. You should be ashamed of yourself. Go wash and come to eat. I forbid you to ask any more questions."

"You have to tell me what happened. On my father's memory, I beg of you."

Fatima still refused to answer. In his mind, Musa cursed the minute he agreed to let his mother take the girl to the old watchmaker.

"She got lost," Fatima said after a long silence. "I know she followed me, because I looked back every few steps, but on Jerusalem Boulevard the traffic separated us all of a sudden, and she," Fatima stopped. Then with a decisive tone she continued, "*Allah chalasna minik,* good riddance."

Without waiting to hear another word, Musa ran out of the house. Where could she be, he thought, walking briskly on the pavement melting under his steps. It was siesta time. Most of the shops were closed, and only a few people ventured out into the street during the hottest hours of the day. Aimlessly he walked through the almost empty bazaar, then through the souk without success. Musa knew he couldn't ask a passerby, "Have you seen a girl with golden tresses and the bluest eyes, wearing a white-sleeved blouse and a long black skirt?" People would think him drunk or crazy. He felt sick at the thought that he had lost her; that he wasn't going to see her again.

Musa found himself in front of the Mahmoodia Great Mosque. He left his slippers at the entrance and entered its refreshing cool walls. The Mosque was almost empty. He prostrated himself and prayed, but instead of the verses of the Koran, he just whispered, "Oh, Allah Akbar, glorious Allah, our light and father, help me find her." After a while he got up and left. His steps directed him toward the beach. It was there he had seen her the first time. He knew that it was ridiculous to think he'd find her on the beach again, but his feet carried him there against his will.

At that hour the beach was usually deserted. No one ventured onto its burning sands when the sun was at its zenith. As he got closer to the place where he had seen her only a day ago, his heart started beating faster. He ran. The sand burned his soles, but he didn't feel it. From a distance he saw a group of boys, barefoot, their pants rolled-up, striding into the water. As he got closer, he heard them yelling, "A girl is drowning. She needs help." His feet grew wings. *It's not possible,* Musa thought, and as he hurled himself into the sea, he saw a blond head, bobbing in and out of water at the mercy of the waves. The sun didn't play a joke on him. It was the girl, his girl. He broke the waves, with the boys swimming after him screaming directions. When he felt a piece of cloth, Musa screamed, "I got her," and feverishly brought her head above the water.

"She is breathing," one of the boys said, after they helped him carry and lay her on the sand. "She hasn't opened her eyes. Should we call a policeman?" asked another boy.

"No, no," Musa said, out of breath.

"Musa," said the first boy, recognizing him. "Musa Ibn-Faud. Tell us what to do?"

The boys, twelve or thirteen year old, looked expectantly at him. Musa had to think fast. He couldn't tell them that he knew the girl, yet, he couldn't lose a minute.

The boys talked all at once, "You could see she didn't know how to swim," said one.

"We called her," said another. "We didn't do anything wrong," said the third.

"You are good people, and Allah will recompense you for your good deed," Musa said, as he covered Shifra's head with his own kafia, to protect her from the sun. "Go home. Don't worry. I'll get the help she needs."

The boys seemed uncertain. "Go," Musa repeated impatiently," I'll be in charge."

"Allah be praised, she's alive," Musa wanted to scream, after the boys left. *What could have been going through her mind? Why would she want to drown herself?*

He had to take her to a safe place as fast as he could. Her body was warm, but her eyes were closed. "First, get her out of the wet clothes. She needs dry clothes," he thought feverishly. Her body seemed so tense. He tried to open her clenched fists. A small piece of folded paper fell out. He picked it up and put it in his pocket. He'd read it later. Where could he take her? There was no safe place he knew, other than his own home. He lifted the girl up in his arms. He ran all the way, his charge seeming to him no heavier than a feather. She hadn't opened her eyes, but he heard her soft breathing. For the moment that was enough.

He pushed the gate wide open. A dozen dumbfounded eyes confronted him. Fatima, completely stricken by the sight, started screaming, "*La, la,* no, not again. *Kafi*-enough. I want none of it. You should be ashamed of yourself, Musa Ibn-Faud. *Chalas,* out, take her out of my house, right now!"

"If she leaves, I leave," Musa answered in a firm voice. Carefully and gently he knelt and placed the girl on the courtyard tiles. "Eumi, this is a sign from the Prophet. I went to pray to Allah at the Mosque and He guided my steps, so that I could save her life a second time. Didn't He say, he who saves one life, saves the entire universe?"

"Go change. You are all wet. You'll catch cold," Fatima said, after looking around and seeing how alarmed her daughters were. They adored their brother and she knew it.

"Don't worry about me. Please, Mother, she's the one who needs dry clothes right now. Look, she's shivering." He moved a lock of Shifra's hair aside from her face. His sisters gasped, "She's so pretty!" they said in one voice.

Fatima clapped her hands, "Girls, go to your rooms. I'll talk to you later," she approached Shifra and placed her hand on the girl's forehead. "She's burning," Fatima said. "What am I supposed to do now? Oh, my son, I don't know if you saved a life, but surely you've brought a lot of trouble for the Masri family."

Musa kept quiet. He already knew that his mother was going to help. "Bring her to my room," she ordered. "There's no need to call Dr. Farid. I'll use my grandmother's old remedies, wash her body in vinegar and wrap it in dry sheets. Then I'll hang wet sheets to keep the room temperature down. She should drink lots of chamomile and elderberry tea. Hopefully by tomorrow there will be no more fever." As they were carrying the girl together,

Fatima added, "Tomorrow the two of us will have a serious talk. Until then, tell your sisters and brother to keep their mouths shut. You know how much our neighbors like to gossip."

There's going to be trouble. Fatima smelled it two nights ago when Musa first brought the girl into the house. Now after she had tried all the remedies she knew, the girl's fever remained high. Fatima had put compresses with potato slices on her forehead, yet her eyes were still shut. From rosy, the girl's face had turned sallow.

All during the night, Musa sat at the girl's side and moved only when his mother asked him to change the compresses. *What am I going to do?* Fatima asked herself, upset that her knowledge did not help.

In the morning she saw that Musa looked agitated. He held a piece of paper in his hands. "Read this," he said, "I found it clutched in her palm."

Though the paper was torn in many places, and the water had erased some of the letters, Fatima could make out its content. It mentioned a missing girl, one of the thousand Teheran Children, saved by a miracle from the Nazis' claws, who traveled from Europe through Siberia towards Teheran, from there to Alexandria before reaching Palestine.

Could Rifka Mendel be the half-dead girl now under her roof?

"How old is this paper?" Fatima asked after returning it to her son. Musa shrugged his shoulders, "I don't know." He looked again at the paper. "What I understand from reading it is that she was brought here, together with other orphans. If she's that girl, she must be an orphan."

After a few minutes of silence Fatima said, "I have an idea. I will take the grandfather clock to Adon Nathan. For some time it hasn't worked properly. Maybe it needs oiling."

Musa looked interested. She continued, "Maybe I'll be able to find out if there is any news in the Jewish newspaper regarding a missing girl."

"Thank you, Eumi," Musa said gratefully, "Allah will bless you for your good soul."

It wasn't long before Fatima returned home, empty-handed. She echoed what Mister Nathan said: "Except for the terrible war ravaging Europe, there was no other urgent news."

5

"So it seems that nobody has claimed the girl," Fatima said looking straight into Musa's eyes. A long silence fell between mother and son.

"What do we do now?" Fatima asked. "I don't want her to die under my roof. You know I've tried everything I know."

While she talked, Samira, her faithful servant, who had been Fatima's nanny, and followed her from Jerusalem to Jaffa after Fatima married, sneaked silently into the room. Samira had been the midwife for each one of Fatima's six children and Fatima considered her a second mother, her confidante and best advisor.

Samira was the one who, during the night, had helped Fatima change the sheets imbued with the girl's perspiration, had washed them quickly and hung them in the courtyard, where the fresh breeze and the smell from the eucalyptus flowers perfumed them. She had also put ice on Shifra's parched lips, while Musa tried patiently to squeeze a few teaspoons of chamomile tea through her lips.

Samira hadn't asked any questions and Fatima knew that she wouldn't, unless Fatima was going to tell her what happened.

Samira had heard Fatima's last words, "Musa, I pity the girl, but it's time to take her to the hospital, or to the French Convent. I have heard that some of the Catholic nuns are trained nurses. Musa, my son, it's time to restore back the calm of this house."

Samira noticed Musa's face becoming darker, "Mother, please don't do anything hastily."

"Can you imagine the consequences of your deed? Have you thought about your sisters? Any young man would have been honored to be married into the Masri family. I've already had matchmakers come from as far as Alexandria making inquiries. Now you want to bring shame to our good name. People will want to know what a Yahud girl is doing in our home."

With each word Fatima had raised her voice. At the end she was breathless. And upset. She turned toward Samira, "Can you bring my son to his senses?" Fatima knew that Samira loved Musa as much as she did.

"We can try Uhm Zaide," Samira said in a quiet voice.

"The witch!" Fatima and Musa exclaimed simultaneously.

"She has cured people. Everybody knows that her mixtures of herbs have saved lives," Samira said. She sounded sure of her words. "Musa could go and bring her, though she lives far from here and moves slowly, poor woman. She's getting up in years."

Musa and Fatima looked at each other. Neither one seemed convinced of the wisdom of Samira's words.

Fatima was on the point of answering, but Samira was faster. She could always guess her mistress' thoughts. "Before calling Uhm Zaide, with your permission, I'd like to try another cure first." Musa's face lightened.

"I need you two to help me," Samira said. "Musa, you bring me a pan with a few burning coals from the hot stove. Fatima, bring a bucket of cold water," she commanded.

After they brought what she asked for, Samira ordered, "Now leave me alone with her." Musa stood undecided "Go, go," Samira said with impatience, when she saw him still lingering.

Alone with Shifra, Samira cooled the burning coals in the water; then placed them on Shifra's chest. Shifra shivered. Samira dipped a clean rag in the water in which the burning coals had been extinguished, and with it brushed Shifra's forehead, cheeks, and arms while whispering, "*Mein kind, mein kind*, my child." The girl's eyelids fluttered. From Samira's lips came a song, one she didn't know she remembered. *Where had she heard it? Did the old man sing it?*

Again Shifra's eyelids moved. Samira could almost see the blue underneath her eyelids. Shifra's lips opened, "Mama," she whispered.

Samira tried to hold back her tears. From around her neck, she took her talisman, the precious amulet that had never left her neck for the last twenty-five years. She kissed it before she placed the string holding it around Shifra's neck.

"It's a *mezuzah*," Samira whispered, "Now I'm placing you in your God's hands. He is going to heal you."

When she was twelve years old, the orphaned Samira was sent by her grandmother to clean the rooms of an old Jewish man who had left his family in the faraway country where he was born and had come to die and be buried in the Holy Land, an old custom of very religious Jews. "He is one of many," her grandmother, who was cleaning for other old Jews, told her.

Mr. Grunwald lived in Jerusalem's Jewish Quarter surrounded by the walls of the Old City. He prayed the entire day, ate very little, and despite the language barrier between them, he smiled at Samira often. His smile warmed her heart. Many times Samira imagined that her grandfather, whom she had never met, must have resembled Mr. Grunwald. His room was full of books and yellowed photographs which Samira dusted with care. For that, Mr. Grunwald added a few piastres to her fee.

Once when he got a cold, he asked her for a *gleizole*, a small glass of tea, and from his signs she understood what he wanted. She served him the tea along with bread and cheese, the only two items she saw him eating at other meals. He smiled gratefully. After he fell asleep, Samira took his hand and held it for a long time. She felt closer to him than to her own grandmother, who never had time for her.

Samira was born in Al Fashha, one of the Arab villages west of Jerusalem. Her father was taken by the Turkish Army to fight in what she learned later was The Great War. He never returned home. From too much work and exhaustion Samira's mother died in childbirth, not long after her father left with the army. The baby didn't survive either. It was then that her grandmother took Samira under her roof. But money was scarce and she had to send Samira to work, too. That's how Samira came to work for Mr. Grunwald.

The seasons passed one after another and with time, a strange kinship developed between the old Jew and Samira. She learned a few of the Yiddish words, enough to be able to serve him, to buy his newspaper and the few groceries he needed. In turn he showed her the photographs of each one of his children and *einikleh*, grandchildren. They were beautiful blond girls and handsome boys, all well-dressed, each one smiling, maybe at their grandfather.

Samira hoped to serve Mr. Grunwald forever. In her heart he had already replaced the grandfather she never knew. But one day he received a letter. He had received many letters before, which he told her were from his children. But that time it was another kind, a terrible letter. The letters on the envelope looked different from the ones she had become familiar with. When she came to work the next day, she saw Mr. Grunwald prostrated on the floor, a burning candle at his side. He seemed unable to move and refused to eat. Not even to drink his tea.

His body was moving forward and backward and he often broke into tears, mumbling constantly, "*Oi, meine kinder,*" Other old bearded Jews came to keep him company, prayed with him and she heard them whispering with dread in their voices one single word, again and again, "Pogrom, pogrom."

One said, "*Wie in the Petliura tzeiten, die gazlan,* like in the times of the monster, Petliura."

At the time she didn't know what it meant but understood that it must have been something terrible. Not long after that the old man took to his bed and despite all her efforts—Samira wanted so desperately to save him—he died shortly afterward. All through his illness he never spoke to her again.

Samira was still holding his hand, now completely cold, unable to move from his side, when the people from *Hevre Kadishe,* the Jewish Burial Society, came to take his body and bury him according to the Jewish tradition. One man approached her, a piece of paper in his hand.

Samira stood up respectfully. The man spoke in a language she couldn't understand. He pointed to something written on the paper after which he gave her money, "From Mr. Grunwald," he said. The money, an amount equal to a full year of service, was not all he had left her. Samira was in shock when the man who had given her the money took the old pictures from the wall and pressed them into her hand, "They are yours, too," he said, "Mr. Grunwald's wish."

Samira waited for the people from the Burial Society to leave. Then with eyes swimming in tears, she went to the door post and kissed her palm after she touched the *mezuzah,* the way she saw the old man do it every time he left home and after he returned. He had told her the mezuzah was holy. A moment later she took a ladder and, with the help of a hammer, removed the mezuzah. She put a piece of string around it and fastened it around her neck. In that way, she told herself, the old man would always be with her.

Now, gently knotting the mezuzah around Shifra's neck, Samira felt she was returning Mr. Grunwald's kindness toward her. The girl's looks reminded her of one of his grandchildren, whose pictures she kept hidden in her closet, in her room behind the kitchen.

Watching Shifra, whose fingers lingered on the mezuzah, a forlorn smile on her lips, Samira was cheered to see that the girl's chest moved at an even pace and she slept peacefully.

Samira's life wasn't easy after Mr. Grunwald passed away. Her grandmother was hit by a car when she tried to cross a narrow street in the Old City. The car was driven by English youngsters, laughing and shouting and probably drunk. Jerusalem was full of English tourists. Her grandmother was almost deaf, and the kerchief she wore on her head didn't help her hearing; neither did the long *jelebia* help her move quickly. Her heart didn't recover from the shock. She died immediately after.

When Samira was hired by Fatima's wealthy parents, she wasn't much older than Fatima. Fatima took a liking to her and taught her to read Arabic. The family was good to her, but they kept her at a distance. For them she was a servant. They never broke bread with her the way old Mr. Grunwald had.

When she missed him the most she'd go to the Jewish cemetery on the Mount of Olives, wash the headstone, light a little candle in the glass box and put little stones on the grave, the way she saw other people do.

After Fatima got married and moved to Jaffa, and especially after the children were born, Samira found a new meaning in life. She adored the children, Musa especially, and they returned her love. She never missed being married. As she told Fatima many times, "I don't need a husband who'd get drunk and beat me." She was only eleven years old when her father was taken into the Army, but she still remembered how her father used to slap her mother after drinking a few glasses of arak.

Fatima entered the room, her eyes full of questions. "I think she's out of danger," Samira whispered, "But I'd like to keep an eye on her, so I want her to sleep in my room." This she added quickly, as she had already seen the frown of displeasure on Fatima's face. Yet Samira knew that Fatima wasn't going to object, because their long history together had created a strong bond of trust between them.

"Whatever you say," answered Fatima, "but the sooner she leaves the better. I warn you. And hopefully next time there will be no return!"

Samira nodded, a little smile forming at the corner of her mouth. Behind his mother, she had seen Musa. He had sneaked along, his brilliant eyes speaking to Samira more eloquently than words.

6

I must have had a moment of weakness when I accepted Samira's idea of having the Jewish girl share her room. As close as Fatima felt toward Samira, she was bothered by the great interest Samira took in the young girl. Fatima had observed how Samira had washed the girl's body, how she fed her, teaspoon by teaspoon, with so much patience, as if this were her own child. Samira helped her get out of bed, when she finally started her first hesitant steps, and sustained her all the way. Fatima noticed that the girl's eyes gleamed when she looked at Samira.

What happened when they were alone? Fatima thought that she had heard murmurs, but she was too proud to ask Samira if she had found a way to make the girl talk. Every noon, Fatima saw Samira boil two soft eggs and place them on a piece of fresh *challah* she had bought earlier in the morning at Abulafia's bakery exactly at the time the warm bread was taken out of the oven.

By now, Shifra wore one of Samira's *jelebia* dresses. If not for her blond hair, she could have passed easily for an Arab girl. All that disturbed Fatima. She would have a talk with Samira as soon as possible. Lately when Samira brought the pale girl to the courtyard, "to get some sun," as she explained it, Fatima saw her youngest daughters approach the girl and caress her hands. They had begged Samira to let them help her. And the young Rama offered to entertain her. Yes, she definitely had to put an end to all this.

To see the light on Musa's face every time he glanced at the girl pained Fatima. Moreover, Fatima thought, suddenly feeling a knot in her stomach, in a few days, the Arab Women's League was scheduled to hold its monthly meeting in her house. What a mess! What was she going to do? How would she explain to those fanatics the presence of the Jewish girl under her roof?

When she had joined the League after her husband's death, she wasn't sure that Faud would have approved of an organization that demanded equal rights for women in the Muslim society. Fatima thought that it would be good for her business. The League did charitable work, following the examples of the British women's organizations that mushroomed during the British Mandate to promote progress in Arab women's lives. Yes, Arab women, especially the well-educated ones, were ready to learn from the British, even if this was in conflict with their feelings. Lately the Arab Women's League had taken stronger attitudes against the British Mandate, because it permitted Jews to settle in Palestine. The Arab newspaper *Filastin* warned daily, "Don't sell your land to Jews. It's a terrible danger. Be alert."

Fatima didn't sell her land. She had made profitable deals with the Jews, but all the same, she agreed with the organization's platform: Palestine belongs to the Arabs and only to them.

Now this girl was like a thorn in Fatima's side. She had to be clear and tell Samira that there was no place for the girl in her house. Fatima clapped her hands. Her daughter Amina appeared, followed by her three sisters. "Amina, tell Samira to see me immediately. I need to talk to her."

"Yes, Eumi," her daughter answered, lingering near the door, unready to leave.

"Then, go! Go!" an impatient Fatima urged her.

"Samira is in the courtyard. She washed the Yahud girl's hair and she let me brush it," Rama said. "Oh, Eumi, I would give anything to have hair like that."

"Enough!" Fatima's voice sounded harsh, "Go, all of you. I am busy."

"Mother," Amina started timidly, "did you give more thought to what we talked about the other evening?" Amina's voice turned suppliant. "Have you made a decision yet? You know the time is running out."

Fatima pressed her palms to her temples. It was too much, Musa, Amina, Samira, the Arab Women's League. It felt like rocks on her head.

"I said, go! We'll talk about this later," with a tired gesture, Fatima dismissed her daughters.

First Musa, now Amina, thought Fatima. *What's happening to my children?* Amina wanted to register as a volunteer for the British Army. The British had made an appeal to the Arab Women's League to help the war against the Germans. The appeal invited English-speaking Arab women to contribute to the war effort, working as nurses, or nurses' aides, cooks, or doing laundry. Already many Arab women had decided to respond to the appeal.

"Now the war is hitting close to home," Fatima thought bitterly. This appeal would be the major issue at the meeting in her house. Fatima knew that her words would weigh heavily in the discussion. She again pressed her palms to her temples. She felt the oppressive heat of the day. And it wasn't noon yet. It must be the *hamsin*, the hot wind blowing from the desert, kind of early in the season, she thought, but always unpredictable.

Fatima saw the door open quietly. Samira entered, her long black garb flowing. At home Samira kept her head uncovered, but out on the street she wore a hijab.

Her eyes questioned Fatima. "The girls said you wanted to talk to me."

"Right," Fatima said. "Sit down, Samira. There are no formalities between the two of us. I want to talk to you about the Yahud girl."

Fatima saw Samira's body stiffen. "I'm listening," Samira said.

"This misfortune has taken too long and has disrupted us in many ways. I don't have to tell you that I'm worried about Musa. He is at such tender age, a child still." Fatima's pitch raised, "Don't interrupt me," when she saw Samira lifting her hand. "What's more, the girls seemed to have taken a liking to her. I don't want and I don't need troubles. I am not asking you what made you take such an interest in this girl, but I warn you that she should leave in the next twenty-four hours. You know as well as I do that the Arab Women's League meeting will be in my house in two days."

Fatima stopped. Her heart beat in her ears like the bells of the Orthodox Church across the street. All through her speech Samira had kept her mouth shut.

"The pastries, coffee and tea will be ready for the guests as usual, and as usual the *Sitat*, the ladies from the Arab League will admire how beautifully you master both your business and your home."

"Stop your flattering," Fatima frowned. She knew that Samira didn't trust that "elite group," as she called the Arab Women's League, whose well-to-do members didn't associate with the *fellaheen*, the peasant women. "Your League worries about the education of their daughters, though they have the means to send them to private schools, not for the education of the poor," Fatima had heard Samira scoff many times.

"You still haven't answered me. Get rid of the girl," Fatima said with impatience, "It's an order."

"I heard it," Samira said. "You seem upset. Let me unbraid and brush your hair, as I used to do when you were a young girl, while I'm going to tell you a true story."

"He was the nearest thing I ever knew to a grandfather."

When Samira finished telling about Mr. Grunwald, she saw that Fatima had been touched by her story. "After his death, I took an oath, though I was so young, still a child, that I'd help a needy orphan as wholeheartedly as Mr. Grunwald cared for me." She looked at Fatima, "Here is my chance to keep that oath. This poor girl needs my help. She's not well yet, and I'm not going to chase her away."

Samira knew that her words sounded unusual for a servant and she expected to be rebuffed by Fatima. But Fatima kept silent.

Samira continued, "Your parents were good to me, and I am devoted to you and your children, but," she took a yellowish picture out of her pocket, "I look every day at the photo of Grunwald *Effendi*'s granddaughter. She and her entire family were killed by bad people. Maybe it's only a coincidence, but I can't stop thinking of the resemblance with the Yahud girl. I want to help her get her health back. Only then will I feel that I've repaid my debt."

"I have to consider the future of my children," Fatima answered. "Keeping her longer will only make Musa think that I approve of her staying here. Who is she? Where did she come from? How long can I extend hospitality to a guest forced upon me? And now you want me to keep her longer!"

"Only until she gains more strength, I promise. She tries to help me with my chores, poor girl, but she's still very weak." Looking at Fatima with a furtive, sly glance, Samira continued smoothly, "Now, about Musa. Would you allow me to give you advice?"

Blankly Fatima stared at her.

"I think that you should send him away, maybe to Ramallah to study, or to work for and learn from your cousin the banker in Jerusalem," Samira said. "I heard in the *souk* that the Brits are encouraging young Arabs to take positions in the government. Our Musa is so bright."

Fatima sighed, "You are speaking my mind. I wanted to keep him close to me as long as I could, but I realize it's time for him to fly his own wings. It just hurts to think that my two older children will leave at the same time. I'm sure you know that Amina wants to volunteer for the British Army."

Samira nodded. She had always been the children's confidante. But she felt sympathy for Fatima. She knew how much her children meant to her.

"As for the meeting of the Arab Women's League," Samira concluded, "you shouldn't worry. The Jewish girl will stay in my room. Your daughters will help me serve the guests. They know to keep a secret when told to do so."

The meeting of the Arab Women's League took place in the *fumoir*, in the men's quarters. It was the room to which Faud, Fatima's husband, used to invite his friends for a smoke, a glass of tea or a little glass of arak. It was the first time Fatima had opened it for her own guests.

The large room was furnished in the Turkish style. Leather ottomans surrounded low glistening copper tables encrusted with beautiful arabesque designs. It was the room Fatima was the proudest of. Heavy Persian rugs in intricate designs of red, blue and black completed the room, giving it a festive look. Samira had aired the room from the smoke that still lingered in the air and washed the carpets with a vinegar solution that brought out the colors to look as fresh as the day they were bought.

Everything, even the smallest details, like flowers in every vase, were ready when the ladies arrived. With low bows, the greeting "*Salaam Aleikum*" and the hostess' response, *Aleikum Salaam*," filled the courtyard. The twenty ladies presented a curious mixture. There was the wife of the *mukhta*r, the Mayor of Jaffa, two Arab Christian women, the wife of a Muslim cleric whom everybody guessed was sent by her husband to spy on the meeting, and two spinster sisters, both teachers in a distinguished private school for girls. Besides Fatima, there were three other Palestinian Muslim women. The others were Lebanese or Syrian, married to notable Palestinian men.

Except for the wife of the cleric, nobody else wore the veil. And even she took it off when she entered the house. The Lebanese women were the most elegantly dressed. They wore knee-length muslin sleeveless dresses in pastel colors. Their French perfume deliciously filled the nostrils of all present. They were also the most educated and everybody in the group looked up to them.

"We have a busy agenda," the *mukhtar*'s wife said, as she opened the meeting." I want to start with the two major propositions we received from the headquarters of the British Army stationed in Palestine as well as from His Excellency, the British High Commissioner."

The ladies nodded. They were familiar with the subjects.

"We'll have to vote this evening if we agree to have our daughters, or even some of us, help the British Army. They've been successful in pushing back Rommel's German Army at Tobruk in North Africa. We can now breathe easier. The Germans will never fight us here in Palestine."

"Hear, hear," the ladies told one another. They applauded. They sat on the ottomans, in groups of three or four around the low Turkish coffee tables.

"Let's vote for the first item. Those in favor of our working for the Red Cross and for the war effort, raise your hands."

The two Christian ladies raised their arms, then the Lebanese ones; Fatima was the last. Amina, her daughter, who had just entered the room with a tray filled with ice water glasses in which rose petals floated, looked triumphantly at her mother.

The only person who abstained from the vote was the cleric's wife. "You are sending your daughters on the way to perdition," she said, a crooked smile appearing at the corner of her mouth.

"Thank you, ladies. We'll move to the next item," continued the *mukhtar*'s wife.

"The British High Commissioner is asking us to recommend educated young Arabs for positions in the government. Even though we don't like to have the British here, my husband thinks that cooperating with them at this stage would only benefit us. For example," she turned toward Fatima, "Musa, our hostess' son, would only bring honor to his family and to us all if he received a respectable position within the government."

Samira, who had entered bringing trays of baklava dripping with honey, and sugar-coated almond pastries, caught Fatima's glance. They looked at one another. Samira saw Fatima nodding imperceptibly.

Following Samira were Amina and Rama carrying trays of small cups filled with Turkish coffee, and glasses with nana tea. Fatima clapped her hands.

"Ladies," she said, "let us take a short break. Samira has worked hard for you. It is my pleasure to invite you to taste her pastries." A murmur of approval ensued.

"So, are you going to send Musa to Jerusalem?" the *mukhtar*'s wife pressed Fatima.

"He'll have to make that decision," answered a noncommittal Fatima.

She got up and as a gracious hostess moved between the different groups and heard snippets of conversation. The two teacher sisters said they had been asked to join the British women's sports club. They wanted to table the proposal and spread the idea among the other members of the League. At another table the cleric's wife was adamant about a woman's need to return to wearing the veil in public.

The Lebanese ladies were eager for the League to encourage women to attend Jaffa's new cinema unaccompanied.

"As they do in Cairo, or Beirut," added the youngest.

"That will never happen!" Fatima heard the shriek of the cleric's wife, who had just heard the last comment. Two other Muslim women nodded.

"It's a shame," one of them murmured.

The League started from the premise that all Arab women were sisters driven by the same ideal, Fatima recalled. But was this still holding true? Her thoughts were interrupted by the *mukhtar*'s wife calling out, "First, I hope all of us agree to say a big *Shukran*, thank you, to Mrs. Fatima for her hospitality."

Fatima heard murmurs of approval.

"And now, my dear ladies," the *mukhtar*'s wife continued, "As we resume our meeting, it's time to take a strong position about what the Jewish call their *aliya*, their immigration. Our newspapers warned us that they have infiltrated our land; many arrived illegally and spread like ants. We have to do our part in helping our men fight to preserve Palestine for Palestinians. This is our fatherland, this is our homeland." Everyone applauded.

Samira, who entered to clear up the tables, heard the last sentence. She glanced furtively at Fatima, and watched the tension narrow her eyes and tighten her lips.

7

Shifra couldn't fall asleep. She had heard unusual noises in the house, many women speaking loudly, all at once. *Where was Samira?* She didn't know what time it was, but it seemed long after the queen of the night had covered the sky with her mantle. Shifra had grown accustomed to the Arab woman's singing in her croaking voice, mixing Arabic and Yiddish words.

How much time had passed since she was brought to this strange house? Shifra remembered the beach. *But what beach, and what was she doing there?* She had opened her eyes to find herself in unfamiliar surroundings, strange people, two women and children who looked at her with worried eyes.

Oh, she felt so tired, so tired. Whenever she tried to think, her head hurt. There was a young man, who had carried her in his arms, she remembered! The blood rushed to her face. He seemed kind, but again, how did she get where she was now? The longer she thought, the more confused she became. And the headache started again. She drank the glass of water filled with nana leaves that Samira had left at her side.

After a slight tap at the door, Rama, the youngest of the daughters entered. By now she knew the little girl's name.

"I brought you pastries," Rama said in Arabic, putting a plate by her side. Shifra didn't understand the words, but understood their meaning and smiled at the little girl.

"You know," Rama said in a mysterious tone, "soon Amina and Musa will go away. I'll miss Amina so much."

Rama started to cry. She wiped her tears and looked hopefully at Shifra. "I want you to live with us and be my new sister."

Neither of them had heard Samira, who had slipped inside the room. "It's time you go to bed, sweet angel," Samira said, taking Rama in her arms and kissing her.

"Samira," Rama pointed toward Shifra, "Do you think I could try to teach her Arabic? Then she could really become my sister."

"Maybe," Samira smiled, "now run, before your mother finds out that you're still up."

At the beginning of the lessons Rama pointed to the objects in the room and named them in Arabic. She waited for Shifra to repeat the words after her, again and again. This child is a born teacher; Samira, proudly, witnessed her efforts. She would love to tell Fatima, but the latter was too busy preparing Amina before joining the British Red Cross.

In time, Rama became bolder. One day when Samira brought Shifra in the courtyard to enjoy the sun, Rama asked Nur, her older sister for help. "Please teach her our letters," begged Rama, who wasn't yet going to school.

"I am too busy, leave me alone," Nur answered. But Rama insisted, "You don't know how fast this girl can learn. She can name everything in the house. Please, Nur, please."

Samira wanted to intervene, but after she heard Rama insisting so much, Nur said, "I'll do it only because you asked me to. I don't see why she should learn Arabic. You heard Mother say that as soon as her health gets better, she'll have to leave."

As much as Shifra wanted to remember her past, now as dark as the sea that almost swallowed her, she made little progress. Vaguely, Rama reminded her of a little girl she had known before, but who? Shifra grew fond of Rama and for her sake, and wanting to make her proud, she took Rama's and Nur's lessons seriously.

"Look how pretty she writes," marveled Rama after a few days. "And she embellishes each word with designs. I have to show it to Amina. This girl's drawings are as beautiful as my sister's."

Excited, Rama took the notebook out of Shifra's hands and went to look for Amina. On the margins of her notebook, Shifra had drawn birds, flowers of paradise, and small animals, each one matching the characters of the Arabic letters.

Amina took the notebook looking attentively at each picture. "Eumi," she called her mother, still contemplating the drawings in her hand, "You were worried that after my departure, you wouldn't find anybody to produce the design which my dear sister Na'ima embroiders on the fabrics. You called us your winning team."

Fatima and Musa joined her. "Now," a triumphant Amina said showing the notebook, "I think that I found the person who could replace me, and this person already lives under our roof."

Amina's words created a commotion. Shifra didn't understand everything, but she felt that something special was going on. Lifting her eyes, she saw Musa nodding, visibly excited.

Amina spoke again, "Yesterday, in the bazaar, I was proud to see how many tourists bought our fabrics. They were snatching them out of each other's hands. I felt really sad thinking that my leaving would stop our work."

Rama clapped her hands. "And it was me! I discovered her." All eyes were on Fatima. They could have heard the buzzing of a fly in the silence that followed, everybody waiting for Fatima to speak. Fatima, who had never addressed Shifra directly, finally asked her, *Sho ismek*, what's your name?

Shifra had heard this question before. Rama had asked her almost daily, encouraging her by pointing to herself and saying, "My name is Rama," but Shifra had never answered.

Now everybody's eyes were riveted on her. Samira looked worried. So did Musa. Shifra tried, "Sh—"she started, then, "Shif—" she continued. Finally, she said on one long, trembling breath, "Shifffrrra."

Rama applauded. "See," she said, "you have a name."

Shifra felt so happy, she repeated it a few times, each time a little louder. Fatima looked puzzled. She opened the torn piece of newspaper that Musa had found in Shifra's fist. "Isn't your name Rifka?" Fatima asked.

"*La*, no," Shifra answered.

"Are you sure?" Fatima asked again. Shifra nodded. Fatima looked at Musa, waiting for an explanation. But Musa was just as baffled as she was.

"What does it matter if she's that girl or not," said Samira, who had followed the entire exchange with growing anxiety. Fatima had told her about the missing girl whom she had read about in the old newspaper and the fact that the Jews were after her. "She's here now," Samira continued, "and she can be helpful."

It took sometime for Fatima to answer. She said decisively "From now on your name is Suha. This is your name. Remember, your only name."

"Suha, Suha," Rama repeated, "what a beautiful name, as beautiful as you are, Suha," and she took Shifra's hand, "I told you, you'll be my sister, now."

But Shifra didn't hear Rama's words. In her heart she heard a continuous chant, *Shifra, Shifra, this is me, Shifra.*

"Come," Samira said, destroying the spell, "You've been in the sun too long. You'll get a headache again." She took Shifra's arm, "You've heard what Sit Fatima said, from now on, you are Suha. That's who you are." Samira pressed Shifra's arm again, "Come, Suha."

Still dreaming, Shifra-Suha felt herself dragged away by Samira. As they were leaving, she saw Amina and Rama hugging their mother, while Musa watched her with moist eyes.

8

So many things had happened in the few weeks since he found the blond girl—his angel, as Musa called her in his heart. Now in the silence of his room Musa loved to repeat her name, "Suha, Suha." Those syllables sounded like a melody, Su-ha, Su-ha, a name so suited to his love.

He felt such an attraction, a desire to touch her, and became dizzy just looking into the pool of her blue eyes. Until that moment, women and girls held no interest for him. He always knew that his mother would find him a match, a girl from a family as honorable as theirs, which was of utmost importance for families of their rank.

And now, was he ready to tell his mother, if she hadn't guessed already, that he had fallen in love with Shifra-Suha, the girl who came from nowhere, and who was, of all things, Jewish! He knew that this was inconceivable. Arabs and Jews didn't mix, as water does not mix with oil.

Like every Arab youngster, Musa had learned the slogans and participated in meetings where the speakers urged those present to fight against Jewish immigration. Yes, he had no doubt that

Palestine belonged to the Arabs. He had known it since he was a little child, and heard the Imam speak with so much fire in his voice, or at the meetings when he accompanied his father. It was there that the men swore to fight the *kafir*, the infidel, to the last one, like the *mujahedin*, the holy warriors.

But he couldn't drive away his feelings, the tremor that filled his heart each time he saw Suha. He followed with trepidation Samira's efforts to heal the girl.

Now, after his sister Amina left with the British Red Cross and thanks to Suha's newly discovered talent for drawing, Musa was relieved to see that his mother seemed inclined to accept her as part of their household. *But would his mother accept Suha as a daughter-in-law?*

Maybe it was too early to think about marriage. If he wanted to obtain his mother's consent, Musa decided, it would be better to wait for her signals and listen to what she encouraged him to do. If she wanted him to go to Ramallah or Jerusalem and learn to become an official within the government, Musa wouldn't oppose her will. He knew that the British would not rule forever. Their empire would crumble.

When the British leave Palestine, Arab leaders will be needed to take over the government. He must be ready for that time.

Yes, everything was working in his favor. If only Suha would smile at him! But she didn't look his way anymore, as if she were avoiding him. Maybe she was too busy with the drawings. But he longed to meet her eyes and see her blush, as had happened that first time, the morning after he brought her to his house.

He watched when Samira gave Suha one of her old *jelebias* and covered her blond hair with a *hijab,* while dark glasses hid the azure of her eyes. Dressed like that, nobody could have guessed that Suha wasn't an Arab woman. Almost daily Samira found reasons to take Suha to the bazaar or the *souk,* and it was usually hours before the two of them returned home. Though they looked tired from carrying heavy packages, Musa observed how exhilarated they were at their arrival. Suha's pale cheeks looked like the first apples he used to pick in the family orchard in the spring.

Musa became jealous of Samira, who shared a bedroom with Suha and, he suspected, shared her secrets as well. He promised himself to have a good talk with Samira before leaving on his journey.

Meanwhile, his mother had been busy writing letters of introduction for him to members of her family in Jerusalem, Ramallah, and even Amman. It seemed to Musa that Fatima wasn't as anxious to see him leave as she had been in the beginning. Amina had been gone for two weeks and Fatima sorely missed her daughter. It was the first time that one of her chicks had left the nest.

When Amina's first letter arrived, everyone crowded around Fatima, who read it aloud,

Esteemed Mother,

The work keeps me very busy, but I'm glad I can be of help. I miss you, my brothers and sisters and Samira, of course. The Brits are very respectful of women. I have in my care a soldier recuperating after a shoulder surgery which closed the wound left by a bullet. Anytime I do something for him he thanks me and kisses my hand. I feel embarrassed and as you taught me, Eumi, I never address him, but he likes talking and telling me about his family. He's from Cornwall, and he says that when he's well, he'd like to show me his country. I never answer. I only do my duty. By the way, his name is George and he has the curliest red hair.

How are you all doing? Did Musa leave already? Are you happy with Suha's designs? Dear mother, I pray *to Allah to keep you and our family in good health. Please don't worry for me. I know how to take care of myself.*

Your loving daughter, Amina

Not one muscle moved on Fatima's face after she finished reading her daughter's letter. Only Musa and Samira, who could read her heart, felt her worry. Silence reigned in the courtyard while each waited for Fatima to speak first.

After Fatima folded Amina's letter, she clapped her hands. "Children," she said, "I've made a decision. From now on, Nai'ma and Nur are going to share Amina's large bedroom, young Rama will come sleep with me, and Samira will take Rama's room."

Fatima stopped, trying to catch her breath. As an afterthought, she added, "Suha can have Samira's old room." Musa raised his head. He saw Suha shivering and Samira looking surprised. Something unusual seemed to have happened.

"Don't stand here and look at me, "Fatima dismissed them, "Go about your business, all but Musa."

When the two of them were left alone, she said, "I have news for you also. My cousin Abdullah, the banker, has agreed to host you during your stay in Jerusalem. You'll like it there. He has a big household full of beautiful girls," Fatima added, a sly smile fluttering on her lips. "I think you should leave tomorrow."

After he heard his mother's order, Musa knew that it had become imperative to talk with Samira. It had to be that very evening after everybody was asleep.

He found Samira singing softly in the kitchen. For once Suha was not with her, and Musa was relieved to find her alone. How was he going to start? He felt as if his head was on fire. He could not just say, "Take good care of Suha while I'm gone," or "At my return I want to find Suha here."

He was still searching for words when Samira stopped singing, looked at his perspiring face and said, "Musa, my boy, why do you look so worried? Jerusalem is not so far away, neither is Ramallah. Go with Allah and make a name for yourself. I know you'll make all of us proud."

Musa blushed. "I came to talk to you about Suha."

Samira smiled. "What about Suha?" she prodded him. "She's working and your mother is pleased with her work. Isn't that enough?"

"I don't want her to forget me," he whispered, blushing hard. "Lately she doesn't even look at me, it's like I don't exist. Now, with me gone—" he did not finish his sentence. Musa's eyes looked imploringly at Samira. *I talked too much*, he thought, *I shouldn't have opened my heart to Samira*. To gather courage Musa reached into his pocket and fingered his gift.

Samira looked straight at him, "I know how you feel," she said, "but you have to be patient. She's been through a big shock. She tells me that though she tries, she can't remember much from her past. She seems recovered, yet I feel there is pain in her heart. Who knows how long it will take until this can be healed?"

"Maybe this will help," Musa said, timidly taking the *hamsa*, the good luck charm worn by both Arabs and Jews, from his pocket. The palm of the five-fingered silver *hamsa* was encrusted with ruby stones shining like fire. "I had the *Imam* bless it. He said it would safeguard the person who wears it."

He held the *hamsa* in his hands, caressed it, and impulsively brushed it with his lips. "Give it to Suha. Ask her to wear it. Tell her that I hope it will remind her of me. I know I'll never stop thinking of her."

Without waiting for an answer, Musa ran out of the kitchen almost knocking down Fatima, who unwittingly heard his last words.

9

Everyone in the Masri household missed Amina, but Na'ima knew that no one's pain could equal her own. She thought about her twin most of her waking hours, and many times at nights before she fell asleep. Amina was not only her sister; she was her best friend and shield. In the intimacy of their room, they shared many laughs and tears while growing up. Na'ima couldn't remember one day when the two of them had been separated.

And yet they were so different. Amina, tall and slim, with a light complexion like their mother's, was the pretty one, whose graceful neck "could make a swan jealous," as Samira, their nanny, said many times.

Na'ima knew she wasn't pretty. She was short and dark. Though everybody lauded her beautiful black eyes, she knew that they seemed lost in her olive-dark face.

Sometimes on lazy summer afternoons when Fatima invited her neighbor friends for a cup of Turkish coffee or a glass of nana tea, Na'ima had heard her mother say, "Twin sisters, and yet so different, like my two Egyptian cousins, the one in Cairo so fair, and the southern one dark like the Sudanese."

Na'ima was not upset anymore by Fatima's remark. Nor when her mother told and retold the story of her birth, so often that she could tell it herself. Amina was born first. The delivery was so easy that after the midwife and Samira explained that the placenta was coming out, Fatima was ready to jump out of bed. "Wait," the women cried, alarmed, "Here comes another one." After so many years there was still wonder in Fatima's voice when she told it. "Another one?" repeated Fatima, "is that possible?" There were no twins in her family as far as she could remember.

"I had no time to think. They asked me to push hard. Five minutes later Na'ima was born. I didn't know whether to laugh or to cry, but my husband wasn't upset. He said, "Allah in his wisdom has sent us two girls to help you raise our future children." After a pause, Fatima added," and he was right, as always."

Fatima didn't mention that it took her a long time to name her second daughter. Amina was named, in respect, after her mother-in-law. If she'd had a boy, she would have named him Ibrahim, after her father. For a time she looked and looked at her unnamed daughter, and no name seemed to suit her. She didn't have the heart to name her after her own mother.

Until one day, when Samira, seeing Fatima's indecision, said, "How about calling her Na'ima, the pleasant one?" It surprised Fatima. "Even though she's not as pretty as Amina," Samira continued, "it surely pleased Allah to give you another girl. And with this name the evil spirits will be sent away."

Except for her sister Amina, Na'ima had no other friends. At school, the girls befriended her lovely sister. Na'ima was nicknamed "Amina's sidekick," and later on, "Amina's dark shadow." The fact that Amina, a brilliant student, was popular, and she was not, did not bother Na'ima. It was enough to know that she was her sister's best friend as Amina was hers.

But now, looking at Suha's blond head bent over her drawings, a pain like a thorn pierced Na'ima's heart. It had been weeks since Amina left to join the British Army, and although their mother had received weekly letters from her, none was addressed to Na'ima.

"Eumi," Amina wrote, "Please embrace my sisters for me," or, "Please convey my best wishes to the entire family."

Had her sister forgotten her? It was not only the work that had bound them together, though they spent most of their time working side by side; it was the product of their combined hands which made Na'ima so proud. Also she cherished the little secrets they shared.

When Na'ima left school at age twelve, after her father's death, her mother did not seem to care. Na'ima knew how to read and write in Arabic and English and that was sufficient. There were things she could help with at home. Amina continued school until she was fifteen. By that time, the matchmakers started to fill the Masri courtyard with proposals. Even a sheik who had heard about Amina's beauty and intelligence sent his emissaries. To all these proposals, Fatima, at Amina's insistence, answered that her daughter was far too young to consider marriage.

Na'ima knew that Fatima was flattered. She kept a file on all the potential bridegrooms. When the girls were small, Fatima invited Uhm Zaide, who could tell the future by reading the sediments left in coffee cups or tea leaves. The fortune-teller declared that Amina was going to make a brilliant marriage.

Fatima, after the matchmakers' visits, looked wistfully at Na'ima, patted her daughter's hand and said, "Na'ima, You'll live with me, to keep me company in my old age."

In the intimacy of their room Amina laughed, "I'll never leave you, "Amina whispered in her sister's ear, "We are going to marry two brothers, maybe twins, and live in the same house forever." It made Na'ima so happy!

When she was thirteen years old, Na'ima noticed hair growing on her arms. Too embarrassed to ask her mother what to do, she started to wear long sleeved *jelebias*. It took her a long time to gather the courage to ask Samira for a way to get rid of her hair.

After Musa brought the Yahud girl into their house, she, Na'ima, like her sisters, had promised their mother to keep the strange girl's presence a secret.

Now Na'ima was forced to work closely with her. She hated the girl, her golden tresses, her nimble fingers and milky arms. How come her sisters liked her so much? Amina, Rama, and now even Nur, who volunteered to teach her Arabic! Where was her sisters' patriotism? If she could, Na'ima would pour black dye on her head!

Na'ima was roused from her troubled thoughts by her mother's joyful shout, "A new letter from Amina! Come, everybody."

The entire household, including Samira and Shifra-Suha, gathered around Fatima. Na'ima sat closest to her mother. Shifra stood a little farther away, but Rama took Suha's hand and brought her into the circle. As she tore the envelope open, Fatima exclaimed with wonder, "She has sent us a few pictures, too."

Na'ima was the first to pick them up. She looked at the three photographs again and again until her mother impatiently snatched them from her hand. "Enough," she said, "let the others enjoy them, too."

The black and white pictures showed Amina in a group of Palestinian girls, dressed in white uniforms; a red cross sewn on each of their starched white bonnets.

They were smiling into the camera.

"This is the *mukhtar's* daughter," exclaimed Samira, pointing to a girl standing near Amina.

"I didn't know she joined the group, too," said Na'ima.

"But nobody is as pretty as our Amina," concluded Rama. Her mother hugged her. Another picture showed Amina with a British woman, tall, slim and serious-looking. "This lady is our head nurse," Amina had written on the back of the photograph,

In the last picture Amina was alone. She was smiling, her hair, freed from the bonnet, flying in the wind. From that picture Fatima sensed a feeling of well-being, maybe something more, happiness.

Fatima began to read the letter.

Most honored mother,

I hope that my letter finds you and everybody I love in good health. For that I pray daily to our Creator, because my family is the most precious gift Allah has given me.

The pictures probably surprised you. It was George, my patient, who took them. It was quite difficult for him, since his shoulder is still bandaged, but he put the camera on a tripod, after which he covered his head with a black blanket. It was hilarious. He rehearsed us until he was happy with our position and smiles. Oh, we all had such a good time!

But, please don't think that this is all we do. We are very busy, learning and working at the same time. George says that my English has improved a lot. He gives me books to read. I just finished reading a beautiful book, Ivanhoe by Sir Walter Scott. I s Musa happy in his new endeavor? George, whose uncle is a member of the British Parliament, told me that as soon as the British Mandate ends, Palestine will need professional women as much as professional men. He encourages me to learn a profession, maybe nursing. He thinks I have a gift for it.

From George's words I understand that a new world full of possibilities can open up for me. It

sounds so exciting. I will wait to hear what you think of it, Eumi.

I'd like to read a few words from everybody, including Rama.

Your most devoted daughter, Amina

P.S. George is leaving in two weeks. He is being sent to a convalescence home in Cairo where there are special therapists to exercise his arm in order to regain movement and strength. It will be sad without him. He has become such a good friend. I am afraid that afterward he will be sent to the front again. I pray for his life as I pray for my family.

Fatima folded the letter in silence. Na'ima burst into tears, "She'll never come back, never!" When she spoke again, Fatima saw hatred in the eyes of Amina's twin.

"You did it," Na'ima screamed pointing at her mother, "It's your fault. You sent her away, but you kept the Yahud girl here. What are you going to do next? Destroy our family? Oh, Allah Akbar, have pity on us!"

Na'ima's outburst left Fatima and everybody else speechless. It was the first time they had heard Na'ima raise her voice. Samira hugged Na'ima, whose sobs softened. "Amina, Amina," she whispered, "You betrayed me."

Tightly holding Na'ima, Samira directed her hesitant steps toward the house. "Samira is going to make you nana tea," she told the girl. "Then I'm going to brush your hair as I did when you were a little girl. That will help you relax, my little lamb."

After Samira and Na'ima left, Nur, Rama, Ahmed and Suha dispersed too with Suha holding onto Rama's arm. Fatima noticed that Suha looked stricken; but she had no time to think about Suha. She had her own worries.

After a while Fatima went into the kitchen to tell Samira about her decision and ask about Na'ima. She found Samira alone.

"She's sleeping," Samira said, guessing the upcoming question, "The storm is over."

"Tomorrow I am leaving for Jerusalem," Fatima said. "I have to see Musa. He is now the head of the family. We have important problems to discuss."

But Fatima could not leave the next day, nor the next, or the next. During the night Na'ima developed a high temperature, and threw up several times. She complained of chills and headaches. Three days later, after the home remedies used by Fatima and Samira did not help, Fatima decided to call Uhm Zaide, the old witch.

"Bring her immediately," Fatima ordered Samira, "she's the only one who can cast out the bad spell." Samira nodded.

In the days following Na'ima's angry outburst, the household became very quiet. Everyone walked on tiptoes, trying not to disturb the sick girl. During that time a delivery man brought a big order of fabrics to be embroidered. "Sit Fatima," he said, "my boss asks to have the order finished in two days. The customer can't wait longer." And he left.

"With Na'ima so sick, that is impossible," Fatima told Samira. "I'm going to send the order back."

Suha tugged at Samira's sleeve and Fatima saw her whispering in Samira's ear. Samira nodded several times. After clearing her throat, Samira said, "Suha told me that she would like to try her hand at embroidering. She said she watched Na'ima at work every day, and she thinks she learned the way to cross-stitch, using different needles at the same time. She asks for your permission."

Since Fatima didn't answer immediately, Samira insisted, "Sit Fatima, let her try. If she succeeds it would mean one less headache for you."

"I'd rather return the fabrics, but," Fatima paused, "she could show me her work tonight, or better tomorrow morning in the daylight. Meanwhile, Samira, go bring Uhm Zaide."

It was almost evening when Samira, followed by Uhm Zaide, returned. The barefoot toothless woman, with her long gray hair flying in the wind and her patched skirt, all rags, wasn't a pleasant sight. Her black eyes looked as fiery as burning coals.

Fatima was relieved that by the time the witch arrived the street was deserted. The neighbors always gossiped after someone called on Uhm Zaide. The witch took Na'ima's palm and studied it for a long time, muttering to herself in a language Fatima didn't understand. In her hoarse voice she asked Na'ima to take her clothes off. Na'ima, scared, looked at her mother, who nodded back to do what she was told. First, Uhm Zaide spit in three directions, to the left, right, and above Na'ima's head. Then she touched the girl's breasts and for a long time rested her gnarled hands on the young one's pelvis. Next she traced her crooked fingernails on Na'ima soles. The girl's body started to quiver. Uhm Zaide seemed satisfied, "Get dressed," she said.

Fatima and Samira watched the witch's doings in complete silence. From previous experiences they knew that Uhm Zaide wouldn't talk until she was finished. The witch took a few packets of herbs out of her pocket, "Samira," she said, "mix the herbs and boil them daily in well water. Make her drink this three times a day. In a few days her appetite and color will return." After she spit three times again on Na'ima's forehead she signaled Fatima to follow her out of the room.

"There's nothing wrong with your daughter," the witch said. "From all the signs I saw the girl is ripe for marriage." Uhm Zaide's toothless mouth was laughing and coughing. "Did you see her nipples?" Uhm Zaide continued, "Dark and hard! And how she shook when I touched her soles! It's a sign that she needs the touch of a man. That's the best medicine!" She laughed again. "Get ready to call the matchmakers."

The bewildered Fatima took out a few coins to pay, but Uhm Zaide refused, saying, "Don't forget to invite me to your daughter's wedding," and, still chuckling, she walked toward the gate, where Samira, who had heard the witch's last words, stood ready to take her back.

Neither Fatima nor Samira could fall asleep the night after Uhm Zaide's visit. In the morning, Samira, seeing that Fatima hadn't left her room, brought her a cup of strong Turkish coffee. The smell of coffee awakened Fatima. She smiled at Samira, "I don't know what I'd do without you," she said, smoothing the bedcover, "Come here. Did you hear the old witch's words?"

Samira nodded, "I think she's right."

Fatima sighed, "I don't want to talk to matchmakers, at least not now. I am thinking of trying another way first. Look here," Fatima opened the letter she had written during the night. "I wrote to my cousin Abdullah for help and counsel. You know that when we were children he was my best friend. If Faud hadn't swept me off my feet, I would have been married to Abdullah."

Samira nodded again. She knew Fatima's secrets. "And he's been so good to Musa," continued Fatima, a tear glistening in the corner of her eye.

"So, now you want to ask him to find a bridegroom for Na'ima?" asked Samira.

"Through his position at the bank, Abdullah meets many young men. I wrote Abdullah that Na'ima will receive a nice dowry."

Fatima picked up a second letter, "I asked Musa to keep his eyes open, too."

Samira looked admiringly at her mistress, "That's what I like about you, Sit Fatima. You don't lose time. When you make up your mind you move straight ahead."

The two women smiled understandingly at each other. "As for me," Samira said, getting up and starting to tidy up her mistress' room, "I also had thoughts that could be helpful. Na'ima can look beautiful too. I will make her bushy eyebrows look pencil-thin. I'll use the Persian way to get rid of hair growing on her arms and legs, which bothers her so much. When she wears short-sleeved dresses, people will admire the firmness and the roundness of her arms."

Fatima hugged Samira; she knew she could trust her. But Samira had more to say, "I'll ask Suha to sew a light-colored dress embroidered in beads of gold and silver. The dress, opened in front, will show off, no more than a little, don't worry, the valley between Na'ima's full breasts. She'll wear it for the bridegroom when he first comes to meet her. I promise you, this view will fill his heart with happiness!"

"You are dreaming, my dear Samira, but it is a beautiful dream," Fatima said.

"Any dream can become real," answered Samira, "Now, get out of bed, and let's start working toward it. "

1 0

Shifra also spent a sleepless night, after the witch, brought to see Na'ima, left. She sat in the small bedroom behind the kitchen, the room she had previously shared with Samira, bent over a narrow table, pearls of perspiration on her forehead. Her fingers ached from working on the embroidery samples Fatima would see the next morning.

She had watched Amira and Na'ima working on the precut fabrics, three or more yards of cotton, linen, crepe-de-chine or silk. Amina would mark with chalk or pencil the ten-inch-wide ribbon running alongside the material, for Na'ima to embroider later. Sometimes there were just curved arabesque lines embracing one another, similar to the ones encrusted on the Turkish coffee tables in their father's smoking room. Depending on the fabric, its color or the demand of the customer, flowers or little birds danced on the ribbon. As a finishing touch, a seamstress would then delicately apply the ornament on the sleeves, around the neck, or hem.

The light from the only bulb was not enough for the delicate work, and Shifra pricked her fingers many times. But she was not going to give up. Samira, whom she now thought of as a second mother, had faith in her, and Shifra did not intend to disappoint her. She wiped away the sweat dripping into her eyes. It was the middle of June, one of the hottest months, and she could feel the *hamsin* penetrating through the stone walls.

A vision of her parents' gloomy faces passed in front of her tired eyes. It pierced her heart. She tried to chase away her pain, to no avail. Slowly she had remembered most of her previous life. But as hard as she tried, she could not remember how she came to be on the beach that fateful day, the day that changed her life forever. *Did she run away from home? Why? Was it only a whim?*

Often she thought that she was living a long dream, and that one day she would awaken in her parents' cold Jerusalem flat.

Shifra looked with satisfaction at the result of her efforts. She saw that she could embroider as well as the twins. For a moment she wished that her real mother could see her now. Her mother thought she was too much of a dreamer, too lazy, not diligent enough.

Shifra suddenly froze as another image appeared before her eyes. It was the image of the *neft* man, spitting tobacco, laughing and telling her, "You'll be mine, you'll be mine; you can't run away from me. I'll find you wherever you go!"

Shifra stood up, her legs shaking. Now she remembered everything. Her father had promised her to the widower, whose daughters were almost as old as she was. Burning tears fell and soaked the embroidered samples, which a minute ago had made her so proud.

She fingered the mezuzah hanging around her neck. Every morning she had prayed, hoping for help, "*Shma Israel: Adonai Eloheinu, Adonai Ehad* – Hear, O Israel: Adonai is Our God, Adonai alone." But there was no way back and she knew it.

Samira opened her door, "Still up," she scolded. "I saw the light under your door and I thought; what is my girl doing?" She hugged Shifra, "I see tears. You'll harm your eyes from so much work. You're too tired. Go to sleep. Sleep makes girls beautiful."

Samira pulled the bedspread away. "Come," she said slyly, "go to bed; you know who wants you to be beautiful at all times."

After Samira left, Shifra still couldn't fall asleep. She knew what Samira alluded to. She touched the second amulet Samira had tied around her neck. It was the *hamsa*, the charm Musa asked Samira to give her, before he left for Jerusalem.

Shifra felt her cheeks burning. Was it a sin to think of him? She had tried to avoid Musa, knowing her heart beat faster in his presence. Now that he was far away, she missed him, the thrill she felt when she heard his voice. Though she did not dare look at him, she knew his eyes followed her every movement.

He was strong. Her body still held the memory of his arms when he carried her. That thought made her blush again. She should not think of him. They were worlds apart. She did not belong in his world. *Then why was she still in his mother's house?* Shifra had to admitt to herself that she was afraid of the outside world, that she felt protected by the house's walls.

What could she expect now after Na'ima's outburst, and with Musa gone? How long before Na'ima, in her hatred, would denounce Shifra to the police? Shifra fell into an uneasy sleep, her troubled mind unable to find an answer.

"Get up! Get up!" Samira's cheerful voice rang in Shifra's ears. "I have good news. This morning while you were asleep, I took the samples and showed them to Sit Fatima. She liked them." Samira drew the curtain and the sun filled the little room, "It's late already," she said, "but I didn't want to wake you up. I knew that you worked late into the night."

Shifra rubbed her tired eyes while Samira continued to chatter. "You have a lot of responsibility now. You have to design and embroider, too. The time is short, but I have faith in you. You can do it."

Shifra shuddered. She remembered Na'ima's wrath. Now she would hate her more. She couldn't remain in Fatima's house. *It wasn't safe anymore.* She had to leave. She had to find a way to do it and the only person who could help her was Samira. *But would Samira help?*

While Shifra got dressed, Samira brought in a tray with tea, leben and pita. "This is for my working girl," she said tenderly.

Now or never, Shifra decided. She cleared her throat, "Samira, I can't remain here any longer." She saw Samira's body turn rigid. "Samira, I know that you care for me. This gives me the courage to talk to you. Please help me," Shifra started to cry as the emotions of the previous night had taken their toll on her.

"I don't understand," Samira said. "Yesterday you offered to double your work and today you want to run away? I think that you are just tired. Maybe you need to sleep more. I know that young girls need more sleep." Samira pulled the curtain back.

"Samira, Na'ima hates me. You've heard her. Now she'll hate me even more if I can do the work she was so proud of. No, it's not safe for me to live here. Not anymore. She'll go to the police, or—" Shifra burst into tears again. "You have to help me, please."

Samira hugged Shifra. "I'm going to tell you a secret," she said holding the girl close to her, "Na'ima's going to get married. Sit Fatima decided that would be best for her. Na'ima misses Amina, as you know, but a good man," Samira paused, while a sly smile passed over her lips, "can make a woman forget not only her sister, but her parents as well!"

"Dry your tears," Samira said, "a lot of work is waiting for you .Finish the customer's order. And pretty soon, you'll start embroidering the dresses for Na'ima's dowry."

11

As usual Fatima got up early. It was dawn. She went to her desk and opened the account book. Once a week since Musa left, she checked the books. The column of numbers was growing steadily. Faud would have been proud of her. She wondered if he'd approve her trust in her cousin Abdullah to invest their money. She didn't want to linger on this thought. She was lucky. Abdullah had made her money grow. At his counsel; she opened accounts in branches of Barclays Bank in other Arab countries, which, he said, were more secure than Palestine. *Yes, she did well for herself.* This morning she planned to go to the port to watch the loading of another big order of her citrus fruits. Her oranges were in great demand.

She fiddled with the buttons of the radio resting on her nightstand. After Faud's death, she had moved his radio from the men's quarters to her room. As a young bride, she was jealous of Faud spending so much time listening to it. When she told him that she would like to listen too, he kissed her and gently made her leave, saying, "You shouldn't bother your pretty head with the problems and the sorrows of the world."

What she loved most of all was listening to Uhm Kultum, the famous Egyptian songstress called by the entire Arab world, "Mother of the Nation." Fatima fell into the habit of turning on the radio early in the morning after reading her daily Koran portion, when everybody else was still asleep.

It was only lately, after Amina left with the British Red Cross, that Fatima started paying attention to the news about the war raging in Europe. *Europe was pretty far away, wasn't it?* Once Faud had shown her the globe and had laughed heartily when she had asked him how such a small ball could contain so many countries.

After the British media announced that Palestine was in no danger of war, world news didn't interest her anymore. But now! She was fingering Amina's latest letter, which came only a week after her previous one. This time Fatima decided to read it alone. She didn't want to provoke another outburst from Na'ima, especially after the girl seemed healed and enjoying the attention everybody bestowed on her.

June 25, 1943

Eumi,

Together with two other nurses I have been asked to escort the convoy of convalescent British soldiers headed for Cairo. George was so happy when he heard that.

Eumi, this is urgent. I beg you to allow me to go. Remember that next month, in July, Na'ima and I will celebrate our eighteenth birthday. Weren't you already married at our age? You know that I can take good care of myself; otherwise you wouldn't have let me join the Red Cross.

Besides, your cousin in Cairo could be my chaperone in that beautiful city.

George says that after he's totally recuperated, he wants to join the army fighting now in Europe until the Germans finally surrender. I fear for his life.

Your loving daughter, Amina

Fatima read and reread the short letter. No, she wasn't going to read it in front of Na'ima. She started to dress. There was a slight knock on the door and when she opened it, Samira entered with a tray of steaming Turkish coffee and sweets.

"I know you have to leave early for the docks," Samira said, ogling the open letter on Fatima's desk. "Oh, I see you've got a new letter."

"Nothing escapes you," Fatima said. She told Samira the content of Amina's letter.

"What are you going to do?" asked Samira

Fatima raised her shoulders, "I did not decide yet. Things are so different now. It's like living in another world."

"Your feet are grounded in our tradition," Samira said, "But you have to keep your head clear and look into the future. There are going to be many changes. I even heard Uhm Zaide say it."

"You and your Uhm Zaide," Fatima smiled. Anytime Samira wanted to make a point, she hid behind 'Uhm Zaide said so, too.' "Better help me get dressed. I have a long day ahead of me."

- - -

Less than two weeks after she mailed the letter to her cousin in Jerusalem, Fatima received Abdullah's prompt answer. The postman joked while handing the letter to her, "Lately you've become my best customer." Fatima gave him his tip and hurried to her room.

July 10, 1943

To my most esteemed and cherished cousin, Fatima,
Salaam Aleikum!

I pray that my letter finds you in good health and
that Allah is smiling upon you. Your letter concerning
your daughter Na'ima's future, Allah keep her in His
Grace, arrived as I was just preparing to leave on
one of my regular visits to our customers living in
the villages around Jerusalem, Ein Karem, Deir Yassin,
Abu Gosh. I took your dear son Musa, a serious and
industrious young man, along with me to acquaint him
with our clients.

Only a few days before my planned visits, Mahmood
Abu-Hassan, a young man from Deir Yassin, came
to see me regarding a loan. I knew his late father
well. Like him, Mahmood is hard-working and a good
person. Unfortunately, he lost his wife in childbirth
some months ago. While taking care of the baby,
he neglected his olive orchard and because of this
year's drought, his harvest is lost. He asked for a
loan in order to buy and plant new trees. I promised
I'd come to visit him as I usually do, to make sure
that our debtors have the means to pay back the
loans.

I don't know if you've ever been to Deir Yassin.
The brown-pink houses are raised in tiers on a
mountainside terrace, three kilometers south of
Jerusalem. Mahmood's house is surrounded by a
thriving vegetable and fruit garden alongside the olive
orchard. And he owns sheep as well.

I had a talk with Mahmood's mother, who now
lives with him and helps to take care of the baby.
She's a sensible woman. She said that she'd like to

see him remarried." Mahmood is only twenty-five years old", she said." He needs a young woman. I am too old to look after a baby."

I hope I'm not too bold in saying that Na'ima's dowry, which you mentioned in your letter, could nicely help him rebuild his orchard and increase his income.

Now, my dear Fatima, please think about what your humble cousin has written. If you decide that it's worth your time, I'd be most happy to be your host, while you visit with Mahmood's mother and gather information about his family. Of course this will be done with utmost discretion.

Allah be with you always, Abdullah

Fatima read the letter again. *A peasant,* the proposed bridegroom is a peasant. It didn't thrill her. She trusted Abdullah's judgment; in his youth Abdullah was called the Fox because he was so quick and bright. He wouldn't have written her about Mahmood unless he was sure of the young man's character.

"Samira," she called from the hallway, "come here quickly."

Samira appeared, wiping her hands on her apron. "What's the hurry," she asked, "are we expecting guests?"

"We might be," answered Fatima with a smile, "but not for a while. Now, listen to this," and she began to read Abdullah's letter.

"Abdullah is right," Samira said. "Go meet his family. And don't look so sad. I don't think you expected Na'ima to marry a sheik."

Fatima didn't answer.

"If he's a hard-working man, as your honored cousin has written, that's worth more than ten lazy sheiks. Na'ima is a strong girl. She is not afraid to work. Together they could blossom. But I know what bothers you. That it's against the tradition for the girl's mother to inquire first. Mahmood is a widower. In such a case the tradition can be bypassed."

Like a poker player using her winning card, Samira, added, "When I hinted to Na'ima that you might consider her getting married, I saw stars appear in her eyes."

The postman was right. Few days passed without new letters. Even though Fatima decided to make the trip to Deir Yassin, as her cousin Abdullah proposed, she couldn't leave immediately. Besides putting her house and business in order, she had to buy gifts for the mother of a future bridegroom, as was the custom.

Her heart was thrilled that she would also be seeing Musa. In one of his first letters from Jerusalem he wrote that cousin Abdullah kept him so busy, he didn't think he would come home before Ramadan, and there were two more months until the holiday. Fatima had sighed when she read it. But here was a new letter from Musa, which Fatima tore open with impatience. Her darling son, the light of her eyes! She knew that she would read it later for everybody, but first she wanted to enjoy it alone, in the intimacy of her room, where she could cry unseen.

July 14, 1943

Most honored Eumi,

I hope that my letter finds you and everybody in your household in the best of health. I am writing in a rush because many things have happened lately and I want to share them with you. First, I got a letter from Amina addressed to me at Barclays Bank. She said that she's accompanying a group of convalescent British soldiers to Cairo. She asked for my blessing as the head of the family.

When I told Cousin Abdullah about it, he immediately called the Red Cross. He was relieved to hear that there is no danger. The convoy will be guarded by military men. Moreover, he called the Barclays Bank in Cairo, and opened an account in Amina's name. He also called your Cairo cousins to expect Amina's visit.

So, dear Mother, please do not worry. She'll return home safe and sound.

Now, about myself! I go regularly to pray at El Aksa Mosque for the late afternoon prayers, when the colors of the limestone and rocks change from the most ardent red to all the shades of blue and violet. What a sight! But you surely know that, as you are a Jerusalemite yourself!

Cousin Abdullah wants me to take classes in International Banking. He says that as Palestinians it's important for our future. An-Najah University in Nablus seems to be his choice, but Al-Quds in the old Jerusalem has a good reputation also.

Meanwhile, I got a letter from our mukhtar, urging me to register for the law and order classes offered by the British Police. In his letter, the mukhtar emphasized Palestine's need for young people to join the leadership when the British Mandate ends. I feel honored by his trust.

In the evenings I take long walks in Bakka, cousin Abdullah's neighborhood. Sometimes I walk as far as Katamon or Musrara. The evening's breeze and the flowers' perfume remind me of our beloved poets. There is no one here to whom I'd like to read a poem. For that I'll have to return home.

Your devoted son, Musa

1 2

Samira was left in charge of the household. It was not the first time. When they were young, Fatima and Faud took trips to visit their families on holidays, for weddings or anniversaries. Samira always proved she could be trusted.

"Now that the children are older," Fatima said, "Na'ima can help you, making your job much easier. Just don't let strangers in."

Samira nodded. She had heard that every time Fatima left on a trip. Maybe Fatima was thinking of the *mukhtar*'s wife who came unexpectedly the evening before Fatima's departure for Jerusalem. She was panting, and instead of the customary greeting, she cackled, "Your daughter, your daughter Amina, whose character everybody admired, has run away with an Englishman. She's gone to Cairo, my daughter wrote me. What shame she brought upon your good name!"

As soon as she uttered the last words, the *mukhtar*'s wife left quickly, without waiting for an answer.

"I cannot delay my departure any longer," a pale Fatima told Samira after the *mukhtar*'s wife disappeared. "I am going to Jerusalem to see my cousin. With Allah's help, I'll call on Mahmood's mother. We need to hurry, before the *mukhtar's* wife spreads her miserable gossip."

"Don't worry," said Samira, putting her arms around Fatima, "I'll give you a little massage to make you feel better. I think the *mukhtar's* daughter was always jealous of Amina. She knew that a letter to her mother would light a fire."

"You are probably right," answered Fatima, "But it doesn't make me less anxious. For all of us, and now especially for Na'ima's sake, no stain should blot our good name. I am leaving tomorrow morning for Jerusalem."

The next day when the children awoke, Samira told them that their mother had left at dawn to go to Jerusalem to see Musa.

Rama said, "For how long? How come she didn't kiss us goodbye?"

"When is she going to be back?" Nur asked.

"Soon," Samira said. "Meanwhile everybody goes by his daily routine as usual."

Only Na'ima didn't seem curious. *Has she guessed the reason for Fatima's quick departure? In the end I'll have to tell her. She should be prepared*, Samira thought .

A few days passed without news from Fatima. Then a letter addressed to Samira arrived. It wasn't from Fatima, as Samira found out when she opened the envelope. From it fell a thin booklet, then a letter written in Musa's delicate handwriting.

It was the first time Samira had received a letter.

July 21, 1943

Allah be with you, my dear Samira,

Many times I started to write to you, but I realized that it might appear disrespectful to my mother. Now that she is here in Jerusalem, I can finally send you this letter.

You know what's in my heart. My feelings are unchanged, or even more ardent because of the distance.

Dear Samira, do you remember the promise you made to me before I left? Are you talking to Suha about me? My heart aches from so much longing. I wish I could be a bird sitting on her window sill and sing to her songs of love, like this verse from a poem by the beloved Egyptian poet, Ibrahim Nagy. Read it to her:

Has anyone been drunk with love like me?
Has anyone seen love as I have seen it?

Oh, Samira, I am burning with love,

Musa

Indeed, it's time to keep my promise. Samira folded the letter carefully and hid it in the drawer holding her other treasures: the photographs of Mr. Grunwald's grandchildren.

For a few days, she concentrated all her labors on Na'ima's appearance. She knew what she wanted to do. First she mashed together bananas and cucumbers to make a paste, which she applied to Na'ima's face. "This concoction does wonders," she said authoritatively. "I've seen how the skin glows after only a few applications and becomes smooth like silk."

After she washed her face, Na'ima ran to look into the mirror hanging in the kitchen above the sink. Seeing that her blackheads had disappeared and her face was without blemishes, she hugged Samira and danced with her around the kitchen.

"Stop it!" laughed Samira. "Now I'm going to shape your eyebrows to look as thin as the arch of the moon when it first appears in the sky at the beginning of each month."

Nur and Rama witnessed Na'ima's transformation with exclamations of admiration.

"Samira," begged Rama, "when are you going to shape my eyebrows, too?" Her sisters laughed. "When you are as tall as Na'ima," Samira joked. For a long time she brushed Na'ima's long hair with perfumed oil, after which she rolled it up to form a crown. Samira admired the result, sighing with satisfaction.

She hadn't forgotten the promise she made to Musa. She would follow the plan she thought of from the day she received Musa's letter. But first she needed Na'ima's absolute trust.

On Friday, the Muslim Sabbath, when the shops were closed, she told Na'ima, "Yesterday I cooked the meal for today, lamb filled with rice. While I made the tabbouleh and baked the bourekas, I was thinking, wouldn't be nice if I take some food to Uhm Zaide too? She's so old and doesn't cook anymore for herself."

Na'ima nodded.

"So I want to ask you a favor," continued Samira. "If you'd agree to look after Rama, Nur and Ahmed, I'll take Suha to help me carry the food to her."

Na'ima nodded again.

As always before leaving, Samira covered Suha's head. Uhm Zaide lived in Manshiya, a no man's land between Jaffa and Tel-Aviv, the Jewish city. It was almost noon when they reached Uhm Zaide's hut. Crouched on the mud floor, Uhm Zaide was scratching a wooden plate of its dried humus remnants.

"Here you are," she cried joyously when she saw Samira. Uhm Zaide sniffed the air with delight. "What goodies do you bring me?" At the sight of her, Shifra hid behind Samira's back.

"You brought food and a girl for me to eat, too?" She laughed, showing the darkness of her toothless mouth.

"Eat, eat to your heart's desire," Samira urged her, taking the dishes from Suha's hands and placing them on the floor. Then she sat next to the witch.

"Nice of you to bring me food," said a satiated Uhm Zaide after a while. Her eyes scanned Shifra from top to bottom. "What is this Yahud girl doing here? Why did you bring her?"

Samira moved even closer and whispered in her ear. Uhm Zaide nodded a few times, while Shifra looked at both of them with apprehension.

"Bo'i ena, come here," Uhm Zaide said in Hebrew, while her crooked index finger signaled Shifra to get closer. "Kneel," she barked.

Seeing Suha tremble, Samira encouraged her. "Do what she says. Don't be scared. She's a good woman. She's not going to hurt you."

Uhm Zaide lit a candle and held it close to Shifra's face.

"Hmm," she said appreciatively, after she looked into Shifra's eyes for a long time, "gorgeous eyes, as clear as the sea in the morning." Then she ordered, "Stand up." Taking a small wooden hammer, she gently hit Shifra's knees and elbows. She watched the girl's reaction with satisfaction.

"There is nothing wrong with her," Uhm Zaide declared.

She got up and spit on Shifra's forehead, then over her left and right shoulders.

"To drive away the bad spirits," explained Samira, seeing how bewildered Shifra looked.

Uhm Zaide opened Shifra's palm and studied it attentively. She turned toward Samira, "As I said, her body is healthy, but her heart is in turmoil. She doesn't know it yet, but her love line," and Uhm Zaide traced it with her finger, "predicts great things. She'll not only be loved, she'll be worshiped like a goddess. And that will heal her sadness."

All of a sudden, Uhm Zaide frowned. "I can't see much more," she said. "Either the future is clouded, or my eyes are too weak."

The witch let go of Shifra's hand, "Go now," she pointed towards the opening of the hut, "go outside." After Shifra left,

Uhm Zaide went to a drawer where she searched for some time until she produced a small envelope filled with powder.

"No one can live without love," she said, giving Samira the envelope, "but it does no harm to push it a bit. Take this powder. Each day, during the three days of the Ramadan feast, pour a little in her tea. There is already love in her heart, even though she doesn't acknowledge it. This powder will make it stronger."

The two women's eyes locked with understanding. Samira wanted to thank her, but Uhm Zaide stopped her short, "You are my friend. I did what you asked me to do. Yet I don't know why you encourage Musa's pursuit of this girl. I can only hope that you'll not be sorry one day."

13

After leaving Uhm Zaide's hut Shifra and Samira continued on their way in silence. It was the first time Shifra had walked through the Manshiya neighborhood. She breathed the salty air with delight, hopping from rock to rock, happy to be far from the darkness of Uhm Zaide's hut. She still didn't understand why Samira had to take her, though she was pleased, for once, to be far from Na'ima's scrutinizing eyes.

It was hot, the sun at its zenith, and few people ventured onto the streets. Shifra saw a path leading to a narrow street with whitewashed walls and old trees shadowing the sidewalks. Gamely, she turned into it, ready for adventure.

"Where are you going?" Samira, suddenly alarmed, cried out. Shifra only hurried her steps without answering.

"Stop it!" Samira ordered, breathing hard, trying to keep in step with Shifra. "This is not the way home."

Shifra shuddered when she heard the word "home." For the two of them, home didn't have the same meaning. Shifra continued to march ahead, letting the old woman run after her.

The sounds of a violin made Shifra stop in her tracks. It was the most endearing, tender, yet sorrowful music, so beautiful and pure, it made her heart cry. It sounded so familiar.

"Listen," she whispered to Samira, afraid that by speaking louder the magic of the music would stop. "Have you heard anything more beautiful?"

Samira looked at the house where violin strains had broken the silence of the placid afternoon. A copper plate was dangling dangerously on the gate. On it in bold letters was written, DR. OTTO SCHRODER, PROFESSOR OF VIOLIN. Whispering, Shifra translated the plate.

"Let's go, let's go," Samira nudged her, taking her arm, but Shifra would not move.

She couldn't break away from the dream state created by the music. *What was the music she heard?* The music had entered her heart. Shifra closed her eyes and, feeling weak, leaned on the wall beneath the magic window.

A vision appeared in front of her eyes. She saw herself in the little room that served as a *shul* for her parents and their neighbors. It was very hot. Through the partition that separated men and women, she saw the men, swaying back and forth, singing the melody that she heard being played by the magic violin.

Then another image superimposed itself upon the first. It was the violin in her friend Chana's apartment, brought by Chana's father when he ran away from Germany. It was kept in a glass compartment and nobody was allowed to touch it.

"My father was a child prodigy," Chana told Shifra. "But he stopped playing the violin after he found out that his entire family was taken by the Nazis and no one heard from them again. His first impulse was to break the violin, but my mother saved it. My father never played it again except for the Kol Nidrei prayer in remembrance of his parents."

That was the music she listened to now, walking on that dusty little street in Jaffa. She was sure she had heard Chana's father playing it one evening long ago. Shifra opened her eyes. *How long had she been dreaming?* She saw a worried Samira watching her. The music stopped. Somebody opened the window and a middle-aged lady peered into the street. Samira dragged Shifra away and both hid behind a tree.

"*Ruhig, die Strasse ist ruhig-* the street is quiet, Otto. There is nobody here." The lady turned her back to the window and called to someone inside the house, "Please, my darling, continue." She had spoken in German, which for Shifra, who spoke Yiddish, was easy to understand. Shifra had noticed the lady's sad eyes and pale face.

"Come on, we have to hurry," Samira urged her. "Na'ima won't understand what took us so long."

Shifra looked at the house once more. Number 34 was written in black charcoal between its two large front windows. All the way back to Fatima's house, the sounds of the violin followed her. Silently, she took an oath never to forget the house, the street and the violinist's name, Otto Schroder. She didn't know yet when and how she would return, but she knew she would be back.

As the two of them approached Fatima's house, they heard a lot of noise in the courtyard.

"What could that be?" Samira hurried, anxiously. Opening the gate, they saw an idyllic tableau. Fatima was seated on a three-legged stool; at her feet, Na'ima, Rama, Nur and Ahmed listened entranced to their mother's tale. Around them were half-opened packages, all gifts Fatima had brought from Jerusalem.

"Oh, here you are!" Fatima exclaimed when she saw Samira and Shifra enter the courtyard. So excited she was, she didn't even ask why they weren't home.

"A friend of cousin Abdullah had business in Jaffa, and he gave me a lift in his beautiful Studebaker. I returned earlier," Fatima explained to Samira, "because we are going to have guests next week, important guests," she stressed the last words, "and it's never too soon to start preparing for them. Look here."

She opened a big package from which a diaphanous muslin material fell to the ground, "We are going to have new curtains to make the house look cheerful."

Shifra slipped away unobserved. In her heart the music never stopped. Impulsively, she took a piece of paper and a pencil and started drawing the cross streets leading to the alley, the violinist's house, the high windows and even the pale woman's features. She wrote the name Otto Schroder and 34, the number of the house on top of the paper. She hid the paper under her pillow. Just in time, as she heard Samira turning the knob to her door.

"Come, don't sit alone," Samira said.

Silently Shifra followed Samira. Even before stepping into the courtyard Shifra heard Fatima assigning tasks to each of her children. Shifra knew that she would be included in those tasks, and that she would have to work hard. But right now, for a few more seconds, she wanted to keep hold of the memory of the music and how peaceful she felt upon hearing it.

14

August 23, 1943

To my dearest and cherished sister Amina, Salaam Aleikum!

It's been more than three months since you left home and so many things have happened that I don't even know where to begin. But I think I'll start by telling you my big news. I'm engaged to get married, with Allah's will, very soon, on Idul Fitri holiday.

Can you imagine, me, to be the first to get married? I never dreamed of it. It all happened so fast. Mother went to Jerusalem to visit Musa, who is working in cousin Abdullah's Bank.

Cousin Abdullah, a wonderful man, introduced her to Mahmood's mother. Mahmood is my fiancé. Isn't that a beautiful name? I feel as though my mouth melts when my lips form his name.

Cousin Abdullah knew Mahmood's father. His people were customers of the bank, and cousin Abdullah knew the family personally.

Have I told you how good-looking my Mahmood is? He's twenty-five years old, you might say, a bit too old for an eighteen-year-old girl, but I think it's good for me to have a husband to look up to, one who'd make the right decisions.

Mahmood sports a mustache, which is very becoming, especially when he smiles, like a little crown above his bright teeth. I hope I'll be able to make him smile every time he looks at me. But I'm getting ahead too fast. Must be the excitement of everything I want to tell you, all at once.

Your letters addressed to our mother were signs of your filial respect, but they never had a little separate section for me. I had hoped that you would write to me, and say that you missed me as much as I missed you.

If I continue rambling like this, this letter will never get finished. I can already hear Samira clapping her hands, asking for everybody to get going. There is so much to do preparing for a wedding.

Do you remember how you said that we would both get married on the same day, two sisters marrying two brothers, and we would live together forever?

Well, Amina, those were beautiful dreams. You are so far away, my heart aches. I'd love so much to have you closer, especially right now. This letter is written with the hope that you'll come home, five weeks from now, when my wedding will take place.

You might ask why so soon? I didn't tell you that Mahmood is a widower, he has a little boy, five months old. His wife died in childbirth. It's for the sake of the little boy that our mother decided to rush our wedding.

Musa has met Mahmood and they like each other. Have I told you that I'm going to live in Deir Yassin? It's a beautiful village perched on the hills outside Jerusalem. I'll live close to Musa and cousin Abdullah's family. I know that I'm going to miss my mother and sisters terribly and you, Amina, most of all.

When our mother returned from Jerusalem she told me to expect a visit from Mahmood's mother, who arrived a few days later, her arms full of gifts for everybody. I received five golden bracelets, which had belonged to her. I wear them even when I go to bed and their ting-a-lings put me to sleep. Mahmood came a week later. I was trembling. What would happen if he didn't like me? I'd become the laughingstock of the neighborhood.

I wore the white dress Suha, the Yahud girl, had embroidered for me, and Samira had done my hair in a new style she saw in a French magazine. My heart beat so fast, I thought I was going to faint. He was respectful to my mother and played shesh-besh with Ahmed, which gave me time to take a better look at him and quiet my rapid heartbeats.

Mahmood said that he couldn't remain long in Jaffa, since he had to return home to plant new olive trees. Last year's drought made him lose a lot of trees. During his visit we decided on the date for our wedding.

Oh, Samira is calling me. She screams " Na'ima, we don't want to deliver a lazy bride to her bridegroom. Time to work, my girl."

Doesn't this sound like her? Amina, I know that you are busy learning a profession. But for the sake of the times when we were so close, please come home and be in my wedding. The wedding will be in Jaffa and not in Deir Yassin, as is usually the custom, in the bridegroom's village. Mahmood said that the villagers might be sensitive to the fact that he is getting married only a few months after his wife died.

As I write to you, I see Suha sweeping the courtyard. She's the only thorn in my life. What made Musa bring her home?

Suha had the common sense, or maybe my mother ordered her, to stay in her room during Mahmood and his mother's visit, but I wonder what will happen during the wedding, when so many of Mahmood's friends and relatives, as well as our extended family, will be here? We can't hide her forever, can we?

Samira has already opened the door to my room and is now threatening to hit me with the broom. It's time to hug you and send lots of kisses. I want to see your smiling face at my wedding,

Your twin sister, Na'ima

15

Musa loved Jerusalem, where the gorgeous sunset descended slowly on the city, and every rock and stone changed its colors from gold to pink, to blue and finally to violet, before being blanketed by darkness. To relax after a hard day of work, Musa took long walks, discovering new neighborhoods, some dating back from centuries before the Sultans' ruling. It was refreshing to walk from the walls surrounding the Old City that had witnessed so many wars and bloodshed to its more modern counterpart, Jerusalem's west side, in the cool breeze of the evening. Jerusalem's evenings were so different from Jaffa's, whose evenings were as fiery hot as during the day.

On Fridays, when in respect for the Muslim holiday his Barclays Bank branch was closed, he had the habit of strolling Jaffa Street, the main thoroughfare in Jerusalem, from Musrara to the *souk*, the market, the Jews called Mahane Yehudah.

It wasn't only the good smells of fresh baked bread or the perfume of the flowers, cut early the same morning, drops of dew sparkling on their petals, which attracted him to the *souk*. Once, as he happened to wander in the maze of streets across from the market, he saw something that astounded him. It was a group of young girls, dressed exactly as his angel, Suha, when he first saw her asleep on Jaffa's beach. They wore long dark skirts, long-sleeved white blouses and black stockings. Their hair was braided, just like hers. But of course no one was as pretty as his love.

He wanted to approach them, maybe to ask ... but what could he ask? He tried to remember her Jewish name, on the day his mother had asked for it. Yes, it was Shifra, wasn't it? Maybe those girls knew her; maybe they could help him solve the puzzle, the mystery of the girl who occupied his mind constantly, awake or asleep.

Musa hurried to catch up with them, but the girls, after taking one look back, disappeared like a flock of birds. Musa didn't understand what could have scared them. He was dressed like an Englishman, in a dark suit and tie. He even didn't wear the *kafia*, which he usually wore at the bank. Was it because his head wasn't covered like the Jewish men he saw in the *souk*?

He sighed. Lately, there were so many events happening at once. Na'ima's engagement and approaching wedding, his mother urging him to write to his sister Amina, now in Cairo, ordering her to come home. As his mother wrote, "If your father were alive he would have asked her to come home immediately. Now, it's your responsibility as head of the family."

Of course, he was going to write to Amina. He was sure Amina knew what her duty was. Besides, Na'ima and Amina had always been so close. What made his mother think otherwise?

Musa was a bit surprised at how fast Na'ima's marriage was decided. He had seen Mahmood, Na'ima's fiancé, a few times already. The first time he saw him at the bank, when Mahmood came to ask for a loan and his cousin, Abdullah, the director of the bank, introduced them. Mahmood's olive trees had been destroyed by the drought and his wife had died in childbirth, a real tragedy. He explained that the loan would help rebuild his livelihood.

Cousin Abdullah had taken Musa aside and whispered, "Remember what I taught you. The bank is the customer's friend and we have to make him feel that he can trust us. We are not loan sharks," Then he turned toward Mahmood and said, "I knew your father. He was an honest man. I hope you are like him. Leave your application here, and come back next week."

A week later his mother, Fatima, appeared in Jerusalem. Soon after, Musa heard that Mahmood was going to become his brother-in-law. Musa looked up to Mahmood, who was five years older than he was and had so much experience. He was a serious man who knew exactly what he wanted to do with his life, while he, Musa, except for wanting Suha more than anything, was still undecided about his future.

He had received a letter from Jaffa's *mukhtar* urging him to register for courses on British laws and customs, "to be prepared for the approaching times when Palestine would belong to the Palestinians," and he, Musa, as the son of an old and well-to-do family, would be called to serve his country in a key position. The *mukhtar* had ended his letter with, "Remember, you represent our future."

On the other hand, cousin Abdullah had only praise for his work. Musa had started as a clerk, but soon after, he was moved to be trained in the department of Foreign Exchange. The department of Letters of Credit followed, and now, two months later, Abdullah started training Musa in the Stocks and Bonds Department.

Many evenings after dinner, Abdullah would look with pride at Fatima's son and say with satisfaction, "Musa is bright and has a bright future." At that Musa's face reddened and he would lower his eyelids, but not fast enough. He still observed the adoring eyes of Abdullah's wife and her three daughters riveted on him.

Government or Banking, Musa hoped that Mahmood would help him resolve his dillema.

Sitting at a corner table in a little restaurant not far from the bank, Musa was waiting for Mahmood to sign the papers that would allow him to receive Na'ima's dowry. Musa himself thought it was premature for his mother to put the dowry's amount in an account in Mahmood's name. It was still more than a month until the wedding. But Fatima had agreed to Mahmood's urgent plea for money.

A perspiring but happy-looking Mahmood appeared in the door frame. "Over here," Musa called, standing up. They ordered a plate of tabbouleh, baba ganoush, hummus and tahini, followed by shashlik and shish-kebab. As Musa was about to start the conversation, he was startled to hear Mahmood say, "I love your family, your sisters and your brother, though of course I haven't met Amina yet. Your brother Ahmed a bright little fellow, beat me at backgammon! My mother told me how polite and well-bred your sisters, Rama and Nur are. Of course," Mahmood laughed, "I'm only a peasant and you are city people. Even your maid, Samira, is so—sophi—"

"Sophisticated?" Musa supplied the word.

"That's it," Mahmood took a large handkerchief and wiped his forehead.

Musa had noticed two things: first, that he didn't mention Na'ima. Maybe, the future husband was too modest to talk about his bride-to-be. But what bothered Musa most was that he didn't say a word about Suha. *What happened? Did they hide her?* His heart ached to know, but he couldn't ask.

Their order arrived and the smell of the roasted garlic and *zaatar* spice invaded their nostrils. A famished Mahmood attacked his plate, while Musa felt his stomach in knots.

"Well, Musa," Mahmood said later, while his tongue moved a toothpick from one side of his mouth to the other, "you said you wanted to consult me on some urgent matter."

For a moment, Musa remained silent. *He had to be cautious.* He could not open his heart and say, *"I am in love with a Yahud girl whom I saved from drowning five months ago, and whom I want to marry."* He would better wait.

Mahmood had opened and started to browse through *Filastin*. Musa cleared his throat. "I wanted to ask your opinion," he said, and told Mahmood about his dilemma, the choice between pursuing a career in banking, to which he seemed suited, or to study the British law and order as the Jaffa *mukhtar* urged him.

"This shouldn't be a problem," answered Mahmood, throwing the newspaper on the table. "You should have made your decision already. The future is clear. *Inshallah,* we'll get rid of the Brits, and after that we'll chase the *Yahudim* out of our country. My father had said it to me in '36, 'Wait and see, all those *Yahudim* are buying our lands and multiplying like rabbits. They are more dangerous than the Brits. The Brits will sooner or later go away, but those Jews are the real danger.' Here, if you want to know more, read this!"

Fishing another newspaper from his pocket, Mahmood pushed it in his direction. It was *Al Wafa,* Loyalty, the newspaper of the radical political party *Istikla,* which Musa never read. He was taken by surprise by Mahmood's outburst. Musa remembered his mother's friendship with Mr. Nathan, the watchmaker, of whom she had repeatedly said, *He never cheats me,* and their chats, his mother seated at Mr. Nathan's working table, drinking the Turkish coffee Mr. Nathan prepared especially for her on hot summer afternoons. Musa's father had not belonged to any political party. He used to say, "I leave the politics to our politicians," while taking a puff from his *nargilea.*

"The Grand Mufti Al-Husseini, warned us about the *Yahudim,*" Mahmood continued, startling Musa. "He admired Hitler for what he did to them in Europe. And what happened next? Our

Mufti, our leader, was forced to run away, and now he is hiding in Germany." There was bitterness in Mahmood's voice.

Only last week, during the coffee break of the meeting with representatives of other Barclays Bank's branches, a young man introduced himself to Musa.

"I am Joshua Goldring. I am with the Rehavia branch."

He was impeccably dressed and had a slight accent, his R's heavy. Surprised, Musa shook Joshua's outstretched hand.

"You have a foreign accent," was the first thing that came into Musa's mind, and he said it.

Joshua smiled, "I was born in Germany. Lucky for me, in 1938, after Kristalnacht, my parents decided to leave Germany. We came to Palestine to start rebuilding our life. My father was a University professor in Munich, but after we arrived here, he worked at building roads. It didn't matter to him, he said, as long as he knew that we were in a safe place."

Musa liked Joshua's honesty. As they were called back to the meeting Musa hoped that he'll meet Joshua again. He wanted to learn more about the European Jews. Maybe it would help him understand Suha.

Caught in his thoughts, Musa barely heard Mahmood. "Yes, the *mukhtar* was right; you can become a great asset for us, Palestinians. You should learn about our activities. I'm going to take you to one of our meetings."

Mahmood got up. He shook Musa's hand and offered him the *Al Wafa* newspaper, "To get better acquainted with us."

When Musa looked at his watch, he realized that he had passed two hours in Mahmood's company. One particular question nagged him: *What would happen when his future brother-in-law learned about Suha, and Musa's desire to marry her?*

16

A week had passed since the fast of Ramadan started. Born into a family of orthodox Jews, Shifra did not know anything about Muslim traditions. She remembered once asking her mother why the Arab kiosks, selling pita-falafel in Jerusalem's Mahane Yehuda market, were closed. Every time Shifra had walked by the kiosk, she had been struck by the strange aromas. Her mother had answered, "It's the month of Ramadan." She did not elaborate and Shifra stopped asking, because she was afraid to trigger her mother's suspicions that, God forbid, she, Shifra had an appetite for non kosher food.

Seated under the courtyard's only shade, Shifra was sweating profusely from the heat. She was alone and in a hurry to finish an embroidery order for one of the prominent merchants in the bazaar. Though all the Arab stores that sold food were closed, the other stores thrived.

She did not want to offend Fatima's feelings by eating or drinking when the rest of the household kept the fast, but it was not easy.

Every day Rama and Nur taught her the importance of fasting during the month of Ramadan. Nur said, "Our Holy Koran was sent down from Heaven." Rama added, "Eumi says that the biggest sin during Ramadan is to lie. One should never lie, but it's worse during Ramadan. If I lie during the fast, my prayer for you to become my sister will never be granted." Her voice sounded serious.

"Girls," Samira said, "Let Suha work. You'll tell her more during *Iftar.*"

After the children left, Shifra's mind wandered. In her ears, she heard Otto Schroder's violin. Since the first time she listened to its sounds, she had wanted to hear it again. She had succeeded in persuading Samira to detour to Otto's dwelling when they were walking nearby. Outside, she saw an elegant lady holding the arm of a boy no older than Ahmed, while in her other hand she carried a violin box.

Excited, Shifra said, "Let's walk slower." But her joy was short-lived. As they approached the house, she heard only the boy's violin exercises, mostly screeches. She was so disappointed she was ready to cry.

When she asked Samira to walk past the house again, Samira looked suspicious.

"Why do you want to go there? I inquired about them. They are refugees, a middle-aged couple with no children, strange people. He teaches or plays the violin all day long, while his wife cries."

Shifra did not answer.

"You don't believe me?" asked Samira. "Their maid is a friend of mine. She told me that the lady's hands are almost paralyzed, she can barely move them. Forget about that violin. It's a devilish instrument."

Shifra would not let Samira destroy her dream. She did not need Samira to guide her to the house. She knew how to get there by herself. She waited for an opportunity.

The opportunity arrived during a Ramadan day, when she had to finish an order quickly. For the first time she was allowed to deliver her work without Samira accompanying her. It was just before sundown and the entire household prayed during *salat*, the third prayer of the day.

Shifra ran all the way from the bazaar, her mouth as dry as parchment, the soles of her feet burning from the overheated pavement. When she approached the house, she heard music that seemed to descend from heaven. It was more than one violin. The other instruments played lower and higher pitches, yet she was able to distinguish each one. The instruments wove melodies that sounded like love songs. Sometimes only one instrument played, embraced later by the other ones. That music made her shiver with emotion.

Shifra touched her amulet, the *hamsa*, Musa's gift. The music awoke in her the same feeling as when Musa looked at her. She missed Musa. The torrid *hamsin* nights were especially difficult for her.

Last night she could not fall asleep; she was sweating and had to take off her nightgown. While she wiped the sweat off her body with a damp rag she imagined how in a month Na'ima's husband would caress his wife's breasts. Shifra knew her thought was sinful, but she could not stop herself. She touched her own budding breasts. They felt like velvet. She imagined Musa entering her room, bending over and kissing the valley between her breasts while his delicate fingers touched her hardened nipples. Shifra jumped, her heart pounding with the shame of her fantasy.

Still under the music spell, Shifra didn't hear it end. She was enveloped by darkness. From her hiding place she saw three people, two women and a man, carrying instrument cases bigger than the violin case she had seen the boy's mother carrying. *Auf wiedersehen,* they said to each other, good-bye, see you *noch ein maal in zwei Wochen.*

Again, in two weeks, in two weeks; Shifra started running in rhythm with their words. In two weeks she would be back, too. Lifting her long dress, she ran even faster. Suddenly she felt the pinch of thirst and hunger. The music had made her forget she was famished.

If Shifra had glanced back at the house, she would have glimpsed the shadow of a woman behind the window's curtains. She would have been alarmed to see her turn to her husband and say, "I've spotted the young Arab girl again, Otto. I don't know why she comes here but I've seen her eyes, blue, like our Ruth's." The woman covered her face with shaking hands while her husband wrapped his arms around her shoulders.

17

Musa stared at the unopened envelope on his desk He recognized Amina's handwriting. Two weeks had passed since he last wrote and told her how proud he was of her decision to study nursing at Cairo's Kasr El-Aini University Hospital. *What could she be writing now?* Impatient, Musa put his work aside and picked up the envelope.

A fifteen-year-old boy, the messenger cousin Abdullah hired to bring tea trays from the nearby *chaikhana,* ran into his cubicle, breathing hard,

"Sayyid Abdullah wants to see you in his office immediately!"

Musa followed the boy, wondering what was so important that Abdullah had to send for him. Fully occupying his leather chair, behind a large mahogany desk covered with papers, Abdullah held a telephone to his ear. He grunted from time to time, but as soon as he saw Musa he said, "He's here. Talk to him."

Abdullah handed the telephone to Musa and whispered, "It's your sister Na'ima."

Na'ima! *What happened? Was there something wrong with his mother, with Suha?* Anxiously, he took the receiver from Abdullah's hands.

"Nai'ma, my dear sister, *Salaam Aleikum,* that's a surprise, where are you calling from?" They had never installed a telephone at home. His father used to scoff, "What for? Good news travels fast, and for bad news there is always time."

"What has happened?" Musa saw Abdullah discreetly leaving the office. On the phone, a weeping Na'ima said, "I am at the post office. Samira is here with me." Musa heard her sniffling.

"Oh, Musa, you have to come home. Mother is not well. She cries all the time and she has taken to her bed. Even Samira can't help her." She paused. "Here, Samira wants to talk to you."

"Musa, Musa," he heard Samira shouting in the telephone, "are you there? Can you hear me?"

Musa thought that all the bank clerks could hear her screams.

"Yes, yes, I'm here," Musa hurriedly answered. "What happened? What's wrong? Stop tormenting me, the two of you."

"You have to come home, my boy. Your mother needs you, your family needs you." Na'ima grabbed the phone again, "Listen to Samira. Please come."

A click ended their conversation. Musa realized that neither Na'ima nor Samira knew they had to add more coins.

Scared and anxious, Musa left Abdullah's office. When he returned to his desk, he remembered Amina's letter. *Could this letter be connected to his mother's illness?* With one movement he tore open the envelope.

Most honored and dear brother Musa, Salaam Aleikum!

First I want you to know that I'll be coming to celebrate my dear sister Na'ma's wedding with all of you and wish Na'ima a life as clear of clouds as the skies of Jaffa in the spring.

But I have news of my own I want to share with you. I hope you remember that when I first joined the British Red Cross I wrote that I took care of a wounded soldier. From the time we arrived in Cairo, we have seen each other often, and the more I saw him, the fonder I grew of him.

He has opened the world for me, by encouraging me to acquire a profession and always treating me as his equal. Because of his love for me, he said, he had started studying the Koran, in English, of course. He wants to learn more about our culture.

He proposed to me a few times, but I always answered, I would be too busy with my studies to think about marriage. I plan to move into one of the apartments the hospital rents to its student nurses, to be closer to the hospital.

Cousin Aiisha, who housed me for the last two months, wasn't happy with my decision, but she understood that it would be for my benefit.

A few days ago George told me, very excited, that his parents are coming to Cairo.

"They want to meet you. They wrote that they can barely wait to see the girl who has stolen their son's heart."

Without giving me time to respond, George took a little box from his pocket and knelt in front of me. "Would you please be my wife?" he asked, opening the box.

He placed the most beautiful sapphire ring on my finger and kissed my hands. Oh, Musa, it's so marvelous to feel loved. At that moment I knew I was destined to marry him. George promised that after he finishes his law degree we'll come to live in Palestine. I know

The girls were asleep. Na'ima had gone to her room, too, and Suha had left for hers as soon as she finished drying the dishes. *Lately she moves like a shadow*, Samira reflected, while walking into the courtyard. It was a beautiful night, full of stars. The hamsin had broken and a cool wind was blowing from the sea. I should open all the windows, and ask Fatima to come outside to breathe the fresh air.

From the courtyard Samira peered into Fatima's bedroom. She saw her kneeling on her prayer rug. She heard a light sound, and wanted to turn around when she felt a hand on her shoulder. As her mouth opened to scream, she saw Musa.

He put a finger on his lips to silence her. *Only three months had passed since he left home, but he seems much older.*

"Have you eaten?" Samira asked, though she knew already the answer. She watched him eat, in her heart a mixture of happiness and sorrow. "You look tired," she said, "Go wash while I put fresh sheets on your bed. You'd better see your mother tomorrow. Oh, my boy, I'm glad you are home."

Musa hugged her. "I think I should see my mother right now," he insisted, but Samira stopped him, "Rest first," she said.

Fatima couldn't fall asleep after Samira told her that Musa had arrived. "Oh, my son," she whispered to herself, "Oh, ibni, oh, my dear son is home."

Amina, in her short letter, read and reread many times, wrote that she was going to move from cousin Aiisha's house. *Is it proper for a girl to live alone in one of the hospital apartments? And what is the important subject that she has to talk to me, about which she couldn't put in writing? What's the mystery?* Oh, her migraine would not stop.

Was not the mukhtar's wife right, when, with a mocking smile, warned what could happen if she, Fatima, let her daughter do as she pleased? Fatima pressed her hands to her temples. Her forehead felt encircled by fire.

Fatima opened the window and was refreshed by the sudden cool air. As she glimpsed outside, she was reminded of the unfinished work, her plan to open the wall between her courtyard and the unused land next door. Faud, her husband, had bought it after Ahmed was born. She could still hear his joyful voice. "Now, with the birth of our second son, we need to enlarge our house. This property is my gift to you for giving me another son."

And he kissed her. She could still feel his lips touching hers. Faud had died before Ahmed's first birthday. She never made use of that property. For years she thought that buying it was a bad omen.

For Na'ima's wedding, she decided to break the wall between the two courtyards to have ample space for the dancers, one courtyard for men, the other for the ladies, as was the custom. But her head could not stand the workers' hammering. She asked Samira to tell them to stop.

Tonight, she sighed with relief, Musa will take over and finish the work. Her daughters would plant the flowers and seeds of cyclamen, roses and hyacinth that Samira bought at the flower market and Suha watered every day. Fatima closed the window and turned off the light.

Allah be praised, Musa is home; and for the first time in a week, she fell into a deep sleep.

Musa woke up early. He heard the muezzin call for the *Fajr,* the first prayer of the day. Certain that his mother was still asleep, he decided to pray at the mosque. Allah knew how much strength he needed to face his mother and appease her.

Last night, during the bus ride from Jerusalem to Jaffa, Musa's heart beat loudly in his ears; he was going to see Suha again! He wondered how he would handle the painful talk with his mother. *And most important, would he be able to make her listen to his own plea?*

Prostrated, his forehead touching the cold mosaic floor, Musa prayed for guidance. "Oh, Allah Ackbar, God of the Universe, in this holy month of Ramadan show me the way, give me direction and I'll follow your will." After the prayer, he felt the weight his heart carried had become lighter. Musa stepped out, and for a moment the sun blinded him. In the few months he'd lived within the walls of Jerusalem, he had forgotten how brilliant Jaffa's morning sun was.

He had not walked for more than a minute when he heard a voice calling him. "Musa *Sayyid*, Mister Musa, wait for me."

It was Yusuf, one of Musa's classmates. Limping more than usual, a big smile on his face, Yusuf caught up with him. He was a sickly child, always dragging his paralyzed leg.

"It's been a long time since I saw you last," Yusuf said, "Where have you been?"

"Salaam Aleikum! Good to see you, Yusuf." Musa kissed him on both cheeks, as was the custom. Then he started telling him about his work in his cousin's bank in Jerusalem. Impressed, Yusuf said, "I always knew you were meant to do great things."

"And what are you doing?" Musa asked.

"I spent some time at the Kasr El-Aini Hospital in Cairo, hoping the doctors could help me walk better. They tried all kinds of boots on me, but I couldn't get used to them, so I returned home."

"This is the hospital where my sister Amina studies to become a nurse," said Musa.

"Good. Kasr El-Aini is the biggest hospital in the mid-east," boasted Yusuf, "people come from all over to study or be treated there. But," Yusuf's eyes looked at him questioningly, "How come you are home? I hope nobody is sick in your family."

"Everything is fine. My sister Na'ima is getting married in a few weeks. I am so glad I met you; I will ask my mother to invite you to the wedding."

"*Mavrook*- congratulations! It will be a real honor to attend."

"My mother is waiting for me." Musa was in a hurry to take his leave. "But we'll see each other again soon, at Nai'ma's wedding."

Samira had already planned the agenda for the day. *Fatima and Musa must be alone,* she thought. So she asked Na'ima to go together with her to check the grocers for the items they needed for the wedding's celebration days, "I think we should place our orders now," Samira said, "to make sure they'll arrive in time, especially the dishes for your henna party. Your mother wants to send the traditional *makhloota*, the sweet pastry, along with the invitations for the wedding. If we order now, we could take this load off her shoulders."

It was almost noon when Musa returned. As he entered the courtyard, he noticed Suha's silhouette between the fluttering curtains of her bedroom. For a second their eyes met. Musa saw her blushing and felt a delicious tremor course through his body.

Fatima came to meet him as soon as she heard the gate open. Mother and son exchanged formal greetings. Then Fatima hugged him and sobbed.

"My prayers have brought you home," his mother said. Fatima handed him Amina's letter, "Read it. Tell me what you know that I don't." While Musa read the short letter, he could hear his mother murmuring, "I have only myself to blame for allowing her to leave home."

Musa knew that there was no way to postpone the talk with his mother. Now or never! But he was saved by the noise of his sisters and brother returning from school. During the Ramadan fast, the school hours were shorter.

"Musa, Musa," they screamed in one voice. "You are home! What a nice surprise. Nobody told us you were coming!"

"If I had known I wouldn't have gone to school," said Rama, pouting her lips. Ahmed took his older brother's hand and wouldn't let go. Nur brought him a chair, and the three children crowded at his feet.

"You have to tell us everything about life in Jerusalem," Nur said. "Our parents took me there once, when I was little, but I remember only that it was crowded, big and noisy."

From the corner of his eye, Musa saw Suha watering the flowers. She stopped and glanced in his direction, her hand playing with the *hamsa* amulet. *Was that gesture meant for him?*

Fatima seemed upset by the children's disruption, "Children, Musa and I have important matters to discuss."

"Eumi, please, we'll talk tonight after *Iftar*," Musa said, "After they are asleep. Now I want to know what they did in my absence, and how many verses of the Koran Ahmed has learned. I want to tell them about Jerusalem too."

Did Suha's shoulders really quiver when she heard the word Jerusalem, or was it only his imagination?

As Fatima left Musa at the mercy of the children, Samira, followed by Na'ima, burst through the gate.

"Musa, Musa," exclaimed Na'ima, bewildered. She had not been told about his arrival. "You came! I'm so happy!"

Musa got up ."*Salaam Aleikum,* my dear sister and future bride! *Salaam Aleikum* my dear Samira."

Na'ima's new looks impressed Musa, "I bring warm salutations from your future husband. I saw him only a few days ago."

"You did!" Na'ima glowed. "You have to tell me all about him."

"Let's get rid of these first," said an impatient Samira. Her arms and Na'ima's were full of fresh flowers.

"Oh, I completely forgot," blushed Na'ima. "I was surprised to see Musa. Here, take mine."

"I'll take them,"Musa offered hoping to be closer to Suha. But Samira was quicker.

"You'll love your future home, Na'ima," Musa told his sister. "Your garden has cedars from Lebanon, and oaks, maybe a hundred years old, also fir, which Mahmood sells to Christians on their holy day. All the people in Deir Yassin sell their beautiful flowers in the *souks* of Jerusalem."

The shrill of the muezzin calling for the third prayer of the day interrupted Musa.

Hurriedly, he said, "I have to go to the mosque, but after I get back you'll hear more." It wasn't the prayer Musa was thinking of, but an urgent call to his sister Amina. He went straight to the Post Office.

Amina cried when she heard Musa's voice, "I'm so happy you called. George contacted the bank this morning, wanting to talk to you, but you weren't there."

Musa couldn't stop the avalanche of words tumbling from Amina's mouth, George this and George that...

"Through the British Embassy, George obtained permission for me to fly on one of the regular British military flights to Lydda airport."

"Why not by train?" asked Musa. He had never been in an airplane and felt uneasy about her flying.

"He said it would be much quicker this way. In two hours I can be at Lydda, while by train I need at least two days each way. Musa, I'll be arriving in time for Na'ima's henna party and stay for the three days of the wedding."

A postal clerk approached Musa and whispered that the office would be soon closing.

"I'll be waiting for you at Lydda airport. I'm looking forward to seeing you, Amina."

"Musa, Musa, don't hang up. Have you told mother about George and me?" Musa heard the anxiety in Amina's voice, but he couldn't lie to her.

"Not yet," he answered, "but I think it would be best for you to talk to her after Na'ima's wedding. And I'll be there to give you support."

The phone went dead. *Probably the clerk's doing. He looked so impatient. I should've given him a tip.* Musa rushed out of the post office, straight into Jaffa's twilight, at the hour the sky and the sea became one.

Musa was home and Shifra could sense the excitement in the air. After Fatima's return from Jerusalem, she heard her tell the children about her trip, and how proud she was when cousin Abdullah praised Musa's work at the bank. Afterward, Shifra's days became so busy helping to prepare Na'ima's trousseau that only during the night, especially during the *hamsin* nights, when the heat and humidity kept her awake, could her mind return to Musa, her savior. She had almost forgotten how he looked. *Was he as strong as Na'ima's fiancé, whom she had watched from behind her window's curtains? Was he sporting a moustache too?* Only her body remembered his strong arms when he had carried her, half-alive, to his mother's house.

Now she could hear Musa giving orders to the workers paving the courtyard or laughing with the children. She also caught his furtive glances toward her window. After Samira brought the sewing machine home, Shifra spent most of the days in her room.

The sewing machine had been Shifra's idea. One day she took the courage to tell Samira, "If we had a sewing machine I could make a dress, from beginning to end, and save the buyer the extra money he spends for a seamstress." She did not add that she enjoyed the work, and wanted to create the whole garment herself, from start to finish.

Samira had looked doubtful. "When did you learn to use a sewing machine?"

Shifra blushed. Her mother had sewn all the children's clothes at home and many times had let Shifra finish a seam or a hem. "I've watched the seamstresses sewing in the store. It's not so complicated. For a *jelebia* one has to seam only the sides of the dress, and add the sleeves. I'm sure I could do it."

Samira didn't seem convinced, so Shifra added, "Na'ima's dowry dresses have to be ready on time, and we also have to keep up with the orders. The work would go faster and easier if we had a sewing machine." Shifra knew that mentioning Na'ima's dresses would lend her demand more appeal.

Samira smiled. "I'll tell Sit Fatima. She'll decide."

Shifra was satisfied. It was the same answer Samira gave her when Shifra proposed embroidering with beads. The two of them were in the bazaar, and Shifra had stopped by a stall selling beads.

"Samira," she asked, "what do you think about doing the embroidery with beads? Nobody has done it yet. Wouldn't that look nice?"

Samira pinched her cheek, "You are some girl, but we'll have to ask Fatima for approval."

The beads were an instant success. More and more orders came their way. Shifra's mornings were filled with work, but in the afternoons she played with Rama and Nur, after the children first checked her progress in Arabic. Her biggest joy was the few times she could steal away to hear the magic violin.

On sleepless nights, she asked herself why she pushed herself to be useful in a stranger's house. *Was she hoping for acceptance, knowing that she couldn't return to her own family? Was it her need to belong, to feel that people cared for her?* She had Samira's trust. *Wasn't that enough?*

After Musa arrived, she hated the sewing machine. It kept her indoors, while in the courtyard Musa was the center of everybody's attention. She could not hear what he said that provoked everybody's laughter.

Perhaps Musa guessed her thoughts. On many afternoons, after the workers left, he sat on the bench, underneath her window, and read aloud from the Palestine Post, the English newspaper. It seemed to Shifra that he especially chose the news which might interest her. Sometimes Fatima joined her son, listening to him.

"Italy's disintegration," Musa read. "After the Allied Forces conquered Sicily in July, in September they landed in Salerno from where they will start the invasion of Italy. This is good news, Eumi."

"If you think so, surely it must be so." Fatima patted her son's hand.

"Everybody who loves freedom thinks so," answered Musa. "On the Eastern Front the Russians are raising their heads and moving against the common enemy. Trust me, before long the Nazi machine will be destroyed."

He folded the paper, "Just a shame that for many people freedom will come too late, like for the innocent children and their parents who lost their lives when the Warsaw Ghetto was burned to the ground."

When Shifra heard the word Warsaw, she stopped sewing. She remembered her mother dreamily saying, "One day, children, we'll visit my family and you'll meet your cousins and uncles."

"My new acquaintance, a German Jew who works at the Rehavia branch of Barclays Bank, said that Hitler decided to exterminate all European Jews. This fellow and his family were saved by coming to Palestine," Musa said.

"Don't listen to hearsay, my son. You are too sensitive. My friend, Mr. Nathan, is also filling my ears about it. How could one man kill millions? Some people have too much imagination." Fatima said with disdain. "What I know is that Jews were and are still smuggled in, through the new port the Jews built in Tel-Aviv.

They violate the British embargo: at the same time their port has caused Jaffa to lose a lot of business."

Fatima's discourse was interrupted by the repetition of a plaintive sound.

"Oh, I hear the muezzin calling for the fourth prayer. Go my son, go to the mosque and pray for the happiness of our family."

Shifra's tears fell on the dress she was making, staining it, but she didn't care. *Millions of Jews were killed? Oh, God!* Then the victory Musa talked about would arrive too late, for her mother and people like her, who lived with the hope of reuniting with the families left behind.

19

M usa enjoyed being home. He knew that his presence made his brother, sisters and mostly his mother,
relaxed and cheerful. *What about Suha?* The few times
their eyes met, he felt that they spoke a language of their own,
without need for words. Yet words would have to be spoken.

One more week was left before the end of Ramadan, which
meant only one more week before Na'ima's wedding. He had to
hurry. He had to talk to his mother. The opportunity occurred one
evening after the *Iftar* meal.

"My son," she said, "I am very pleased with everything you
have done in the short time since you've been home. I really don't
know how I could have managed all by myself."

She took his hands, "You are a good son. I've been always proud
of you. Come sit near me," she patted the pillow next to her.

It was true that Musa had done everything she had asked him
to do. He had hired the musicians for the wedding. Under his
supervision the extension of the courtyard was completed. And
conforming to the Muslim tradition, he personally invited the
neighbors and his friend Yusuf, to Na'ima's wedding.

"Eumi," Musa said, "There is something I want to ask you." He stopped, searching for the right words.

"Go on," Fatima encouraged him. "You know I'd do anything for you."

"I want you to invite Suha to be at the wedding party."

"You want what?" Fatima was almost screaming. "How can you ask me that? You are going too far, my son. First you begged me to give her shelter because she was sick. Then you asked me to keep her because she was an orphan and had no place to go. I've done all this, isn't that enough?" Her voice grew louder.

"Hush, hush," Samira said, entering the room. "You two will wake up the neighbors."

"Samira, listen to him, listen to my son." Fatima was choking. "What insolence! I don't want to hear any more about it. I'll try to forget it. Never again! Go to bed, my son. When you wake up tomorrow morning you'll realize how foolish you have been tonight!"

"I'll ask you again tomorrow, and after tomorrow, and every day after," Musa said. "Suha is already part of our household. You've given her an Arabic name. She has learned to speak Arabic, and all of her embroidery work has made you not only proud but wealthier, too."

Fatima brought her hands to her throat, as if she were suffocating.

"Think about it, Sit Fatima," Samira offered, "maybe Musa is not entirely wrong."

"What are you talking about? I've shared my children with you, Samira. You want this girl in this house as much as Musa does. The two of you want to kill me tonight? Think of Na'ima, what would she say? She never liked the Yahud girl. Oh, I should have gotten rid of her long ago." Fatima pressed her temples. "I'm getting a migraine again. Leave me alone. This is an order."

"If Suha doesn't take part, I'll not be in the wedding either," Musa persisted.

Though he tried to sound firm, his insides were shaking. He had never spoken to his mother in that way. By the Muslim code, he was being seriously disobedient and disrespectful.

"Musa, you are going too far. This is no way to talk to your mother," Samira said, taking charge. "Please, Sit Fatima, reconsider. Wasn't she the one who sewed all nine of Na'ima's wedding dresses, one more beautiful than the next? Wouldn't you have invited such a talented seamstress to the wedding? The girl has been living with us long enough, and though it might not be your will, I think she deserves it."

Samira turned to Musa, "Apologize to your mother and leave us alone."

She never gave him orders, but Musa understood.

Fatima sat prostrated while Samira paced the room, mulling over how she could dissipate Fatima's anger, and more than that, convince her that Musa was right. She couldn't say like in the old days,'a good night's sleep will cool you off', or, 'Pray to Allah and He'll show you the way.'

She loved all of them so much, Fatima, Musa and Suha, that orphan who was trying so hard to please, just the way, she, Samira was. "*You are a good person, Samira, you'll find the way,*" a voice seemed whispering in her ear, a man's voice with a Yiddish accent, Mr. Grunwald's voice? The time was short. Samira had witnessed the scene in the kitchen, that very evening, just before she served the Iftar meal. Musa came in and seeing Suha, he asked her feverishly, "Are you happy here?" Samira saw Suha's neck suffused with color before she nodded. No words, but for Samira that was enough. Suha wouldn't need the love potion from Uhm Zaide.

"I want to brush your hair," Samira started, as in other times of stress.

"Not now," Fatima answered. "I have no patience for it. Leave me alone."

"Now is the best time," insisted Samira. "Besides, I want to talk to you."

"Didn't you say enough? Now, leave."

"You'll have to hear me, Fatima Masri, even if you fire me afterward. For more than twenty years, I've worked for you. You know that I'm ready to sell my life to the devil to save yours."

"Say what you have to say and leave."

Samira was undisturbed by Fatima's harsh tone, "Please, help me remember. Didn't Faud *Effendi* have a good friend in Alexandria? If I'm not mistaken, he was French, married to an Egyptian woman, wasn't he? He was one of Master Faud business partners."

Fatima was surprised, "That's true, but why are you asking me that? It was a long time ago, before Faud died. What's so urgent? You make it sound as if it's a matter of life and death."

"You told me that only death could separate them. Something happened to that fellow before Faud *Effendi* died. What happened?"

Fatima stared into Samira's eyes. Samira returned the most innocent of looks.

"He died in a car accident, both he and his wife. Faud was inconsolable. For days he couldn't eat or sleep". Fatima seemed to be looking into a gallery of ghosts, "Why do you ask me? I have no time for charades."

"Wasn't there a child, a girl?" Samira softly asked, "What had happened to her?

"I don't know what got into you to ask those questions tonight. Yes, there was a girl. She was two years younger than my twins. Some said that she escaped alive from the accident. Faud tried to find her, ready to adopt her, but he lost track. She was such a pretty child."

Silently and gently, Samira undid Fatima's long hair. She started to brush it when Fatima, as if waking from a dream, asked sharply, "Samira, why did you bring all this up? You knew what happened, didn't you? What's on your mind?"

"You said it yourself. You would have adopted the girl, if you had found her." Samira took a deep breath. "Think of Suha as being that girl."

Abruptly, Fatima snatched the brush from Samira's hand, "What nonsense. How dare you compare the two, and come to me with such a proposition? That girl, I loved her with all my heart. Oh, Samira, you not only disappoint me, you make me angry!"

Fatima got up. "Go, and don't talk to me again."

"Please, Sit Fatima, think," Samira insisted. She knew she had to play her last two cards, "Think of Musa. You heard him. Maybe he has fallen in love with the Yahud girl."

Seeing the flicker of shock in Fatima's eyes, Samira changed her approach. "Maybe not, but for sure he has some warm feelings for the girl he saved from drowning. He feels responsible for her. He is also stubborn, especially when he thinks that he is right."

Fatima didn't answer.

Samira played her trump card, "You don't want to lose your son, your comfort and consolation at old age."

While Samira talked, Fatima prostrated herself on the rug, "*Allah Ackbar, Allah Ackbar,*" she wailed, "Save me, save me, and give me sustenance."

Samira waited. When Fatima raised her head, Samira helped her up. Fatima's eyes were red. She cried as she said, "In this holy month of Ramadan, you want me to commit the biggest sin, you want me to lie. I wouldn't do that, not even for the Prophet Mohammed."

From the tone of her voice, Samira knew she had gained some ground. "I am not asking you to lie. Besides, the wedding takes place after Ramadan ends."

"What do I say to people who ask me who she is? That she is the Yahud girl Musa saved from drowning?"

"Nobody will ask you. Everybody's attention will be on the bride and groom, or on Amina and Musa returning home after a long absence: Suha will wear a hijab and *jelebia*. She will stand near me."

"And what if somebody addresses her? You seem to have thought of everything, but have you thought of this possibility?" Fatima's voice was breaking as she said, "Samira, Samira, seeing how sly and cunning you are now, could I trust you in the future?"

Samira fell to her knees. She was moved by the bitterness in Fatima's voice.

"Sit Fatima," Samira took the hem of Fatima's dress and kissed it, "maybe not today, but sometime later, you'll think again, and you'll not judge me so harshly. I had nothing in mind but the happiness of your family."

She looked up at her mistress. "As for what you asked me before, if Suha is questioned, I'll make sure that I answer for her. She is too shy."

Fatima sighed. "Don't be sure you've convinced me. Have you thought about Na'ima's reaction? She has a right to decide if she wants Suha at her wedding."

That was a consideration Samira hadn't foreseen. Fatima was right. Na'ima could be an obstacle.

"See, as clever as you are, you don't have answers for everything," Fatima said. "Go now. I'd like to say that I am going to forget our talk, but it would be a lie."

Samira left. Although she had not achieved what she wanted, she did not doubt that the seed she had planted in Fatima's mind would bear fruit. Yes, talking to Fatima was important, but who would approach Na'ima?

"I'm counting the days," Na'ima had told her. "Four more days until Amina comes home. Oh, we'll have so much to talk about." Suddenly, she hugged Samira, "And by this time, next week, I'll be married! I can hardly believe it."

20

Amina was expected to arrive one day before the start of the wedding festivities. At dawn Musa left for Lydda airport. Though it was still early, the entire Masri household was already on its feet.

From her window, Shifra watched the bustle. Young boys from the neighborhood hung colored lanterns in both courtyards. In her guttural voice, Samira gave short orders, pointing to where they were to be placed. Nur and Rama filled baskets with the traditional sugar-coated Jordan almonds, while Fatima checked Na'ima's dresses once more for any small defect that might have escaped her critical eye.

Exhilaration was in the air. Shifra, to whom Samira had explained the customs of a Muslim wedding was as excited as the bride. At Samira's urging, Shifra had used the remnants of a material matching the color of her eyes to sew a dress for herself. It was a modest *jelebia*, without any of the adornments she added to the dresses she made for Na'ima, for Fatima or the white dress awaiting Amina. Samira had bought a white *hijab* to cover Shifra's head.

Na'ima, meanwhile, was busy opening the boxes of gifts she received from the groom's family, from neighbors, from Aiisha, her mother's cousin in Cairo, and especially the little packages with which Amina had showered her every day for the last week.

"Eumi, come see," Na'ima exclaimed with the opening of each new package as the mailman delivered them: an Egyptian shawl, a bottle of perfumed oil, a papyrus with her and Mahmood's names encircled in elegantly designed hieroglyphics.

Later in the morning, after the rented long tables had arrived, Ahmed arranged the borrowed chairs and ottomans around them, while Rama and Nur set the tables with the starched embroidered tablecloths that Fatima kept in a chest in her bedroom, gifts she had received twenty years earlier at her own wedding.

In the kitchen, the baskets of fruits and vegetables, delivered and ready for the big event, were competing for space with pots and pans lent by neighbors. Moving around in the kitchen was so treacherous that Samira, the kitchen's supreme chef, had to chase the children away, "This is not the time to fall and break a leg."

At noon, a cheerful voice called out from beyond the gate, "*Inshallah*, I'm home. Nur, Rama, Ahmed, open the gate quickly and give your sister a big hug!" Musa followed Amina with a suitcase in one hand and a big package in the other.

As if by command, the entire family, including Samira, ran out into the courtyard. Shifra came out too, but kept a few paces distant from the family circle. Seeing Amina, her eyes opened wide. Amina's family looked as surprised as Shifra. *Where was the Amina they all knew?*

She was dressed in a gray two-piece suit, the skirt barely covering her knees, with high cork-soled wedged shoes which made her look much taller than Shifra remembered. Her perfume invaded the courtyard. But the most unusual sight was her hairdo. What happened to her beautiful thick braids? Had she cut them?

Her hair was jelly-rolled, like the models Shifra saw in the old magazines which wrapped the fish bought in the market.

Amina was all smiles, "*Salaam Aleikum*, honored Eumi," she addressed her mother. "I'm happy to see you in good health."

Fatima seemed hypnotized by her daughter's new looks. Anger and disappointment played on her face. How was she going to react? Samira and the children watched her, waiting for a sign. But as fast as a flicker, Fatima's clenched muscles relaxed and she opened her arms. Amina hugged her mother in the middle of the deafening noise made by Rama and Ahmed, each one pulling at her dress.

"Welcome home, my daughter," Fatima said. "Now, with you in our midst, we can celebrate Na'ima's wedding as she deserves."

When it was the impatient Na'ima's turn to embrace her sister, both had tears in their eyes. "I have so much to tell you," whispered Na'ima. Amina whispered back, "So do I."

Rama and Nur took hold of Amina's hands, while she bent and kissed Ahmed three times on his cheeks, exclaiming, "It's hard to believe that all of you have grown so much in the five months since I saw you last. *Salaam Aleikum* to you, my dear Samira," Amina said. Freeing her arms from her sisters, she embraced her old *morabia*.

During the commotion created by Amina's arrival, Musa took Amina's suitcase and package inside, and intentionally or not, brushed against Shifra and felt a sudden, thrilling tremor in her body.

"Put her suitcase in my bedroom," ordered Fatima.

Na'ima and Amina looked surprised. Didn't Fatima guess that the sisters had hoped to be together the few nights before the wedding? But Fatima had other designs regarding her prodigal daughter.

While Amina told the children about the gifts that awaited each one and the stories she was going to tell them about Cairo, Fatima approached Samira and murmured in her ear. "It was smart of us to make a dress for Amina to wear at the wedding, a dress that befits the daughter of Faud Masri, a daughter of Islam."

"You have to thank Suha for it. She was the one who worked on it during the nights you slept so well," answered Samira.

Amina's ear caught the name and turned around, searching. "Suha," she exclaimed, "I'm so sorry. With all the emotion and the commotion, I didn't see you. I am glad to see you again."

Rama, who couldn't keep the secret anymore, interjected, "You have to see the dress she made for you. It is really beautiful. She sewed all our dresses."

Shifra blushed. "She's my sister now," Rama took Shifra's hand in hers, "During Ramadan I prayed for it every day."

"Then she is my sister, too," Amina said, smiling at her youngest sister.

If she had looked at Na'ima, she would have seen the bewilderment in her eyes. On the way home from Lydda airport, Musa had opened his heart and told Amina about his wish to marry Suha. Brother and sister promised to support each other in their quest for their mother's approval.

Na'ima's wedding festivities were to start on October 1st with the traditional henna party, when the hands of the bride and her sisters are dyed red. Fatima decided to have the henna party on the first night of *Idul Fitri*, the three-day holiday following the fast of Ramadan, usually celebrated with food, music, and visits.

Mahmood, his mother and a number of relatives had already arrived in Jaffa, and were hosted by Fatima's neighbors and friends. Abdullah and his family also descended from Jerusalem and took rooms at a famous *khan*, an inn close to their neighborhood.

Though the henna party is for women only, sometimes a groom is allowed to participate. But since no party could be a real party unless there is music, from early morning the musicians had their instruments, the *tabla* and the *oud*, ready to start.

Seated on the chair of honor in Fatima's large living room, Mahmood's mother waited for her future daughter-in-law to pay her respects. In their bedrooms, the sisters checked on one another for the last details. Wearing a splendidly adorned red velvet dress and a tulle head scarf covering her face, Na'ima followed by her three sisters and her mother made her entrance.

While Na'ima's future mother in-law was busy telling the other guests her recipe for henna dye, Samira entered the room with the henna preparation, accompanied by a helper holding trays of crescent walnut pastries and tall glasses filled with ice water and nana leaves. Hearing the last words, Samira exclaimed, "This henna was made with the same recipe!" The mother-in-law took the henna and smeared it over Na'ima's fingers and her forehead, "The henna will keep you and your future family in good health," she said.

Afterward each one of the sisters got their fingers smeared with henna, a lucky sign for finding a good husband. Amina allowed her fingers to be smeared. She did not wear her engagement ring. She wanted to talk to her mother first. But Musa had asked her to wait for the day after Na'ima's wedding, and she agreed.

Mahmood entered the room, and after he bowed respectfully in front of the old ladies, his mother smeared henna on his little finger. It was the first time Amina saw him, but she would have recognized him anywhere from Na'ima's descriptions as well as from Musa's letter. *A hunk of a guy,* Amina concluded.

In spite of the loud music, they heard the cries of a baby.

"It must be our little boy," Mahmood's mother said, getting up quickly. A woman entered the room holding in her arms the five-month-old child.

"I'm sorry to disturb, but I can't make him stop. Maybe he has colic." Mahmood and his mother jumped at once, but Na'ima was quicker.

"I want to hold him, please. In two days I'll be his mother, we'd better start getting used to one another." She cradled the little boy in her arms, and as if by magic, he stopped crying and smiled at her.

Amina's eyes shone with admiration, while   N a ' i m a ' s mother-in-law gave her a kiss. "That's a good omen," she said. "You'll have a good marriage."

At noon the next day, the *Imam,* accompanied by Mahmood and two of his friends, his witnesses, arrived at Fatima's house for the religious wedding ceremony. Na'ima was told she could choose to participate or not, since Musa would represent her, but she wanted to be a part of it. Cousin Abdullah was her second witness. Only male witnesses were accepted by Islamic law.

The *Imam* started by reading the Surah Nur from the Koran, "Marry those among you who are single and those who are fit," after which he added the words of the Prophet, "No house has been built in Islam more beloved in the sight of Allah than through marriage."

The Imam asked Na'ima first, "Do you agree to marry Mahmood?" With tears in her eyes, but in a clear voice, Na'ima answered, "Yes, with all my heart." Then the Imam asked Mahmood the same question. Mahmood nodded. He and his witnesses were asked to sign the *Nikaahnama,* the marriage contract.

Following the ceremony, Mahmood was led to the women's section to receive the blessing of his mother, Fatima, and the other elderly women from both families. Fatima had decided to bypass the obligatory gifts that the groom was supposed to give to his bride's sisters as well as a money dowry due to her family. *"Inshallah,"* Fatima had said to him at their engagement, "We'll talk again when you sell the first harvest of your new olive orchard."

Fatima bypassed the old tradition concerning the meal following the ceremony; instead of eating separately, at their first meal together, Na'ima and Mahmood were seated at the head of the table, with the Koran between them, while a long scarf covered their heads.

The many dishes and delicacies brought to the table, one by one, were greeted by the guests with admiration. In the kitchen, the fine chopping of dill, parsley and green onions ready for the tabbouleh salad never stopped; while the shashlik and shish-kebab sizzled on the skewers.

The fame of Fatima's kitchen and her exquisite dishes had reached beyond the circle of her family. Now that she was honoring her son-in-law's family and his friends, she served the best. Scents of the Mediterranean spices *zaatar*, *sumac* and roasted cumin danced in the air, and the guests, already cheered by the glasses of arak and the sweet wine made by the Latrun monastery monks, felt their appetite renewed with each dish.

To those who congratulated her, Fatima modestly answered, "Wait until tomorrow, when you'll eat the real feast."

For dessert, there were dates, nuts and the honey-moist baklava. The dates, according to tradition, were symbols for happiness and for a fruitful life.

One by one the guests left saying again, "*Mavrook Wa-barak Allah Fecum*," the usual blessings and good wishes offered to a young couple. Only Mahmood remained. According to tradition he had to sleep in the bride's home and share one of her brother's bedrooms.

Musa, who would have loved to linger in the kitchen to watch the preparations for the next day's banquet, and mostly, to be close to Suha, had to host Mahmood, who, with the perennial toothpick in his mouth, grinned with satisfaction,

"If your sister knows how to cook the dishes we ate today, our marriage will start off on the right foot." Musa refrained from telling Mahmood that his sisters were never allowed in the kitchen.

Mahmood stretched out on the bed, opened his belt and after a big belch, he groaned, "I need to rest. The wine from those devilish

monks has gone to my head. Tomorrow will be another long day."
He yawned, "A good night's sleep will help to lead the *Debka*."

Musa was happy to leave him. He went into the courtyard
where he found Amina and Suha hanging garlands of flowers
between the lanterns. When Amina saw him, she whispered, "Be
quiet; Na'ima and our mother are asleep. *Inshallah*, everything has
gone as planned. We couldn't have wished for anything better."

"Can I help you?" Musa offered.

"You can help Suha," Amina answered with a smile. "Since
she's shorter than me, it's harder for her to reach so high." Musa
looked at Suha, whose face glowed in the lanterns' lights. Silently
she passed the garlands to him. The two girls had woven cyclamen,
tulips, irises and narcissus, and their perfume intoxicated Musa.
He took hold of Suha's hands and for a moment they felt their
rapid heartbeats pulsating in their wrists.

Musa could not refrain any longer. "By this time next year,
Inshallah, you'll be my bride. I promise." His eyes burned. He'd
never been so direct, but he needed to say it. He would be going
back to Jerusalem to work at Abdullah's bank and there should be
a clear understanding between them. He saw Suha's eyes suddenly
brimming with tears. The garlands fell from her hands and she ran
into the house.

Mahmood woke up in the middle of the night. For a moment
he didn't know where he was. He was completely dressed. Still
half-asleep, he started to undress. These were the clothes he was
going to wear the next day and they had to look fresh. As he
moved, he heard a sigh. It was Musa, who slept peacefully at his
side, a smile on his lips.

Mahmood yawned. He had eaten and drank too much, but it
had been a long time since he had such a meal. He still felt his head
spinning. Yes, he was getting married again, and at that thought,

he felt that he was getting an erection. Na'ima will be all right. Of course she's not as pretty as her sister Amina, but who needs beauty?

His first wife had been beautiful, but did that help him? She was so skinny she couldn't even work in the yard, much less take care of the olive trees. She moaned during her pregnancy, and begged him to take her to a doctor because she passed blood when she urinated, but he knew that all she wanted was to be spoiled. She wanted attention. As for making love, at the beginning of their marriage he had to beg her, until one night he beat her to make her understand he was the boss.

After she became pregnant, she mostly stayed in bed and told him that if he wanted a boy, he should not touch her until the baby was born. She died giving birth. Mahmood was sure that she put a curse on him.

But now—now, he was sure that his star was on the rise again. Na'ima had strong arms, good for work, good to embrace. Plump like a fattened goose farmers sell in the *souk* in Jerusalem. And her breasts! Even through the loose *jelebia*, he could see how firm they stood, those two little melons. Oh, he felt his desire mount. If only he could find her room! He'd go right now, open her fat thighs with his knowledgeable hands and enter her with all his might. When he laid his strong body on top of her, his semen would spill into her as from an open tap. He felt feverish, excited. Yes, he'd go right now and surprise Na'ima.

Wearing only his long shirt, Mahmood climbed carefully over Musa's body but as soon as he was at the door, he heard Musa's sleepy voice, "Where are you going?"

This stopped Mahmood in his tracks.

"I'm going to pee," he answered sheepishly.

"I'm coming with you," Musa said, getting up. "It's dark in the house and you don't know the way. You could make a mistake and wake somebody up."

Damn you, cursed Mahmood. "There's no need," he answered, "I think I can hold it until the morning."

Na'ima was awake, but lingered in bed. It was the day of her wedding party, and her mother had told her that she could stay in bed as long as she liked.

"You'll have to be as fresh and beautiful as a flower," Fatima said. Amina, who entered the room together with her mother, said, " I see you haven't opened the gifts I brought you.."

"You've already showered me with gifts," Na'ima answered, "every day last week the mailman brought gifts from you. For me, the biggest gift is that I have you here with me. I was so afraid you wouldn't come," and Nai'ma kissed her sister.

But her curiosity was aroused. She took one package from Amina's hands and caressed the wrapping paper, "Let me guess," she said, closing her eyes and playing their childhood game. Quickly, Amina opened the first gift.

"Oh, how beautiful," gushed Na'ima at the sight of the exquisite Turkish coffee cups. The second gift was a set of tall tea glasses with silver holders. "Amina, you spoil me."

"Not yet, look what I brought you, to wear tonight when the two of you will be alone." In front of Na'ima's wide-open eyes, Amina displayed a diaphanous see-through nightgown.

"And before you put it on," Amina expertly continued, "oil your body with this perfumed oil. It's a recipe from Queen Hatshepsut, King Tut's wife. It will make your skin as soft as silk."

Na'ima blushed. "Where did you learn all this, Amina? I'll tell you a secret, I can barely wait to have Mahmood all to myself, yet somehow I feel scared, too."

"Girls, girls," an impatient Fatima called, knocking at the door, "do you want to wait until noon to get up? Did you forget what day it is?"

"We are coming in a minute," Amina answered. While she spoke, she took from underneath a pillow where she had kept it hidden, the sapphire ring, George's engagement gift, and showed it to Na'ima.

"I am engaged to a wonderful man. The gifts I brought you are from both of us."

Na'ima was speechless.

"Who is he? Do we know him? Does Eumi know?" Na'ima fired the words rapidly when she regained her voice.

"Not yet," whispered Amina, hugging Na'ima and dancing her around the room. "It's a secret, but she'll find out very soon."

Shifra woke up early. She had promised Samira to prepare *fattoush*, the vegetable salad mixed with big toasted pita pieces, which had to be served as fresh as possible. And all for at least a hundred people!

But it wasn't that chore that troubled her sleep. She dreamed of Musa saying to her again and again, "By this time next year, you'll be my wife." In her dream she heard his voice accompanied by a violin, little bells and angels' voices. Her savior, her hero, how handsome he was, so much better looking than Mahmood!

Thinking of last night made her blush. *Why had she run away from Musa? Why didn't she answer him? What would Musa think of her now?*

"Suha, what's taking you so long?" Samira's clear voice startled her. "The guests will arrive soon, and we are far from being ready."

Dear Samira, always worried, the entire household resting on her shoulders. The meal they had after the wedding ceremony, was such a feast, Suha wondered how the guests would be able to eat again just twenty-four hours later. In all her life she had never seen such a rich meal, and, as her mother would say, "Such a waste of food!"

She remembered the *kiddush* following the weddings held at their little *shul* in Geula, where the men clanked the glasses filled with schnapps, screaming *L'chaim, L'chaim*, while the children ate the yellowish and already dried *leikeh*.

"There was nothing to eat but herring, boiled eggs and *challah*," Shifra had heard her mother say sometimes, to which her father would answer, "*Ureme kinder*, poor youngsters, what did you expect, they couldn't even pay the Rabbi."

Samira burst into the room, "Suha, what's happening to you today, of all days? The musicians are at the gate. The minute they start playing will be the signal for the guests to arrive. And you are still in your nightgown!"

It was true. By the time the violinist and the clarinetist finished tuning their instruments; the *tabla* player started drumming and the gate bell rang. Suha watched the guests from her window. Mahmood's family and their friends arrived first. On the low tables, plates with *sharbat* and water glasses filled with nana leaves waited for the guests.

Fatima, flanked by Amina and Musa, welcomed the guests. She looked splendid in her rich attire, embroidered with gold and silver, and wearing her most expensive jewelry.

"Dear Guests, *Tafadaloo Tasharafna Fecum*, thank you for honoring us with your presence," bowing slightly, Fatima said to the well-wishers. Besides neighbors and family, she had invited Faud's former friends and partners, as well as her own business contacts. She introduced her children, "My eldest son, Musa, may Allah grant him long life, who's going to be a banker, and this is Amina, *Benti Al-Azeeza*, my dear daughter, who studies nursing in Cairo." There was unabashed pride in her voice. Like raindrops, the congratulatory *Mavrooks* fell on the three of them.

Everybody eyed Amina, whose see-through hijab was constantly sliding, showing her modern hairdo.

"Look, look at her," the women guests elbowed one another. The first to talk was the *mukhtar*'s wife, whose daughter was at her side.

"*Salaam Aleikum*, Amina," she said, honey dripping from her mouth, "We are so glad to have you home. I hope you are here to stay." The group of women around her, members of the Arab Women's League, became quiet, their eyes riveted on Amina.

"I'm glad to see you," Amina answered gracefully, "but I'm sorry to have to disappoint you. The day after tomorrow I will return to my classes. I have to study two more years before obtaining my nursing license."

"Your mother will miss you very much, now with Na'ima married and living far from her," the *mukhtar*'s wife continued in a vinegary voice, "Weren't you taught that a daughter's first duty is toward her mother?" The other ladies nodded their heads in approval.

As Amina looked at her mother for help, Cousin Abdullah, who was just passing by and heard the last sentence, saved her.

"Cousin Amina," he called joyfully, "you are more beautiful than ever. Cousin Aiisha from Cairo is so proud of you and your accomplishments."

Then he turned toward the *mukhta*r's wife. "I'm sure you know that Amina was accepted to study at Kasr El-Aini, which is the best hospital in the Middle East."

Another group of guests arrived, including Mr. Nathan. "*Salaam Aleikum*, Musa," he said shaking Musa's hand vigorously. "I almost didn't recognize you. Where's the boy I knew? You are now a full-fledged young man, and your mother tells me a lot of good things about you."

"*Salaam Aleikum*, Mr. Nathan, you are too kind," Musa smiled at his mother's friend. "I don't deserve your compliments."

"Don't be so modest, my friend," Mr. Nathan answered.

He moved along with the guests in line waiting to congratulate the newlyweds. Na'ima wore the *thobe*, a red wedding dress, whose sleeves were embroidered, like her mother's, with thick threads of silver and gold. Standing tall, next to her, Mahmood was dressed in a white shirt, white pants, white *kafia* and black boots. He was surrounded by his friends who, like him, seemed anxious to show their prowess dancing *Debka*.

The young children respectfully directed the older guests to places of honor at the heads of tables, either in the house, where it was cooler, or outside under the shade of the palm trees. Nur and Rama, after being pinched, kissed and spat upon by the old ladies to ward off the evil eye, arranged the pillows on the low chairs behind them. While the ladies, their faces hidden behind their fans, commented on everything and everybody, the old gentlemen smoked the *nargilea* and discussed politics.

One by one, the dishes were brought to the tables. M*elouchia*, a goulash, *kube*, the Arab moussaka, a concoction of rice and lentils, and Shifra's *fattoush* disappeared as quickly as they were brought in. The piquant spices made the arak and the wine flow like rivulets. The cheerful assembly, after raising their glasses numerous times, first in honor of the newlyweds, then in Fatima's honor, and that of the *mukhtar*, Abdullah, and other dignitaries, clapped their hands, demanding the *Debka*, the dance the youngsters waited for with impatience.

The young men started lining up for *Debka*, the Middle East national dance where men show off their strength. Mahmood, the groom, stood proudly, his arms high in the air, the chosen leader, powerful as an oak tree. *Debka* in Arabic means "stomping feet." Twirling a handkerchief in his raised hand, Mahmood's continuous shouts urged the dancers to keep the rhythm and the energy of their stomping.

Second in line was Musa, as befitted the brother of the bride. While he danced, his eyes searched feverishly, until they found her, his Suha. Their eyes locked and sparkled. Every time he turned, Musa fixed his gaze on her. And in her eyes he read the response he hoped for.

There was someone else who watched Musa. It was Mr. Nathan. He followed Musa's gaze. Surprised, he looked at the girl. Who was she? He had never seen her before. With her light complexion and her azure eyes she didn't look like any of the Masri family. *Who could she be?* He would ask Fatima.

Meanwhile the nationalistic spirits provoked by the dance soared.

"Palestine to Palestinians," an old man screamed. He was followed by others, shouting, "Soon we'll get rid of the Brits."

"The Brits and their cohorts, the Jews, too!" yelled one of Mahmood's friends.

"Yes, yes, right you are, we should throw them all in the sea," the first man said. Sensing the danger in the air, Fatima discreetly approached the music band and ordered them to stop playing.

"The young musicians are getting tired and it's time to serve dessert," she said. But spirits didn't quiet down so quickly. A few men continued to shout at the top of their lungs.

At Fatima's signal, the women started singing and dancing. A proud Fatima took Na'ima and Amina's hands and asked Mahmood's mother to join them. The women danced with small steps, slowly swinging their bodies to the rhythm of the music.

All of a sudden, Amina took off the scarf that held her hair, kicked away her high-heeled shoes and asked the musicians for a fast dance.

"Women can dance the Debka too," she said provocatively. The women laughed, surprised.

"We are as good at dancing as men," Amina insisted. "Let's prove it!"

The young girls cheered. With her beaded necklace in her raised hand, the leader' sign, Amina urged the women to join her.

Rama took Shifra's hand. "Dance with me," she said.

"I don't know how," Shifra answered, embarrassed.

"I'll show you," Rama said. Amina heard her younger sister, "Come, come, you too," she said, but Shifra declined and went to sit by Samira.

Earlier, she had heard the men's shouts. Though Musa wasn't one of them, Mahmood was. She had quivered at the sound of hatred in his voice.

A tired and perspiring Fatima dropped on the seat next to them.

"Wonderful party, Sit Fatima, *Mavrook* again, may God grant you a long life," Mr. Nathan wished his friend.

"Thank you for coming," Fatima said. Then she added. "I hope you didn't pay attention to the youngsters. They got carried away. They were drunk."

"I know, I know," Mr. Nathan answered, a thin smile on his lips. He was about to leave, when he changed his mind, "I meant to ask you, who is this beautiful girl?" He pointed to Shifra, "A relative of yours?"

For a minute Fatima looked blankly at him, but Samira was quicker. "She's an orphan, Mr. Nathan. Her parents were killed in an accident. She escaped, but the shock made her lose her voice, poor girl. Her father had been a good friend of our master, Faud *Effendi*, now resting in Allah's Paradise. Sit Fatima, in her kindness, has taken her in."

Musa, who heard Samira's last sentence, saw his mother nod. Mr. Nathan raised an eyebrow, but said nothing more. He bowed to them and left. Other guests started leaving, too. It was growing dark. The party was over and Mahmood was anxious to return to his home, though not before collecting all the money purses, gifts from generous guests.

Abdullah, who had arrived at the wedding in the bank's chauffeured limousine, offered to take the newlyweds to Deir

Yassin, which was on his way to Jerusalem. There were tears and embraces and tears and hugs again.

"I'll send all your gifts tomorrow in one of our trucks," Fatima said.

"Promise you'll come soon to visit us, Eumi," Na'ima said, kissing her mother's hand.

"When are you coming back?" Abdullah asked Musa, "There's a lot of work waiting for you at the bank."

"As soon as I finish helping my mother get the house in order and after I take Amina to the airport."

The four sisters were still clasping their arms together.

"Enough," said an impatient Mahmood, seizing Na'ima's arm. "It's time to go."

Amina raise a quizzical eyebrow when she saw his gesture.

"I'll write to you," a wet-eyed Na'ima said, tearing herself from her sister.

"And I'll write back," Amina called after her.

"The house seems so quiet," dead tired, Fatima yawned. Then she asked,

"Amina, you had something you wanted to talk to me about."

"It can wait until tomorrow," Amina answered, "Let's rest now."

2 1

"Finally we have some time for ourselves. The last few days have passed like a whirlwind," Fatima said the next morning. "I didn't even welcome you as you deserve," she continued, caressing Amina's hand. "It's been five long months since you left home. Everybody missed you, but I most of all."

Fatima, Amina and Musa were seated at the kitchen table, drinking nana tea. No one touched the breakfast Samira had spread in front of them.

"I ate so much yesterday, I'm sure I can't touch any food for the next two days," Musa said.

"Me too," echoed Amina. "Na'ima had a very beautiful wedding and you should be very proud, Eumi," Amina addressed her mother.

Fatima smiled at her daughter. "What I plan to do for your wedding when the time comes, *Inshallah,* and I hope that time is not too far away, will exceed this one by far."

Musa coughed. "I think I should go take down the lanterns and return the chairs and tables to the neighbors."

Amina looked at him with reproach.

"But I'll be back soon," he said, reassuringly.

"Go, go, my son," Fatima told him. "You'll find us still here. We are going to take things leisurely today. Besides, Amina and I have a lot to talk about. Though, thank Allah, she wrote me every week; those letters were too short for the heart of a mother who aches to hear more, to know more. Cairo is so far away," Fatima sighed.

"Not as far as you think," Amina said. "It took only two hours by plane. Now that we live in modern times, the distances grow smaller every day. That's what George says, too."

Amina felt she made a faux pas. This was not the way she planned to tell her mother about George. She should have bitten her tongue before saying the last sentence. She saw her mother's eyes grow bigger.

"You are right." Musa, who hadn't left yet, tried to come to his sister's rescue. "Soon, there will be no frontiers between countries. I mean, when the war ends, and there is peace."

"Also no more hatred between people," Amina responded, happy at her brother's intervention.

Fatima looked from one to the other, keeping her mouth shut. Only her eyes betrayed her feelings.

Samira started clearing the table. "Why don't you go to the living room and let me clean the kitchen?" she asked. "Everything in here is still a mess."

Fatima stood. "You are right. Come, Amina."

There was harshness in her voice. Amina read the astonishment on Samira's face. Walking behind her mother, she put a finger to her lips while the other hand cupped her ear, a signal Samira understood well.

"So, these are modern times, my daughter, and you seem to have become a modern girl. I saw the change the minute you arrived. The way you wear your hair and your clothes show nothing of the modesty the Prophet asked from Muslim women. I wonder what else you hide from me."

No, thought Amina, *it wasn't going to be easy. It was going to be a fight.* Oh, how she hated the idea. She stopped in front of the credenza and picked up the framed photograph taken on her parents' wedding day. Her father stood proudly by his bride, but Amina could barely see her mother's features underneath the voile covering her face.

"Were you in love with my father before you got married?" Amina asked, caressing the picture.

Fatima looked surprised "What kind of question is that? Your father was a good husband, a good father. I think I didn't disappoint him, either."

"But did you fall in love with him?" insisted Amina.

"I saw your father for the first time at our henna party. Our parents met first and in their wisdom decided that it would be a good match for both families. I didn't need to meet him. I trusted my parents, the way Na'ima trusted me. *Inshallah,* I hope she'll have as good a marriage as mine."

Amina abstained from disclosing her doubts about Mahmood.

Fatima continued, "And you would be married already if not for your stubbornness. Since you were fifteen years old, the matchmakers filled our courtyard with proposals. Wealthy and powerful sheiks asked for your hand. But let bygones be bygones. I have no doubts that with Allah's help I'll still find a most successful match for you."

Amina could not wait any longer. "Eumi," she knelt in front of her mother, "I've already found him and he is the most wonderful man. Look," she showed her mother the sapphire ring, "I'm engaged to be married. Oh, Eumi, my most honored mother," words stumbled from Amina's mouth while she saw that anger and pain changed the color of her mother's face from fiery red to pale white and back to red, "Please hear me. I am here to beg for your consent and blessing."

Fatima rose from her chair.

"Is he a Muslim?" she asked, wringing her hands, her knuckles as white as ivory. "Is he also a modern man, and shameless, like you? Who could be the Muslim man who bypassed our tradition and forgot to send his parents to talk to me first? Answer me!"

"Eumi," Amina whispered, her eyes close to tears, "he's not Muslim. He's not going to pay you a dowry, as my father's parents did. George loves and respects me. He considers me his equal."

When she heard his name, Fatima shuddered. Amina's voice grew passionate.

"George is the British soldier I wrote to you about. Our love grew slowly and steadily. If not for him, I wouldn't have chosen to study to become a professional nurse. Because of his love for me, he's studying Arabic and the history of our people. His parents are now in Cairo waiting to meet me, but George felt that my duty was to be together with my family. He was the one who made it possible for me to attend the wedding."

Amina stopped talking. She was out of breath. With her back to her daughter, Fatima picked up her wedding picture.

"Faud," she cried, "Did you hear our daughter? Did you hear the insult? Oh, Faud, Faud, these are bad times when our daughter wants to marry the enemy! You left me with a great responsibility and I failed you."

"That's not true. You didn't fail our father. Eumi, you had to fight for your place in a world full of men. A widow at thirty-four with six children and a business to run, you worked hard, much harder than a man. And you succeeded!"

"If you have come to ask for my consent, the answer is no. I'll never give my blessing to such a union. It's against everything I believe in. It's against our faith."

Fatima's words hit Amina like stones; torn between her wish to marry George and her wish to obey her mother. After a long silence, she said softly, "With or without your blessing I'm going to marry George. My future is with him."

Neither one of them was aware that Samira and Musa witnessed their fiery exchange.

"Mother," Musa started, but an angry Fatima stopped him, "I'm sure the two of you plotted this. You knew what she was going to tell me. You are now the head of the family. Hasn't she asked for your approval?"

"I know she's in love," Musa answered.

"Love, love, don't talk to me about love. You are both too young to talk about it. Love comes slowly, with time. My mother taught me about it and she was right. Children benefit when they listen to the experience of their elders."

"I'm going to marry George," Amina said again. "Musa understands me. It's my own life I'm going to live, not a repeat of my ancestors' lives."

Fatima's hand went to her throat, for she found it hard to breathe.

"You both want to destroy the family your father built. You want to destroy our honor. Go live your lives! I will never give you my blessing. Never!"

Samira signaled to Amina and Musa to leave her alone with Fatima.

"Drink this cup of strong coffee," Samira lured Fatima, "I made it the way you like it, boiling water, no sugar."

Fatima covered her face with her palms.

"I don't need anything. After what I just heard I feel devastated. I'm sure I don't have to tell you; you who always knows everything happening in this household before I do!"

"Sit Fatima, please calm down. Think of yesterday's gorgeous wedding. People are going to talk about it for a long time."

"That was yesterday; today the sky is falling over my head."

"Fatima, how many years have we been together? You were eight years old when I started working for your family. That would make…" and Samira counted on her fingers, "more than thirty years."

Fatima waited. Anytime Samira started talking about the past she always had something in mind.

"I remember you as a young girl, how old, fourteen, fifteen, when you were so much in love with your cousin Abdullah. You had eyes only for him. I still remember how bitterly you cried when your mother said that first cousins can't marry."

"This has nothing to do with what's happening today," Fatima replied sharply. "My parents had the right to decide whom I was to marry. They were wise in choosing Faud for me."

"But did you love him? The night before your henna party you cried in my arms and do you remember what you said to me? You, the daughter of a most honorable Jerusalem family, wanted to run away from home!"

Fatima's cheeks were suffused with a flush of red.

"I don't know why you bring those forgotten things up. Faud was a good husband, a good father, a good provider. And yes, I loved him and you know that. I learned from my mother that marriage builds love, day after day, month after month, and that's what happened to me. I was lucky. So don't remind me of my foolish youth."

"It's true that you were lucky. But how many Muslim women are as lucky as you were? My mother wasn't one of them. After drinking a few glasses of arak, my father beat her so badly that she had a bloody miscarriage. For one lucky woman like you, I know ten unlucky ones locked in unhappy marriages."

"You are talking a lot today, and I still don't know the purpose of it. What do you want? Do you want to change my mind? This will never happen, so don't bother!"

Samira decided to try another angle. "The times are changing," she started, "even the customs are not the same. You've given a good education to Amina and Musa and you encouraged them to taste the life of big cities, Cairo, Jerusalem. You allowed them to have freedom. And freedom comes with a price."

"What price? What are you talking about? You think it is my fault that my daughter wants to marry a Brit? I am sure he'll ask her to convert." Fatima rubbed her temples. "Just the thought of it makes me crazy."

"Why don't you ask her, instead of imagining it? Maybe you'll learn something, rather than falling prey to your dark thoughts, to your nerves and worries. Talk to her, you still have time, she's not leaving until tomorrow."

Fatima raised her eyes.

"And when you talk to her," continued Samira, "tell her again how much you love her and worry for her. Don't let your pride get in the way. If you could ask the Prophet Mohammed what to do, he would say that it's a bigger sin to lose a child than to lose your pride."

Behind the door, Amina and Musa tried to listen through the keyhole, but the two women spoke in whispers. "You promised to help me," Amina said bitterly.

"Eumi didn't give me a chance," answered Musa. "But we both know that Samira can move mountains. Have patience."

PART II:

Palestine, 1944–1948

22

Deir Yassin

N a'ima tried to turn over. Six months pregnant, she felt as big as an elephant. Her hand inched across the bed sheet but she didn't find what she was searching for. The place beside her was empty. It was still dark outside. Where could Mahmood be? She tried to find a more comfortable position. Was it her fault that she got pregnant on their wedding night? She closed her eyes and remembered their arrival in Deir Yassin.

When cousin Abdullah ceremoniously opened the limousine door and she stepped out, still dressed in her red wedding gown, the entire village was there to welcome her. Mahmood, proud and a bit tipsy, took her in his arms and lifted her over the threshold. "You'll have time to meet her tomorrow," he turned away the well-wishers, "tonight she's mine."

All the men cheered.

The house, though small, looked clean. She saw the empty wooden shelves along one wall and thought to place there Amina's gifts, the coffee and tea sets. Mahmood took her arm and guided her to a small alcove off the main room. A large iron-framed bed and two chairs were the only furniture.

"Here," he said, "you can undress while I go to check on the sheep and the chickens."

As she still seemed unsure of what to do next, he impatiently repeated, "I want to find you undressed and waiting for me. I'll not be long."

Unpacking the filmy nightgown that had been Amina's gift, Na'ima felt herself invaded by heat from her soles to her head. The only window had no curtain, and she made a mental note to make one, first thing in the morning. She turned off the single bulb and undressed. She sat on the bed and felt the coarse sheet prickling her skin.

Mahmood came in, his breath smelling of arak. With one hand he turned her on her back, the other reaching to knead her breasts. He lowered himself on top of her. "You don't need this," he said, fumbling with her nightgown and throwing it over her head. He forced his hands between her thighs, and before she knew it a sharp pain made her scream. He was pounding her, his breath short and heavy, while she felt that something sticky trickled down her legs. The pain didn't stop. He moaned. The sheet scratched her shoulders. When he was finished, he turned his back to her. She wanted to get up to clean herself, but he stirred and she became afraid.

"Where do you go?" he asked in a drugged voice. "I'm not done yet."

He pushed her back and entered her again. Na'ima wept.

"Don't," Mahmood said. "I am fed up with you women. The other one cried, too. You must've been told what your duty is."

He laughed. "In time you're not only going to like it but you'll beg for it."

The next morning when Mahmood's mother brought the baby, who had slept with her that first night, a proud Mahmood showed her the bed sheet covered with bloodstains. His mother embraced a dumbfounded Na'ima.

"I was sure of it! Now I'm going to show it to the neighbors, too. They were making bets that my son wasn't marrying a virgin, you being a city girl. I'll keep the sheet to show it to your mother as well."

The following nights continued in the same fashion. Na'ima became used to it, and though Mahmood's touch wasn't tender, Na'ima liked to feel his strength overpowering her. To please him she started to move her hips in rhythm with his movements.

"I told you you'd like it," her husband laughed, pinching her nipples.

During the day, Na'ima kept busy putting the presents away, cooking for Mahmood and taking care of Nassum, Mahmood's little boy. She loved the baby, who reminded her of her brother Ahmed at the same age, when she and Amina competed to be the first to bathe or feed him. She felt that Nassum returned her love from the way he smiled at her while his eyes followed her every move.

She started feeling tired and nauseous six weeks after her wedding. When she told her mother-in-law, Mahmood's mother kissed her on both cheeks and said, "*Mavrook, Mavrook*, I'm sure it's going to be a boy. I'm running to tell Mahmood. What a breeder my son is," and she laughed happily.

But it turned out to be a difficult pregnancy, and Mahmood's memories, still fresh from his first wife's pregnancy, left him continuously upset and preoccupied. Na'ima saw that he didn't seem as happy at the prospect as his mother was, and she didn't know the reason. Months passed and she felt sicker every day. "You'll feel better when you feel the child moving," her mother-in-law told her, but Na'ima felt just the opposite.

"Why don't you invite your mother to come be with you for a little while?" Mahmood's mother proposed. When Na'ima finally wrote to her mother, she didn't dream that the thought of a grandchild would revive her mother's old energy.

After her three older children left home, Fatima suffered from lassitude and fatigue. Samira tried to lure her by cooking her specialties, but Fatima left most of the food untouched.

"You should go somewhere," Samira said one evening. "You need fresh air. Go to Jerusalem, go to Abu-Gosh. How about visiting Na'ima?"

"It's too soon," Fatima said. "She has to get used to her new life first."

"Nonsense," retorted Samira. "You refused to go to Cairo to Amina's wedding; now you don't want to go to Na'ima, though you know very well that you'll enjoy being close to Musa and the rest of your family. You need them. The older one gets, the more one needs family."

"Don't harass me. If not for you, Amina wouldn't have married that Brit. You pressured me," Fatima said bitterly. "'For the sake of not losing her,' you said. What kind of wedding was that, with the British consul marrying them? And how do I know that she is not going to convert, if she hasn't already?"

Fatima's cheeks burned from the pathos of her words, but Samira didn't concede. She said, "Read me again your cousin Aiisha's letter. Was there something in it about Amina's converting? I don't remember."

Reluctantly, Fatima rummaged in her pockets until she found the letter.

To my most honored cousin, Fatima, Salaam Aleikum,

Fatima stopped to search for her glasses. Samira saw that the letter was stained from dried tears. Who knew how many times she had cried over it?

I just returned from the British Embassy. I promised Amina, for whom I was a witness at her civil ceremony, to write to you. Though only George's parents and I were there, we felt that it was a very moving event. Your daughter looked splendid, dressed in a mother-of-pearl gray suit and a petit chapeau of the same color with a veil that covered half of her face. She held a bouquet of white roses in her gloved hands. A white rose was in George's lapel. His face radiated happiness.

The consul, an aristocratic-looking gentleman, asked if they want to say something to one another before taking their vows. Blushing, Amina nodded. She then read in English a love poem by Omar Khayyam At his turn George, looking into her eyes, recited a poem by Lord Tennyson. I cried, and George's mother had tears in her eyes, too.

Oh, my dear, dear cousin, I know that reading this letter pains you, but I believe in destiny, fatma, your name. Amina and George were destined for one another. After the ceremony, we drank champagne in their honor. The young couple left immediately for their honeymoon, a cruise on the Nile.

Dear Fatima, I wish you good health and joy from all your children.

May Allah bless you, Aiisha

Both women remained silent. Samira stood up and hugged Fatima. The gate bell rang. It was the mailman, bringing a letter. "Na'ima," Fatima said, impatiently opening it. As she read, Samira saw Fatima's features relax, a smile on her face.

"She's five months pregnant," Fatima said her eyes suddenly clear.

"Already!" wondered Samira.

"Young people, hot blood," Fatima said. "She's asking me to come. She doesn't feel well."

"And she wants her mother. It's natural. Tell me what to pack for you."

"Not so fast, not so fast, though I know you want to get rid of me," laughed Fatima. It was a happy laugh. "Would Mahmood be pleased to see me visiting there so soon?" She remained pensive. "But my daughter is calling and my heart aches to go."

"What else has she written?" Samira asked. "I see she covered two full pages."

"Oh, yes. The news that she's pregnant was such a surprise, I didn't read the rest!" Fatima's eyes scanned the letter. "She writes that the weather has changed and she needs a warm blanket. She's not used to Deir Yassin's cold nights. She wants me to buy rolls of wool for her to knit sweaters for Nassim, for herself and for the coming baby."

Fatima continued to peruse the letter. "She writes, 'I could play with Nassim all day long. He's such a good baby. When he sees me, he stops crying, smiles and stretches his little arms toward me. Oh, Eumi, I think that motherhood is marvelous. I promise myself to try to be as good a mother as you have been for us. Come soon. It will be an honor to have you with us."

"What did I tell you?" Samira said, her eyes dancing in her head.

"I'm going to the bazaar," an energized Fatima said, "There is a little store that sells the best quality wool. I want to knit an afghan for Na'ima. Meanwhile, take out from my chest the goose-feather blanket that my mother made and we never used. Air it out and clean it. I want everything to be ready by tomorrow, do you hear me?"

"That's my girl," gushed Samira happily. "I'll do more than that. Remember the patchwork quilt we started and never finished? We called it the patchwork of love. Wouldn't it be a perfect bedspread for Na'ima's new baby?"

Watching Fatima leave, Samira felt overjoyed by her sprightly steps; Fatima was almost dancing as she unlocked the gate and disappeared beyond it.

23

During the months following Na'ima's wedding, Musa's life became busier. Thanks to his command of the English language and his cousin's satisfaction with his aptitude for banking, Abdullah promoted Musa to Assistant Manager of the Foreign Exchange department. Musa was ready for the challenge. It was in step with the plan he had made the day he returned to Jerusalem.

The plan included a managerial position at Barclays Bank in Jaffa, which he was sure he could obtain with Abdullah's recommendation. But he was not going to disclose his plan to his cousin yet.

Musa still basked in the memory of Suha's brilliant eyes watching him dance the Debka at Na'ima's wedding. Her eyes had been full of promises. In his new position he traveled to other Barclays branches. During a short visit to Jaffa, he could steal a few hours to kiss his mother's hand and to see Suha. Once when he mentioned that he might move permanently to Jerusalem, he saw Suha's face freeze and her eyes take on the fearful look of a wounded rabbit. Somehow he understood that for her Jaffa was a safe place. Maybe later, after their marriage, he would ask her about her fears, or remind her of that day … or maybe he'd never ask. So many things are better left unspoken.

Contemplating their future, Musa knew that he would not want them to live in his mother's house. He was sure that Fatima would expect it and would be hurt, but that was not part of his plan. Since he would not want to live far from her, Musa decided to rebuild the old house on the adjacent plot of land, his father's gift to his mother.

When he told Fatima about his idea to repair and modify the old building, she was suspicious, "Why?" she asked. "There is more than enough space in our house, especially now with Amina and Na'ima married. There was plenty of space even before. What is in your mind?"

Cautiously, he answered, "We need a guest house. Na'ima and Mahmood will visit you, and Inshallah, after her baby is born, there will be two children. The day is not far when Amina and George will visit, too."

"As always, you think of everything, Ibni," Fatima kissed him, "You are right. Talk to Attia, he's the best builder in town. Tell him you have my blessing."

Musa had seen a few elegant dwellings in Jerusalem and wanted to model his Jaffa house after them. From Petra, that magic place, he wanted to bring red rocks and have them cut into tiles. The new house would definitely have a bathroom, the sides of the bathtub covered in blue tiles, the color of Suha's eyes.

He had seen such a bath advertised in a Cairo magazine. In his mind he could see Suha's alabaster body lying in it, her face turned toward him with a big smile, while he would be ready to dry every drop of water on her body with his kisses. Every night he dreamt a different variation of this scene.

"I'm in no hurry," he told Attia, the contractor, whose powerful muscles seemed to coil under his shirt. *Fatima would probably faint when she heard the cost.*

Rebuilding the house gave Musa a reason to visit home more often. As he said to his mother, "I trust the builder, but he has to know I am the boss. Without control, he might use cheaper materials and charge for more expensive ones."

Musa told no one he was building his future love-nest. He kept it a secret even from Samira, his usual confidante.

There was only one cloud on Musa's clear sky: Mahmood. Since their talk in the Jerusalem restaurant, he had been after Musa, pressing him to join his political group.

"Don't you see what's going to happen?" Mahmood asked in a harsh tone, "The Brits are going to leave, or we'll make them leave. But the Yahudim remain. After pressure from our leaders, the Brits' White Paper reduced the number of Jewish immigrants to 75,000. Even this number was too big. The future will confirm it. We have to prepare ourselves for a fight, my brother!"

From his mouth, "my brother" sounded like a sneer. Mahmood was waiting for an answer. And Musa was caught unprepared. Finally, in order to end Mahmood's insistence and fearing that a refusal would arouse his suspicions, Musa agreed to come to one of the group's meetings.

It was held in Abu-Gosh, the village well-known for its vineyards. Musa saw young people, the *Mujahedeen*—holy warriors, Mahmood called them with pride, as heated as his brother-in-law was.

There was a lot of smoke and screams of "Out with them," meant for the British or the Jews, Musa couldn't tell which. One thing was certain. A young man to whom the others seem to look up told the crowd, "Soon we are going to receive arms from our brothers in Syria, Egypt and other Arab countries. The forests around Jerusalem," he added, "would be the perfect training ground."

"See," a satisfied Mahmood said afterward, slapping Musa's back, "we are making progress. Sooner than you think, your mama's darling boy will learn to put a gun to good use."

After he left Mahmood, Musa decided that first thing in the morning he would tell the builder to hurry and finish the house.

24

I t had been more than a year since that fateful day when Musa found her on the deserted Jaffa beach. Lately she had started thinking of herself as Suha, as everyone called her. Only in the intimacy of her room did memories of her past intrude her. Days like today, when the rain finally burst out of the skies, a vengeance after the long dry winter, reminding her of the dismal day in Jerusalem when the *neft* man had pinched her cheek with his oily hand smelling of kerosene. The next thing she knew, her father had promised him her hand in marriage. The memory still made her tremble.

"Brrrr," Samira suddenly entered, "it's almost as cold as the Jerusalem winter. Come into the kitchen to warm yourself. I'm making tea for the two of us."

The children were in school and Fatima was visiting Na'ima. It was one of her bi-weekly visits. At the beginning of these visits, Samira told Shifra, "Fatima seems to be reliving her life as a young bride. She goes to the bazaar and buys trinkets, a flower vase, or another prayer shawl, all for Na'ima. And when she goes there, she cooks Mahmood's favorite dishes, *kafta, a meatloaf,* and fattoush. After she leaves, Na'ima and Mahmood have food to last a week."

"Fatima said it was your fault that Na'ima didn't know to cook," Shifra said smiling, warming her hands around the cup of tea, "She said that you spoiled her children."

"It wasn't me, she did it and she continues doing it now. Look how much knitting and quilting we've done already. She has less and less time for her children here at home."

Shifra knew what Samira meant. The children's grades had declined, especially the thirteen-year-old Nur. The English teacher had sent a letter complaining of her lack of interest in the class and that she was not doing her homework.

"Why should I break my head with it, when in a few years I'll be married? How much does Na'ima use her English now?" a stubborn Nur had answered her mother's reprimands.

"I might be able to help her, though my English has become quite rusty," Shifra whispered timidly in Samira's ear. Nur had told Shifra that her school, Tabeetha, run by the Church of Scotland, offered intermediate and advanced evening classes for adults. Shifra became excited; she would love so much to go back to school. *Could she find a way to register?* She confided in Samira, but to no avail.

On one of Musa's visits home, now more frequent since the rebuilding of the house next door, Fatima complained of Nur's laziness, to which he answered, "It must be a phase, it will pass." But it did not.

Lately, Shifra observed with delight that Musa was coming home often during his mother's visits to Na'ima. Musa would show Shifra the plans for the guest house. He asked for her suggestions, to choose the paint color for the walls in different rooms, or to select the window frames and tiles, nodding approvingly at her choices.

Her heart beat faster when she was alone with him, and it warmed her soul to see how attentively he listened to her. He brought her flowers at almost every visit. During one of his visits, Shifra told him about her wish to study take a English class, "In that way," she said, "I could help Nur to better prepare her lessons."

Musa did not answer immediately. *Was he still afraid that she was going to run away?*

At breakfast the following morning, a smiling Musa said, "Last evening I talked to Samira about your wish, and like me, she thinks it's a good idea since," he emphasized, "You'll be able to tutor Nur. Samira offered to accompany you and wait until the end of the lesson."

I am not a prisoner, Shifra was displeased, but she knew that it was better to have Samira on her side; especially if Fatima would do more than raise an eyebrow at hearing her latest request.

Seeing the anxiety with which Musa waited for her answer, Shifra thanked him with a gratifying smile, happy to see the color returning to Musa's face.

25

"A child brings happiness," Fatima told Na'ima, putting a cold compress on her daughter's forehead. "Our Prophet, in his great wisdom said, 'Go and multiply.' One more month and you'll be up and running. Then you'll remember my words."

Na'ima moaned, "I wish you would stay longer, or send Samira. Oh, I miss Amina so much. Where is she when I most need her?"

"I'd rather we don't talk about her. There's no reason to aggravate ourselves."

"You and Mahmood," cried Na'ima. "He doesn't let me answer her letters. He says, 'When she married her Brit, she stopped being your sister. No wife of mine has a British brother-in-law.' He tore up her letters. Eumi, you are as cruel as he is."

Fatima did not answer. She also missed Amina, who had written long letters describing the cruise on the Nile during her short honeymoon. They had the most elegant cabin, and George made sure that every morning the cabin steward brought fresh flowers and a box of Swiss chocolates for his bride. "Eumi," she wrote, "it feels so good to be loved."

Fatima thought how different the lives of her twin daughters had become. At Mahmood's commands, Na'ima had to wake up at dawn and feed the chickens, prepare breakfast for him, change and bathe Nassum, then dress and feed him. No wonder she was exhausted.

Amina wrote about the large apartment overlooking the Nile George rented for them in Zamaluk, Cairo's most elegant neighborhood with two bathrooms, and a sleep-in maid who learned from Amina the recipes for Samira's delicacies.

Fatima's eyes turned toward the well-worn clay floor. *Mahmood should install tiles.* She made a mental note to tell him. She feared for Na'ima, who could easily get a cold, especially during the winter rains for whom neither she nor Nassum were equipped. Meanwhile, she'll buy a few carpets in Jerusalem's bazaar when she'll go visit with Musa and Abdulah.

Fatima, who had stopped listening to Na'ima's flood of words, heard suddenly, "I wonder... If Mahmood is so adamant about Amina marrying George, how will he react when he hears that you hide a Yahud girl under your roof?"

Fatima's heart skipped a beat. She was aware of Mahmood's nationalistic views, with which she basically agreed, but she was alarmed at the hatred that flared in his eyes anytime he talked about the "unwelcome strangers who grabbed our land," as he called the Jews.

She knew her daughter tolerated Suha only because she was liked by the other members of the family. "She's an orphan girl, whom nobody claimed," Fatima answered, "and she's learned our ways."

Taking Na'ima's hand in hers, Fatima continued, "My mother, Allah bless her memory, said on the eve of my marriage, 'Even if you adore your husband, there could be times when things would be better left unspoken.' Mahmood is quick-tempered. A few weeks before giving birth, if telling Mahmood about Suha could provoke his wrath, it wouldn't be healthy for you or for your child. I see no need to bring it up."

Na'ima sighed, "You speak the voice of wisdom, Eumi." She kissed her mother's hand.

Something will have to be done quickly, Fatima thought. The minute I get back I'll tell Samira, the girl has to convert or leave. Tomorrow I'll see Musa and let him know my decision.

A child cried in the adjacent room. "Oh, it's Nassum. He's up from his nap," Na'ima said, climbing out of bed, as cumbersome as a whale. "Eumi, please bring him while I get his snack ready."

Yes, Fatima thought again, *the sooner I talk to Musa, the better.*

Musa was waiting for his mother at the central bus station in Jerusalem. She had called him at the bank and asked him to meet her at the station. Her voice sounded tense. She said she needed to talk to him about an important matter, a matter which could not wait.

He held in his hand the Palestine Post. Since the Allied Armies' debarkation, Musa had followed the news with excitement. The war in Europe was going to end soon.

At the bus station, a mob and noise surrounded Musa. Peasant women, their babies tied in blankets on their backs, carried cackling chickens. People descended or climbed the old yellow buses, while the stink of burned tires and smoke brought tears to their eyes.

"Musa Masri! Mr. Masri!" Musa turned when he heard his name. The caller was Jonathan Goldring.

"Unbelievable," said Musa, shaking Jonathan's hand, "What a coincidence to encounter you in the midst of this hullabaloo."

Musa barely recognized Jonathan. He was dressed in a khaki uniform, with the red beret's ribbon flying in the wind. Proudly Jonathan raised his hand. "A member of the Jewish Brigade salutes you. There are five thousand of us who have finished training with the British Army and are ready to fight the Nazis."

A vision flashed through Musa's mind; Mahmood and his cohorts training in the woods as he unwillingly watched them, too afraid to arouse his brother-in-law's suspicions to object.

Does Jonathan know what Mahmood and his friends are doing in the forests around Jerusalem? Their training is not only to get rid of the Brits. Musa heard Jonathan say, "I was chosen because I speak German and I could obtain important information during prisoner interrogations. I never thought I'd be facing Germans again. My parents hope that I can find out what happened to the family we left behind. I'm scared of what I might discover."

"Good luck to you," Musa said shaking Jonathan's hand. "May Allah guide you," Realizing his mistake, Musa blushed. "I'm sorry."

"Don't apologize," Jonathan smiled, "we need everyone's God praying for us."

"Deir Yassin local bus arrives on line 4," the loudspeaker announced.

"Excuse me," Musa said, "I am here to meet my mother."

From afar, he saw Fatima. His mother looked tired. She descended the steps with difficulty.

After the customary greetings, Fatima blurted out, "Either she converts or she has to leave."

"What are you talking about?" Musa asked, though he had little doubt who she meant.

"It's Suha. She's been with us more than a year. We healed her and brought her back to life; we fed and clothed her. She has a safe roof above her head. For everything we did, has she ever mentioned that she wants to become one of us? No! How do we know she's not a snake in our midst?" Fatima ended out of breath.

What happened to her all of a sudden? Why this outburst? She never spoke like this before. Musa couldn't understand his mother's anger. *She sees Na'ima too often,* Musa thought, knowing that only Na'ima didn't like Suha. Mahmood's face flashed again through his mind.

"It's because of Mahmood, isn't it?" Musa asked.

"No," answered Fatima, "he doesn't know yet. But Na'ima might tell him any day."

Then I have no time, Musa thought. He should immediately proceed with his plan.

"Eumi, you shouldn't worry," he said, trying to calm his mother, "everything will work out for the best. Now let's go meet Abdullah for lunch. He's invited us to be his guests at the French Quarter's finest restaurant."

Musa knew that he wanted to marry Suha. His dream was to live in the renovated house, where he could wrap his arms around her and never let her go. And the walls of the house would witness their love.

But had he ever asked Suha, whose love he was now sure of, if she would renounce her religion to marry him? Would she convert to Islam? Could the strength of his love be enough to convince her? She seemed docile, but he'd heard Samira say more than once, "One never knows what lies under quiet waters."

And if she didn't convert, what would be their alternative—to run away? He knew that his father had amassed a fortune, which, thanks to Abdullah, was tucked away in safe places; Alexandria and Cairo, even London. It would be so easy for him...No, that wasn't in his nature. He wasn't going to hide. He would marry Suha in the open, proudly facing the world.

Musa tossed in his bed, unable to fall asleep. As much as he disliked the Brits, he could try, as a last resort, to be married by a British judge. Then he remembered that Suha didn't have a single document to prove her identity. No birth certificate. It was as if she never existed. Oh, what a mess.

But, maybe this wasn't so bad. He remembered what Samira told Adon Nathan, the Jewish watchmaker, at Na'ima's wedding. She said that Suha was an orphan whose parents died in the accident, in which she lost her speech. It was a thin line to walk on, but it might solve his problem. He would need only two witnesses. It wouldn't be too difficult to persuade two people; he knew that money's power to convince is stronger than a thousand words.

Musa fell into a deep, disturbed sleep. His first dream was of Jonathan fighting with Mahmood, in the Abu-Gosh forest. He woke up and went to drink a glass of water. The second dream was worse. His brother-in-law was grinning at him. "You thought you and your Yahudia whore could hide from me. I'll find you even if I have to walk to the end of the world. For me the lovers of Yahudim are the enemies of Islam. You are a sinner, a sinner, sinner…"

The following morning when a tired Musa looked in the mirror, he saw a pale face and fatigued eyes. But he had made a decision. He would take the first bus to Jaffa where soon the wheels would start turning.

26

What Musa had asked of her was difficult. Yes, Samira loved him as she would have loved her own child, but even for one's own child, there are times when a parent can refuse to comply with his wishes. Musa had asked Samira to convince Suha-Shifra to convert to Islam. And he told her that it had to be done quickly. No time to wait.

Musa had arrived at dusk, had kissed the children, but she noticed his impatience when he immediately went to check the progress on the new construction. When he returned, he said, "Samira, after dinner, I need to talk to you." He barely glanced at Suha, who looked as happy as the children when he arrived.

And now, the news! He wanted to marry Suha as soon as possible. *But how could a Muslim man marry a woman of another faith?* Samira knew as well as Musa that this was unlikely.

"She'll have to convert," Musa said. "You are the closest to her." His eyes begged Samira. "From the beginning you helped our love blossom. I know she loves me, I feel it in my soul. But does she love me enough to convert? We know that it's only a formality; it can be accomplished in front of you or another witness. Samira, Samira, do you listen to me?"

Everything he said was true. Now she had to face the result of her foolishness, of her romantic notions, of her unfulfilled life. What was she thinking when she took the girl to Uhm Zaide and asked for the love potion? Wasn't she encouraging a forbidden love? And now she was responsible for that dream. Oh, she's going to be punished. The Prophet doesn't forgive trespassers.

Samira turned her face toward Musa. "He's still a child," she thought, seeing how anxiously he waited for her answer. She remembered Adon Grunwald, the man who had made her miserable childhood bearable. He was a wise man. *If he was alive what would he say?* She sighed. *On the other hand, where would Suha go?* Samira's heart cringed at the thought of Suha lost in the midst of strangers.

The first step would be to find out who Suha thinks she is, an Arab, a Jew?

For sure Suha loves Musa. She didn't need the love potion. The girl was already in love with Musa from the minute she opened her eyes and saw him.

"I'll talk to her," Samira said after a while. "I understand it would be easier for me than for you, but," she added when she saw Musa's eyes lighting up, "I can't promise I will succeed."

Musa kissed her hands.

"Think of tomorrow, your big day," Samira's eyes were wet, "when you'll tell Suha how much you love her and ask her to be your wife."

The next morning, Musa left early to apply for a position at Jaffa's Barclays Bank. During a sleepless night, Samira thought of different ways to approach Shifra, but when the two of them were seated at the kitchen table, she only said, "Musa is in love with you. And I know you share his feelings."

Shifra's face reddened as Samira continued, "Last night he told me that he wants to marry you. That's the reason he came home."

Samira stopped, waiting for a reaction from Shifra, who didn't move.

"Doesn't it make you happy?" Samira asked. "Do you realize that half of Jaffa's girls would want to be in your place?"

Still no response from Shifra, though her blue eyes looked brighter than ever. Samira became impatient. "What would you say to him if he asked you today?"

Shifra lowered her head. Almost imperceptibly, she nodded. When she raised her head, Samira saw tears in her eyes.

"Come here," Samira said, opening her arms. She cradled Shifra. "I have something else to say to you. A Muslim can't marry a woman of another faith unless that woman converts."

A tremor passed through Shifra's body and she tried to release herself from Samira's embrace, but Samira tightened her grip.

"Listen to me," Samira said. "For more than a year you have shared our life. Nobody asked you where you came from or who you are. We accepted you and cared for you, and you became a part of our household. Now Musa wants to marry you. It's time you prove that you want to be one of us."

"Even if I wanted to, "Shifra sobbed, "I can't."

"Of course you can," Samira caressed her hand. "You'd only have to say the *Al-Shahada*, the acknowledgement that you accept our God. It's very simple and I can teach it to you."

No answer. Samira felt tired. Was it Shifra's limp body, which suddenly felt too heavy for her arms, or what Musa had asked her to do that was oppressing her soul? She shouldn't have involved herself in their affairs of the heart, and now it was too late for regrets.

"If you really love Musa, you'll do it. You need only one witness to hear you say the *Al-Shahada*,' she whispered, "And I will be your witness." Gently, Samira pushed Shifra out of her arms.

- - -

After Musa heard that Suha took the declaration of faith and became a Muslim, he knew it was his duty to tell his mother without delay. His conscience wouldn't be at peace unless he received her blessing. First he went to see Abdullah. It was only fair to tell the man who considered him like his own son, and who had had hoped that one day Musa would marry one of his daughters.

Musa was relieved that Abdullah didn't ask any questions after he told him that he wanted to marry a girl he had met in Jaffa and had fallen in love with. Musa prayed that the encounter with his mother would be as easy.

With his arms full of gifts for Na'ima's newborn baby, he descended from the yellow screeching Jerusalem-Deir Yassin bus. The sun was already fading. Even before knocking at the door he heard Mahmood screaming at the whimpering Nassum.

"Don't slap him, don't slap him," Na'ima pleaded, "he didn't do anything wrong. It's my fault. I told you it's my fault."

"Then you should stop encouraging him," Mahmood turned his fury on his wife. "You are lucky you're still recovering, otherwise you'd get it from me."

"Be quiet, somebody's knocking at the door," Musa heard Fatima's voice.

"It's Musa!" Na'ima screamed, her face radiating happiness, "Musa, my darling brother is here."

"*Salaam Aleikum, Mavrook,* may your child find grace in the eyes of Allah!" Musa wished them, shaking Mahmood's hand and kissing Na'ima."

Then he turned toward his mother. "And to you, Eumi, our most honored mother, I wish many more grandchildren to sweeten your life like honey."

"So be it, so be it," Mahmood muttered in agreement. Only Nassum stood in a corner crying.

Musa marveled at little Faud's good looks, which pleased his sister. Later, during supper, he complimented his mother on her tasty food, "I understand now why Na'ima wants you here. You're cooking her favorite dishes."

"Just don't fatten her up like a cow," said Mahmood, "she won't be able to move."

"A nursing mother should eat well," Fatima said, annoyed.

After the meal, Na'ima yawned, saying she was tired and wanted to go to bed. Mahmood invited Musa to the village meeting, but Musa, happy for the opportunity to be alone with his mother, excused himself.

"Eumi," he said after Mahmood left, "let's take a walk in the orchard. The mountain air is so refreshing I can't get enough of it."

His mother took his arm, "I'm so happy you came," she whispered.

Musa wanted to ask Fatima why Mahmood seemed so angry when he arrived, but he restrained himself.

To his surprise, Fatima brought it up. "Mahmood has a quick temper, especially after he drinks one or two glasses of arak. He scares me."

Musa stopped in his tracks. He had never been fond of Mahmood. "What happened?" he asked, almost against his will.

"Nassum is still a baby. He's jealous of little Faud. When he saw Na'ima nursing him, he climbed on the bed and pursed his lips close to Na'ima's breasts. We laughed. Na'ima nursed both boys, one at each breast. Nothing wrong with it, except that Mahmood got mad." Fatima shook her head, "It's no good, no good."

Musa didn't know what to say. He took a deep breath. The rosebushes planted by his sister filled the air with their perfume.

"It's stupid of me," said Fatima, "I shouldn't worry you."

She walked to a bench underneath a pear tree. "Sit with me, Ibni," she said, brushing away dried leaves.

Musa cleared his throat, "I have good news. According to your wish, Suha has converted to Islam. She took the *Al-Shahada*. Samira was her witness."

He waited, but his mother was silent. In the dark, he couldn't read her face, which made him nervous.

"And I am here to tell you that I'm going to marry her."

Again silence. Maybe he should have said, "I want to marry her, and I came to ask for your blessing." Now it was too late for that. He continued, "I wouldn't do it behind your back. I fell in love the minute I saw her asleep on Jaffa's beach. Since then, my love for Suha only grew. And I was happy to see how well she adjusted to living with us, and the way she's been almost adopted by our family."

A star fell. In its light Musa saw his mother's angry eyes.

"How do you dare?" she said. "What do you know about her? Even if she converted, she's not one of us. Where does she come from? Did she tell you who she is? You want to marry a strange girl you know nothing about? You want to destroy our good name? You should be ashamed of yourself!"

Fatima started to cough, nearly choking. It was difficult for her not to raise her voice. "First you brought her home, begging me to give her shelter. I should have known better, oh, I should have known."

"Eumi, I respect and love you. It's because of this respect that I'm here to ask for your blessing."

"Never, do you hear, never!"

The fury in Fatima's voice grew with every word. "I should have guessed that she would bring *nakhba*-disaster, upon us. Look what has happened. Amina is gone, married to a Christian. And now you want to marry a Yahud girl! Is that the example you want to give your brother and sisters? What about your responsibility to your family? Have you forgotten your duty towards our ancestors?"

"My wife will become a Masri and she'll honor our name," a stubborn Musa answered. Suddenly they heard footsteps, a neighbor's squeaking gate, a sign that the meeting was over and Mahmood would be home any moment.

"There's going to be a war soon," said Fatima through clenched teeth. "You'd better keep your eyes open, my son. Forget about marriage. This is not a good time. More important events are on the horizon, events that are going to shape our lives forever."

She took a deep breath, "Go now. For your sake I'll try to forget our talk tonight."

The night Musa returned from Deir Yassin, after being rebuffed by his mother, he decided to have a civil marriage as soon as possible. As always, he confided in Samira.

"It's easier to say it than to go through with it," Samira said, "Do you know the requirements?"

Musa nodded, "Two witnesses—and they must be males, of course!"

The boy she raised had become a man and seemed now more determined than ever, Samira thought.

"Who could I ask to witness? I need people who can be trusted and who won't ask too many questions." His words lingered in the air.

"First, let me bring you some fresh nana tea. You look so tired. Then we'll put our heads together and try to solve the problem," Samira said.

It was almost midnight, when Musa, his face lightening, said, "I'll talk to Yusuf."

"I remember him, the limping boy who followed you like a shadow, when you were kids. Even if he would be as faithful to you as a dog to his master, he's no fool. He's going to ask you who she is, where she is from, which family. Have you thought of it?"

Musa remained silent. "Then who should I ask?

Samira heard the impatience in his voice. "There are not many options."

She got up and paced the room, "What about Mr. Nathan?" she said after a while, standing behind Musa, her arms massaging his shoulders. "Do you remember at Na'ima's wedding he asked who Suha was and I told him she was Hassan *Effendi*'s daughter, your father's friend from Alexandria."

"Are you kidding?" scoffed Musa, "A Jew? You want to bring a Jew as a witness in front of a Muslim Judge? Come on, Samira, you know better."

"Don't answer so fast, young man. First, Mr. Nathan is your mother's good friend. He's a Moroccan Jew whose reputation both as an excellent watchmaker and a good person is recognized in the Arab community."

Musa shook his head in disbelief. "Still, you are going too far."

"At least he could give you good advice," Samira insisted. "I have a feeling he can be of help. At Na'ima's wedding, I told him, that Suha is an orphan, the only survivor from her parents' car accident. With no close family, her neighbors remembering that your parents were good friends of the family, they asked your mother if she would take her in."

"It's a moving tale, but it isn't going to work"

"It could work if you start believing it. Ask Uhm Zaide. She could tell you. When you believe in something strongly, it becomes reality."

"I don't want to build my future on a lie." Musa answered.

Having raised him, Samira knew how honest Musa was, but she stood her ground. "When there is need, even an honest person can bend a bit. Moreover," she continued, "I told Mr. Nathan that the accident and the death of her parents caused her to lose her voice. Now that she has regained it, she still has trouble speaking."

"You've thought of everything, haven't you? So people who'd hear Suha speaking Arabic wouldn't detect she wasn't born an Arab."

"It's only because I love you, my boy, and I want so much to see you happy."

Samira got up, "Listen, it's past midnight. Tomorrow you will feel better. A new day renews each one of us."

But Samira had difficulty falling asleep. If Musa agrees with my plan, she thought, I'll pray to Allah to punish only me since I am old, and my life is half over. She knelt. Allah Ackbar, let him live and enjoy his love.

Mr. Nathan said that he remembered Suha, the beautiful blue-eyed girl who had eyes only for Musa during the men's Debka dance at Na'ima's wedding.

He added laughing, "And you, Musa, seemed to be dancing for her and her alone."

Mr. Nathan was courteous, listened with attention and said that he understood the situation when Musa explained that Suha had no papers to prove her identity and needed two witnesses to sign an affidavit declaring they knew who she was.

"If only my mother could have been here, instead of taking care of my sister and her new baby," Musa said with false innocence, "she would have helped find the right witnesses."

After a long silence Mr. Nathan said, "I think I can help."

He called, "Habib, come here, I want you to meet Mr. Musa Ibn Faud, my friend."

Habib, his young Arab apprentice, wiped his hands on his apron before answering his master's call. He listened respectfully and agreed with a smile to be a witness, after Mr. Nathan ended by saying, "Everyone has to help a man in love."

After he left Mr. Nathan's store, a jubilant Musa thought, now I have more courage to talk to Yusuf. He started running, feeling wings carrying his feet.

"Yusuf accepted without asking any questions," Musa told Samira when he returned home, still wondering at how easy it had been.

And so it came to pass that Suha Hassan, seventeen years old, born in Alexandria to a French mother and an Egyptian father, received an affidavit signed by Yusuf and Habib. A grateful Musa bought new kafias for the witnesses and invited them to join him at Jaffa's famous Turkish baths. Later that evening the three of them continued to celebrate the event by clinking together numerous glasses of *arrack*.

At breakfast, the morning after he had the affidavit in his hands, Musa said, "Now we have to obtain a legal union."

"Today is a beautiful day, no clouds, the sky as limpid as the sea, a perfect day to get married," said Samira, smiling.

"We are going to *Baladia* in the afternoon and after that, *Inshallah*, our troubles will be over. We'll have our marriage license and Suha and I will spend our entire lives together."

Musa had planned everything. Samira admired him, even though it wasn't the wedding his mother dreamed of for him.

Samira held Suha's hand as they entered the City Hall where Musa and his witnesses, Yusuf and Habib, were already waiting. Suha, modestly dressed in a blue jelebia and hijab of the same color, kept her eyes locked on the floor. Musa handed Suha's affidavit, her new identity, to the registering clerk. The room was filled with smoke. The Muslim judge barely looked through the papers presented to him.

Samira noticed that Suha's body was trembling when asked if she agreed to marry Musa. She lifted her eyes to Musa as if searching for the answer there. Samira felt the importance of the moment. She glanced at him. In Musa's eyes she saw the gleam of intense love. Suha must have seen it too. Almost imperceptibly, she nodded her head in agreement.

After Musa effusively shook hands, thanking the witnesses, the three of them returned to the young couple's new home. Flowers were displayed in every room. Musa must have bought out the entire flower market, thought Samira.

They shared a meal, which Samira had prepared in advance, lamb with rice and fattoush for Musa, cold lebenia soup and tabbouleh salad for Suha. After two years of living with us, Suha still didn't touch meat, Samira mused to herself.

From time to time Musa touched Suha's hand as if wanting to reassure himself he wasn't living a dream. After Samira put a pitcher of fresh nana tea on the table, she retreated, not wanting to disturb the young couple in love.

Not the usual Muslim wedding, three-day affair, with lots of food and drink, music and dancing. The newlyweds had three days in which they ate and drank in their love, sang and danced to it. For three full days, the worried Samira didn't see them. *Weren't they hungry?*

Each day she discreetly left trays of food in front of their door. She tried to listen, but then felt ashamed of herself, an old maid spying on young lovers. The trays remained untouched most of the time.

On the fourth day after the marriage, a bewildered Samira prayed, Oh, Allah Ackbar, I didn't know that love can be so strong that it can forgo all other needs. She watched the sky. Gray clouds chased one another as before a storm. Suddenly Samira felt a pressure on her chest. *Was that a premonition of days to come?*

27

"It's been a long time since I last saw the pretty blue-eyed Arab girl," Gretchen whined while peering through the window. "

Otto stopped practicing the minute he heard her voice. It wasn't the first time Gretchen had mentioned the girl. His wife seemed obsessed with her. The girl, half-hidden behind a cypress tree, would listen to his music for a half hour, then leave. She never approached them. Even if she had, which language could they have in common?

Gretchen looked forward to the girl's appearance. *Poor Gretchen!* She even saw a resemblance to Ruth, their daughter. No, he mustn't think of Ruth! It would destroy him as it destroyed Gretchen, and then who would take care of his crippled wife?

"*Please, my darling,*" Otto said, "I'm sure she'll be back soon and then we'll ask her to come inside and listen, rather than stand outside. Who knows, one thinks of these people as ignorant, but we might discover that this girl has a real sensitivity to music."

"One reason I fell in love with you was that you were such an idealist." Gretchen turned to her husband, her expression more a grimace than a smile. "I remember how you used to say, 'People who love music cannot be bad people."

Otto panicked; afraid she might slide into one of her dark moods. He took the skeleton his wife had become into his arms.

"Thank you, my dear. Even after twenty years, your words warm my heart. And speaking of warming, how about two nice cups of tea for ourselves? This stone house chills my bones."

Gretchen clasped her trembling hands, "You know I can't," she whispered, raising her blue eyes to him, the same luminous blue eyes their daughter had inherited from her Aryan mother.

"You sit here while your husband serves his lady," Otto said, gallantly helping her to a chair and covering her shoulders with a shawl. Gretchen's features looked relaxed. For how long, he didn't know, but he was grateful for even a few moments.

When Otto Schroder arrived in Leipzig from Wrotzklav, (Breslau in German) he held his violin in one hand and his slim suitcase containing one change of clothes, the socks his mother had knitted for him, his father's hat, and sheets of violin music in the other. But most important, he had his teacher's letter of recommendation for the *Leipzig Hochschule fur Musik's* most famous professor of violin.

His German wasn't great. It was mixed with the Yiddish he spoke at home and the Polish he learned in school. His father, the owner of a small grocery store in a shtetl close to Breslau, had never encouraged him. "Violin, *shmiolin*," he said, "What do you want to be, a *klezmer*, playing for *bar-mitzvas* and *chasanas?* That's not a profession. You go and learn accounting. Then you'll become somebody."

But Otto loved playing the violin more than anything else. He knew that in her heart, his mother approved. When he left, she gave him a kerchief in which there were a few zlotas, her last months' savings.

His teacher told her, "Your son has a magic talent. He can make the violin cry or laugh at his will. He's already an artist. What he needs is to be heard and encouraged."

First he lived in his Leipzig professor's home after the teacher learned that Otto was born in a Polish *shtetl* not far from his own place of birth. With the help of his professor's acquaintances, Otto started teaching children and soon was able to move into his own place. His colleagues at the Hochschule acquired a new respect for him after they heard him play at one of the school's concerts. They didn't giggle anymore at his out-of-fashion clothes or at his flying hair, the Paganini Jew.

That same concert brought him another reward, one he never expected—Gretchen Trammer. She was the Hochschule's most talented pianist, and a beauty for whom, he was told, many of his colleagues wrote poems of burning passion. Her diaphanous blond hair framed a high forehead, strong cheekbones, a mobile, smiling mouth, and eyes, the bluest Otto had ever seen, the way he imagined Lorelei's, Goethe's sea enchantress.

He would have never approached her; he was too timid, and besides, she was always surrounded by a crowd of admirers like a queen bee. It was Gretchen who came to him one afternoon.

"I heard you play," she said, "and I was moved like never before. At the end of your recital, I had tears in my eyes."

Gretchen stopped, waiting, but Otto, overwhelmed by her presence and her compliments, couldn't get a word out of his mouth.

"The other violinists play correctly, but you, you are a magician; in your hands the violin is as alive as a human heart." Gretchen's tone changed. "I came to ask you," she said timidly, "if you'd agree to play with me in the chamber music class. I want to learn from you."

Otto felt dizzy. His teeth were clenched so tightly he couldn't open his mouth. She was asking him to play with her. He would gladly give ten years of his life for the courage to address her. And here she came to him!

"Of course," Gretchen said quickly, "if you've already committed yourself, I understand."

"Oh! No! No!" Otto stammered, "I'd be happy to, more than happy, I'd be honored. I admire you," he stammered, "I'd be most honored," he repeated, afraid that he was babbling and she was going to think him a complete idiot.

"Can we start tomorrow, then?" Gretchen asked, "I'll bring a few Mozart sonatas to read through." She smiled, "I'm sure we'll get better acquainted through our music than through words."

He walked and walked that evening, rehearsing in his head what he'd say to her the next day. Then he panicked. Maybe he dreamed the whole thing. Suffering from too much practice and little sleep, he'd probably had a vision. It hadn't been Gretchen. Yet, since he couldn't fall asleep, he took out the Mozart sonatas and played until the gray light of dawn announced a new day.

- - -

"My dear lady, the tea is served," Otto clamored, bringing in a tray with two tall glasses and two pieces of cake. But Gretchen had fallen asleep, a forlorn smile on her wrinkled face. She must be dreaming of Ruth, Otto thought. And when she wakes up she'll scream again, "Where is Ruth, where is my daughter?" and thrash around to look for her. Otto put Gretchen's medication on the tray and carefully rearranged the shawl that had slipped away.

In the evening Otto wrapped his arms around a still sleeping Gretchen and gently directed her steps toward the bedroom. He had already put a hot-water bottle on her side of the bed. Her feet were usually so cold he could feel her shiver even in her sleep. But tonight, Gretchen seemed calm, while he turned and turned, his head flooded by memories.

- - -

When did he realize that she was in love with him? Was it when she took him to the imposing Thomaskirche, the church where almost two hundred years before, Johann Sebastian Bach played the organ and conducted the choir? Inside the cold, empty church, as the late afternoon light filtered through the stained-glass windows, she whispered, "Please, play for me."

Otto stood quietly for a moment, then began playing Bach's Air on the G String.

He played with closed eyes. Still immersed in the music, he felt her burning lips touch his. A tremor went through his body. He responded with the passion he had tried to hide for more than a year. Only when they played together had Otto's violin declared his love for her.

"I know that you love me, too," Gretchen said, breathing hard, when he finally let her out of his embrace. Then she kissed him again.

What a marvelous time! During their long walks, after they finished practicing, Gretchen introduced him to the beauties of Leipzig, its famous University dating back to the 15th century, and its beautiful parks. She took him to Auerbach's Keller, the beer hall where Goethe had been a frequent visitor. They talked frequently about their future, but very little about their past.

Otto knew that Gretchen was born into a well-to-do family. She told him that her father owned a number of factories that manufactured fine luggage, not only in Leipzig, but also in other cities in Saxony.

"My parents live in the past. Almost ten years after the end of the Great War, their hearts are still wounded by Germany's defeat." Gretchen sighed, "My parents are very conservative."

Was that the reason she never introduced him to them? Otto was sure that she hadn't told them about their making music together. He imagined how her father would raise an eyebrow and say, "You play with a Jewish Pollack? Couldn't you find another partner?"

Be realistic, Otto said to himself, what kind of life could you offer Gretchen? The basement you live in? But luck or fate was on his side. His professor retired from his position with the famous Gewandhaus Orchestra. A competition to fill his position was posted. Otto was known to the orchestra members from his recitals, and the many times he substituted for sick orchestra members or was available when the orchestra needed additional players.

Otto was doubtful that at his age, twenty-two, and without much orchestral experience, he could win. But his teacher encouraged him, and so did Gretchen.

"You have to try," she said. "Remember, I believe in you."

Before he started to play behind the curtain, as was the rule, the judges not being allowed to see the candidates, Otto took an oath. "If I win, I'll ask Gretchen to marry me."

Closing his eyes, he began, Gretchen constantly present in his heart. After he finished he heard a storm of applause; the jury applauded him.

Yes, Otto thought, those were beautiful times. Beautiful memories! But those times were long gone and by thinking of them he was only twisting a knife in his heart. Gretchen turned and murmured in her sleep, "Ruthie, Ruthie, *wie bist du?*" It scared Otto, but he saw that she hadn't awoken. Otherwise she would scream inconsolably until the wee hours of the morning.

- - -

When Otto was informed that he was accepted in Leipzig's Gewandhaus Orchestra, one of Germany's best, he became delirious with joy.

Gretchen, as thrilled as he was, said, "I told you, I was sure you'd be chosen. This calls for a celebration."

She wouldn't tell him what her plan was. "It's a surprise," she said.

The same evening, holding a bottle of champagne, she took his arm, "Tonight we are going to have a lot of fun."

They went through barely lit streets until they arrived before a gate. After Gretchen rang the bell, she whispered her name, and the gate opened. It seemed so mysterious. Only after they entered, Otto understood. They were inside one of the city's famous underground cabarets. Through the smoke, he saw skimpily dressed women, dancing languidly between tables topped with champagne, whisky and brandy. He breathed in the acrid odor of cigarettes, alcohol and something else that he couldn't determine, hashish maybe?

Seeing that Otto seemed uncomfortable, Gretchen said, "You didn't know that places like this existed, did you?" She laughed, "Neither do my parents. But we are not doing anything wrong. We're just having a good time."

From a table in a corner, somebody called, "Gretchen, Gretchen, over here." Otto recognized some of his colleagues from the Hochschule.

"Finally you succeeded in bringing your prodigy to join us," one of his colleagues said without malice.

Gretchen smiled mischievously. She took Otto's arm. "At least here," she addressed her companions, "we can forget what's happening in Germany today. We don't cry for its lost status in the world."

Hearing a storm of applause, Otto turned his head. On the stage, a woman dressed in a black tuxedo jacket, her long legs in black stockings and high heels, stepped into a spotlight and began to sing with a voice as smoky as the hall itself.

"It's Marlene Dietrich," Gretchen whispered, "our blue angel."

The champagne or the way Gretchen leaned so close to him, her legs intertwined with his, made Otto almost lose his head.

The toasts never stopped. "Prosit," one called, followed by the others. "To your success," they raised their glasses. Otto had never felt so happy and relaxed.

Leaving the cabaret, Gretchen whispered in his ear, "Let's go to your place. We'll continue to celebrate." As much as he wanted to, Otto thought that it would not be proper. "I'd better walk you home," he said. "It's already very late."

"For only a minute," she said, snuggling to him, "I want to see your place."

How could he resist? He thought of his wet socks hanging in a corner of the room, his unmade bed, and the sheets of music scattered on the floor.

He had planned to propose to her after receiving the first paycheck from the orchestra, when he would be able to rent an apartment and buy new clothes. Then, with his heart thudding in his chest, he would go talk to her parents. That was the right thing to do, Otto knew. He was a decent man. His parents had instilled in him the moral code they themselves inherited from their parents.

"It's too hot in here," Gretchen said, and without waiting, she took off her fur coat and her dress. "Come," she said, throwing her arms around his neck, "I want you to make love to me. I knew from the very beginning that we are made for each other. If we wait a minute longer it would be a lost minute."

Her perfume, her willowy body, her lips! He couldn't deliberate anymore. He threw all caution to the wind. She belonged to him! That night their bodies made the most beautiful music.

"I'm going to ask your parents for your hand in marriage," was the first thing Otto said, the morning after their night of ecstasy, "This afternoon, in fact."

Gretchen laughed. "They'll never agree," she said. "You don't know my parents. But since I am twenty-one, the law gives me the right to decide my future, and my parents can't stop me. This morning we'll go to City Hall and get our marriage license."

Gretchen had thought of everything.

"Sweetheart," Gretchen said, "aren't you happy? You are so quiet. Did I make a mistake by throwing myself into your arms? Don't you want to share your life with me?" Tears filled her eyes.

Was he happy? Of course he was, but the idea of getting married behind her parents' back as well as his—oh, he'd better stop thinking of his parents. He knew that his father's desire was for Otto to marry the daughter of one of his friends.

Otto knelt in front of her, "You are my love and my life. I am just in shock by so many surprises all at once." He kissed her hands, "I can't live without you, you are the air I breathe, my sun by day and my moon by night."

Gretchen closed his mouth with a kiss. "Let's get dressed and stop by a coffee house on the way to the City Hall. I want to hear a forceful yes when you'll answer the registrar's question if you want to marry me!"

They both laughed. Oh, Gretchen, impetuous Gretchen, the girl more precious to him than his own life!

Dawn. Shortly the Mediterranean sun will appear at the horizon, the signal for Otto to rise. Another lost night sifting through his memories. In his forties, he felt the burden of a man twice his age. Barefoot, he went to the kitchen. Jaffa oranges, Palestine's pride, filled the small place with perfume. Patiently, Otto squeezed one after another preparing Gretchen's breakfast. Soon he would have to go to the Palestine Orchestra's rehearsal, where he occupied the third chair of the second violin section.

He was worried every time he had to leave the house, though by now he trusted the Arab woman who came daily to clean and cook, and most importantly to be with Gretchen while he was away. Third seat in the second violin section, not even section leader, was not a great accomplishment. And yet he was lucky, lucky to be alive, to have employment, to put bread on the table, and to be able to pay for Gretchen's medications.

He would have had another position if he had followed Bronislaw Huberman, his Polish landsman, when he came to Germany in 1936 and proposed to all Jewish musicians fired from German orchestras to come to Palestine and join him in establishing a Jewish orchestra. Gretchen had said, "What a dreamer. He wants to build an orchestra on sand. What's happening here, now, it's only a temporary situation. I know the German people, I am German myself. Soon we'll get rid of this mustached clown."

They remained in Germany. He couldn't blame Gretchen. At the time they lived in Berlin, the musical capital of the world. It had been another stroke of luck that the principal cellist of the Berlin Philharmonic, Heinrich Schultz, came to hear one of their recitals, while visiting Leipzig. Enthusiastic about their performance, Mr. Schultz offered them a chamber music partnership, a violin, cello and piano trio. Gretchen was excited. "Herr Schultz," she said, "what you propose is a dream come true."

She tried to convince the doubtful Otto that it would be a good move. "Leipzig is still a provincial town. Everything happens in Berlin. You deserve to be heard there. This is your chance! We can't turn down Heinrich." She already called Schultz by his first name.

That was in 1929, a year after their marriage. Ruth was two months old. "It's too soon," said Otto, "I joined the Gewandhaus orchestra a year ago. Nobody leaves such a good position for a dream. How are we going to manage in Berlin? It'll take months of practice before the trio is ready to perform. We'll have to pay rent, hire a nanny for Ruth. My love, forget it for the moment. I think this is impractical."

But Gretchen had made up her mind and she was not going to be defeated. "You know," she said, "we can use part of my inheritance."

The subject of her inheritance had been a sore point with Otto. It wasn't the first time she had offered it. Otto would not hear of it. He felt that a husband had to support his wife, not otherwise. To Gretchen's chagrin, he took in more students in order to pay his loans.

"You're wasting your talent," she said. Then Gretchen tried another tactic. "When my parents refused to see or talk to us, I decided that unless they accept you, I'll have nothing to do with them. Still, it is difficult to live in the same city, where I know everybody and everyone knows me. In Berlin we'll turn over a new leaf."

Otto sighed. He suspected, though Gretchen never complained, that her parents' attitude was a constant wound. They moved to Berlin, where they found a small apartment close to Heinrich Schultz's residence, not far from Unter den Linden, where on beautiful afternoons they pushed the baby's carriage, under the alleys of linden trees, proud to see people stop and compliment Ruthie's beauty.

Otto heard Gretchen's moans, "I'm coming, *Shatz*. My princess' breakfast is ready," he called in a voice he forced to sound cheerful.

He had only one hour to shave, shower, get dressed, and ride two buses in order to be on time for the rehearsal of the Palestine Orchestra. Sometimes he regretted that he hadn't rented a place closer to his work, on a street like Shenkin or Allenby, where other members of the orchestra lived. But he had been worried about Gretchen's feelings. By living in Jaffa, he wanted to protect her from the other musicians and their wives, from their gossip or a negative attitude toward his German wife. He wouldn't use Gretchen's pain to gain their sympathy.

Otto heard the gate squeak, a sign that Nabiha, their faithful servant, had arrived.

Otto's colleagues pressed him to move to Tel-Aviv. "You are sitting on a volcano," they told him. "The numbers of Jewish immigrants from the displaced persons' camps are seen as a threat by the Arabs, and are not welcomed by the British. Jaffa is an Arab city. Be careful. The English mandate ends in 1947 and we have to prepare ourselves for turbulence."

After four years of living in Palestine, Otto had only a limited knowledge of Hebrew, but he knew what they were talking about. He read the Palestine Post daily and was aware of the English proposal to divide Palestine between the Arabs and the Jews, a proposal that met with Arab anger. *How long was it safe to remain in Jaffa?*

When he returned home, he found Gretchen trying to work the beads brought by Nahiba. It was painful to watch Gretchen's deformed hands passing a thread through the center of the bead. Her beautiful, agile fingers had once made the piano keys dance with joy. Her entire life seemed described by those fingers.

When they reached Switzerland, after the trip that could have cost them their lives, the Swiss doctor they consulted took him aside. "There is no hope," he said. "Her knuckles were broken into small pieces. Those little bones cannot be attached again. Maybe if I inserted metal platelets between the fingers, the hand would look less deformed, but she'll suffer more and it would not be of great help."

Otto wept. "I'm sorry," said the doctor, "I heard that your wife was a great pianist."

To his orchestra colleagues he had said that their last years of living in Berlin, with no heat and Gretchen waiting in line for hours for bread, had produced the acute, debilitating rheumatism of her fingers. His colleagues commiserated, they knew how it was, but they did not know all of it. And he could never bring himself to tell them what they had lived through.

Otto took off his jacket and hat and hung them on a coat hanger. From a pocket he fished a large handkerchief and wiped his forehead. He kissed Gretchen's cheek.

"How is my lovely wife today?"

"Look," she said the blue of her eyes as bright as ever, "I think I'm making progress."

Nahiba nodded. She caressed Gretchen's hands. She's beginning to understand German, thought Otto. Gretchen held in her hand ten little beads strung together.

"Oh, *liebchen*, sweetheart, this is beautiful," exclaimed Otto and kissed her again. There was a time when he was afraid he would lose her, that when she realized that she could not play the piano anymore, the life would drain out of her. But now this kind, simple housekeeper's patience started to bear fruit. That slow, repetitive work could be the therapy Gretchen needed. As long as Nahiba was with them, Otto decided, they would not move away from Jaffa.

28

These last months I have become quite lazy, Shifra thought, stretched out in bed, her hand caressing the warm spot where her husband had slept. She turned and embraced his pillow, which had the hollow left by his head and his familiar smell. Musa, her husband! It was every morning's pleasure to remember that she was married to Musa; she had to pinch herself to recall that it was not a dream. And yet how could it have been a dream when Musa's baby was kicking hard, playing football in her belly.

Shifra smiled. Could it really be that she would be a mother soon? She did not know if she was ready for it, but she was happy to see how excited Musa was to become a father. Still in bed, Shifra's thoughts returned to the events preceding her marriage.

First Fatima's wire, telling them that Na'ima's baby came sooner than expected,

"*Inshallah*, we have a new Faud in the family," she wrote a few days later. She would remain in Deir Yassin until Na'ima felt stronger.

In Jaffa the Masri children became ecstatic. "Can we go see the baby?" Rama and Ahmed asked in one voice.

It was hard for Samira and Musa to calm them down. "Not right now," Musa said, "In a few days, when Eumi writes that Na'ima is ready for guests, we'll all go."

The same day after the children left for school, Musa took Samira aside. "Allah is on my side. Now or never," Shifra heard him say.

Samira nodded. The look on his face was enough for Shifra to know that he was talking about her. He surely meant her conversion to Islam.

Oh, God, what should I do? Shifra remembered brooding. Where could I turn for advice? Yes, she loved Musa, whenever she looked at him her heart fluttered. Yes, she felt comfortable in the Masri household. The children loved her, Samira loved her, and even Fatima had good words for her work. But wouldn't God, her God, the God of the Jews, punish her? Didn't she learn in school that the Jews of Spain preferred to be burned at the stake rather than convert? Why does life have to be so difficult?

She knew she had to make a choice. But hadn't she already made a choice when she ran away from home, afraid to become the wife of that bad-smelling old man to whom her father had promised her?

"Suha," Shifra heard Samira calling her. They were alone in the house.

"Today is the day," Samira said quietly, taking her hand. "You will be taking the oath. There's nothing to be scared of. Think only of Musa and how happy it will make him. Now repeat after me, I acknowledge that there is no God but God."

Shifra repeated the words.

"I acknowledge that Mohammed is the messenger of God," Samira continued.

Shifra recollected the Jews of Spain who did convert, but continued secretly to observe their ancient religion. Samira looked at her, waiting. Shifra's mouth felt as dry as parchment, when she whispered, 'I acknowledge that Mohammed is the messenger of God." Then she closed her eyes, but there was no thunder, no blow to her head. There was only Samira, who embraced her.

"I witness that you took our sacred oath, that you said the *Al-Shahada*. You have become a Muslim. Now you are really one of us. *Mavrook.*"

Seeing that Shifra remained quiet, Samira added, "You know how pleased Musa will be. Nothing could stop him now from marrying you. Doesn't it make you happy? Musa, the most sought-after bachelor in Jaffa, has chosen you. You should be dancing and cheering with joy!"

Shifra's eyes were swimming with tears. She did not understand why, while her heart palpitated with hope, she still felt so uneasy after taking the oath.

"I'm telling you, girl, you are becoming lazier by the day. Do you know what time it is? The sun has been out long ago and you are still in bed. If I had known what a lazy wife you'd become, I would never have encouraged Musa to marry you!" Samira's outburst made Shifra smile.

"Have you forgotten that we are going to the bazaar today? The earlier we go the better—fewer people, better prices, enough time to bargain."

Dear Samira, thought Shifra, she truly enjoys bargaining. How many times had Musa told them to stop hassle the merchants? "Everybody has to make a profit," he would say. Oh, Musa, her dear husband was such a fine, caring person.

Slowly, Shifra got out of bed.

"It's hard for me to walk," she answered. "I am so heavy. I don't think I can get any bigger. And still another month to go!"

"You are doing fine. You're just too spoiled. I haven't seen yet a husband pampering his pregnant wife as much as Musa does. If not for me, you'd be in bed all day long."

Shifra hugged Samira, "You are right." She looked around the room, searching, "I know that last evening I finished sewing the stitches on the baby's blanket and now I can't remember where I put it."

"Here it is," a triumphant Samira brought forth a little package. "I came early this morning while you were still sleeping. I brought a cup full of fresh coffee for poor Musa, who leaves at dawn for prayers, then goes straight to work."

Shifra understood what Samira's words meant. She, his wife, should have prepared the coffee for him.

"I took the blanket to see how far have you've gotten with it," continued Samira. "All you need to finish are the ornaments, silk and beads."

No compliments. That was Samira. But Shifra knew that she admired her work. They both had been sewing and knitting the baby's layette for the last two months.

"Maybe it's too early," Shifra had said at the time, "we don't know if it's a boy or a girl." She remembered that her parents never prepared clothes before a baby was born. Her mother said that it would bring bad luck.

"It's going to be a boy," Samira said. "Look at your belly. All in front like a sugar loaf. With a girl you'd have larger haunches. Don't laugh. I know it. I saw many pregnant women in my life. Besides, I'm sure Musa expects a boy."

It was mid-morning by the time they entered the bazaar. It seemed quieter than usual. Shifra and Samira approached the stall of their favorite bead-seller. They weren't the first; a tall lady in European clothes that hung in disorder on her slim body, and an Arab woman were looking at beads.

Samira exclaimed, "Nabiha, *Salaam Aleikum*, I haven't seen you in a long time!"

The woman turned, and seeing Samira, answered with great joy, "Samira, what a surprise!" She bowed. "I am here with my mistress." She lightly touched the woman's arm.

Nabiha's mistress, whose shaking, deformed hands Shifra had already observed when she touched the beads, raised her head. Seeing Shifra, she put her hand over her mouth, her eyes wide. Shifra heard her murmur, *"Dieselben blauen Augen."* The woman's intense stare disturbed Shifra.

"Saleim, Shailam," the unknown woman tried to address Shifra, *"Enstschuldigen Sie mich,* excuse me," she continued in English, "I have the feeling that I've seen you before, *es ist nicht wahr-* Isn't that so?" Her eyes traveled down Shifra's body, surprised to discover her pregnancy.

Shifra noticed the web of wrinkles on her face.

"I don't think we've met before," Shifra answered in her best English, and she bowed, "My name is Suha Masri."

"Ach, you speak English, *sehr schon,* very nice." The woman's eyes never blinked; she continued to look at Shifra as if she wanted to swallow her up. Shifra felt embarrassed. She searched for Samira, who was chatting with her friend.

"Suha," Samira said, guessing the question in Shifra's eyes, "Mistress Schroder is the violin teacher's wife. Nabiha, my friend, works for them. She tells me that working with beads helps—" but Shifra had already turned to the woman,

"I'm sorry," she said, "I don't know you, but I heard your husband play while I walked on your street. The music seemed to descend from heaven. It spoke to me more than a thousand words." Shifra stopped, suddenly feeling shy.

"I knew I had seen you, "Mrs. Schroder said, "and I was right. You were hiding behind a tree. Now you don't have to hide. Please, come, *Kommen sie bitte,"* her swollen hands shook harder, trying to touch Shifra's hand. "You'll be more than welcome in our home."

"We have to go," Nabiha said quickly. "My lady seems excited and it's late, it's the time she should take her medicine." Gently taking her arm, she directed her mistress toward the exit, while Gretchen kept turning back to look at Shifra.

What a strange encounter! Shifra would have loved to find out more about Mrs. Schroder and her husband. Why is she so ill? It was nice of her to invite Shifra to visit, but, would she do it? *Would she tell Musa about the meeting?* She had never told him how much music meant to her, how listening to the sound of Otto Schroder's violin soothed and caressed her soul, like the healing of a pain she didn't know she had.

Would Samira tell Musa about their unexpected encounter? Shifra glanced at Samira's pursed lips. Better not to ask her.

29

Descending from the Tel-Aviv bus, Otto decided to walk home rather than taking Jaffa's bus full of people sweltering from heat. He still heard the cheerful waltz of Mahler's First Symphony, which the Palestine orchestra had just finished rehearsing. For a moment he was flooded with the memory of the KuBu orchestra's performance in Berlin in 1938. KuBu, the Jewish Kulturbund orchestra, was designed by the Nazis to play only for Jewish audiences. No good remembering; when we left Germany, I decided once and for all that the past is dead.

Even before he turned the key, he heard Gretchen's moans. Alarmed, Otto hurried inside. Gretchen sat near the table covered with the scattered pages of the Palestine Post. There were feverish red spots on her face and her body shook more than usual.

"Here," she said, a trembling finger stabbing the paper, "it's written, black on white, *sha-li-chim*, emissaries, have succeeded in smuggling people from the displaced persons camps into Palestine. How many times have I asked you," her angry eyes locked on his, "have you looked for Ruthie? Have you inquired where my Ruthie is?" The last words died in Gretchen's throat.

Otto looked at Nabiha, to whom he had specifically said, "Don't show newspapers to Gretchen."

"Gretchen, my Gretchen, my darling, you are tired, you should rest."

"No, no rest for me, you promised we'd find Ruthie, Ruthie, my dear child," Gretchen sobbed.

"I told you," Otto spoke slowly, as to a child, "there are thousands of people in the Displaced Persons Camps. We have to have patience. *Ich bitte dich,* I beg you, my love." *Oh, how long am I going to have the strength to continue?* Otto's head started to spin. *I should have ended my life that night, but who would have taken care of Gretchen?*

Quick, get Dr. Hoffman's syringe and morphine. When the doctor gave the kit to Otto, he had cautioned that it was to be used only for emergencies. With Nabiha's help, Otto injected Gretchen's limp arm.

No *shaliach* can help us, Otto thought with bitterness, waiting for Gretchen to fall asleep. *Would he ever bring himself to tell Gretchen the truth, the ugly, brutal truth?*

It was Heinz, Gretchen's little brother, who couldn't get over the fact that his beautiful sister had married the Jewish caricature, as he called Otto. Six years younger than Gretchen, a failure in school, he drifted from job to job, unable to keep one for very long. His parents were so upset that they refused to continue to support him. Then he joined a youth organization.

Though her husband had never reconciled with his daughter, Gretchen's mother continued to correspond with her. In a letter she wrote:

"For the first time, I have wonderful news about our Heinz: Only a year after he joined the organization he has impressed his superiors. He is now a Hitler Jugend Gruppe Kommandant. He is training young people as enthusiastic as he is about Germany's future. Would you have believed this of our little Heinz? Your father is very proud of him.

P.S. Heinz says that he wants to visit you soon."

When Gretchen handed the letter to Otto, his first impulse was to say, "We have to move." Instead, he folded and returned the letter. There was no need for words.

Shortly after 1933 a dreadful law was enacted which forbade all Jewish artists, musicians, actors, composers, conductors and playwrights to perform or have their compositions or plays performed in German concert halls or German theaters. At their daily rehearsal, Heinrich Schultz, their trio partner, shared the news with them. During the four years of performing together, their trio had become famous in Germany as well as abroad.

"It's absolutely inconceivable," Heinrich Schultz said, holding the paper with a trembling hand. "Our best artists are Jewish. This law is ridiculous! You'll see. German artists won't stand for it."

But Herr Schultz was wrong. The German musicians, actors, playwrights, composers, many of them second-class artists, enjoyed the benefits of the new law. Not long after that, Schultz, embarrassed and avoiding looking at Otto, proposed to Gretchen to continue their concerts as a duo, cello and piano. "We'll still rehearse our trios," he said encouragingly, "but while waiting for better days to come, we could...." He let the sentence die in the air.

Gretchen looked at Otto. "Of course, Herr Schultz is right," Otto graciously conceded, though he felt a thorn in his heart. He had never called Schultz by his given name. "We are lucky that Gretchen kept her name, Tramer, for the stage, a true Aryan name."

Gretchen looked distressed. "Otto, if you think that's not a good idea...."

"Just the opposite, *liebchen*," Otto hurriedly assured her. "Thank you *Heinrich*, you are a good and caring friend."

Otto was jealous, but he was able to hide his feelings. Heinrich was an old bachelor. Otto had suspected that he was a little in love with Gretchen, but who wouldn't be? In the ensuing years, Heinrich proved that he was a good friend to both of them, but it was only at the very end, in that *Gotterdammerung*, their twilight days in Germany, that Otto learned to trust him completely.

As the Nazi claws started to close around them, Heinrich's advice proved to be a Godsend. First, he proposed they divorce. "For Ruthie's sake," Heinrich quickly explained.

"Never," Gretchen said.

Otto believed the pain would burn him alive. Yet he understood Heinrich's motive,

"Think of Ruthie," Otto turned to Gretchen. "In these times we're not supposed to think about ourselves. Ruthie has to start school soon. An Aryan last name won't arouse suspicion."

Soon after, Gretchen and Ruthie started wearing big gold crosses, especially after Ruthie went to the Carmelite nuns' school. "At least she'll get a good education," Gretchen sighed.

They changed apartments almost every year after 1933, always trying to find inconspicuous neighborhoods. The last little house, far from the center of Berlin, had a concrete basement where Otto could practice his violin and rehearse their trio without being noticed by the neighbors.

In her letters to her mother, Gretchen gave a Berlin postal office return address. She never told Heinrich about her brother Heinz. *Maybe if she had....*

When Otto started playing in the KuBu orchestra, Gretchen came to listen to their concerts, but later Otto decided it was too dangerous for her. The SS people were guarding the place.

"Why would a German woman want to listen to the Jewish orchestra?" he said to her.

Heinrich agreed. "You can never be too careful." He continued, "I think it would be better if Otto sleeps at my place after concerts.

One never knows if he's followed or not." That was especially true after the Jews were ordered to wear the yellow star with JUDE woven into it.

Gretchen, Otto and even Heinrich, had deluded themselves about the Nazi regime, Otto reflected with bitterness much later—too late. They failed to notice that Ruthie was developing into a young woman, with eyes like two pools of blue diamonds and rich, golden hair.

30

How quickly time passes, Fatima reflected, while observing her grandchild, hidden as always behind her window's curtains. Samira was playing with Selim in the adjacent courtyard, and the little boy's happy laughter had awakened her from a sleep filled with dreams in which she, Fatima, was holding him in her arms.

It seemed only yesterday that Selim was born. Fatima did not reconcile with her son, even though Musa had brought his child and asked for her blessing. In her mind, what Musa did could not be forgiven. Musa married Suha against his mother's will.

Even now, almost two years after her family's *nackba*, as she called it, she felt the same anger taking hold of her, like the day she returned from Deir Yassin, two weeks after Na'ima had given birth to Fatima's first grandson.

Musa was waiting for her in the house and said, as if there was nothing unusual about it, "I want to tell you that Suha and I were married a few days ago." She did not faint nor did she scream. Instead she raised her arm and slapped his face. Fatima saw his black eyes change from surprise to shock. The red marks left by her rings were visible. Without a word, Musa turned and left.

He had used his mother's absence to work up his defiant plan! It wasn't just on the spur of the moment! How did she fail to guess what might transpire when he offered to rebuild her property next door?

"We'll use it for a guest house," Musa had told her when he asked her approval for the expense. Yes, it was her fault from the very beginning, from the day she let the Yahud girl enter her house. Afterward, everybody seemed to conspire against her, asking her to keep the orphan girl, when nobody knew where she came from or who she was. Even her devoted Samira, especially Samira, duped her and concocted a lie that now she, Fatima, was forced to go along with. Oh, the shame of it all!

"One day there will be a terrible punishment. Allah Ackbar sees all and knows all," she wanted to scream at Musa, but he had already left.

That night she had a strange dream. She was walking on the street when she saw a long line of women dressed in black jelebias. As she passed by them, each one turned her back to her, one by one, the *mukhtar*'s wife as well as all the ladies from the Arab Women's League. "This is the mother whose son has betrayed her," one of them pointed a finger in her direction. The wind blew their long skirts making them look like old crows, foreboding ill omens. Fatima woke up, drained. She dressed, her decision made: she would fire Samira.

"You leper," she charged, "You are worth less than a wandering dog. Was this the reward for my trust in you? Miserable creature, it was your idea to teach and witness Suha's conversion." Fatima felt her blood boiling. "You said that seeing the love in Musa's eyes convinced you to help him realize his dream. Have you asked yourself how I would feel? What were your duties toward me? You forgot your place! You were and never would be anything but a servant."

She had never spoken like that and Fatima knew that those were words that could never be erased.

And Suha, "the intruder," with that clever and cunning Jewish mind, she knew how to make herself indispensable!

Her heart was seething with rage, thinking that Musa could have married into one of the rich and honorable Palestinian families. He stole from his mother what she rightly deserved. *From whom could she ask advice now? Who would lend her a sympathetic ear?* Not her cousin Abdullah, who was probably as upset and disappointed as she was. And Allah forbid, she couldn't share her feelings with Mahmood. She knew how much he hated Jews.

Talking to Na'ima wouldn't be a consolation. Na'ima complained about being constantly fatigued from hard work, crying children and an irritable husband. Thank Allah she had had the good sense to ask Na'ima to keep Suha's origin a secret.

If only Amina had stayed at home! Everything started going downhill after Amina left. She affronted her mother's dignity by marrying a British soldier. That was the start, easing the way for Musa to follow in his sister's path.

It had been almost two years since Fatima screamed at Samira. The same day, Samira moved into Musa's house. Now Fatima longed to be in Samira's place, playing and laughing with Selim.

"Suha decided to call him Selim, peace," Musa told his mother when he showed her the baby, "and we hope that he'll bring peace into our family."

"Never," Fatima answered.

Now her heart ached to be the one playing with little Selim. She lost patience with her own children, who slowly began to take refuge at Musa's house, where they competed to play with the baby.

"Musa's house is so cheerful," Rama told her mother. "We all sing, and you'll not believe it, but Selim, who's only ten months old, sings with us!"

When a letter arrived from Nur's English teacher praising her progress, Fatima knew that Suha's tutoring had helped Nur to achieve that result.

The last blow came from Ahmed, her baby, who said, "Everything tastes so good at Suha's. You should ask Samira for Suha's recipes."

His words burned Fatima's heart. It reminded her how much she missed Samira, their evening chats when Samira would undo her hair, brush it and braid it again. She felt lonely inside and outside, in her own home.

She never replaced Samira. She went to the *souk* herself to buy the meats and vegetables that for a small tip were brought to the house by a young boy. When she was shopping at the bazaar she avoided the shop of her old friend, Mr. Nathan, the Jew who helped achieve the successful "plot" against her.

Ahmed, Rama or Nur never asked her why she had not stepped even once over the threshold of her firstborn son's house. Did they guess why? Maybe the fourteen-year-old Nur, now as beautiful and bright as Amina at her age, had guessed it, but she was busy whispering secrets with her girlfriends, giggling together and chasing Rama out of her room. Her mother's problems were of no interest to her.

Fatima spent most of her time praying. She prayed fervently, "Oh, Allah Ackbar, in your great wisdom, give me a sign." Many times she would address her dead husband, "Faud, you who loved me so, and entrusted me with your children, give me a sign." And she waited.

How could she know that the cry of the newborn, Selim, would be the answer to her prayers? She knew only that her heart was pierced with pain when she heard Selim call Samira, *Jeddah-*grandmother. "It's not right," Fatima wanted to scream, "This is my right. I am his Jeddah."

But pride stood in her way.

31

With a satisfied smile, Musa stretched his legs in his office, at the busy Jaffa Barclays Bank. He could not believe that he had been married two years. Though only a few hours separated him from the time he would be with his wife and their baby, the joys of his life, he already missed them.

He would love to have a framed photograph of Suha and Selim on his desk, as he had seen the British colleagues display their families. So many things were forbidden by Islam.

But he was happy knowing that his darling wife waited for him in their nice home surrounded by the beautiful things her hands created. Like the Prophet had said, what makes a man happy is a beautiful wife, a beautiful home and pleasant surroundings. He had all of that and more.

Since the birth of his son Selim, he felt blessed. At first he wanted to call him Rashid, like the sultan, but he yielded to Suha's wish. Even when he heard her call him Shalom he didn't mind.

The young boy, who usually brought the tea trays from the *chaikhana,* the nearby tea house, entered Musa's office. In less than a year, Musa had been advanced to assistant manager of the branch.

"Mail!" the boy said, placing it on his desk. Opening the package, Musa noticed a letter bearing British stamps. It was a letter from Amina. Since their mother would not answer her letters, she wrote him at the bank. Impatiently, Musa tore the letter open.

September 3, 1946

To my dear brother Musa, Salaam Aleikum,

Inshallah, I hope that my letter finds you and all our family in good health. I am so excited about your baby. I can barely wait to meet my nephews, Na'ima's Fauad and your little Selim. It's been too long since I've seen you all. We are planning to come for a visit two months from now, when cold and dreary England makes us dream of the nice Mediterranean sun. George is as excited as I am.

You know from my last letter that I've graduated with honors from nursing school. We moved to Bath, a quiet city, where George's family owns an adorable cottage. Here he landed a job with a prestigious architectural firm.

I am not working yet, though I received a few offers. George says that my life has been too tense for the last two years and I should relax for a while, maybe do a bit of gardening. You'd laugh seeing me early in the morning, wearing a pair of George's old pants, a large straw hat, my gloved hands armed with clippers and long scissors ready for my daily dialog with my plants. My roses and azaleas have taught me how to take care of them.

I don't know why I bother you with my foolishness. Maybe it's the sadness that in two years of marriage I haven't been able to get pregnant. Oh, how I envy

213

*Na'ima and your Suha. To comfort me, George said
that maybe we should adopt and what could be better
than a little Palestinian baby? Now I'm glad that I got
it off my chest,*

Your loving sister, Amina

Folding Amina's letter, Musa sensed again how blessed he was. In a few hours he'd hold Suha in his arms and watch the smile lighting Selim's face.

32

"This child grows by leaps and bounds," Samira said, spitting three times, above Selim's right ear, left ear and his forehead. "I think we should take him to Uhm Zaide," she continued as she bent to knot Selim's shoelaces.

"Take him to the witch?" Shifra asked, remembering with a shiver her own visit to the witch's hut, "What for? He's a perfectly normal child." Shifra felt a terrible urge to take Selim in her arms, while the boy chimed Samira's words, *Uhm Za-i-de, Uhm Za-i-de*.

Samira spit on him again. "When have you heard a child speak at his age? They barely crawl. Forget about standing. Our boy, may Allah preserve him and give him a long life, walked at ten months and now, not yet sixteen months, he speaks like an old man. Even Musa thinks so."

Shifra hugged Selim. He was so handsome. Selim had inherited her complexion and blue eyes, but the strong nose and his jet-black hair were unmistakably his father's. "Forget it, Samira. Selim is a bright little child, but he's not unique. Some speak earlier, some later. I just read it," and Shifra patted the book opened on her bed."

"I am older than you, and I know better," Samira continued. "If you don't want to take the boy to her, I'll go and ask her for an amulet to protect him from the evil eye."

"Evil eye, evil eye," Selim chanted until his mother closed his mouth with a kiss.

"Play with *Jedatha* Samira, but don't run," Shifra cautioned. "She can't run after you. Play nicely. I'll come out and join you in a little while."

From her bedroom window, Shifra saw Fatima watching the child from her courtyard. *She shows up like a clock. She doesn't utter a word.* Shifra felt sorry for Fatima, but, as Musa said, it was her loss.

Thinking of Musa brought a smile to Shifra's lips. The pillow next to her was still warm. She embraced it. After almost two and a half years, she still blushed at the memory of their first night together.

They were both so innocent. They started by holding hands, too timid to look at each other. Then he caressed her arms farther and farther up. When his arms touched her shoulders, he pulled her toward him until his strong chest almost crushed her breasts.

"I'm going to be gentle," he murmured, "don't be afraid."

Shifra's body was shaking like a leaf under rain.

"I'll be gentle," he said again and repeated it, taking off her dress. When the last of her clothes fell to the floor, he knelt in front of her.

"Oh, Suha," he said, "I was waiting for this moment from the time I saw you asleep on the beach. You are my angel, my goddess."

He took her in his arms. Just as in the dream she had before Na'ima's wedding, she could feel a strong desire mounting from her body to feel him closer, to melt into him.

"I'll be gentle," he whispered again, his voice trembling. She closed her eyes. She trusted him. Her heart throbbed when he parted her legs with his impatient hand. He must have felt her tension because he stopped. But she didn't want him to stop!

Awkwardly, she raised her arms and encircled his neck lowering his face to hers. He read in her eyes that she trusted him.

He crushed her lips the moment his body entered hers. They screamed simultaneously. Later he dried her tears with his kisses before he entered her again. She was moving with him in ascending and descending waves. She breathed in his body odor, a mix of perspiration, orange fragrance and cigarettes. It excited her then as it excites her now.

Only much, much later did Musa confess that he had been a virgin. "I wanted it to be the first time for both of us. Since I met you I vowed to keep myself chaste for you."

Yes, Shifra thought, her marriage was bliss. There wasn't a day that she didn't hear Musa declare, "*Euti Aumry WaHayati*, you are my life and my soul." But sometimes she found Musa looking pensively at her. "You still are a mystery to me. You have never told me about your life." Her heart stopped for a few seconds. Like a cloud passing over the sun, his questions pained her.

What would she tell him? That she ran away from her family? In her mind she saw two men shaking hands, her father and the kerosene carrier. Shifra shivered.

She was a renegade. Her former self was dead. It died the afternoon Musa carried her limp body into his mother's house. In her heart she still thought of herself as Shifra, though after Fatima renamed her Suha, she wanted to believe that she had started a new life.

"I hope that one day you'll trust me enough to tell me," Musa sighed.

Almost every day her husband brought her gifts; once perfumed oil, another time, French cologne from the Lebanese lady's store, then a transparent blue nightgown, "the color of your eyes," he said, which she felt bashful to put on.

"Wear it on the nights you want us to make love," he whispered. Her face burned. He meant she should wear it every night.

Six weeks after their wedding, pregnancy surprised her. So soon, she thought, but Musa glowed with happiness.

"It's going to be a boy," Samira said. *How could she know?* Shifra's mother gave birth to two girls before the desired boy arrived. Shifra remembered the advice her mother gave to a neighbor while both were at Mikve. The distressed woman had four daughters already and the Rabbi was of no help. "Your husband shouldn't touch you for two or three months. His sperm will become stronger and you'll deliver a boy."

"And what if it's a girl?" Shifra asked Musa, knowing that the Arabs, like many Jews, prefer males.

"I'll love her as much as I love you," Musa kissed her, "but I know it's going to be a boy."

Life really was bliss for Shifra. The only cloud on her horizon was Fatima.

"Eumi, *Ima*,"—Shifra had taught him the Hebrew word for mother—Selim burst into the room, breathing hard and stumbling over his R's, "Come, come quick. Jedati Sami-a, butt-fly." He cupped his little hands.

"Samira caught a butterfly?" Shifra asked.

"Yes, yes, come see, many colo-s," Selim's eyes shone from the marvel of discovery.

At fifteen months old he could speak not only words but also short sentences. *Was he an exceptional child, as Samira seems to think?* Even so, taking him to Uhm Zaide was out of the question.

Before she left the room, Shifra glanced out the window. Fatima was at her post, as usual.

"She spies on us," thought Shifra.

Was Samira thinking of Fatima when she said the child should be protected from an evil eye?

33

"Let's take Selim to the beach," Samira declared. "It's a beautiful day, clear skies, not too hot and almost no wind. This child is too pale. The sun and the seawater will be good for him."

Shifra's heart throbbed when she heard the word "beach." Since that day when she almost drowned, she had avoided the beach. The memories it conjured up scared her. "He's too young, maybe next year."

"He needs to play with other children," insisted Samira. "We are too old for him. How long do you want to keep him attached to your skirt? When Musa was his age, he played out in the street with the neighbors' children."

Always Musa had done this or that. It was Samira's best argument, her weapon. Shifra could have told her that her brothers went to *heder* at that age.

"I told you that playing in the street is dangerous; besides, I don't want him playing in the dust or mud."

Shifra was annoyed because in her heart she knew that Samira was right. The child seemed bored. Maybe the beach wasn't such a bad idea. They could go now, before the crowds arrived. They could teach Selim to build castles on the sand. Shifra could imagine his surprise at seeing the immensity of the water. "*Eumi, wa-te no-end,*" he might say. She smiled at the thought.

"You are right," Shifra conceded. "We'll go to the beach, but not for long. Selim's skin is fair. I don't want him to get burned." She would conquer her fear, Shifra encouraged herself. Really, it was a shame to live so close to the beach and not take advantage of it.

When they arrived, they found few people on the seashore. Selim's hands held tightly onto his mother and Samira. But when he saw the sea he tore himself away and ran toward it. "Eumi, look," he screamed, "big, big wa-te.."

"Don't get too close," Shifra called, running after him, with Samira out of breath behind her. But Selim had already stopped at the water's edge. He was excited. "So big, so big," he repeated, opening his arms, as if to seize the entire sea. "Go high, high," Selim addressed the waves, clapping his hands.

While Samira brought buckets of seawater, Shifra, patiently showed him how to mix the water with sand. "Together we are going to build a castle," said Shifra. The child started to work in earnest, both women delighted by his enthusiasm.

"What did I tell you?" Samira said with satisfaction. "The children born in Jaffa have the sea in their blood. After they get the taste of it, they become its lifelong lovers."

They were seated on the large beach towel that Samira had stretched on the sand, not far from where Selim industriously carried his little bucket back and forth. Shifra was happy that he didn't try to go farther than the edge. "Eumi the wa-te tickle," he screamed, when a small wave touched his feet. For a while he kept busy going back and forth. Then suddenly he cried, "Eumi, Jedah Sami-a, Selim thisty, Selim wants dink," and he cupped his hands around his mouth.

The two women looked at each other. In their haste, they forgot to bring a bottle of water or juice. They peered along the beach. No vendor was in sight. "I'll go," Samira got up quickly, "I know a kiosk not far from here. It will not take long."

"Let me go," offered Shifra

"You watch Selim," Samira said. "If you play with him he'll forget he's thirsty."

Shifra saw Samira climbing the rocks toward the street. Selim was playing quietly. She felt a kind of torpor. She fought to keep her eyes open, but they had a will of their own. Her body relaxed, her eyelids dropped.

When she opened them, she didn't see Selim. Only a minute ago he was here, she thought. "Selim," she screamed his name in continuous crescendo, "Selim, come back, Selim!" No answer. She was terrified. The sea looked at her with angry eyes. "Oh, my God, help me." She started to run in one direction, but the long *jelebia* kept sticking to her legs. She lifted the dress and threw her slippers away. "Oh, God, please, please!"

She turned back and looked the length of the beach. The sun was in her eyes, she couldn't see far. She ran in the other direction. The wind blew her hijab away.

"Selim," she cried, "Selim!" The hot sand burned her feet, but she didn't feel it.

Suddenly, she stopped, her feet glued to the scorching sand. A girl, five or six years old, was dragging a crying Selim toward a woman sitting underneath a beach umbrella.

Shifra could almost make out the girl's Hebrew words, "Doda, Doda, Auntie, look. I found this little boy crying. Maybe he lost his mother. He said something I don't understand."

At that, the woman got to her feet. *This can't be true.* A shiver went through Shifra's body. *I am dreaming. It's a bad dream. This woman is not who I think she is.*

"Stop, stop! Selim, come here. It's me, Eumi!" Shifra screamed. She was afraid to get closer. Her heart was an amalgam of thoughts and feelings, the happiness of finding Selim mixed with fear. The woman was dressed in a garb she recognized too well, the dress of orthodox Jewish women. Selim didn't hear his mother, but the woman did. She turned her head. Suspicion, suspense, the surprise of recognition all played in a matter of seconds over Chana's eyes, while Shifra, scared, could only think *why is she here? Who is this girl with her? What am I going to do now?*

"Selim, you naughty boy, you scared me, come here immediately!" Shifra ordered in Arabic, hoping that her voice didn't reveal the tumult in her heart.

"Shifra, Shifrale, it is really you, isn't it? Oh, I think I could recognize you from a thousand faces. Oh, Shifra, when your poor parents hear that I saw you—"

Shifra interrupted, "*Tesmaneli,* excuse me. *Hada Ibni,*" this is my son." She picked up Selim in her shaking arms "You just wait," she said to him in a threatening voice, "Until I tell your father how much you scared me today."

"Shifra, Shifra, look at me," Chana implored. "It's me, your old friend, Chana. And I know that it's you."

"I'm sorry," Shifra said in English. "I don't understand you." Addressing the girl, she bowed. "*Shukran,*" she said, before turning rapidly and walking away. In her ears she still could hear Chana calling after her, "Shifra, you are making a mistake, a big mistake. *Hashem* sees everything. You can't hide forever!"

"Eumi," Selim whined," I want to play with the gi-l." But his mother just pressed him closer to her. From afar she saw Samira descending the rocks with difficulty. Just in time, Shifra thought.

"Eumi," Selim asked, turning his face to her, "You know the lady? Why she said, Shif-a Shif-a?"

"It was a mistake. She thought I was somebody else." Shifra was happy that Selim couldn't hear her heart, which beat like the bells of the nearby Armenian Church.

"Look," she pointed her finger, "here comes Jedatha Samira. We don't want to upset her, right? So not a word about what happened. If you'll be a good boy, I'll try to forget it, too."

"Jedati Sami-a, Jedati Sami-a," Selim called, running to her and snatching the bottle from her hand. In seconds he gulped down its entire contents. "He really was thirsty," Samira said, stroking his hair.

"It's time to go home," Shifra said, folding their towel. She didn't want to look at Samira just then. Samira could read her face better than her own mother. Shifra double-knotted the kerchief on her forehead, "Let's go," she repeated, forcefully, walking ahead of them.

You can't hide forever. You heard Chana. You thought that you were safe. You became somebody else, and oh, how much you wanted to believe it! But now just look at yourself, your insides shake. To see Chana was to feel the ground tremble under your feet. How easily you lied to your best friend, the girl who told you about the magnificence of the sea and inspired your desire to come and see it with your own eyes. Aren't you ashamed? And who are you? Is Suha a real person? In your mind don't you call yourself Shifra? Do you have the courage to tell Musa about today's encounter? Would you tell him about your real identity? An identity you just denied and ran away from, like a coward?

The two halves of her conscience fought with one another. *I love Musa*, one said. *Yes, but do you love him enough to disclose everything?*

Her feet were burning, but Shifra didn't dare tell Samira that she had lost her slippers on the beach. Though troubled by her thoughts, her ears could still hear Selim babbling, "Jeddah Sami-a, tomowow- again beach, yes? I want to play with the gi-l."

"What girl? Tell me Suha, what's he talking about?" Samira asked Shifra.

"Oh, look, we are already home," Shifra sighed with relief, "I feel tired. I think I've got a headache from too much sun." She feigned a yawn. "Selim met a little girl while gathering shells. I don't know who she is. I didn't ask."

Shifra opened the gate. "What we all need right now is a good bath," she said, forcing her voice to sound cheerful. "We are filthy and perspiring. Selim, you'll be first. Quick"

She saw Samira glancing at her furtively, somewhat puzzled, but no words came out of her mouth. Shifra took a deep breath. One thing she knew for sure. There would be no more trips to the beach.

34

When the letter with the British stamps arrived, the children recognized the neat writing on the envelope. "A letter from Amina," they chanted and brought it like a precious gift to Musa. All crowded around him to listen. Samira was there, Suha too, while Selim played on the floor not far from them. Musa tore the envelope open and began to read:

November 9, 1946

To my dear brother Musa and his household, to my honored mother, my sisters and little brother, Salaam Aleikum!

From the beginning I have to say that I am afraid this letter is going to disappoint you. Three years I have waited for our reunion and yet, with a heart full of distress, I have to let you know that strong reasons oblige us to postpone it.

My husband, George, says that the political situation in Palestine is too unstable to take the risk of visiting at this time. Oh, dear brother, I wanted *so much to hug you and be again under one roof with all of you!*

It's hard for me to understand what's happening. We always lived in good relations with our Jewish neighbors. I loved to buy pastries from Mr. Abulafia's bakery, who never forgot to add a sweet baklava, just for me, without charge, and there was Mr. Nathan, mother's friend, who always advised her wisely. Our mother gave shelter to Suha, a survivor of the war in Europe, who now is your lovely wife.

What do the Jews want? George agrees with me that Palestine belongs to us; we inherited it from our ancestors, it is our country from time immemorial. It seems that bands of Jewish terrorists attack the English troops stationed in Palestine, and now, he says, England is forced to send more troops to keep the spirits quiet. But, I am sure you are well aware of what's happening and I am not telling you anything new.

At that point, Musa stopped reading, and looked anxiously around him. Nur, Rama, Ahmed, and Samira kept their eyes locked on him. Not Suha, whose attention seem concentrated on Selim, who suddenly clapped his hands, and said, "Auntie Amina, Auntie Amina, come, play with Selim."

Nervously, Musa folded the pages, "There is nothing else interesting for you," he addressed his listeners, putting the letter back in its envelope. "Go tell Eumi," he said to his sisters and brother, "that Amina has postponed her visit." It was through her younger children that proud Fatima heard news from her favorite daughter.

While Samira and Suha were busy in the kitchen preparing the evening meal, Musa reopened the letter.

George told me what happened at the King David Hotel in Jerusalem. It was Jewish hoodlums, he said, and their explosives that killed some of their brethren together with British and Arab officials. The British are worried. They sent 100,.000 troops to Palestine, to calm down the situation.

So I am sad and pray for you and talk to my flowers about my faraway family. My garden has grown and awaits guests. In my mind I see a child like Selim playing there, but for now I have to postpone my dream.

George is adding a few words too.

Good bye for now. Your loving sister, Amina

— — —

Honored Family,

Though we have not yet met, I feel as if I already know you from Amina, who talks constantly about you with love and longing.

Probably you, my dear brother-in-law, are well aware of the situation. We, the British, have always felt solidarity and obligation toward you, and more so right now, when our troops have daily skirmishes and harassments from those ultra-nationalistic Jews. We had to retaliate and even hang a couple in Accra in order to teach them a lesson.

They want a Jewish state! Never! Mr. Bevin, our Prime Minister, is definitely opposed to it. Palestine belongs to the Palestinians, he declared only yesterday. We cannot permit those ships with survivors to dock in your ports; we don't want any more Jews in Palestine.

Only united, the British and the Arabs, will we be able to have absolute control and make sure that no one lands on Palestine's soil, indifferent of the consequences.

As a student and admirer of your history, I know you will prevail. Hopefully, we'll meet in quieter times.

I remain your respectful brother-in-law, who hopes that soon could call you, my brother

George

The first thing Musa did, was to hide the letter. Suha should not see it. He wanted to keep her far from the turbulent problems, which he was only too familiar with. He entered the bedroom, his mind preoccupied with the letter, not noticing that Suha followed him. Quickly he placed the letter under the mattress. Suha backed off silently.

Tonight, I'll tell Suha that I'm going to the chaikhana for the last time. She always waits for me when I'm out at night. I have to talk to the mukhtar, I'll say, I have a young wife who wants me at home. I hope he'll understand what I mean. Lately, I am so tired I can not even enjoy her.

Shifra was not upset when Musa told her that he was going out again that evening. She wanted a chance to read the letter, especially after she saw Musa hiding it. Did he hide it from her?

She waited patiently until Samira put Selim to bed. Then Shifra went to sing for him, and as always when they sang together her heart filled with happiness. He did not know all the words, but his pitch was better than hers. *Should we take Selim to Uhm Zaide?*

Alone in her bedroom, she plucked the envelope from under the mattress. With each sentence she read, she felt a whirlwind in her head. Since encountering Chana on the Jaffa seashore, her heart cringed at the pain of keeping secrets from Musa. Reading George's letter—easier for her to read his English than Amina's Arabic handwriting, full of flourishes, she discovered that Musa had secrets to keep from her, too.

What she read was devastating. And so hard to understand!

What was happening in the world, the real world beyond the fences of her garden? She did not know that Jews fought the British. Who were those Jews? Jews, like her father, who feared God? And what did Musa know? George, in his letter, seemed sure that Musa knew what was happening: skirmishes and killings and people being hanged.

Shifra shivered, rereading George's missive. It was clear he liked the idea of a coalition between the Arabs and British against the Jews. How could that be possible? Didn't the Arabs hate the British?

She had more questions to which she didn't know the answers. What would happen to those boats filled with Jewish survivors not allowed to land? And those words, *no matter what consequences,* flitted back and forth in her head. Did it mean that those who tried to set foot ashore would be killed and thrown into the sea? Maybe one of them was a member of her mother's family, an escapee from the war, seeking a final shelter only to be killed at the gates of the Holy Land.

Tears fell from Shifra's eyes. She cried for the *weltshmerz,* the world's grief, as her mother called it, and for her own distress; the pain of a girl who thought she had found paradise only to realize that paradise existed simply in her imagination.

Under a sudden impulse, she went into Selim's room. The child was sleeping peacefully. Shifra wanted to take him in her arms and hold him close to her heart forever. She took a deep breath. From what she discovered that night, after reading the letter, she knew she could pretend no longer that her life would continue as before.

3 5

The emergency call from Mahmood had taken Musa by surprise. It was the first time Mahmood had called him at the office. He sounded angry, his voice hoarse.

"I have bad news," Mahmood started, bypassing the conventional greetings. "Na'ima woke up this morning in a pool of blood. She lost the baby. Neither my mother nor other women in the village were able to help. I took her to Al Maqassad Hospital in Jerusalem."

"I didn't know she was pregnant," Musa answered, his voice shaking.

Mahmood stopped him short, "She asks for Samira. She cries that she wants her mother and Samira to come. That's the reason I'm calling. Tell them. Me, I have no time to pamper her." Mahmood hung up.

As he was on the watch for the boats bringing Jewish illegal immigrants, something Musa had done often in the last few months, he thought of Mahmood's call. Hidden behind a rock, rifle in hand, he was watching the sea, waiting, in the company of

Jaffa's other young men summoned by the *mukhtar*, to help turn away those who ignored the British orders.

His mind turned back to the events preceding Mahmood's call. How pleased he was when during the Ramadan holiday his mother had made peace with Samira. *Was it the holiness of Ramadan, which demands that Muslims pray for forgiveness, or the fact that his mother missed Samira's company?* Whatever the reason, it had been an important step, he hoped, toward improving the relations between the two households, his mother's and his. Furthermore, he understood from Samira's words that Fatima seemed more inclined to accept Suha as her daughter-in-law.

"Your mother loves your child. For hours she watches Selim playing in the garden. She's his real Jedah, blood from her blood and flesh from her flesh." Samira said. "You'll see, pretty soon she will turn around."

And maybe that was about to happen, but the call from Mahmood changed everything. Hearing the news, Fatima burst into tears. Then, without skipping a beat, she took control, as strong as ever. "We are all going. Not only Samira and I. Rama and Nur can help take care of Faud and Nassum. Ahmed," she addressed her youngest child, "you'll work with Mahmood in the orchard. It will do you a world of good."

Musa did not interfere. He was not going to oppose his mother's decision. When he told Suha, she complimented his mother's solution, "Na'ima needs their help, not only for cleaning and cooking. She needs the closeness of her family, the people who love and care for her."

Musa was touched by Suha's sensible words, yet he insisted, "But we need Samira. Who'll help you watch Selim, cook, shop? With me at the office, you'll be alone all day."

Suha closed his mouth with a kiss, "Trust me," she said. *Was she going to tell him that she took care of her own brothers and sisters, at a much younger age?* She kissed him again, "Don't worry, Selim and I will be fine and I promise you that the *Iftar* will taste as good as Samira's."

So spoke his darling wife, whom he was betraying this very moment, armed to frighten away her brethren who wanted to enter the Holy Land. At least, he reasoned with himself, he didn't aim at them, like the others; he shot into the air trying to scare them. But he knew that lately, bands of armed Jews waited on opposite hills ready to open fire on whoever attacked the boats. What misery! Could he ever dare tell his trusting wife what he was doing? His heart ached at that thought.

Suha is Muslim, he tried to assure himself, not Jewish. She took the *Al-Shahada*; she is a good, obedient wife. Stop being suspicious, her lovemaking alone should be enough proof for you.

He waited, but no boats arrived that night. It must have been a false alarm. Relieved, Musa returned home. Peering at his dark bedroom windows, to assure himself that Suha was asleep, he slipped furtively along the wall, toward the shed behind his house where they kept the gardening tools and the bric-a-brac. He wrapped his rifle in a piece of fabric and buried it deep in the soft earth. Then he washed his hands at the garden pump.

His wife smiled in her sleep. But his sleep became disturbed by unusual dreams. Mahmood screamed, "I know she did it to herself, she's not a real Muslim wife. Na'ima doesn't want more children! She wants to shame me!"

Musa arose to drink a glass of water. It took him a long time to fall asleep. The second dream was no better. He dreamed of the *mukhtar* speaking to the group of volunteers for the nightly watch. "It's your duty to be vigilantes. We can't allow strangers in our land. Palestine belongs to Palestinians! Musa, I want you to be in charge, you have experience. I've been told about your training in the Jerusalem forests. All of us," and he gestured to his audience, "Are proud of you. I always knew you were born to be a leader."

One Palestinian shouted, "Inshallah, you spoke well, *mukhtar.*"

"We trust Musa," screamed another with enthusiasm.

Musa woke up sweating. *It was a dream, only a dream*, but it kept him awake, reminding him that he had to talk to the *mukhtar*, before, Allah help us, such a dream could become a reality.

36

On September 1st 1947 the day of the first rehearsal of the eleventh season of the Palestinian Orchestra, Otto Sch-roder entered the Ohel Shem Hall in Tel-Aviv dressed as usual in a suit and tie. He came earlier to practice a few scales for warm-up. To his surprise quite a few of the Orchestra members were already there.

His stand colleague, his former pupil Hugo Myerson, who changed his name to Chaim Ben-Meir after he arrived in Eretz Israel, grinned at him, "A *Guten Morgen*, Herr Professor." The young man wore knee-long khaki pants and sandals without socks, which Otto considered completely disrespectful to their profession. "*Was Machst Du?*" he asked.

Otto shrugged. He was sure that Hugo had purposely changed the polite address, *Wie Sind Sie,* into the slang version. But he didn't answer because his attention was caught by a fiery discussion taking place between other members of the orchestra.

"What's happening?" Otto asked, bewildered.

"Didn't you read the papers?" retorted Hugo. He took the Palestinian Post out of his pocket. "Here, read for yourself."

**The British Government Ends Mandate in Palestine.
Because of the inability to arrange an understanding between
the two parties, Arabs and Jews, regarding the British proposal
for a partition, the British Government announces that it
will end its Mandate on May 15, 1948. The newly formed
United Nations will take over. The UN has already formed a
commission to study the proposal and present its report as
soon as possible.**

Musicians crowded to peer, one over the other's shoulder, and
read aloud from DAVAR, the Hebrew newspaper.

"It's going to be chaos," said the burly trombone player.

"We'll never agree to part with Jerusalem. Jerusalem is ours," a
defiant oboist replied.

"You and your *Etzel* terrorists would do better to listen to the
voice of wisdom," thundered a cellist. "Without compromise we'll
never have a state." He was one of Otto's former colleagues from
Berlin.

"What was the reward the European Jews got for their pacifism,
for compromising? Nothing but a slaughterhouse!" screamed a
second violinist.

"*Palmach* is forming special units. My son was called to serve,"
whispered the French horn player.

"It's going to be war. We Jews are like a drop of oil in a sea
filled with Arab hatred."

"You European Jews were always fearful of your own shadows.
Enough of that! Here we are raising Sabras. We teach our children
to know no fear," shouted the Etzel sympathizer.

Otto thought there was going to be a fight. At that moment
the concert-master appeared. All took their seats, but the anger
lingered in the air.

Suddenly, Otto remembered that he hadn't warmed up. *All
those arguments, what for, they couldn't resuscitate the dead.* He looked
at the two pieces of music in front of him and turned pale.

"Attention, please," the concert-master called, striking a stand with his bow. "In his desire to identify with our brethren, martyrs who perished *Al Kidush Hashem*, the conductor has decided to change the initial opening program of our season. Instead of the Beethoven Third and Fifth Symphonies, we'll perform Mahler's Second Symphony-The Resurrection, and Mussorgsky's Kindertotenlieder-The Children's Death Songs."

Otto's eyes blurred. His fingers fought to open his tie. He needed air. Water, he thought, I need water. But he was unable to move. Would he be able to play this concert without fainting?

The tragedy befell him after a rehearsal of Mahler's Resurrection with the KuBu orchestra in Berlin. It was a starless night. Still haunted by the beautiful poem which Mahler himself had added for the chorus to sing at the end of the Symphony, and so fitting for the terrible times they were witnessing, "Believe you were not born in vain. Stop trembling. Prepare to live," Otto decided to take a detour and share its glorious and encouraging message with Gretchen and Ruthie before returning to his hiding place in the basement of Heinrich Schultz's apartment..

As Otto arrived at the back door of their house, he peered first anxiously to see if anybody was around. He held the key ready in his hand when he heard screams that made his hair rise, "*Muti, Muti, Mutter*, save me," followed by a long, desperate wail.

Oh, my God, it was Ruthie's voice! He hid behind a bush. He saw a man dragging his daughter, while two others laughed.

"Now," the man smirked, "you are going to become a real German woman, not a mongrel. And you'll never bite a German soldier again or I'll break your teeth! Stop yelping!"

He crashed his whip on her back. To his horror, Otto recognized the voice. It was Heinz! Heinz, Gretchen's brother, dressed in the sinister SS uniform.

Where was Gretchen? Shaking, Otto fell to his knees. *What should I do? If I go to her they'll take us both away. Maybe, yes, if I run to Schultz for help! His brother is a general in the Wehrmacht. Yes, yes, I'm sure he'll get Ruthie out.*

Crying, Otto plugged his ears until he could no longer hear his daughter's wails. Yes, it had been Heinz, his brother-in-law! And Otto knew that he would be condemned to hear Ruth's wailing and carry the weight of his cowardice for the rest of his life.

"Everybody ready for tuning," the concert-master said. "Please, give us an A," he asked the principal oboe player. A cacophony of sounds followed as all were tuning their instruments.

"Herr Schroder, Herr Schroder," whispered the violinist behind him, "have you fallen asleep? The concert-master has called for tuning."

Obediently, Otto put the violin under his chin.

37

Shifra was excited to have Selim all to herself while Musa's family and Samira were away. She thought the child was too spoiled by Rama and her brother Ahmed, whom Selim adored. Throwing their schoolbooks away the minute they arrived home, they came over to play with him. Lately, during the Ramadan, they played together all the time.

After the first two days alone, Suha felt she had exhausted the games and the nursery books that Selim knew by heart.

"Your fig tree must be thirsty," Suha said, "let's go water it." In honor of his child, Musa had planted a fig tree in the garden the day Selim was born. The child loved to watch his tree grow. He called it his little brother, though the fig grew taller than he was.

"How about singing our songs?" Suha asked Selim afterward. She loved to hear his silvery voice, which matched hers so well. But after a few songs the child seemed bored.

"Beach," he said, "See big wave," and he raised his arms to show his mother how high the wave would be.

Hearing that, Suha's heart skipped a beat. Since the day she saw Chana on the beach, she had avoided the seashore.

"I have a better idea," she said brightly. *Samira wasn't home, Musa was at the office and during Ramadan he doesn't return home before dusk. Nobody would know where they went. She felt a desire, almost like an ache, to listen again to music.*

"You'll hear beautiful music today," she told her son. Without waiting any longer she brought his hat, tied her kerchief and off they went. It was hot, and Suha realized that in her haste she had forgotten to take Selim's stroller. After a short time, the child wailed, "Selim no more walk," and sat on the sidewalk.

"We are almost there," Suha said. "It's the next street, just around the corner." She took him in her arms, her heart full of expectation. The Schroder's street was empty and silent, not even a dog was barking. As she drew near, she heard the violin's exquisite melody. Suha's heart vibrated in the same rhythm. She realized how much she had longed to hear Otto Schroder's violin.

She lowered the child. "Let's walk slowly and listen," she whispered. From the first sounds, Selim's eyes grew bigger. He seemed mesmerized. At the gate, he stopped. His little hands grabbed the rails. He tried to peer inside.

"It's not nice to stand in front of other people's houses. We have to keep moving."

"My ears want to see," Selim said stubbornly. Suha picked him up in her arms, but the child jerked away. The gate opened. Instantly Suha recognized the Arab woman, the maid, Samira's acquaintance, whom they met in the bazaar.

Alongside her walked a man dressed in a dark suit and tie, his head bent, counting banknotes into her hand. Suddenly, the shrill of a woman's voice interrupted the silence.

"Otto, it's her. It's the girl I told you about, your secret admirer."

"Excuse me," Suha said in Arabic, "It wasn't polite of us to stand in front of your gate."

"Otto," the voice insisted, "Talk to her; invite her to come in."

"Please, don't go." Otto's English had a strong German accent. He watched the window anxiously. "It seems that my wife knows you, she said that you remind her of our daughter."

Then he addressed the child, "Would you like to see the violin?"

Selim frightened and about to cry, looked at his mother. He clutched her hand tightly, hidden in the folds of her dress.

The servant, who was watching the scene, said quickly in Arabic, "Don't be afraid. She's a good woman. And she likes children."

Otto continued, "My wife is not well. Please excuse me, we haven't been introduced." He bowed slightly. "My name is Otto Schroder. I know I have no excuse to ask you to come in." His voice sounded nervous, excited. He took a handkerchief from his pocket and wiped his face. "I talk too much."

Suddenly Shifra realized that Selim had disappeared. He had slipped away and entered the courtyard.

"Selim, Selim, come back," Shifra called, but the child laughed and ran toward the steps. "Selim," Shifra screamed again. When he saw the door opening, Selim stopped, looking back at his mother, scared by his own daring. Otto Schroder stood in the doorframe holding the violin under his chin.

He began by playing a children's tune. Selim smiled. Close to Otto his little body seemed to be one with that of the tall man. It was such a beautiful picture, Shifra thought; a picture she would remember for a long time.

It started first as a game. Otto played a few notes, and stopped, waiting. The child sang, repeating the melody. Otto raised his eyebrows. He tried again. And again Selim sang the notes, his voice like the sound of a delicate flute. He seemed to enjoy the new game tremendously.

Otto's wife appeared at the door, "Otto," she said, "it is incredible. This child has perfect pitch."

She addressed a bewildered Shifra, who had followed the scene, hardly believing what was happening, "How old is your child?"

Shifra, alarmed, stopped daydreaming. "We have to go! Excuse us." And to Selim, she ordered, "It is late. We have to go. Say goodbye to the nice people."

"Please stay," Gretchen Schroder begged.

Shifra bowed her head and repeated, "We have bothered you enough. We must go home. It's very late. Thank you."

Selim seized Otto's hand which held the violin. Oblivious to their talk, the boy timidly touched the violin, caressed its shiny wood, and courageously plucked one string. He laughed with delight, and plucked another, then a third, singing the sounds of the strings he plucked.

Otto joined his wife, "Please, come in. I'd like to talk to you about your son. He impresses me as being an exceptional child."

Suha's eyes moved from Otto to his wife, who looked, like a ghost, even skinnier than the time she saw her in the bazaar. Otto's words played like a record in her mind. *What should she do?* Really, it was time to leave, Musa could be home soon. Yet her feet refused to move.

"Maybe another time," she said.

Selim cried, "Eumi, I want dink, to dink." For the Arab maid, who witnessed the scene from the beginning, those were the first words she understood. "Come inside," she said, "and you can choose any drink you like."

Not waiting for his mother's approval, Selim followed her. The two Schroders gestured invitingly at Suha. This wasn't my decision, Suha thought, as she walked into the house. Maybe it was *bashert*.

As she stepped inside the Schroders' home Shifra was surprised by its darkness. The high windows shielded by heavy curtains seldom let the sun in. The big room had spartan furnishing; around a coarse wooden table were a few mismatched chairs. Between the windows Suha saw two violin stands covered with music sheets and more sheets were spilled on the floor or spread out on top of a huge box covered by a black oilcloth.

A sofa and an old carpet, its colors faded from use, completed the furnishings. The walls, without any adornment, looked blank to Shifra. She thought of the overgrown weeds in the courtyard; both the house and the courtyard needed a caring hand.

Meanwhile three grown ups fussed around Selim. The Arab maid sat him at the table and gave him a glass of orange juice.

"I'm so sorry we have no cookies," Gretchen Schroder said, hiding her shaking hands in her skirt pockets. "Please, tell him," she addressed Suha, "next time you visit, we'll have many goodies for him."

Otto, who had taken off his jacket, couldn't take his eyes off Selim. Seated near him, he took hold of one of his little hands.

"Otto," Gretchen scolded in German, "where are your manners? Please, offer the young lady a glass of tea." The last sentence was said in English for Shifra's benefit.

"Oh, we will leave soon. Please don't bother," Shifra said.

But Otto, looking apologetically at Gretchen, got up immediately.

"It will take only a minute," he said and disappeared.

"Please sit down," Gretchen said. "You know who we are, but we know nothing about you, your name, and your little wonder child's name." The tone was warm, inviting. Shifra noticed that her voice, when calm, sounded as melodious as Otto's violin.

"Otto already told you," Gretchen continued, "your son is a little gem, or a little budding rose, which with proper care could develop into the most beautiful flower."

While she talked, Gretchen rested one hand on the table, but she retrieved it when she saw Shifra watching her disfigured fingers. Even without knowing what illness afflicted the woman, Shifra's heart filled with pity.

"His name is Selim," she answered, "In Arabic it means peace." Then she ventured to say, "The same as *Shalom* in Hebrew. He is not yet two years old."

"And who are you?" asked Gretchen, with so much gentleness in her voice that Suha almost lost her composure. "Shif..." she started, instinctively ready to give her real name. She caught herself in time. "My name is Suha, Suha Masri."

The Arab maid nodded.

"Suha Masri," Gretchen repeated. "And you love music, Suha Masri. I know it because I spotted you when you stopped to listen to my husband's violin practice. Not only once, but quite a few times. I had also noticed your beautiful blue eyes, *dieselben blauen Augen,* the same as...."

"Tea is ready," Otto clamored in the same instant, appearing with a tray on which the steam twirled up from glasses filled with boiling water.

Shifra watched the Arab maid. She had to remind herself that she was a Muslim now. As thirsty as she was, she wouldn't dare drink during the holy month of Ramadan.

"Thank you," she declined, embarrassed, "It's the Ramadan holiday. We are prohibited to drink before sunset."

"Find me, Eumi," Selim screamed. Following his voice, she saw him hidden underneath the big box covered with oilcloth, and standing on sturdy legs, which she had noticed when she entered.

"Ach, he has discovered the piano," Otto Schroder said, looking at his wife questioningly. She nodded slightly.

"Get up and come here, you naughty boy," Shifra called. She hadn't noticed the exchange of glances between husband and wife. "It's late and we have to go home."

But Otto had already moved away the oilcloth, revealing the instrument. The finishing wood had a reddish texture to it. Otto gestured Selim to come out. "I'll show him how this box makes music, too," Otto said. "Actually it makes the most beautiful music, because it can replace a full orchestra. That's piano's magic."

Intrigued, Shifra pulled Selim from under the instrument, and holding his hand, approached Otto, who had raised the lid. The shiny ivory keys intrigued the two guests. "Try to play it," Otto offered, but neither Selim nor his mother dared to get closer.

A piano; Shifra remembered that in her childhood, one of her schoolmates told her she played piano, but Shifra had never seen or heard the instrument. Timidly, she pressed a key. It produced a clear sound. The entire room resonated. She pressed the next key. On his tiptoes, clinging to his mother, Selim sang the two notes, repeatedly, creating a game with the two syllables, Eu-Mi, Eu-mi. Impatiently, he cried, "Me, too," raising his arms to be lifted to touch the keyboard.

At Otto's sign, the Arab maid brought a chair. After Selim was seated, he tried one key, after which, with a confidence incomprehensible to Shifra, he pressed the same keys his mother had pressed. The child laughed with delight. The old couple nodded.

"It's as we thought," said Otto in German, addressing his wife, who had tears in her eyes. "This child really has it in him."

Knowing Yiddish, Shifra understood his words, but didn't comprehend their meaning. Probably Selim likes to play with sounds, like another child plays with toys, she thought.

"Your son was blessed by gods," Otto said solemnly. "Of course, he is a bit too young to start playing an instrument, but his talent is like a gold mine."

He thought for a while, "Maybe I could borrow a quarter-size violin from one of my colleagues. It would be worth a try. Gretchen, what do you think?"

"I agree," Gretchen answered.

It was a talk between two professionals, which excluded Shifra. She picked Selim up. "We had a wonderful afternoon," she said, "for which we thank you very much."

"You'll be back, *Ja*, yes?" Gretchen asked anxiously. "You've heard what my husband said. Your son is a gold mine. No one can bring out the gold from that mine better than my husband."

"Oh, Gretchen," Otto said, reproach in his voice.

"Don't be so modest, *sweetheart,* I just told her the truth."

In front of the gate, with Selim in her arms, Shifra turned to wave to the Schroders. With one arm around his wife's slim shoulders, Otto waved back. On the way home, Shifra felt she had wings under her arms, as Otto's words continued to resonate in her ears, "Your son was blessed by gods, blessed by gods."

Though she was happy, a cloud pressed on her heart. Could she share Otto's discovery with Musa? How would he react? Would he let her go back to their house? If she didn't tell him, he might still find out. The Arab maid was friends with Samira. One word from her would be enough. Oh, what a dilemma! But she was sure of one thing. Nobody could hold her back; she would return.

3 8

W*hen would she be able to see the Schroders again?* Shifra wondered. Before that meeting, the music was what brought her there, the need to fill her soul with sound. Now she wanted to know them better. But with Samira and the rest of the Masri family due to return any day, she knew it wouldn't be possible. Samira watched each of her movements.

The afternoon Nur's letter arrived, Shifra immediately recognized the fifteen-year-old girl's neat handwriting. She placed the letter next to Musa's plate. When Musa arrived home, hungry as a wolf, he pushed aside his Iftar meal and tore open the letter. "I don't understand why my mother didn't write the letter herself?" He muttered.

Most honored broth\er,

My mother asked me to write to you to dissipate any worries you might have. She decided that for the time being we will remain in Deir Yassin until the end of the Ramadan month, but we'll be back home before Idul Fitri festivities.

Na'ima is doing better, Allah be praised, but is still very weak since she lost the baby. She can't stop crying. The doctor told mother that with all of us around her, she'll heal faster. He said, "It's not the first time that the spirits of a woman who had a miscarriage are low. It's your duty to encourage her to enjoy life again."

Rama and I play and entertain Nassim and Faud, but neither one is as smart or sweet as our Selim. Ahmed has become a real farmer. He wakes up with the roosters and works until late in the evening, since Mahmood mostly arrives home in the middle of the night and is seldom here during the day.

Oh, I want to tell you how much we enjoy the fresh mountain air. Our mother says that the air here is so much healthier than Jaffa's humidity this time of the year. We sleep with our windows open, but other times we lay our blankets in the orchard and fall asleep under the sweet smell of the honeysuckle and pine trees. Mahmood was furious when he found us. He said that in these troubled times what we did was really dangerous.

We'll see you in two weeks.

Your loving sister, Nur

While Musa read the letter aloud, Shifra's mind wandered. Her first thought was, two weeks of freedom, time she could visit the Schroders. Good for Selim too. After Musa finished reading, she said quickly, "I'm glad that your sisters and brother enjoy their stay. As always your mother made the right decision."

Musa's face relaxed when she said, "It's time to get back to your meal. You know that cold meat has no taste."

After he ate, Musa wiped his mouth, satisfied, "You've learned all of Samira's kitchen secrets. Now you are a real Muslim wife."

Why did he emphasize the word "Muslim"? After they married he seldom went to the mosque and never demanded that she read the Koran or pray. His words seemed out of place, even strange. But she wasn't going to ask him. Maybe Musa meant it as a compliment. At any rate it was too late to ask him, because, with Selim cushioned in his arms, both had fallen asleep.

She had no intention of waking them up, so she cautiously cleared the dishes from the table. Her mind raced, trying to find a plausible reason to return to the Schroder's home. She was aware that such a visit could arouse the Arab maid's suspicions. Bringing them flowers to thank them for their hospitality seemed like a good reason. She would offer to clean their yard and plant new bulbs, an idea which had already crossed her mind.

From the kitchen she could hear Musa's light snoring. *Lately he comes home so tired.* After a furtive check on her husband and child, her thoughts returned.

Mrs. Schroder would enjoy the sight and smell of fresh flowers. She could already picture her standing in the window, a smile lighting her face. Flowers have the power to heal. And Shifra would have a reason to return again and again; to water, to weed, to teach Nabiha how to take care of the garden.

Selim's cry woke her from her reverie. "I'm here," she whispered, taking him in her arms, and covering him with kisses. The child rubbed his eyes. "Music," he said, and he repeated the word, music, his fingers tapping on her arm the way she had seen him touching the piano.

"You had a dream," Shifra said, kissing his fingers one by one. "Now, I'll tuck you in bed and you'll continue to dream about music."

The next morning, Shifra tried to think of ways to explain to the Schroders the purpose for her return visit. *Can I just go and say,*

I'd like to take care of your garden? They seem so private. Who knows if they would agree to my offer? Yet I can't go empty-handed. Just flowers, would that be enough?

While preparing the Iftar meal, her face and arms sprinkled with flour dust from kneading the dough for kafta, Musa's favorite dish, the pouch filled with lamb and rice, she was still preoccupied with her plan to visit the Schroders. *How about baking something for them?* Their house looked empty of sweets. What should she bake, almond cookies or bread rolls, or both? She tied the apron again around her waist. In her ears she heard her mother's voice whispering, it could be *a mitzvah*. Now she felt driven by a mission.

Selim played quietly near her, on the kitchen floor. "Smells good," he sniffed, "you make cookies for Selim," and he clapped his hands.

"For Selim," Shifra answered, "and for other people also." Selim nodded, as if he had guessed his mother's intentions.

Taking the trays out of the oven, Shifra thought, *why am I so obsessed with them?* Those people are not my family. What draws me is not only the music; it is the suffering I read on their faces. It makes me feel close to these strangers and eager to help. Shifra's heart was filled with pity recalling Gretchen Schroder's tormented face and her deformed hands timidly inching toward hers on the table surface then retreating fearfully.

3 9

Selim's whimpering awakened her. Shifra's hand touched the spot alongside her. It was empty. Musa is with him, she thought. He was the first to get up at the smallest sound coming from the child's room. But Selim's cries continued. Barefoot, Shifra ran to his room.

"Hush, hush, my sweetie, sleep well, my son," she murmured, rocking him to sleep, thinking, "Where can Musa be?"

Suddenly she heard a screech. Somebody was unlatching the gate. Quickly she set the sleeping Selim back in his bed. *Could it be Musa? Where has he been?* Weren't the coffee houses closed during the Ramadan? Some time ago, Musa had explained to her how important it was in his position at the bank to socialize with his clients.

"The bank benefits from it," he said, "and so do I. I've been promoted twice since I started. Even the *mukhtar* is my client." But seeing her sad eyes he promised to go out less often.

With her heart beating like a drum, she saw Musa carefully walking toward the shed behind their house. Kneeling near the kitchen window she followed her husband's silhouette with her eyes. What was he doing in the shed? What was taking him so long? What time was it? The hands on the clock hanging on the wall above the sink showed two in the morning. She saw Musa washing his hands with the garden hose. She quickly returned to bed, feigning sleep.

But sleep evaded her. Shifra thought of the last few days' events. Maybe that would calm her. They had visited the Schroders twice. Before the second time, she stopped at the *souk* and bought the flowerpots she intended to fill with plants. Then her eyes caught sight of a pair of shoes in the bazaar next door. Solid leather shoes, not slippers, similar to the shoes stolen from her on the beach, on the day Musa found her. Impulsively, she bought them, the first item of clothing purchased since her marriage. Now they were hidden in her closet.

While Shifra and Nabiha were cleaning the weeds in the courtyard, Otto Schroder told her, "At your next visit I'll have a surprise for you."

She hadn't noticed him coming out of the house, where he was playing a new game with Selim. While Otto touched a piano key, Selim, underneath it, held the pedal with the entire weight of his little hands, enchanted by this new discovery, an endless sound.

"Eumi, Eumi," he screamed, "Come quick and listen."

Perspiring, Shifra tightened the head kerchief and straightened her back. It was so hot. She would love to go into the house, but she didn't want to leave Nabiha to work alone.

"My lady's eyes are clearer and she cries less since you came," the Arab woman told her, with wonder in her voice. "She looks forward to your visits."

"Nabiha, let's take a break to go see what Selim is doing," Shifra proposed.

They found him dozing on the sofa, while Gretchen Schroder sat near him holding his hand and humming a lullaby, love pouring from her eyes. Shifra had never heard the song, but moved by the scene, she was ready to cry, especially after Otto picked up the violin and accompanied his wife. Later, he told her that it was a lullaby by Brahms, a German composer.

The Schroders were Jews, yet so different from her parents, or her friends' parents, from all the people in the community where Shifra had been raised.

As soon as Musa left for work, Shifra stepped into the shed looking for garden tools, a small hoe and a rake, to put in Selim's stroller before going to the Schroder's house. She had forgotten Musa's previous night's foray into the shed. Her eyes caught sight of Selim's old blanket. It looked dirty and was partly buried in the ground. *Why is it here?* Curious, she tried to pick it up, but it was heavy. She unearthed it and found a rifle enveloped in it, its unfriendly eye aimed at Shifra. Her hands started shaking.

Oh, my God, what's that? She saw herself, a four-year-old child, whose father, with bulging, red eyes, locked her and her sisters in their stuffy old apartment for what seemed to be days and nights without end. "Nobody leaves," he screamed, while the windows shook from the shots outside.

"*Rebono Shel Olam,*" he knelt, "*Hob Rachmoones,* they are murdering Jews." She saw people running in the streets. One man suddenly fell, blood all over him.

Much, much later she learned about the 1933 events, when many Jews were killed by Arabs, and about the dreaded bullets which have that power.

Why does Musa keep a rifle? Is he hiding it from me? Where was he last night?

Shaking, Shifra went to look for Selim, who held a branch of his fig tree. "This is for *Hada Jedi,* Grandpa, and my new *Jedati,*" he said. "I will plant it myself."

Only yesterday on the way home from the Schroders he had asked, "*Hadola kaman Jedi wa Jedati?* Are they your parents, my grandparents? Why do they speak in such a funny way?"

Shifra picked up the child and his fig branch and hugged him tightly. She did not know what she'd do after her discovery in the shed, but she knew she'd never be the same.

Shifra couldn't get ready; as she was loading the stroller with the garden tools, she stopped again and again to think about the hidden rifle. Had it been buried for a long time in the shed, or did Musa bring it last night? If he meant to protect his family from, God forbid, thieves, why didn't he keep it in the house? Is he protecting somebody who committed an ill deed, by hiding the offending object?

"Let's go, let's go," an impatient Selim interrupted her reverie. "Look, I dressed myself."

By the time they left home, the sun was high above their heads. As they walked on Jerusalem Boulevard, Shifra heard the newspaper sellers scream, *Falistin!* Big news! The Brits decide to end the Mandate. The Palestinians reject the proposal to divide the country." Men were snatching the newspapers, shouting with excitement.

"I'll ask Otto about it," Shifra decided, hurrying her steps. In her mind she already called him Otto. At the Schroder home they were greeted joyously by Gretchen and Nabiha.

"I'm sorry Otto is not at home," Gretchen said when she saw Selim inspecting the rooms. "But he'll be back soon. Please, tell Selim," she addressed Shifra, "he looks disappointed."

"We'll plant the flowers, and he'll help us," Shifra said brightly. "Have you shown *Jedatha* Gretchen the fig branch?"

"For you," Selim said timidly, looking up at Gretchen, who didn't need translation. Her eyes were already brimming with tears.

We feel so good here, Shifra thought, *a home away from home.* Shifra and Nabiha had finished planting when Otto arrived with a package under his arm. He was panting.

"This is for you," Otto said, bending down to Selim. "The surprise I promised you." His voice sounded excited. "It's yours, my boy," he repeated.

"Otto," Gretchen called reproachfully, "Please, not in the courtyard. Come into the house."

"Right," he answered quickly, taking Selim by the hand, Shifra and Nabiha following.

"It's a quarter-violin," Otto explained, "perfect for a small child."

Like a pro, Selim propped it under his chin, the way he saw Otto do, his eyes glistening like blue diamonds.

"Now let's try the bow." Otto showed Selim how to hold it. Hearing a scratch, Selim cried.

"It takes practice," Otto smiled. "Take it home and practice and show me tomorrow, yes?"

"We can't take it," Shifra whispered. *How would she explain it to Musa?* "Please, excuse us." She ran away from the Schroder's home, crying, while in her arms a whimpering Selim poked at her ribs.

Shifra was sorry for the hurried way she left the Schroders' home. Otto Schroder had the best of intentions, and she was rude and ungrateful. In less than a week, the entire Masri tribe was expected to return home, and then it would be impossible for her to sneak away, especially under Samira's hawkish eyes.

She would go apologize during Selim's afternoon nap. *But what if he were to wake up scared by not seeing her?* He would leave the house in search for her. She had no choice but to take him. An idea passed through her head. Long ago, Samira told her that her aunt, a poor woman, dribbled drops of arak between the lips of her baby to make him sleep longer, while she was at work. It seemed so primitive, Shifra thought.

Before his nap, she squeezed a drop of *arrack* into Selim's sleepy mouth, but lacking the will to leave him, she put him in the stroller, and hurried toward her destination. Otto and Shifra almost bumped into each other in front of the house. Otto looked worried. With a tired voice, he stopped Shifra when she tried, her cheeks afire, to apologize for her conduct.

"Maybe it was for the best," he murmured, making an evasive gesture with his hand.

Shifra didn't understand, so she looked at him, waiting.

"Let's go inside," Otto said. "It's not something I want to talk about in the street."

The house was quiet. Gretchen was asleep on the sofa, a shawl covering her feet, while Nabiha, seated near her, mended old towels. She got up when she saw them enter, Shifra carrying the sleepy child. Nabiha raised her arms, and Shifra, grateful, settled Selim on her lap.

Otto took off his jacket and loosened his tie. He bade Shifra to follow him to the corner farthest from the sofa. He whispered, "We have to move away from Jaffa. It might be dangerous for us to continue to live here. That's what my colleagues tell me. They have warned me for a long time, but I wouldn't listen to them."

Shifra kept silent. She had no idea what Otto meant. Otto filled two glasses with water, offering one to her, but Shifra refused.

"Since we came to Palestine my only desire has been to protect Gretchen. She has gone through so much," he paused. "I thought that living in Jaffa would protect her from gossip from people who'd find out she is not Jewish."

"Gretchen never converted," Otto continued, "I knew that if I had asked her she wouldn't oppose it. Yet I didn't. I knew that our souls were one." His eyes became dreamy.

Shifra felt that Otto had just opened his heart to her. He looked distraught. Maybe he forgot to whom he was speaking. Shifra coughed slightly.

"I'm sorry," Otto said, suddenly blushing, "the British have ordered a curfew for the Jews. We live in difficult times. I probably don't have to tell you that."

When Shifra didn't answer or nod, Otto said, "Next month the orchestra is starting its season of concerts. The curfew doesn't allow Jews to travel after dusk. I'll be unable to return home. Unfortunately it reminds me of another curfew... years ago." His shoulders shivered.

"We'll move to Tel-Aviv," Otto said decisively, "the sooner, the better. Gretchen doesn't know it yet, neither does Nabiha. We'll be sorry to part with her."

"What makes me even sadder," he said, "is the thought that we'll not see you and Selim anymore. Gretchen will be inconsolable. She has become very attached to you. You mean so much to her."

It was the first time Shifra heard him speak at such length. It was a miracle that Selim and Gretchen were still asleep. Nabiha, who didn't understand Otto's words, kept humming a lullaby in Selim's ears. Shifra's thoughts leapt from one to another.

"Why," Shifra asked, "why," she repeated, as if it was the only sound she could utter. *What were her hopes when she thought of a home away from home? Suha Masri, how stupid can you be? You dream the impossible.* She felt she was sinking.

Otto raised his eyebrows, "Don't you read the papers? I'm sure it's in all the Arab newspapers. Don't you listen to the radio? The British plan to divide Palestine into two states, one Jewish, one Arab, didn't succeed. Why didn't the Arabs agree? The future is unclear. There are skirmishes, I hear, on the way to Jerusalem. Hopefully there will not be another war. Enough Jewish blood flooded this century. Our only daughter...."

Suddenly Otto got up. "Take the violin," he said. "One day, your son might become a great violinist and if I'm still alive, I'll be proud to think that I was the first one who discovered his talent."

"I can't," Shifra said, crying. "My husband doesn't know that I—we, come here. He's a good husband." Shifra thought of the rifle she found in the shed and shuddered, "He, I don't know, he might not understand my need to listen to your music or our visits. This was a beautiful dream," Shifra sighed, "and like all dreams...."

"It doesn't have to end," Otto whispered. "I'll keep the violin for Selim. The violinist who lent it to me said he doesn't need it anymore. Here," Otto rummaged through his pockets until he found a crumpled piece of paper, "this is our future address, 31 Yehuda Halevi Street, entrance B, third floor. Take it. I hope we'll meet again."

In an almost inaudible voice, Shifra said, "*Danke Schon, Danke Schon.*"

Impulsively she bent and kissed Otto's hand. Then she took the still sleepy Selim from Nabiha's arms and hurried out.

Otto ran after her, "Stop, stop, please. Please look at me." Breathless he caught up to her at the gate. He turned her face, streaming with tears, toward him.

"Who are you?" he asked in the gentlest of voices. "Who is this young Arab woman who loves classical music and speaks German?"

Dusk was approaching. Shifra let her *hijab* drop. The last rays of the sun lit up her hair. Unable to speak, Otto stared at her, his eyes wide.

"I was born Jewish," Shifra said in a hoarse voice, "but unlike your wife, I converted."

She pushed the stroller so fast it was a miracle Selim didn't fall out. For a long time Shifra felt Otto's eyes following her. The crumpled paper was still in her hand. She'd have to hide it. What did Otto mean by skirmishes on the road to Jerusalem? *Who's fighting whom?* She feared for Fatima, Samira and the children soon to be on their way back. Musa's hidden rifle haunted her again. *What was its purpose?*

She had to find out soon, but would she have the courage to tell him about her discovery? Selim woke up and she covered him with kisses. "My treasure," she whispered, praying for her child to grow up in a world in which the word "war" would cease to exist.

40

"My family is coming back tomorrow," an excited Musa told Suha as he entered the house, "Abdullah called me at the bank. We'll be together for Idul Fitri."

He didn't kiss her, neither did he pick up Selim, nor ask them how they spent the day. He seemed preoccupied, nervous.

"Don't worry, I'll shop early tomorrow morning," Suha said. "Everything will be ready for Samira to start cooking after their arrival. You'd better open the windows at your mother's house and let the fresh air in."

"Good idea," finally Musa kissed her, while Selim started dancing around them, "Jedati Samira, Jedati Fatima comes home, Ahmed, Rama, Nur too."

The wrinkles on Musa's forehead disappeared. He lifted his son. "Come, help me open *Jedatha* Fatima's house and see if there is a wolf hidden inside."

The child laughed with delight.

The return of Musa's family filled Shifra's heart with anxiety. She knew that she couldn't visit the Schroders anymore, much less investigate the rifle. Dark clouds were fencing her in.

Musa took the day off from work waiting for his family's arrival. Every few minutes he peered down the length of their street. Shifra felt his mix of impatience and tension. At midday, even before the black limousine stopped in front of their house, Musa had run to open the gate. "Inshallah," he sighed with relief.

"*Salaam Aleikum*, welcome home, my honored mother," he bowed to her, as he opened the car door to help her descend. "I'm happy cousin Abdullah offered you the bank's car for the trip."

The children and Samira crowded around Selim, exclaiming, "Look at you, you grew so big in only two weeks," kissing and passing him from one another. Shifra watched the scene. She saw a tired and older-looking Fatima whispering something in Musa's ear. Musa's face darkened suddenly.

It was time for Shifra to welcome them. She went out and bowed, "*Salaam Aleikum*, welcome home." Only Samira and Rama turned to her. "You are prettier than ever," Rama said, blowing her a kiss.

"It's good to be back," Samira sighed happily. "But I have no time to waste. *Idul Fitri* is almost upon us and little time to prepare for it."

"Don't worry, Samira, I went to the *souk* this morning and brought everything fresh and ready for you to cook." Fatima heard what Shifra said and nodded in her direction, her only gesture acknowledging Shifra's presence.

In the evening, after he finished his meal, Musa said, "I'm going to visit my mother. I want to hear news about Nai'ma's health, also about cousin Abdullah. You go to sleep. Don't wait for me."

Fatima saw Musa coming. She motioned him to follow her to her bedroom. Musa's quick eyes saw the Egyptian *Al Ahram* and other Arab newspapers stacked on her desk. Under a half-opened letter, a page of an English newspaper showed its headlines.

"Sit down, *ibni*," Fatima said. Musa felt warmth flowing in his heart. She hadn't called him "my son" since he married Suha. "We have grave and important matters to discuss."

It must be Mahmood, Musa assumed. *She must have discovered his real nature, a fox with the face of a lamb.* Fatima shuffled through the newspapers in front of her. "I don't know how up-to-date you are on what's happening in the country, but Abdullah is worried and warns me that war is imminent." *So she wasn't going to talk about Na'ima's health, nor about Mahmood.*

Musa raised his hand in protest. "Let me talk," Fatima said. "You are still a child. You got married against my will. Your eyes are only for your wife. And you are a father. Now you have become responsible for your son, but not only for him. As a good *Muslim*," and she emphasized the word, "You are responsible for your widowed mother and for your young siblings."

Musa waited. His mother handed him the newspapers. "Read what the Egyptians, Lebanese and Syrians think. In the beginning I doubted him, when Mahmood talked about the Yahudim threat, but no more! This morning when Abdullah came to say goodbye, he brought me the newspapers. He told me to pass them to you after I finished reading. You'll see that our real enemies are not the English. They have washed their hands of us, and let the United Nations decide our future. And what do they mean by our future?" Fatima spat. "We've been in this land for thousands of years. The Yahudim intruded on us little by little, and now they want to throw us out?" her voice raised its pitch.

"I know," Musa answered, "that Palestinians refuse to consider partition." He continued emphatically, "There will never be two states."

"Don't be so naïve, my son. The Jews have powerful friends, even the American president is on their side. Everybody deplores the crimes committed by the Nazis, but it wasn't our fault, and Palestine shouldn't have to pay for it. Now a committee has to decide our future. What does this committee know about our history, about our culture?"

His mother was right. Musa's eyes stopped over a quote from Azzam Pasha, secretary-general of the Arab League, "If the General Assembly ratifies the decision for a Jewish State to be established, there will be war. There would be no other option. We have to try to prevent Jews from achieving something that violates our emotion and our interest. It is a question of historic pride. If there is to be a decision, that decision will be taken only by force."

Musa folded the newspaper. The dye was cast, he thought. He hoped a war could be avoided.

His mother continued, "Abdullah thinks that we should transfer more of our savings to Cairo and Alexandria. As long as the Brits are still here, there is time. When their Mandate ends, in six months or so, it might be too late."

"Cousin Abdullah is right," Musa said. "He's a cautious man and has always held your best interests at heart."

Did his mother blush? Even if she did, his mother's affairs of the heart never interested Musa, and definitely not now. His eyes fell on the half-opened letter.

"It's a letter from Amina," she said, visibly embarrassed. "It's addressed to Abdullah, but meant for me."

"Can I read it?" Musa asked.

"Later," Fatima put the letter in a drawer. Musa was surprised by his mother's reaction. She had never refused to share her news with him.

After he left his mother's house, Musa lingered in the courtyard. He was keyed up after their meeting. Without stars, the sky looked bleak, its sliced moon hidden by clouds dipped in black ink. *Like my thoughts.*

Why didn't Fatima say a word about Na'ima's health? Wasn't it the reason they all went? Of course he could ask Samira tomorrow, but still it seemed peculiar. And what about her admiration for Mahmood! She said Mahmood was the first one to be aware that the Jews were the real danger.

Would he tell Suha about tonight's talk? Lately, he had been hiding so many things from her. It bothered him because she was so loyal, trusting and loving, so devoted to him and their son. His mother said that Selim, like the rest of the family, needed Musa's protection, but she made no mention of Suha. His mother should have known by now that he was ready to kill for Suha.

And Suha! How would she feel about her husband fighting her brethren, maybe her brothers? She converted to Islam, he told himself. Yes, because it was the only way they could get married, his other self answered. But in her heart, does she really feel Muslim? She never prays. It's true that he didn't ask her to, but she respected the holy days. Suha didn't eat meat, only fish or vegetables, which didn't bother him until now, when he thought of it. Why? Because she tried to keep faithful to the way she was raised?

Does Suha know anything about the disturbances happening outside the walls of their home, about the tension in the air? Musa read the newspapers only at work or at the *chaikhana,* careful not to bring them home.

He knelt in the dark *Oh, Allah Ackbar we all need your help.* Musa rose, shaking. He felt tired, very tired. As he slowly opened the front door, a new thought troubled him. *What did Na'ima tell Mahmood about Suha? How could he find out?*

His house was quiet. How long would it stay as peaceful as tonight? Trying not to make noise, Musa took off his clothes and climbed into bed with a heavy heart.

41

The smell of brewing coffee awoke Shifra. It was early. The sun wasn't up yet, but she realized that Musa was already gone. In the kitchen the rattle of pots and pans continued—Samira is back, Shifra smiled. Her face froze midway. It also meant that she wouldn't be free to move about as she pleased. *I should go and help her.*

"Oh, it smells so good," she said, entering the kitchen, "I hope you had a restful night. I imagined how hard you worked at Na'ima's, cooking for a legion." Shifra embraced Samira. "And now you are starting all over again. But I am here to help."

Samira laughed, "You forget that I am used to cooking for as many, or more people. When master Faud was alive, the house was filled with guests." She sighed, "But those times are gone. I am sad that Na'ima and Amina are not with us to celebrate the holiday."

"How is Na'ima? Is she well? Completely recovered?" Shifra poured hot water over nana tea leaves. She returned Samira's penetrating gaze with innocent eyes.

"She'll be fine," Samira answered, busy with the pots singing on the stove.

She doesn't want to talk. Musa will tell me tonight. Strange, why did Fatima call her son last evening? Was there an emergency or secrets from which I am excluded?

"If you don't need me," a disappointed Shifra said, "I'm going to see if Selim is up."

"Don't wake him," ordered Samira, "Sleep is the healthiest thing for a child, healthier even than food."

Shifra entered her bedroom. For a second, she stood undecided. Then, she remembered. Quickly she took the Schroders' new address from her pocket and hid it inside her new shoes on the bottom of the armoire. The remnants of fabrics saved from the time when she embroidered dresses to be sold at the bazaar caught her eye. The light yellow cotton would be enough for a short-sleeved blouse. After rummaging further, she found two different fabrics, dark green and brown, which together could make an adorable short pleated skirt. She'd start sewing right away. Musa would be pleased, she thought. For a long time he had asked her to wear modern clothes instead of the perennial *jelebia*. And he'd never suspect what she had in mind.

"Eumi, Eumi, come, Selim is up," her son called.

Shifra smiled, "You are going to have a nice morning. Everyone is back, waiting to play with you."

"Are you ready to eat breakfast?" Samira asked Selim, her arms wide open for him to nestle.

"Jedati Samira," the child said and repeated with delight, "Jedati Samira," returning her kisses.

"You are as hungry as a wolf," Samira said with satisfaction. "Didn't your mother feed you while I was away?"

The child nodded; his mouth full. Leaving her pots and pans, Samira sat on a chair next to Selim. "You are like your father," she said, caressing his hair. "He was always hungry. *Inshallah,* you'll grow up to become as big and strong as he is." Shifra smiled at the tableau of her son and Samira together.

"Now you tell *Jedatha* Samira what you did while we were gone."

"He watered his fig tree every morning," Shifra hastened to answer. "He loves doing it."

"And what else did you do?" asked Samira.

Selim looked at Shifra, then at Samira, and said smartly, "I went to see my Jedi and my other Jedati."

"Who? Say it again, I didn't hear well," an astounded Samira said, while Shifra's ears rang with warning bells.

The child got off his chair and with a serious face turned his left arm toward his shoulder as if holding an imaginary violin, while his right hand mimicked the movement of a bow. "Jedi Otto," he said.

Moving the imaginary bow, he tried to sing the sounds of the five open strings. Samira turned toward Shifra, her eyes changed from surprise to fury. *"What?"*

"Selim, that's enough. Go play with Rama and Ahmed," Shifra said, trying to gain time. When she finally looked at Samira, she knew she couldn't lie.

"Selim was bored at home, so we went for a walk. As we approached their house, Selim heard the violin. You should've seen him! He was transfixed; he didn't want to leave. Otto Schroder saw us and invited us in."

"Does Musa know?" Samira asked after a long silence. Shifra made a negative gesture.

"You are playing with fire," Samira said harshly. "You have to stop it. You are not a child. Promise, you'll never go there again."

"Samira," Shifra cried with enthusiasm, "he discovered that Selim has a talent for music, a wonder child, he said!"

"More reason to stop," Samira said. "I'll take Selim to Uhm Zaide to cast out his spell."

"There is no need for it, Samira," Shifra whispered. "The Schroders have moved away."

- - -

Samira sighed with relief; finally, a quiet moment. The Holy Days were over. Since their return from Deir Yassin, she had been busy shopping and cooking, washing and ironing clothes for the children's return to school. The memory of her conversation with Suha still simmered in her mind. But yesterday she had proof that Suha didn't lie to her as she accidentally ran into Nabiha at the *souk*. She told Samira that her employers had moved away.

"Do you know where?" Samira asked.

Nabiha raised her shoulders. "Somewhere in Tel-Aviv, I believe. I am sorry for my poor lady, who is so sick. Schroder *Effendi* said he doubted they'd find somebody as devoted as I was. I know I'll miss them." Then she added, "They became very fond of your Selim, Allah grant him a long life. I believe your young mistress will miss them too."

If they moved away, Samira thought, *there is no need to alert Musa. Why was I so worried? There was no threat in Suha's listening to the violin music.*

The two weeks at Deir Yassin were worrisome enough, she didn't need extra worries. *Musa and Suha should have another child. Both are young and strong. Now is the right time*, Samira decided. I'm sure Musa would like another boy. I am going to nudge him. Then surely Suha will forget her violin dreams.

As she was about to turn off the light, Samira heard the gate unlock. She ran to the window. She saw Musa'a shape slip by. A few minutes later there was a light knock, and without waiting, Musa entered her room. *It's after midnight, what is he doing up at this hour?*

"*Salaam Aleikum*, Samira," Musa said, "I saw a light, and I guessed you weren't asleep yet. Since your return I have wanted to talk to you."

"Sit down, my boy. Though you are a father now, you are still my boy," Samira said affectionately.

Musa took her hands, "Samira, I don't want to beat around the bush. I am worried. Since her arrival my mother hasn't once mentioned Na'ima. I saw she received a letter from Amina, but she found an excuse to hide it from me. I know my mother confides in you. What's happening?"

His reddened eyes prove how much he cares, thought Samira.

"I really shouldn't talk, but you are now the head of the family. Things are not good at Na'ima's. She must have had wrong notions about marriage." Samira sighed, "Mahmood is a strong man, too strong for her. He says that she's lazy by day and not willing by night."

Musa nodded. "I had a bad feeling about him from the very beginning."

"Once when he returned home at dawn, while your mother filled his *nargilea* with water, we heard him say, 'Tonight I shot into the air. You should've seen how scared those Yahudim were! But next time I'll shoot straight at them.' Later, Fatima said that Mahmood was right, good for him, he's not waiting for others to make decisions for him; he's taking the law into his hands.

'And he's doing the same with Na'ima,' I answered. 'Last night I heard him beat her.' To that your mother had no answer."

"This is breaking my heart, especially knowing that I am unable to help her," Musa got up and started pacing the room. After a while he whispered, "What was in Amina's letter that made my mother refuse to show it to me?"

"When Na'ima was taken to the hospital, the night of her miscarriage, she wrote a letter to Amina and asked one of the nurses to mail it. If Mahmood were to find out about it, he would kill her, Na'ima said. That's why Amina addressed it to your mother, yet mailed it to Abdullah. When he showed up, Abdullah explained to Mahmood that the reason for his unexpected visit was to lend your mother the bank's limousine. He was afraid, he said, that we might encounter trouble on the way from Deir Yassin to Jaffa. It calmed

Mahmood, who is suspicious anytime Abdullah visits. Abdullah slipped the letter into your mother's hand."

"Na'ima! It was a mistake that my mother agreed so fast to her marriage."

" Fatima read the letter in the car. She looked sad and put it aside without telling me much. Maybe she was afraid Nur was listening."

"Do you know what Amina wrote?" Musa asked.

"A few days ago your mother was less distraught and said now she could read the letter to me. To tell you honestly, I understood only the parts about Na'ima and what Amina asked your mother to do. The other things she wrote went a bit over my head."

"Would you please tell me what you know?"

"It sounds like a crazy idea. Amina wants Na'ima to leave Mahmood, take her baby and come live with her and her husband in England. She begged your mother to understand Na'ima's unhappiness and not to judge her harshly. No woman, she wrote, should submit to her husband'—and here I try to remember the word, but I can't—it sounded like sodo or sodm. Your mother cried. She said that everyone has his own fate and that must be Na'ima's."

Musa pressed his hands to his temples. He gestured to her to go ahead. Samira whispered the words she had memorized. "Bring Na'ima to England with her little Faud, the bearer of our father's name. We'll raise him together. George fully agrees with my plan and urged me to ask you to do it sooner rather than later. Please don't wait until November."

Samira stopped. "Does it matter which month? Why November,' I asked your mother.' In November' she said, 'Palestine's future will be decided.' Amina mentioned something about war. 'War is a terrible thing', she wrote; three years after it ended, the British still suffer the aftermath of the European war."

"Thank you, Samira," Musa said, while his fists were locked from tension. "You did well to tell me."

269

Samira kissed Musa's forehead, "You'll not solve anything this minute. We are all in Allah's hands."

Life could have been so beautiful, Musa mused, remembering the day he first saw Suha asleep on the beach. He was only nineteen years old. His future looked like Jaffa's azure sky, no blemish on it. Now, four years later, he felt a terrible weight on his shoulders. He wished he had a close friend to unburden to and receive counsel. He couldn't talk to Suha! To Abdullah, yes, Abdullah, their perennial protector! He'd have to leave soon for Jerusalem.

42

Tel Aviv

How cozy it felt to sit around the dining-room table, covered with a starched white damask tablecloth, Otto thought, sipping the strong Turkish coffee and nibbling from the Cream torte, a product of Charlotte's skilled hands. Only one month had passed since they moved from Jaffa, but to Otto it seemed much longer.

"Willkommen, welcome to our little German colony, and you must call me Lotte," Charlotte Gruber had greeted him on the day he came to see the Bauhaus building on Yehuda Halevi Street, where an apartment on the third floor was available for rent.

Sigmund Hochmeister, the double-bass player and a friend from their days in the KuBu, informed him about it. He lived across the street and had nagged Otto, "Nowadays those apartments are in such demand, they go like hot bagels; you'd better hurry." At the front door of the balconied building, Otto met Bruno Herbst, an oboe player and an acquaintance from the Leipzig Conservatory who, besides teaching oboe, had a job on the side as a real-estate broker.

"The rooms are spacious," Otto said after visiting the apartment, turning his hat in his hands, visibly embarrassed, "but I doubt that my wife could walk the steps to the third floor. She is not well. *Entschuldig,* I am sorry to have bothered you."

"*Warten,*" Charlotte Gruber who followed them upstairs shouted, "Bruno, wait! Not long ago I heard you say that you'd love to have a view of the entire city of Tel-Aviv. Here is your opportunity. Switch with Herr Schroder. He could take your apartment on the second floor while you move up to the third."

"I would never impose," Otto started, but Bruno Herbst laughed and stopped him in mid-sentence. "A woman's brain works much faster than ours. Welcome to our building, Herr Schroder. Have your movers take my furniture up before they move yours in."

The Schroders didn't own much furniture. Otto had sold the piano. It had been paid for with Gretchen's jewels at a time when he still hoped she'd play again. But now he needed money for *schlisselgelt,* the initial deposit, and the only way to have such a large sum was by selling the piano. Otto promised himself that as soon as he acquired more students he'd buy an upright. Anyway, the stairs couldn't have accommodated a grand.

"Herr Schroder," the gentle voice of Hugo Gruber woke him from his reverie, "we haven't heard your opinion. You've been very quiet this evening."

They were again discussing politics. And Otto knew that they'd continue to talk until late at night. *What's the need? Didn't I participate in intellectuals' discussions in Germany? And where did that lead?* These talks don't serve any purpose, but his European manners stopped him from speaking his mind.

"Excuse me," Otto arose, "I'm worried about Gretchen. I left her asleep two hours ago. I must go upstairs to check on her. She doesn't sleep more than two hours at a stretch."

"I could go," offered Charlotte, moving her chair aside.

"You are doing too much for us as it is, Frau Gruber. Please sit, *Danke Schon.*"

As he closed the door behind him, he heard Charlotte say, "I pity him so much, I pity both of them. It's terrible, they move like living cadavers."

True, Otto recognized. But since moving to Tel-Aviv, he observed the beginning of changes in Gretchen, changes for which he was grateful to Lotte. Charlotte Gruber was keeping his wife company while he was at rehearsals or concerts. Gretchen wasn't yet part of the colony's evening meetings, but the fact that they spoke her language gave her sustenance and to Otto, new hopes.

Maybe I was mistaken when I chose to live in Jaffa. Why did I think my co-religionists would be unkind to Gretchen?

Gretchen was peacefully asleep, but Otto tossed from side to side, on the broken sofa in the living room. He began the habit of sleeping alone after his nightmares intensified. He could hear himself howling, the same long howl he had heard from his daughter that fateful night when she was dragged away by that monster Heinz, "Muti, Muti, help me!"

Had she seen her father hidden behind the bushes? The look in her eyes told him that she did. She screamed, "Papa, Papa," though she was told not to ever mention his name. Yes, she probably saw him. A little girl of thirteen whose cowardly father, *coward, coward, coward,* heard the ugly laugh of his brother-in-law, *"Mieschling,* mongrel, your father cannot hear you. He's rotting in jail, or already in hell, the dirty Jew."

The train took a grieving Gretchen and a petrified Otto out of Germany to freedom, to Switzerland, in a dangerous escapade with false passports, obtained at the last minute with the help of Wolfgang Schultz, the cellist's brother, a Wehrmacht general. But Otto could see only Ruthie's eyes and hear his inner voice, *coward, coward, coward,* ringing in his ears.

Ruthie was never found. Otto visited many survivors who arrived in Palestine straight from the DP camps. He asked, he begged, but they had no answer. Otto even got an appointment with Chief Rabbi Herzog, who headed the search for displaced families, to no avail.

"Ruthie," Gretchen sighed.

Otto's body arched, ready to jump. It was a false alarm. His thoughts returned to his neighbors. Yes, it was a good move. Nice people, Hugo and Charlotte Gruber. Doctor Hugo Gruber, former professor of Greek and Latin at the University of Dresden, a man without a profession in Eretz Israel. They and their twin boys arrived in the early thirties and enthusiastically joined a kibbutz. "We loved it," Charlotte told him, "we were old Zionists; it was our dream come true. Not for one moment did we think of Hugo's asthma. Even after he got sick, we still didn't want to leave. It was our home, though it was difficult for the *Frau Doktor*," she pointed at herself," to clean the toilets." Everybody has a job to do,' I told Hugo, who wanted to protest. When his cousin offered Hugo a job to keep the books in his haberdashery, we moved out. Our boys cried."

"But I understand they live on a kibbutz now," Otto said, a bit confused.

"After high school they returned *livnot uleibanot.*" She translated, "To build and be rebuilt, physically and spiritually. But we are worried now, after they joined the *Palmach*."

Otto remembered the ardent conversations between his friends. Sigmund's son joined the *Irgun*, an underground and very aggressive organization. *Why couldn't all Jews, for once, be on the same side of the fence?*

The one who regularly tried to make peace between the friends was Bruno Herbst, a lanky man, whose German wife had divorced him shortly after she became a member of the *National Sozialist Partei*. A former cabaret dancer, she was inflamed by the Nazi propaganda about the purity of the German race. "You Jews should go to Palestine," she told him. Without malice, he repeated it to his friends saying, "It was her best advice."

Mazal was Bruno's girlfriend, a Moroccan with luscious copper skin, eyes like two black pearls, and kinky hair in which no comb could make its way through. She wore big golden hoops in her ears and laughed wholeheartedly, showing her small regular teeth, when she tried to teach her *Yekim* friends the correct Hebrew pronunciation. The two women, "the *Shwarze*" as Charlotte called Mazal, and Charlotte, competed as to which of them could help Gretchen recuperate faster.

43

It would take a knife, Shifra felt, to cut the tension building around her. Lately Musa had acquired a new habit almost every evening; closing himself up in his mother's house and conferring with her. When Shifra asked him what was happening, his mouth was as closed as a bank vault. He became impatient even with Selim.

"Selim, not right now, I am tired," she heard him say when the child chimed, seeing his father return from work, "Abu Selim, Abu Selim, it's time we play!"

She knew how much Musa loved to hear his darling son call him "Selim's father."

If he wasn't busy with his mother, then he was at the *chaikhana*, or at meetings with the *mukhtar*. When he returned home frowns furrowed his forehead. Shifra still felt elated when Musa's arms tightened around her body, his warm breath on her nape, thrilling her as at the beginning of their marriage. But his attention to her had changed. Gone were the poems he recited while his eyes watched her like two burning coals. Gone too were the long caresses which made her body shiver with pleasure. He was always in a hurry.

At Musa's request, Ahmed started to teach Selim rudiments from the Koran and now the child was chanting them all day long, making her head spin. Though she still coached Nur on her English, and sometimes sewed dresses for Rama, Shifra felt that she had too much free time. She had finished sewing the skirt and blouse she made for herself. The hem of the skirt was just below the knee, but she didn't dare wear it yet.

She missed the time when she had been busy sewing and embroidering, when at the end of the day she was so tired that she'd fall asleep like a log. She didn't think much about the future then. She had a roof over her head, Samira hovered over her like a mother hen, and Musa made her heart beat faster anytime he looked at her. She tried to forget where she came from. Anytime she thought of her parents, she chased those memories away. For them she was dead. She was an outcast... *but was she really?*

Thinking of the day she met Chana on the beach, Shifra's heart cringed at how she lied to her old friend. Now she longed for her old way of life; she missed Shula and Chana and their open, confiding friendship. In her ears, Chana's shouts of surprise and happiness when she saw her that day on the beach, still rang.

And shortly after she found Musa's gun in the shed she realized that he, too, kept secrets. Would he ever tell her what he was doing with a gun in the middle of the night?

The visits with Otto Schroder and his wife were special. At the time she tried to convince herself that their enthusiasm about Selim's musical talent was the reason for her desire to go back. Now she knew that she found solace in their company, just as the violin music soothed her anxious soul.

Did their haste in moving out of Jaffa have anything to do with Musa's secrets? Or with Amina's letter postponing her visits to Palestine because she foresaw troubles in the near future? She remembered Otto's words, "My friends advised me to move. It is not safe for us to continue to live in Jaffa." Seeing her astonished eyes, he said, "Don't you read the newspapers? Don't you know what's happening? We are sitting on a bomb ready to explode."

Musa never brought newspapers home. Lately when she went shopping with Samira, Shifra became aware that Samira was watching her intensely when she stopped at a newspaper stand, "Don't throw Musa's money away; he knows better what you should read."

How long would she continue to live in a vacuum? Shifra was relieved when Musa told her that he planned to go to Jerusalem. "I am going on behalf of the bank. I'll be gone for a few days. It will be a chance to meet with cousin Abdullah. I hope I'll be able to see Na'ima, too."

He took her in his arms, "I'll not be gone for long. Don't worry." Seeing her clouded eyes he continued, "What would you like me to bring you? Silk for a blouse, or ribbons to braid in your beautiful hair?" When Musa smiled his frowns disappeared.

And now she was waiting for his departure, her head full of plans to spend the time he'd be away from home. It wouldn't be easy to find her way in Tel-Aviv. She'd been there only once, for a bar-mitzvah in her father's family. She remembered her father, looking at the streets bursting with groups of people who were laughing or seated around tables outside Beit Kafes, speaking loudly, watching passers-by. His words were full of contempt, "A city of *epicorsim*, nonbelievers, no fear or respect for the Almighty." And to her mother, "Tell the girls to keep their heads down. No need for them to watch this Sodom and Gomorrah debacle."

She knew the Schroders' new address, 31 Yehuda Halevi. She repeated it to herself every day. From fear that Samira might find it, she had torn the little paper into pieces. She would go alone. Maybe she could convince Samira to take Selim to the beach. The child had begged for a long time to go back to see the "big water." She would feign a headache. It would not be a complete lie. Lately, the restlessness tightening her heart made her temples throb, while her entire body felt weak.

Samira only smiled at her complaints, "Your sickness will soon have eyes. Inshallah, it will pass. But you certainly must rest."

Samira was happy to take Selim to the beach. "Just be careful," Shifra called after her, "Don't keep him in the sun too long; take his drinks and, please, don't let him get too close to the water."

After they left, Shifra feverishly readied herself for adventure. She put the new blouse, skirt and shoes into the bag she used when she went to the *souk*. She did not leave before watching Fatima's windows to make sure she wasn't being spied on. Dressed in her *jelebia* and *hijab*, Shifra knew that she wouldn't attract attention.

She would enter the St. Peter's church halfway between Jaffa and Tel-Aviv, go to the rest room and change clothes—enter as Suha and exit as Shifra. That was her plan. Then with the money she had saved at the *souk* the last few weeks, for which Samira clicked her tongue in admiration, "I didn't know you were such an expert shopper," she would pay the bus fare. Here her plan ended. She didn't know if she would find the street in Tel-Aviv or what she would do after she found it.

Shifra was lucky. Aside from two women kneeling in front of the altar, the church was empty. Shifra changed her clothes in a hurry, the smell of the burning candles giving her a headache. Outside she breathed with relief. For the first time she was not wearing stockings, as she did as a religious Jewish girl, nor the long *jelebia*, as an Arab woman. She felt embarrassed thinking that people could watch her naked legs, so she walked along the seashore.

Walking did not scare her. On Shabbat, her family would walk for hours from their Geula neighborhood to visit their uncle in Mea Shearim and back.

"Hey, *ialda*, hop up, we'll give you a lift." The Hebrew words startled her. The voice belonged to the driver of a small truck filled with watermelons, which stopped near her. Among the watermelons she saw two girls and a boy, about her age, smiling at her. They were dressed in short pants, and Shifra could see the tan of their naked arms and legs. Shifra hesitated.

"I don't have an entire day to wait for you to make up your mind," the driver said, "are you coming, yes, or no?"

The girls extended their arms to pull her up. "We are delivering the melons to *souk* Hacarmel," one of them said, while the other made a place for Shifra on the narrow bench. "My name is Aviva, this is Ayelet," she pointed to the second girl, "and Amnon here is the *leitzan*, the comedian of our moshav Yarkona."

"I am Shifra," Shifra found her tongue. She felt overwhelmed by the way her adventure was turning out. "I must've been dreaming. I guess I lost my way."

"Aren't you lucky?" said the girl called Ayelet. "Avram, our driver, knows Tel-Aviv like the back of his palm. Where are you going?"

"To Rehov Yehuda Halevi," Shifra answered.

"That's really close," Avram, following their conversation, remarked. For Shifra's benefit he continued to call the names of the streets he drove on, while Shifra tried to memorize the way, as well as note the turns he took.

"What number?" Avram asked.

"*Bevakasha*, please, leave me at the beginning of the street, I don't remember the number, but I know what the house looks like," Shifra lied. She hopped down from the truck, saying "*Toda raba*, Avram, many thanks to all of you, *lehitraot*, goodbye."

The boy called Yehuda said, "Hey, Shifrale, wait, catch this," and he threw a small watermelon into her arms, "Enjoy it!"

Shifra walked on the even-numbered side of the street, thinking how friendly and helpful the young farmers had been. She found a passage, across the street, from where she thought she could watch unobserved the house at No. 31. On the third-floor balcony a beautiful dark-haired woman with dangling earrings was hanging wet clothes on wires stretched in three rows outside the balcony. *Who was she?* Wasn't that the Schroder's apartment? Was she their helper?

"Mazal," called a plump woman walking out the front door of the house. "Mazal," she repeated, looking up, "are you done? It's time we take G'veret Schroder to the park." The woman rolled her R's with a strong German accent. Behind the woman, Shifra saw Gretchen Shroder's frail silhouette. When both women accompanying her were on the street, Gretchen Schroder raised her hand to protect her eyes from the sun. Suddenly Gretchen screamed, "Ruthie," pointing her finger at Shifra. "This is Ruthie, my sweet child," She opened her arms, "Ruthie, *Commen sie, bitte,* come, please."

The heavy set woman took Gretchen's arm, whispering in her ear, while Shifra squeezed behind a group of passers-by. The woman named Mazal was faster. Like an arrow, she crossed the street and tugged at Shifra's sleeve. "Who are you?" she asked. When Shifra didn't answer she repeated with impatience, "Who are you? Answer me."

At that moment the strident sound of an ambulance stopped all movement. Everyone, including Mazal, watched it. A British policeman appeared from nowhere and whistled for people to disperse. Feeling Mazal's grip on her arm lessen, Shifra quickly disengaged herself and disappeared in the crowds.

"It was too soon," she tried to calm the rapid beats of her heart while hurrying her steps. "That wasn't in my plan. I wanted only to see where they lived, maybe to hear the violin."

Shifra was still running long after she knew she was out of danger.

Now that they lived in Tel-Aviv and Lotte and Mazal were watching over Gretchen, Otto mostly walked home after the orchestra rehearsals. He liked to unwind after the intense work. It was October, his favorite month, which reminded him of Berlin in October when, holding Gretchen's arm, they would walk on Unter den Linden, under the trees' fine rain of flowers. One could not get much shade under Tel-Aviv's palm trees, but it was a short walk from the orchestra's residence on Rehov Balfour to his apartment.

Otto thought of the concert schedule for the month, Joseph Rosenstock conducting his friend from Berlin days, Szimon Goldberg, in the Mendelssohn violin concerto in Tel-Aviv and the Beethoven concerto in Jerusalem. "Beethoven for the connoisseurs, the *yekim* in Jerusalem," laughed one cellist, a *Sabra*.

Otto did not like the cellist or his big mouth. What worried him were the rumors concerning travel to Jerusalem, the terrifying fights between Arab and Jews. The concertmaster, who might have guessed Otto's thoughts and probably others' too, announced, "We will travel by armored car. We live through troubled times, but the show must go on. This will be a contribution to our brethren who fight to create a state for all of us."

Otto was thinking how he would break the news to Gretchen. When they lived in Jaffa, Nabiha was with her until late at night when he returned from Jerusalem or Haifa, but what would he do now?

He didn't realize that Lotte and Mazal were waiting for him. Lotte opened the door to her apartment and whispered, "Herr Schroder, Herr Schroder, please come in. We have to ask you a question."

Mazal was standing next to Lotte. *Where was Gretchen?*

Guessing his thought Mazal quickly said, "Your wife is asleep upstairs. She drank two cups of chamomile tea, and we watched over her until she calmed down. Now she sleeps peacefully."

"Something happened?" Otto asked alerted.

"Who is Ruthie?" Lotte asked in return.

Otto saw both women's eyes riveted on his lips. He never told his neighbors details about their family. But he wasn't going to lie. Otto swallowed hard, his mouth dry, "Ruthie was our daughter."

Otto's eyes became moist. "We don't know if she's still alive. I asked many people returning from the camps. No one knew about her. Neither did the Red Cross. I took great care to prepare Gretchen that Ruth might not be among the living," Otto took out a handkerchief to wipe his forehead, "but she refused to believe it."

"It's horrible, so horrible," he fell onto a chair, his hands covering his face.

Lotte put her hand on Otto's shoulder, while Mazal, looking reproachfully at Lotte, brought him a glass of water.

Otto struggled to stand on his feet with difficulty. "I have to go."

He stopped, "If my wife talked to you about Ruthie, why did you ask me who she was?"

Lotte turned to Mazal, "You tell him."

"We planned to take Mrs. Schroder to the park. I was hanging laundry on the balcony when Lotte, always thinking I'm going to be late, called—"

"Oh, you always talk and talk," Lotte interrupted her. "We were on our way when Gretchen pointed across the street and screamed, 'Ruthie, this is Ruthie, my Ruthie,' she was trembling, then Mazal—"

"I saw the girl," continued Mazal, "and crossed the street like a bullet. She was blonde, her eyes the color of sapphires. I took her arm, but she slipped from my hand and was gone. It must've been a coincidence. Mrs. Schroder became upset."

"Maybe it wasn't a coincidence," said Otto thoughtfully. The women looked at him, questions in their eyes.

"Did she have a little boy with her? Otto asked.

"No," said Mazal

"When we lived in Jaffa," Otto said, "a young Arab girl stopped many times to listen to me practicing. Gretchen loved to watch her. The girl's eyes were as blue as our Ruthie's, she said. We didn't see her for a long time, but when she showed up again she had a little boy with her. We got acquainted. We discovered that her son, the little boy, was a musical prodigy. Gretchen and I were fond of him." Otto fell silent. Then he raised his head.

"Please forgive me. I have to go attend to my Gretchen."

"What happened next?" asked Lotte, "Don't leave us in the middle of your story!"

"That's all. When I told her that we were moving to Tel-Aviv because the British didn't allow Jews to travel by night, she confessed that she was Jewish, too."

"That's all you know?" Mazal seemed disappointed. "No name or how to get in touch with her? Maybe this girl was abducted, maybe she's in danger."

"You, and your romantic soul!" exclaimed Lotte. "You read too many cheap five-piaster books."

"Why do you think she might be the girl we saw?" Mazal asked Otto. "Do you know her name?"

"She said her name was Suha. Our Arab maid knew her and her family."

"The girl we saw wasn't dressed like an Arab," Lotte said. "She was dressed like one of us."

"Now I remember. Her Hebrew name was Shifra." said Otto.

"Suha or Shifra," Lotte suddenly turned sour, "I hope, for Gretchen's sake, she'll not bother us anymore."

Otto picked up his violin and started to retreat, "I'm very sorry," he muttered.

But Mazal had one more question, "How did she know where to find you? Do you think she asked your Arab maid? Did you leave your new address with her?"

"Perhaps you'll think I made a mistake. After she told me she was Jewish; her Yiddish sounded so sweet, I was astounded. I scribbled our address and gave it to her. I said, if you ever need anything, here is where you'll find us."

Otto bowed and left. Lotte and Mazal remained standing looking at each other.

"What do you think?" Lotte asked after a long silence.

"The girl must be in trouble. Maybe we should find her," answered Mazal. "I scared her today, but I don't think we've seen the last of her. She'll come back."

"And give Gretchen a heart attack?" Lotte responded. "Are you ready for another crisis?"

"Maybe by helping this girl, we can help Gretchen, too."

"Mazal, what's cooking in your head full of straw?"

"If my head is full of straw," Mazal smiled, "you'll have to fill yours with a lot of patience, my dear lady," Mazal curtsied, "because I'm not going to tell you."

Mazal left laughing, her earrings tinkling. She stopped for a second in front of the Schroders' apartment. It was quiet. Pleased, she mounted the last flight of steps to her lover's apartment.

Panting and out of breath, Shifra finally stopped running. While her heartbeat returned to normal, she observed the crowds around her, groups of people gesticulating, laughing and slapping each other's backs; some were eating falafel, others spitting pistachio shells, young boys barely making their way balancing tea glass trays on their heads.

Shifra walked slowly, reading the names of the streets, trying to remember the ones Avram drove his truck on earlier. People talked so loudly that Shifra could easily make out their conversation.

"It's only through negotiations that we can succeed. Patience, only one more month until we hear what the United Nations decides," a middle-aged man said, "Why rush into action?"

"Foolish dreamer, like the ones who went to the slaughterhouse," his friend said. "You know that we can't expect anything good from the goyim. Where were they in '42, '43?" The man rolled up his sleeve and Shifra could see the blue seal of a number. "I swore on my parents' memory that nothing like it would ever happen to my children."

"You are right, Hershel," said a young man who joined them. He wore khaki shorts and a *kova tembel*, "It's only Begin's Etzel, and not Ben-Gurion's Haganah which could solidify a Jewish state."

Though she wanted to hear more, Shifra did not stop walking. She was afraid to attract attention to herself. She crossed the street, her mind in turmoil. *What were they talking about?* She understood their Hebrew, but the names she heard were unknown to her.

Shifra saw a man pointing to the newspaper in his hand. "We Jews are like a drop in a sea full of Arabs. We have to be cautious if we want to obtain statehood."

"This country is ours! It belongs to us. We were here more than two thousand years ago," a man wearing a skullkap answered.

With so much tension in the air, Shifra felt her head would explode. She turned onto a street lined with cypress trees. Two women, perhaps mother and daughter, sat at an improvised outdoor café. "You can't marry him, a man without a profession. How is he going to make a living? Stealing?" the older woman screamed.

"We love each other. We'll work," the girl answered. "We are young, a beautiful future awaits us. We will join a *hashomer hatzair* kibbutz, and raise strong, free children."

Oh, how much she wished she had that girl's courage, Shifra thought.

From afar, Shifra still heard the mother crying, "Do it and you'll kill us both, your father and me!"

The smell of fried onions and garlic filled Shifra's nostrils. Women cooked the midday meal with their kitchen windows open. In a narrow alley Shifra saw a man's arms clasped around a young woman's waist. "Let me go," she said, struggling.

"Not before you kiss me." the man nuzzled the girl's neck.

"Here in the street? Itzik, you have no shame. What would the neighbors say?"

"Everybody knows I love you." His mouth closed on hers.

How beautiful life can be, thought Shifra. She suddenly panicked. She had to return home! Hurriedly she passed a flower vendor. "Hey, *Yafeyfia*, you gorgeous one," he called. Shifra wasn't sure he meant her. He threw a rose in her direction "Pin it in your hair," he winked. "Come by tomorrow and I'll fill your arms with flowers."

Shifra ran. What was she going to do now? She couldn't return to change clothes in the church. It was dangerous. Yet, she had to become Suha again. She heard the noise of a creaking gate. The house behind it seemed deserted. She could hear only the wind and her heartbeats. Quickly she took out the large *jelebia* from her bag, wide enough to slip over her blouse and skirt. Then she knotted the *hijab* under her chin.

On her way to the bus station she saw on an empty bench, the scattered pages of a Hebrew newspaper. She snatched it and put it in her bag underneath the watermelon. She would read it during Selim's afternoon nap, when the house was quiet. She would better understand what was going on.

Waiting for the Jaffa bus, Shifra recalled the day's adventure. Why hadn't she planned what she was going to do after setting eyes on the Schroders' flat? *What were her expectations?* She could still hear Gretchen Schroder's outburst. It had caught her totally unprepared. What would Gretchen and the other two ladies think of her running away? It seemed that she could never escape from making mistakes.

With a screeching noise, Jaffa's old yellow bus stopped in front of her. An exhausted Suha mounted the two steps. It had been a draining experience.

Samira and Selim were not at home when she arrived. Shifra breathed relief, but only for a minute. *Where could they be so late?* Her first impulse was to hide the newspaper, but she was impatient to read it. She smoothed the wrinkled pages of *DAVAR*. Her eyes ran over the headlines; for the first time she was reading a newspaper written in the *lushen kodesh*.

LATEST NEWS ABOUT UNSCOP

At Hotel Eden in Jerusalem, the United Nations' Special Committee on Palestine (UNSCOP) has finished its consultations with Jewish, Arab and British representatives. The committee favors the idea of partition, two states, side by side, Jewish and Arab, with Jerusalem being an International City under UN control and presented its conclusion to the General Assembly on October 9.

In the name of the Jewish Agency, Ben-Gurion has accepted the partition, but Irgun's spokesman, Menachem Begin, rejected it saying, "Jerusalem belongs only to Jews." Meanwhile the Palestinian Arabs as well as all Arab countries are furious and promise to boycott and fight the Commission's proposal.

Shifra did not fully comprehend what she read. She did not understand the meaning of the words: United Nations, General Assembly, UNSCOP. Only this afternoon on the streets of Tel-Aviv she had heard for the first time the names Ben-Gurion and Begin. *Who were they?* Her father had never mentioned those names. Did the Jewish Agency or Irgun represent her family also? Those questions burned her lips. *Who could she ask?* Not Musa, for sure. *How about Mr. Nathan?* It would be easier to ask him rather than return to Tel-Aviv. She could find a reason to go to the bazaar the next day.

Her eyes jumped to another headline. **NEW GARIN WILL START A KIBBUTZ NEAR NAHARYA.** Shifra started to read slowly, her lips moving to the rhythm of the words.

The members of the new kibbutz, Iehi-Am, are mostly young immigrants from Hungary, Holocaust survivors and former Hashomer Hatzair members.

Shifra closed her eyes and saw the girl at the outdoor café who told her mother about joining a kibbutz with her future husband. Maybe Iehi-Am was the kibbutz where she wanted to raise strong, fearless children, strong like Aviva, Ayelet, Avram, with whom she had shared the ride to Tel-Aviv. How she envied their easygoing ways.

What she read next made her blood freeze. **PALMACH, OUR YOUNG ELITE FIGHTERS, ESCORT CONVOYS OF ARMORED TRUCKS BRINGING FOOD AND WATER TO JERUSALEM.**

Did Jerusalem lack food? Shifra remembered going with her mother to the Mahane Yehuda *souk* to shop for Shabbat, where mountains of fresh fruits and vegetables waited for customers. They never had enough money for the goods spread before them. Anxiously she read:

Our Palmach young boys and girls are real heroes. Armed only with home-made guns they risk their lives guarding the convoys from the Arab terrorists attacking from the heights of the hills surrounding Jerusalem.

Those were the lovely hills changing colors from eerie pink to shadows of deep blue which she admired on her bus trip from Jerusalem to Jaffa. Oh, my God, could Mahmood be one of those attacking the trucks? He and his friends dancing the Dekba at Na'ima's wedding, and screaming, "We'll get rid of the Brits and the Yahudim too!" At the time she thought they were drunk.

Because of daily threats and danger, she read, the British police had divided Jerusalem into security zones, encircled by wires. People trying to bypass the curfew were arrested.

Jerusalem is under siege. Shifra's temples throbbed. *What was happening?* She could not believe that her father could be barred from going to shul. Is it possible that her brothers and sisters lacked food? Were they waiting for the trucks from Tel-Aviv to deliver water as the paper says?

Her heart ached remembering how fussy her mother was about having the cleanest tablecloth and napkins, especially for Shabbat. *Oh, Shabbat! Is there enough flour in the cupboards for my mother to bake challah?* Her eyes filled with tears.

Musa's rifle! *Why does he keep it, and keep it hidden? What did she know about the man she had married, other than that she was in love with him? Was he prepared to kill her brethren?*

The gate squeaked. Shifra quickly hid the newspaper and wiped her eyes.

"Where have you been so late?" she called even before opening the door.

"Where have *you* been?" retorted Samira in an angry voice.

"I dreamed of watermelons," Shifra answered quickly, "So I went to the *souk* and bought one. Here it is."

"Eumi, Eumi, look what Jedati Fatima gave me," Selim shouted happily. He proudly displayed two small toys, Arab soldiers dressed in kafias, with rifles on their backs. "Jedati Fatima said that soon we'll go on a big trip, where I'll see many beautiful places."

"What's this?" Shifra questioned Samira, who took her time before answering, "Since you weren't home we went to see Sit Fatima. Don't pay attention to Selim. He didn't understand…"

"But I did," the child said stubbornly. "You said to her, I'm too old to travel, Sit Fatima, when Jedati said that you'll come with us."

"Go play now," Samira frowned. "A child shouldn't listen to old people's talk."

"Let's cut the watermelon," Shifra proposed while her mind was racing. She needed answers to her questions and the time seemed shorter with every day that passed.

I am growing old, Samira thought, *and I can't seem to be in step with what's happening around me.* She couldn't understand Fatima's overwhelming news, when, after returning from the beach with Selim, and discovering that Suha wasn't home, she entered her former mistress' house. Her first thought was, *where could Suha have gone? She had complained of a headache earlier.* Then Samira remembered that she saw her wearing a pair of shoes she had not seen before. *Why new shoes? For the souk, a pair of slippers would serve as well. She is quite secretive lately. Are those the caprices of a pregnant woman?*

"In what world do you live, Samira?" Sit Fatima asked, seeing how perplexed Samira became after she was told about the war they would all soon face." Such a war as we have never seen before."

"What do you mean, Sit Fatima?" Samira asked, though she remembered observing, while shopping at the *souk*, how tense and agitated people were. Fewer people sat in front of the *chaikhana* smoking a *nargilea*, or playing *shesh-besh*. They were snatching the newspapers out of the vendors' hands, without even demanding the change back.

Although now she worked for Musa, Samira felt that Fatima would always be her mistress. She could not erase thirty years of being together. Waiting for Fatima to talk, Samira saw new wrinkles on her face, wrinkles she had not seen before, and her luscious black hair streaked with white threads.

"The world nowadays is not as we knew it, Samira. We have no control over our lives, not anymore," Fatima blurted.

She stopped and Samira was sure Fatima would speak again about Amina marrying her Brit and leaving home, or about Na'ima's unhappy marriage. She wouldn't complain about Musa and Suha, with Selim playing at their feet. She knew the child understood everything.

"We'll have to leave, Samira. We'll have to leave the country. Cousin Abdullah says the sooner the better."

Samira felt that her heart would stop. She cried, "What do you mean, leave the country, where do you want to go? Are you making fun of me in my old age?"

"Now the governments of other countries hold our future in their hands." Fatima said, sadly. "They want to divide our land, the land of our fathers and grandfathers, to split Palestine between the Yahudim and us. The decision has been made, but we don't accept it. The entire Arab world is on our side. As I said, it will be war, a terrible war. We have to protect ourselves."

Samira was scared and she didn't want to hear anymore, but Fatima would not stop. "Egypt and Syria, Lebanon and Jordan, and our own Arab Legion fighters are getting ready. A bloodbath awaits this country, and the Arab Brotherhood advises us to leave."

Fatima must have seen the fear creeping over Samira, because she added quickly, "*Inshallah,* we will return when it's all over. We'll be gone for only a short time. And Samira," she patted her servant's hand, "Be assured we aren't going to leave you behind. You'll come with us."

"I don't know, Sit Fatima. My bones are too old to travel. I'd better stay here and watch over your property." Tears blinded Samira's eyes.

Selim asked suddenly, his lips trembling, "Jedati Fatima takes Selim too?"

Neither Fatima nor Samira had paid attention to Selim, who had stopped playing and was listening. Fatima took him in her arms, "Oh, the light of my eyes, the love of my old age, it's you I'm thinking of first."

"My Eumi and Abu too?"

"Yes, yes," Fatima said impatiently. "But this is a secret. Can you keep a secret, Selim?"

The child nodded proudly. But minutes later, when Samira and Selim entered Musa's house, it was the first thing that came out of his mouth. Suha's face reflected surprise, followed by fear.

"Don't pay attention to him," Samira hurriedly said, but Selim continued, "All of us will go, you, Eumi and Abu Selim, too. Jedati Fatima has promised. Only Samira said she's too old to go. Eumi, please ask Samira to come with us." He started crying and kicked his feet, "I am not going without Jedati Samira."

Oh, my sweet angel, you touched Jedah Samira's heart. Instead she said, in a harsh voice, "Stop talking nonsense, Selim. Samira will give you a glass of fresh-squeezed orange juice and you'll go take your nap."

It was too late to find out what Suha's real reason for leaving the house was, thought. Samira, who didn't believe her words, that she craved watermelon. *She couldn't fool me. I'll have to watch her more closely, especially now. Does she suspect why Fatima wants to leave? Has Musa told her?*

I need to talk to someone, Shifra thought. *Will Musa answer me if I ask him straight out if there is going to be a war? And if he said yes, should I ask on which side he will fight? Maybe there is not going to be a war, and I am only tormenting myself. Then what about the rifle in the shed, and his secret conversations with his mother?*

Shifra hoped so much that the visit with the Schroders would clear up her burning questions. Now while Samira watched her like a hawk, she suspected that it would be too dangerous to try to go there again. She suspected that Samira never believed the watermelon story.

"What happened here?" Samira cried when she walked in and saw the broken fragments of the clock's glass on the kitchen floor.

"What's gotten into you?" She sounded angry, "You know that you can't reach that high. Musa is going to be upset."

"I wanted to clean it and it fell out of my hand. Please, no word to Musa. I am going to the bazaar to Mr. Nathan's shop. I hope he can replace the glass on the spot. I saw he has all sizes. If you don't tell Musa, nobody will know," Shifra answered.

Was Samira convinced? She looked doubtful, but at the end she said, "If I didn't have to help Sit Fatima for the guests coming tonight, I'd go with you." After a second she added, "I don't know who they are but the *mukhtar* stopped by yesterday and talked to her at great length and asked her to host two foreigners. That's all I was told," Samira added when seeing Suha's eyes open wide.

"It won't take me long," Suha assured Samira. "Ask Nur, who has no school today, to play with Selim. I can't carry the clock and watch him too."

Shifra never walked so fast. When she reached Mr. Nathan's store, the shutters were closed. Where could he be? She saw spider webs hanging along the shutters. Anxiously, she went to the back of the bazaar where vendors delivered merchandise. Picking up her *jelebia*, she walked on the unpaved path to the back of the watchmaker's store.

"God be praised," whispered Shifra, when she saw the door slightly open. Inside, it was completely dark.

"Is anybody here?" she called, as she stepped in. From somewhere a figure appeared. It was Habib. He rubbed his eyes. "Is this you, Sit Masri?" he asked and immediately bowed, "*Salaam Aleikum, Salaam Aleikum.* I don't know if I can find a chair for you in this mayhem."

After Shifra got used to the dark, she saw the broken windows, the overturned working table, and Mr. Nathan's magnifying glass in pieces, "What happened here, where is Mr. Nathan?"

"Oh, mistress, hoodlums have attacked our store. Fortunately, I was the only one here, and I hid behind a cupboard. They screamed,

'Where is the Yahud, where is Nathan?' but when they didn't find him, they broke what you see, then left."

"Why, why?" Fear gripped Shifra's heart.

"Because the Arabs don't want us,—Jews—here." Shifra heard Mr. Nathan's voice. He had entered surreptitiously and now faced Shifra.

"I came," Shifra started while unpacking the clock, "because I broke the glass and I'm afraid Musa will be very upset with me." She was almost in tears.

"Dear lady, as you see, they stole most of my tools and what's left doesn't amount to much. Habib is helping me with what can be saved from this disaster as I move to my new place in Tel-Aviv."

"Are you moving?" Shifra asked with a tremor in her voice.

"Of course," Mr. Nathan's eyes penetrated hers, "I am not going to stay here and wait to be slaughtered, but you shouldn't worry for me, Musa Masri's wife."

Shifra gathered all her courage, "I need to talk to you too, but…." she glanced in Habib's direction.

"Habib, come here," commanded Mr. Nathan. "Do me a favor. Sit Masri needs her clock fixed. Go to Abu-Amir, across the street. I taught him our profession. Tell him that for the money he owes me, I am asking him to put a new glass on this clock. Go right away. Neither Sit Masri nor I have time to wait."

After Habib left, Mr. Nathan asked, "Does Sit Fatima know that you are here?"

Shifra shook her head.

"I guessed as much," Mr. Nathan said. He was rummaging inside a broken case and sighed with relief, bringing out two heavy silver candelabras. *"Baruch Hashem,"* he whispered in Hebrew, then for her in Arabic, "those candelabras belonged to my grandmother. She brought them from Egypt to Morocco, then all the way here."

"Adon Nathan," Shifra started hesitantly, "I am frightened by things happening right now. I know I can trust you." She cried, "I live in a bubble, Musa doesn't tell me anything. I just found out that Fatima wants to leave the country and take the family with her."

"So it is," Mr. Nathan said with bitterness. "*Sauve qui peut*, people with means are quick to save their skin," he added. "So how can I help you? What do you want from me?"

Shifra let the *hijab* fall at her feet, freeing her curly blond hair. She whispered in Hebrew, "I was born Jewish. I took the *Al-Shahada* because Musa said it was the only way we could get married. Don't mistake me, I love him with all my heart, but the same heart tells me not to leave. Please help me. I am scared...."

As she spoke, she saw the surprise mounting in Mr. Nathan's eyes. He muttered, "My suspicion was correct." To her, he said, "Young lady, I can't advise you what to do. It's too big a responsibility. What about your parents? What do they say?"

"I am an orphan," Shifra blushed deeply.

"I am sorry," Mr. Nathan said softly. "I think that you'll find the answer in yourself."

He peered through the shutters. "I see Habib returning with your clock." He signaled to Shifra to cover her head. Quickly scribbling on a piece of paper, he handed it to her. "Here you can find me if you need more restorations."

Habib entered breathlessly, and Mr. Nathan took the clock from his moist hand. "It's good to still have a few good friends here, Sit Masri. Habib is one of them."

Looking into Shifra's eyes he added, "He's going to watch over the store for me."

Shifra bowed her head, "*Shukran*, thank you to both of you."

She stretched her arms to pick up the clock, but Mr. Nathan objected. "Sit Masri, let Habib carry the clock and see you home. Please convey my respects to Sit Fatima."

At their gate, Shifra turned to Habib, who had followed her in silence, "Thank you," she said, taking the clock and squeezing a few piastres into his hand.

"Honored lady, Mrs. Musa Masri," Habib started timidly. He stuttered. It was clear to Shifra that he wasn't used to talking to ladies of her status.

Gathering courage, he continued, "If you'll ever need me, I want you to know that I guard the store day and night. I sleep near the back door."

Then he slipped away.

44

"Don't kid yourself, Musa, my boy. The war has already started," Abdullah said impatiently. "How long are you going to wait before making a decision?" He had called Musa's office in Jaffa almost daily. Due to Abdullah's high position, nobody bothered Musa during those calls.

Abdullah's words echoed in Musa's head during the monotonous train ride from Jaffa to Jerusalem. Since he was a little boy, he had been in love with trains. His father used to smile when he told him that he wanted to be a train conductor. "You are meant to do better things, my son," Faud had said.

Now he was at such an impasse. Musa, who considered Abdullah not only his mentor but a second father, was on his way to discuss with him the future of their family.

It isn't fair, Musa reflected, while the train passed orange groves, some known to him since his childhood; that at my age I have to make such important decisions. In light of the latest events, Fatima, no doubt influenced by Abdullah, was pushing him to leave Jaffa, maybe even the country. But where would he go, to Jerusalem, Ramalla, Aman?

"The Arab High Committee has decided to call for a three-day strike in Jerusalem and other cities," Abdullah told Musa in one of his calls, "but when I went out into the streets, I found only about fifty people, without a leader, and a lot of chaos."

On the evening before Musa left for Jerusalem, his mother was visited by the *mukhtar*. He came to ask her to host "two Iraqi volunteers who are coming to fight alongside us, Palestinians. I expect that each of our families will do its duty and contribute to our holy war."

Fatima's face turned pale. Musa knew what she was thinking. The Iraqis were known as rough, coarse people, and she had two daughters to protect, especially Nur, who at fifteen was as ripe as a peach. Musa was stricken by another thought too: Suha, his wife, alone at home, while he would be burning with worry at the office. Two households full of women, and he, Musa, their only protector, away from them.

The *mukhtar* had more to say: "The city guard I am organizing needs people like you, Musa Ibn Faud. I know that I can count on you. I don't doubt your love for your country nor your patriotism."

The train had left the plain and now, puffing and squeaking, was mounting the hills toward Jerusalem. The skies looked gray, *even the skies seemed to weep for what was happening in this country*. Musa's mind returned to the scene of his parting that morning. Suha nestled in his arms as if she didn't want to let go. He felt her shaking slightly as he kissed her. When she asked why he had to leave so abruptly, he pulled away. "It's a business trip," he said. "But I'm glad I'll be visiting with cousin Abdullah, and I'll steal some time to see Na'ima, Mahmood and their boys."

She clung to him so lovingly that he was already sorry he was parting. *Could she be pregnant?* As much as he would love another boy, it could not be a worse time. Musa sighed. One doesn't choose the time to be born, Allah decides these matters. If only he could find out why Suha seemed so strange lately! *Women are such a mystery.*

Slowly the train entered the Jerusalem station. Musa heard that the British had divided the city into sections, and the train station was in a section controlled by them and close to Bakha, Abdullah's neighborhood. Abdullah had encouraged him to take the train rather than coming by bus. "Though our Arab rebels control the hills, it's still safer to travel by train," he advised.

What awaits me here that I am not aware of already? Musa asked himself as he entered the rose garden of his cousin's stately house.

"*Salaam Aleikum,*" Abdullah, with his wife and three daughters, welcomed him in one voice.

"*Aleikum Salaam,*" Musa replied, bowing to the ladies while he bent to kiss Abdullah's hand. Instead, Abdullah hugged him and kissed him on both cheeks.

"Let's go into my study," Abdullah said after Musa was served with the traditional sorbet and nana water. "We won't be disturbed there."

Abdullah's voice was serious. "The situation is critical," Abdullah said, before asking, as usual, about the well-being of Fatima and the other members of Musa's family.

"We are poorly prepared for war. As I told you, the strike was disorganized; it ended by breaking windows, looting and setting fire to stores on King George and Ben-Yehuda streets. Of course, the Jews were quick to retaliate by blowing up the Semiramis Hotel."

"Can't the British control the situation? Their Mandate isn't over until May. It's their duty to protect the people."

"They couldn't care less. After the British Government announced that they would evacuate their forces from Palestine on May 14, they refused to involve themselves further."

"What's most disquieting is the fact that the Mufti wants to command the war from his hiding place in Cairo," Abdullah continued, "Syria and Iraq dislike the idea of the Mufti calling the shots. King Abdullah of Jordan is in doubt if he'd ally himself with the others. Musa, if the leaders of the Arab countries don't agree among themselves, we might suffer the consequences."

"What you just said is new to me," Musa felt as if a bucket of ice had poured over his head. "Maybe I was too optimistic in thinking that we could resolve our differences without bloodshed. I doubted that the Yahudim would want a war after so many of their brethren were killed by Hitler not so long ago. Couldn't we find a way—"

Angry, Abdullah stopped him, "Musa, are you blind or deaf? I don't want to hear more of this nonsense. You are a man responsible for your family. Everybody waits for you to decide their future, your mother, your brother your sisters, and the little boy you fathered." Abdullah shouted, "It's time to prove that the man they love and respect is worthy of their trust."

Musa had never seen his cousin so upset. He thought of the *mukhtar* obliging his mother to host two Iraqi "volunteers" in her house. He shivered.

"Of course I want to protect my family. I'd gladly give my life for them. I think I knew what was on your mind, but I wanted to hear it straight from your mouth."

"My boy, I love you as if you were my own son. All I want is to make sure that your family is not going to suffer during the approaching bloodshed. Your mother has amassed enough money in Cairo, Aman and Alexandria banks for you to live comfortably. When the fighting is over—and hopefully soon, as our Arab allies promise—we will all return to our homes. Other people in your mother's position have left already."

A flood of thoughts crossed Musa's mind. How could he face the *mukhtar*? He would certainly think Musa was a traitor. What about his own pride, and his deceased father's pride? What would Faud do in his place?

What about Suha? He felt a pinch in his heart. He had not told her anything. Would he be able to persuade her to leave Jaffa or would she agree to it without objecting?

"And Mahmood," Musa asked, "is he ready to leave?"

"Not Mahmood!" Abdullah said. "He's made of another alloy. He fights in al-Jihad al-Mukaddas led by Abdul Kader al-Husseini, Mufti's representative. They are enforcing the siege at Bab al-Wad to prevent the Jewish supplies and men from reaching Jerusalem's Jewish quarters."

The Barclays Bank messenger brought Musa's letters, one for his mother, one for his wife, delivering them both to Samira. Musa had been gone for more than a week, and the letters were the first signs that he was alive and well.

Suha snatched her letter and opened it with trembling fingers. With a gesture of her hand she dismissed Samira. *Musa, my boy, you chose the worst time to leave for Jerusalem.* Samira sighed and readied herself to deliver the second letter to Fatima. Since the two soldiers from Iraq arrived, boisterous and commanding, Samira had grown cautious and avoided them when she could.

It was a nice day, the rains had stopped and Selim, cooped up in the house for the last couple of days, asked to play outside. Samira took him along with her on her errand. They were traversing the courtyard, when the soldiers, bursting noisily, came out.

"Boy, come here," one of them called. Selim hesitated. "Come, come, we want to show you something," the one with the silver tooth said. Selim looked scared.

"I'll go with you," Samira pushed the child in front of her. "The uncles are good people."

"They are not my uncles," cried Selim. "I want my father, I want Abu Selim."

Samira saw Shifra and Fatima watching the scene behind their closed windows. At the beginning, the men played with Selim, throwing him from one to another, like a rubber ball. The child laughed.

"You see, Selim," Samira said, relieved, "you have no reason to be afraid."

"We'll teach you to be fearless. A sheik's son should be brave," the unshaven one said.

He took the rifles propped against the wall. "Let's show him," he said to the second soldier, who seemed uncertain of the first one's intention. They put the rifle muzzles under the child's armpits. "Hold on to them," the first one commanded. In a second they lifted him up in the air while Selim clutched the muzzles with his small hands.

Howling, Fatima ran out of her house.

Panicked, Samira shrieked, "In Allah's name, what are you doing? Put the boy down immediately!"

They laughed.

Wailing, Selim urinated in his pants.

Samira took the shaken child in her arms. "Despicable men," she spat on the ground, though she wanted to spit on them, "Shame on you, to frighten a small child."

Thank Allah, Suha was not in sight. But when Samira entered Musa's house, carrying Selim, she found her unconscious on the floor.

"Eumi, Eumi," Selim cried.

Samira threw cold water on Suha's face and was able to arouse her. Later, Suha shivered even under the warm shawls Samira enveloped her in. After both Suha and Selim were settled comfortably, Samira discovered that she still held the second letter.

Fatima opened the door, her finger on her lips commanding silence. The fear of the Iraqi soldiers made her house as quiet as a tomb. In her bedroom Fatima eagerly opened Musa's letter. Her face went pale as she read it: she handed it to Samira without a word. Samira started to read it aloud, slowly deciphering his dense writing,

Jerusalem, December 1947

Salaam Aleikum, Dear Eumi, My Honored Mother,

Cousin Abdullah has shared with me his thoughts and worries about our immediate future. I am grateful to him for the concern he's always shown our family.

I haven't yet spoken with Mahmood. If it will come to pass that we leave Palestine, even for the shortest time, I think that neither you nor I would want to do it without Na'ima and her family.

Unfortunately, the visit with Na'ima filled my heart with sadness. If I leave and take the children with me, she cried, Mahmood will find us and kill me.

I know how fanatic Mahmood is, cousin Abdullah knows it too, yet I want to convince Mahmood that Abdullah's plan is wise. Leaving Na'ima's house, I couldn't stop thinking that not all marriages are made in heaven like mine."

Samira stopped reading and looked at Fatima. Seeing no reaction, she continued.

Yesterday, I went with cousin Abdullah to Ein-Karem, the beautiful village in the valley west of Jerusalem. One of the bank's clients defaulted on his payments and his house was slated for foreclosure.

"I want to sell it," the man said, "but in these unstable times who would buy it?"

I suddenly thought that with some restoration the house could be a nice, cool summer place for us. We'd all be happy to stay away from Jaffa's

merciless summer sun. I gave the man a deposit. He kissed my hand in gratitude.

"Can you believe this?" Fatima screamed. Samira was startled; it had been a long time since she had seen her mistress so angry.

Though it is winter, and the rains never seem to stop, I don't think it will take long for the house to be fixed up. Meanwhile I will work in Abdullah's bank while I keep an eye on the builder.

Dear Eumi, I think that we should all wait in Ein Karem to see how events develop further. There is no need to rush.

Your faithful son, Musa

Samira looked at Fatima. "What are you going to do?" she asked cautiously. "Are you going to answer him?"

Fatima burst into rage, "What's going on with him? Is he irresponsible? Why does he want to stall our departure? Does he realize the danger we are in? Did I raise my son to be a coward? I am going to order him to come home immediately. There is no time to waste. He doesn't know the danger his son, and all of us are in since the arrival of our guests."

She sat at her desk and started writing, while Samira, with fear in her heart, made her way back to Musa's house and the other letter. She was wondering what he wrote to his wife and whether Suha would tell her.

Though nestled under a mountain of blankets, Shifra felt frozen. Since the terrible afternoon when the Iraqi soldiers played cat and mouse with her child, laughing as they tossed him up in the air, she could not stop shaking. A feeling of dread had taken root in her heart. Musa was away when his son needed him most!

Now what she had from him was a letter! *Not a piece of paper ... Musa, you should be home to protect your family.* Her trembling hands found it difficult to tear open the envelope.

> *To my sweet wife, Suha, My Dove, Salaam Aleikum!*
> *It's hard for me to be away from you and from our son, for whom I constantly pray to Allah to grant a long life. Yet I have to ask you for more patience, because I am delaying my return. For a good reason! I'll tell you about it when I get home. I'm sure you'll be pleased!*
> *Take care, my love, and don't spoil Selim too much,*
>
> *Musa*

While still puzzled by Musa's letter, Shifra heard Samira' steps approach her door. The older woman coughed. *Has she caught cold?* Shifra wouldn't be surprised. *The ceilings in the Arab houses are so high that it makes it impossible to heat the rooms properly. Maybe she coughed to let me know she was back.* Shifra wanted to know what Musa had written to his mother, but she felt tired. She closed her eyes. She heard Samira gently open her door; stand for a minute, then retreat.

Shifra knew Samira was worried about her, particularly about her loss of appetite. The more Samira pushed, the less she ate. After seeing the two Iraqi soldiers holding Selim at the tip of their bayonets, Shifra could not stop throwing up.

A worried Samira said, "You have to see Uhm Zaide," her face wrinkled with concern.

"I was so afraid Selim would fall and die," Shifra said, her eyes filling with tears,

"Ssh, it's over. Nobody will touch a hair on Selim's head. Not as long as I live," Samira said.

Yet almost every day, Samira insisted Shifra should call on Uhm Zaide.

"If not Uhm Zaide," Samira said, disappointed, "maybe we should go to the English nuns. They might know of a cure," though Shifra could guess from her tone that Samira had doubts. As sick as she felt, Shifra wouldn't see Uhm Zaide nor would she consult the English nuns.

She dreamed of resting in her mother's arms, while her mother sang a forlorn Jewish song. In her dream, following her mother's song, she heard the siren of an ambulance. *Where did she hear that lately?* Feverishly awake now, Shifra searched her memory. Yes, it was on Yehuda Halevi, the street where the violin teacher lived. People said that a hospital was close by. *Was that an omen?*

For a few nights the dream returned, first her mother's song, then the siren's howl. *What was the dream telling her?* It surely had a meaning: go back, go back.

Otto's image floated before her eyes. Yes, her dream had a meaning. She has to go back! To see Otto, to confide in him and ask for his advise; Otto, in whose eyes she saw the love and care for her son, was the only person whose sincerity she did not doubt.

But could she leave home without arousing Samira's suspicions? She is so worried about me; especially after I refused to see Uhm Zaide, or go to the English convent.

"I need a doctor, a woman doctor," I'll say to her, "and soon." I know that Samira suspects that I am pregnant. "I am out of the pills she had prescribed for me and my headaches kill me." *What should I do if Samira opposes this or if she wants to go with me? I'll be adamant,* "Musa trusts me, and so should you. You don't want me to complain to Musa about your attitude, when he returns home."

With or without Samira acquiescence, she would go the coming Friday afternoon, when Otto surely would be home. Shifra remembered that when he lived in Jaffa, he used to teach home on Friday afternoons.

45

Otto felt relaxed sitting in the familiar ambiance of the Grubers' home, with its needlepoint curtains, and Charlotte's family portraits on the wall, her mustached grandfather, looking like Emperor Franz Joseph, holding the chain of his onion-sized vest watch, standing proudly behind the chair, where his petite wife was seated holding three children on her lap. Lotte never missed a chance to point out that she was the youngest of them.

During that night of terror when Otto had dragged an unconscious Gretchen out of their house, photos weren't on his mind. His thoughts were focused only on the need to escape from Germany. It pained him to watch the display of Charlotte's family pictures when he had not been able to save one image of his daughter Ruthie.

After a tiring day of rehearsals with the Palestine Philharmonic Orchestra, Otto was grateful for the cup of steaming coffee and the *apple strudel* Charlotte placed in front of him. Yasha Horenstein, whom Otto knew from Berlin, was a very demanding conductor, and though the members of the Orchestra were anxious about an imminent war, Yasha wasn't going to lower his standards.

"In times of turmoil, making good music is our way to encourage the young fighters, and to let them know, that on the home front, everything is all right."

Though the conversation in the Gruber home was always about politics, to which he had little to contribute, Otto felt good to be included, that feeling of *gemutlichkeit*, the comfort and intimacy of being among friends. The thought that from the beginning they should have lived in Tel-Aviv, rather than Jaffa, nagged Otto again. But what was done couldn't be undone. Otto was grateful to Charlotte Gruber and to Mazal for the time they spent with his Gretchen. It was clear to him that she liked being with both of them, as different as they were from one another. She conversed in German with Charlotte, but both women were serious about teaching her Hebrew.

Sie leben in diesem Land, müssen Sie sprechen ihre Sprach, when you live in this country, you must speak its language, Otto heard Charlotte say time and again when Gretchen complained that it was too hard, or she was too old to learn Hebrew.

"Nonsense," answered Charlotte, who wouldn't take no for an answer.

Mazal, twenty years younger, brushed Gretchen's now mostly gray hair as she whispered in her ear, "You are beautiful."

"Only conversation, *b'ivrit kala*, in easy Hebrew, commanded Charlotte, and Gretchen, like the good student she once was, tried hard. Otto noticed that her nightmares had become less frequent.

Sigmund Hochmeister, the bass player, with the perennial cigar in his mouth, played with the radio knobs. "Nine o'clock, time to hear the broadcast from *Kol Zion Halochemet.*"

"You are obsessed with Etzel. Begin should listen to Ben-Gurion. This should be a time of restraint, not of war. At least until May, when the British Mandate ends," said Hugo Gruber.

"You want us to sit with our arms crossed, when every day we lose people? We are no cowards, *nicht so*, Otto?" asked Sigmund, Sigi to his friends.

Bruno Herbst was quicker. "The *Haganah*, as Ben-Gurion has determined, is not going to initiate fights. It will only retaliate and punish a violent attack."

"It is that simple? Have the snipers on top of the minarets of Jaffa's Manshya's Mosque, or the terrorist bands hidden in the hills along the highway to Jerusalem, been silenced? How many victims have already fallen prey to them?"

A moment later they heard the sound of bullets from the areas of Shchunat Hatikva and Kerem Hateimanim, the two oldest Tel-Aviv communities, and the closest to Jaffa.

Sigi got up and paced the room. "You see that they are not afraid of the Brit's curfew. Why should we be?"

"We have to stay calm and not give way to hysteria. Haganah is strong and well-organized. All you think about is revenge. In the long run this is not what we want," Hugo Gruber said in a quiet voice.

"We are as concerned as you are," Charlotte Gruber, who was knitting a sweater, joined the conversation. "Only the other day, the kibbutz of one of our boys, Ef'Al near Tel-Aviv, was under attack. Thank God, the attackers were repelled."

"Good evening, you are listening to the news from Kol Zion Halochemet."

The stern voice of the broadcaster brought silence to the room. "Again, Arab attacks and violence occurred simultaneously, at *Kfar Uria*, near Ramla and other settlements in the North as well as at the edge of towns. *Lehi*, in retaliation, has attacked and wiped out the Arab villages of Yazur and Tira."

"It's really a war," whispered Otto, bewildered.

"*Sheket*, silence," demanded Sigi, who bent his cupped ear toward the radio.

"Syrian Bedouins attacked Kfar Szold," continued the announcer, "but were quickly defeated and pushed back across the frontier."

"Bravo," Mazal clapped her hands. Unobserved, she had entered the room. Otto stood up, his eyes worried, but Mazal gestured for him to sit down.

"We have noticed that most of the wealthy Arabs are leaving. They are going to Damascus, Amman or Ramalla," the broadcaster continued. "They think they are taking a holiday, and will be back soon. The Mufti Al-Husseini is upset, because not only women, children and old people are leaving, but also young men who should serve in the towns' militias and the Arab Liberation Army."

Sigi turned off the radio. Nobody talked, but each one could guess the others' thoughts. Arabs could leave to get protection from the neighboring Arab countries, but where could Jews go? They had no other place. Their brethren, even if they wanted to help, lived in faraway countries.

"For better or for worse, we are going to stay and fight until the last one," said Charlotte, speaking for everyone in the room. "Our son, Uri, is training orthodox Jews, who volunteered for the Haganah. Isn't this extraordinary? Can you imagine, a Jew with the Torah in one hand and a rifle in the other?"

Everybody smiled. They knew that she wanted to raise their spirits. Otto kept his eyes shut. He thought of the little boy, Selim, who showed such a rare gift for music. *Where were they, the child and his mother? Had they left already? He felt sorry for the boy. Would he receive the musical training he deserved?* He remembered that Charlotte and Mazal had told him that the mother came looking for him and Gretchen. *Should he try to find her, the girl with the bluest eyes, Ruthie's eyes?*

"I am sorry," Otto said, blushing, when he saw five pairs of eyes riveted on him, "I dozed. I am getting old."

"You were dreaming," said Mazal. "You had such a serene smile. What did you dream of?"

Otto was amazed by Mazal's boldness, but he knew that she had the gentlest of souls and cared so much about Gretchen.

"I was thinking of the little Arab boy, such musical promise, the one I told you about. Where would he be? Has he any chance to develop his talent, a refugee in an Arab country?" Otto answered.

He saw Mazal's eyes open wider, as if his words took on a special meaning for her. "We have to find her and tell her the truth," Mazal said. "No Jew can feel safe in an Arab country. My mother thought that Morocco was heaven, until Arab hooligans burned her store. Poor girl, she doesn't know what awaits her and maybe her son as well."

For a long time before falling asleep, Otto thought of Shifra and Selim. How could he find out what happened to them? Maybe Nabiha, his former housekeeper in Jaffa, would know. *But where could he find Nabiha?*

It had been by chance that Otto hired her. He was shopping in Jaffa's *souk* when he noticed a strong woman crouched on the floor, cleaning the entrails of a freshly butchered chicken. Though he hated the stink, Otto admired her efficiency. Through sign language and a volunteer interpreter, he made her understand what he wanted. She wiped her hands, ready to follow him. Every day for four years, she took care of Gretchen and their needs, but he never knew where she lived.

Otto fell into a deep sleep, dreaming that he had offered his life in exchange for his daughter's, his obsessive dream.

Mazal also had difficulty falling asleep. She kept thinking of the young girl who had enough courage to approach them, before

Mazal let her slip away. She was sure the girl didn't come just to pay a courtesy call. Maybe she needed help. She turned over in bed. It was hot and Bruno's snoring annoyed her.

Mazal arose and went onto the balcony. The February night was bleak and cold and made her shiver. She thought of a plan. She knew it could be risky even in peaceful times, now it would be plainly dangerous. If she told Bruno, he'd say, "You want to abduct somebody? *At ishtagat*-are you crazy?"

Back in bed, Mazal threw her arm around Bruno's large back. His body warmed hers. Before falling asleep her last thought was, *"Why would I want to play with fire? Is my desire to protect a Jewish girl strong enough to take such a risk?"*

Shifra awoke with a start. *What was that noise?* It was still dark outside. Careful not to wake up Selim curled next to her, she rose and peered through the window. The neighbors across the street were busy loading their household wares into a donkey drawn cart, already filled with mattresses and pillows. A weeping child carried a load of pots and pans taller than himself. When one of the pots fell, the father, his arms filled with chairs, screamed, "Not again, Ali, you good-for-nothing, you break one more thing, and I'll break your back."

Shifra sighed. What she saw had become a familiar sight. People were leaving Jaffa. *Where were they going?* A few days ago Samira told her about the two Lebanese ladies who came to visit Fatima.

"You must remember them," Samira said, "The owners of the French Perfume Shop. Cool, beautiful and elegant as ever. Fatima was so happy to see them. It had been a long time since she had visitors. She called me to help her serve the guests, but they said, no need, they had stopped by for only a minute, to say goodbye to Fatima. They were leaving, returning to Lebanon."

Shifra did not need to ask the reason. The answer was everywhere. Menace floated in the air, the clouds of war becoming denser every day.

"Fatima cried," continued Samira. "She had ordered Musa to come home, but he answered that there was still time, not yet reason to hurry. Now is the orange picking season. He had consulted with other orange-grove owners who said they would leave by the end of March or the beginning of April, after the oranges were boxed and shipped to their regular customers."

Shifra waited to hear more. Samira had yielded to her pressure and told her already that Musa had written to his mother about the house he bought in the village of Ein Karem.

"Another reason for Fatima to be upset with her son," Samira had said. "Who needs to buy a new house, when we don't know what tomorrow will bring?"

Shifra knew that Samira repeated word for word what Fatima said. She was seized by tremors. *So that was the surprise Musa had for her! To live close to Jerusalem!*

Musa's sister, Nur, came home crying one day, saying that most of her classmates had left, and she did not want to return to school. Only when Fatima threatened to whip her, did she relent. Samira told Shifra that Fatima said, "Our life must continue the same way as always. That's your brother Musa's wish."

But life was not the same. Every day when Samira returned from the *souk*, she complained that the prices for flour and eggs had gone up, and sugar and butter were scarce. "More stores are closing. The farmers are scared, they stopped harvesting and many have even left their villages." Gone was the old Samira, the one who only a few years ago, had sung Yiddish songs to help her fall asleep.

During those anxious days, Selim had a good time. Fatima had hired a tutor at home for Rama and Ahmed. "They don't learn that much in school," was her excuse, but Samira knew better.

She told Shifra, "Fatima is afraid of the militia men patrolling the streets. She's heard about small children being stolen. She's like a mother hen."

The children loved the tutor, an unassuming young man with a face marked by chicken-pox scars, and long, bony arms hanging away from his shoulders like a marionette. He taught the children that chanting the verses of the Koran would help them memorize quicker.

The minute he heard singing, Selim ran to his grandmother's house and begged to be included in the lessons.

"You know that Fatima can't refuse Selim anything," Samira told Shifra, without adding that Fatima also said, 'Musa is away, and I don't believe the *Yahudia* would give the child a proper Muslim education.'

The tutor was surprised by the speed with which Selim learned everything he was taught. Fatima and Samira delighted in his singing, "Like a muezzin," Samira commented, amazed.

For Selim it became a new game. He sang from the minute he woke up in the morning until he went to sleep. Samira spat on him a few times. "To chase away the evil eye," she told Shifra, casting her eyes meaningfully toward the two Iraqi soldiers who were just leaving the house. They weren't often at home now that they were training the Jaffa militia.

One evening before falling asleep, Selim whispered, "I want to sing my new songs for Jedi Otto and Jedati Gretchen. It'll cheer them up. When are we going to see them?"

Shifra was astounded. *Her son hadn't forgotten the violin teacher and his wife.*

"A letter from England," announced Nur. She had waited by the gate, hoping to receive mail from friends who had left Jaffa not so long ago. "From Amina and addressed to Musa," she added, somewhat disappointed.

Fatima stepped out. "Eumi, a letter from Amina," Nur repeated, though she had already handed it to Shifra.

Fatima stood undecided. "Let me have it," she ordered. Silently, Shifra gave the letter to Nur, who handed it to Fatima.

Fatima's children and Samira surrounded her, like bees around their queen. Before opening the letter, Fatima said, "Nur, take Rama and Ahmed to your room and help them with the Koran recitation." Disappointed, the children left.

Fatima's fingers trembled as she tore open the envelope. She signaled to Samira to come closer to her. Their gray heads bent over the letter, as they started to read, Samira mouthing the words in silence.

March 15, 1948

To my dear brother Musa, Salaam Aleikum,

I pray that Allah continues to protect all of you in these difficult times.

Even though we are far from you, our hearts and minds are constantly with you as George and I have followed with increasing anxiety what happens in our dear Palestine.

I have good news. George's uncle, the member of the British Parliament, has obtained a position for George to assist Sir Alan Cunningham, the British High Commissioner in Palestine, with the withdrawal of the British Army at the end of the Mandate. He will arrive in two weeks.

George says that what the British government wants is to maintain law and order, now, and also after it leaves Palestine. Although the British troops were ordered not to intervene between Arabs and Jews, sometimes they have had to do it.

I know that George made his decision because of my constant worries about my family. He promised he'd not only protect you, but he'll see to it that you'll come to England, for a short vacation, until things quiet down in the Middle East. He is convinced, as most British people are, that after the intervention of the Arab Liberation Army, the brotherhood army of five Arab neighboring states, peace and calm will be restored in Palestine.

Dear brother Musa, please convince my mother of my undeterred love and respect, and that my concern for the well-being of our family is sincere.

Be assured that George is as devoted to my family as I am.

Your loving sister,
Amina

Fatima groaned, "Her Brit husband is coming to save us? She should be ashamed of even mentioning it!" She spit the words out, "Amina married without my consent, she left us, and now she's worried about our well-being!"

Fatima crumpled the letter and threw it away. She paced the room, "We have to leave before her George sets eyes on us. We don't need his help. Samira," she ordered, "Bring my shawl. We are going out now."

"Going where?" Samira asked, while she picked up the crumpled letter and smoothed its pages, before pocketing it.

"We are going to the Post Office. I want to call my cousin Abdullah. Musa has to come home immediately. I've waited long enough. It's time to take action, no dreams of romantic summer homes in Ein-Karem."

"There are long lines at the Post Office," Samira said. "You don't know because you haven't left the house lately. All Jaffa is at the Post Office making calls. You'll have to wait for hours!"

"If I can't call from the Post Office, I'll go to the *mukhtar*'s office," Fatima answered stubbornly. "I must get through to Abdullah today."

Fatima is right, thought Samira. *Suha needs her husband around, especially now that she is pregnant. It is what I suspected all along, but more so, after she decided to go alone to see the woman doctor, last Friday.*

Sighing, Samira followed her mistress.

Shifra saw her mother-in-law and Samira leaving. Where were they going? She felt hurt when Fatima ordered her to hand over Amina's letter. *She still considers me no more than a servant.* Four years after their marriage, Fatima still would not recognize her as Musa's lawful wife. Sad and embittered, Shifra started to pull the curtains. *Wait! Who is that woman standing on the sidewalk across the street? Is she taking a stroll?* She seemed to look with persistence toward Shifra's house. Had she seen her at the window? Shifra took a step back. The woman dressed in Arab garb looked familiar.

When the woman rearranged the *hijab* on her head, Shifra caught a glimpse of big golden hoops gleaming in her ears. Shifra approached the window again. She saw the woman raise her hand, an inviting smile on her lips. In an instant Shifra recognized Mazal, Otto Schroder's neighbor. Shifra felt a tremor in her heart.

"Were you looking for me?" an out-of-breath Shifra asked Mazal.

"We want to help you," Mazal said. "The time is short."

Shifra nodded, a knot forming in her throat. They spoke in the shed, Shifra fretting that Fatima and Samira might return any minute and find the unknown visitor.

"Come with me now," there was urgency in Mazal's voice.

"I can't. They'll be back soon, my mother-in-law and Samira. They will be suspicious," a disheartened Shifra answered.

"There is no time to wait. It's your decision. We can be here at midnight. If you wait longer, it might be too late."

"I'll be ready," Shifra answered

"You'll hear our signal, three howls of a jackal," Mazal's black eyes seemed to burrow into Shifra's soul.

After they returned from the Post Office, Samira told Shifra that Fatima telephoned Abdullah, who promised her that Musa would come home the next day.

At supper, Shifra poured a bit of *arrack* into Samira's tea. Shortly afterward Samira's head fell on the table, asleep. *But she could wake up before midnight. And who could tell if Musa wouldn't change his mind and arrive earlier?*

She let a fully dressed Selim fall asleep in her bed. *From tonight your name is Shlomi,* she whispered in his ear. Lying near him, Shifra trembled with anxiety.

Mazal was so mysterious. She did not say who would come to pick them up. *Who would bypass the Brits' curfew and put their lives on the line for Shifra and her boy?* And even if they pass the curfew unobserved, another danger awaits: the nightly exchange of fire between Arabs and Jews through the Manshya quarter.

Feverishly, Shifra took a piece of paper and started writing.

Musa, my darling,
Things happen so fast. There were so many words left unspoken between the two of us. I was too shy to tell you about my former life. I felt my life really

started when I woke up in your arms. Then on one of your late nights out I saw you hiding a rifle in the shed. It scared me. Your secret talks with your mother which you never shared with me made me wonder if I really knew you...

Why didn't you tell me your plans? Why was I kept in the dark? If you shared your thoughts with me before deciding to leave, maybe I would've shared with you my fears and also my hopes for our son's future.

What could be our son's future in a strange and unwelcoming country? The Palestinians didn't welcome the World War Jewish refugees, what makes you think that another country would welcome us, a Yahudia and her son?

Now it's too late.

I want to think that I love you less but this would be a lie. I love you today as much as ever, but I know that uprooted, I'd wither like a flower without water. My heart bleeds at the thought of not seeing you again.

I pray to have the courage to leave you this letter. I hope that one day you'll be proud of the way our son was raised.

On the floor, close to Shifra, a small bag was packed with one change of clothes for Shlomi and a blouse and the short skirt she had sewn for herself. Shifra closed her eyes and took a deep breath. *"I'm doing it for the future of my child."* She repeated the words in her mind; it helped her relax. The clock chimed nine times; three more hours to wait. Shifra closed her eyes.

In her dream, her mother entered the room, arms outstretched. Shifra wanted to jump up, but she felt nailed to the bed.

Shifrale, her mother said, *I didn't sit Shiva for you. For me you never died. I always hoped to find you. For a full year, the year the family mourned you, I took an oath, not to speak to your father or let him touch me. I separated our beds like during the weeks I am impure.*

Your father was upset. "It's not enough the bishe your daughter brought upon us, you want to shame me too." After the year of mourning ended, I said to him, "Our Shifra is not dead. I feel in my heart that she is somewhere not far from us. She ran away because our home was stifling. She wanted to learn. She wanted to sing."

"Shifra inherited your streak of independence," your father accused me.

Shifra heard a sob; she couldn't tell if it was hers or her mother's.

I don't know what you did during the years since you left us. Maybe you joined a kibbutz. Often I dream of you coming toward me, dressed in a white blouse and navy skirt, your golden hair cut short. What did you do with your beautiful curls? I see a baby in your arms, and a tall young man walking at your side.

All the time I waited for a sign. But now I'm scared. I see you less and less, only as a shadow. You are moving away from me. Shifrale, the war is at our doorstep and I am afraid for you... afraid for you... for you.

Shifra awoke with a jolt, her face wet. It seemed so real, if she had extended her hand she could have touched her mother.

Ten o'clock. It was still early. Her throat was dry, but she was afraid to move. She saw a smile on Selim's lips; it reminded her of the responsibility she was taking by deciding his destiny. Shifra stood up and paced the room. Who could predict how he would judge her, when he grew up? Better not to think of it. She heard Mazal's words, "The child's future is in this country. You'll not be welcome in an Arab country. You'll feel like a stranger wherever you go." Those were Mazal's words, a woman she barely knew, but who was ready to risk her life for her. In Shifra's mind, the wreckage she had seen in Adon Nathan's store in Jaffa's *souk* was still fresh. It was done not by strangers, but by his lifelong neighbors.

What about Musa? Her heart would break if she thought of his shock, his anger. *No, she shouldn't think of Musa now, because if she did, she'd lose her courage.*

The jackal's howl, three times, their signal! Shifra enveloped the sleeping child in her cloak and took him in her arms. With wavering steps, she left by the back door, straight into the dark night, the letter for Musa crushed in her fist.

PART III:

New York & Israel 1968-1972

46

"I know so little about you," his lover said, tracing her finger slowly over his body. "Since we were children, you seemed so mysterious, so serious."

Shlomi laughed. His lips covered her mouth. They were in bed, still naked after an afternoon of making love.

"Let's either rehearse or make love again," he gamely proposed.

"Shlomi Gal, violinist and the latest recipient of the Leventrittt Award, performing tomorrow night at Carnegie Hall, can you for once answer my question?" She turned toward him, her elbow propped on the pillow.

In the silence that followed they could hear the hiss made by the old heating system. Shlomi Gal and Beatrice D'vora Sonnenfeld were lucky to find an apartment in a building where the renters were all musicians. At any hour of the day or night they could hear a practicing cello or a soprano gargle her scales.

Shlomi climbed out of bed and approached the window. He looked down from their sixth-floor apartment and saw an almost empty street. Here and there the wind swept away the leaves gathered on the wet pavement. "I can answer you in two sentences.

I was raised by my grandfather, Otto Schroder, violinist and member of the Israeli Philharmonic Orchestra. He's due to arrive tomorrow morning from Israel."

D'vora pulled the blanket over her shivering legs. "I remember him. He used to come with you to the Gadna rehearsals, always carrying your violin; a neat man who wore a jacket and a bowtie even in the summer. But so did you, which our *hevra* found so peculiar. Was he your mother's father?"

A cloud passed over Shlomi's face. "No," he answered shortly.

"Oh, your father's then," she insisted.

"D'vora," Shlomi liked her middle name and always used it. "Why all these questions? I love you. Isn't that enough? Love doesn't come easy to me. I barely remember my mother. I have no pictures of her or of my father. She died in a car accident. Grandpa Otto told me that my father died during the War for Independence. Nobody knows where he has been buried."

"Oh, my love, my sweetheart," D'vora threw the blanket away, her arms outstretched. "Come here. I promise I'll never ask you anything anymore. It will be up to you when, if ever, you want to open your heart to me."

That night Shlomi could not fall asleep. His grandfather's impending arrival brought back so many memories. It had been three years since he last saw him, on the day he left Israel after he received a scholarship from the Israel America Cultural Foundation to continue his violin studies at the Juilliard School of Music.

And now, on the telephone, after he heard about the award, Otto said, "I'm very proud of you. I'm coming and bringing with me a surprise." *What did he mean?*

But mostly, Shlomi was troubled by D'vora's questions. He had tried to get rid of that riddle regarding his parents. When Shlomi had almost succeeded in shutting the unanswered questions out of his life, D'vora, his darling D'vora, had to reopen that sealed box.

Forgotten images appeared in his mind's eye: Grandma Gretchen crying at his mother's grave and screaming, "Ruthie, Ruthie, *wo bist du?*" when it was clear that his mother's name, Shifra, was etched on the headstone. Lotte and Mazal later told him that Ruthie was Grandpa and Grandma's daughter who disappeared during Hitler's Germany. If not for Lotte and Mazal, Otto's neighbors, his adoptive mothers, as fondly Shlomi called them, his daily life with Otto, continuously worried about Gretchen's mental instability, would have been a wasteland. He thought many times of running away, but always stopped short, thinking of the pain it would inflict on those two old people, but more than that, he knew that without Otto, who had opened the path for him, he would never have found his passion—the violin.

Otto was not easy to please, and Shlomi cried many times, especially when Otto decided which pieces he should perform in public. "You are not mature enough to play the Mendelssohn concerto," he said after the conductor of the Gadna, the Israeli Youth Orchestra, asked Shlomi to solo with the orchestra. "You'll play the Beriot Third."

"But Grandpa Otto, I've been practicing the Mendelssohn for a year. All the members of the orchestra know that. I'll be embarrassed." cried Shlomi.

"You are not ready. You are only twelve years old. You have an entire life in front of you to perform it. I am preparing you to become a solid violinist, not a child star." Otto was firm, and Shlomi knew that it wouldn't help to discuss it further.

D'vora turned in bed and nestled in his arms. She puffed slightly during sleep and he teased her about it. "You snore," Shlomi told her one morning. He laughed, "Sometimes in A, but mostly in B flat."

"I do not," a hurt D'vora answered.

"And when you are tired, it sounds like C sharp." The following night, D'vora took her pillow and went to sleep in the living room. He had to kneel in front of her and beg her to return to bed.

Sweet D'vorale, the cello player, a head taller than he when both were fourteen years old. "What a player, this D'vora, she has a lot of fire!" Otto said with admiration. To have fire was his best compliment. Yet they never became friends during their Gadna years. Shlomi was too shy; besides, he knew the children called him names behind his back, the kindest being, "Herr Professor," because his shirts were always pressed and he wore shoes and socks, never sandals.

After his Beriot performance, Beatrice D'vora Sonnenfeld was the first one to congratulate him. He stammered, *"You are a bee in a sunny field."* The translation of her name was all he could find to say.

Surprised, D'vora asked, "Do you speak German?" Shlomi nodded. He'd heard Otto, Gretchen and Lotte speak it for so many years, he not only understood, but if need be he was able to speak it, too.

"It's not proper for two individuals of the opposite sex to cohabitate," an upset Otto wrote to him.

"But it is cheaper to share an apartment," Shlomi had written back to him.

The Old World man replied, "You know that we never touched Gretchen's German war reparations. They are yours to use." Otto relented only after he heard that Shlomi and D'vora were playing chamber music together. By then, the love between them had flourished. "I've always liked you," D'vora told Shlomi with sparks in her eyes, after their first night of lovemaking, "I only waited for you to grow taller."

"Don't come to the airport," Otto said when Shlomi offered to pick him up on the day of the concert. "Better practice a bit, scales and arpeggios. Try to rest and save your strength for the concert. I'll call you from the hotel."

On the day of the concert, Shlomi woke up at dawn. He liked to run early in the morning, when most of West 104th Street was still in the throes of sleep. The pavement was wet, but it didn't bother him. Shlomi was a good runner; it was the only sport he allowed himself.

He began running on the Tel-Aviv beach, where Mazal brought him as a young child almost every day. She believed that inhaling the salty air would heal him, especially after his long sickness. But Shlomi had no recollection of his illness, which Otto told him happened after his mother's sudden death.

Running became a passion. If somebody had asked him why, he would not know what to answer. Maybe it gave him the same feeling of complete freedom and control he had when playing the violin.

Seated across the aisle from the three women, his flight companions, Otto took a furtive glance at them. Animated, Mazal and Charlotte were talking to their guest, the woman in the middle, an attractive lady in her forties. Nobody would have guessed that she wore a *shaitel* unless they knew that she was an orthodox woman.

It wasn't Otto's first visit to America. He had already been on tours with the Israeli Philharmonic Orchestra, from which he would soon retire. Sighing, Otto tried to find a comfortable position on the eleven-hour-long flight to New York. He knew that he would have little time to rest before the concert. Although the solicitous El-Al stewardess had given him an extra pillow and blanket, sleep eluded Otto.

He closed his eyes, but his mind was awake. He thought of the last twenty years, during which Shlomi, the name his mother Shifra called him, an orphan, became the center of his and Gretchen's universe. Was it wrong to keep the truth away from him all those years?

Though it was against her wish, Otto's first thought was to try to contact Shifra's family, but the child became frightfully ill after his mother died, and not understanding what had happened. Otto decided to wait. Shlomi had fought death with temperatures soaring up to 42 degrees Celsius. If not for Mazal's and Charlotte's devotion, changing places day and night to wash his small body in baths of vinegar, change his soaking clothes, pouring with painstakingly slow motion drops of water and medicine between the child's dry lips, Shlomi would have joined his mother. *Would Shifra's family have labored to save the child's life as Charlotte and Mazal did?*

After he recovered, Shlomi became everybody's child. When Gretchen, with tears in her eyes, in one of her bright moments whispered to him, "I think Ruthie has sent him to us," Otto's decision was taken. But as in past years when Ruthie's vision disturbed his sleep, Shifra's pale image in the hospital bed, as life dripped out of her body, haunted him.

She was doing so well as a volunteer at Shaarei Zedek Hospital in Tel-Aviv, preparing to become a student nurse. "I prefer to work nights," Shifra said, "while Shlomi is asleep. During the day he needs me. He's confused and at times asks how much longer we'll visit, before we return home. It's nice that Mazal and Charlotte try to entertain him, but he feels more secure with me around."

What a courageous girl she was! She threw herself whole-heartedly into her work, only two months after she arrived trembling, in the middle of that night, when Mazal and Bruno brought her with the child asleep in her arms.

As much as he tried, Otto couldn't understand how the accident occurred.

Shifra thought she heard a voice screaming "Suha," her Arabic name. That's what she told Otto through her great pain minutes after he arrived at the hospital, called in by the emergency ward. The scream petrified her. She looked to see where the voice came from. *Could it have been Musa, her husband?* The whistle of bullets made her throw herself onto the pavement, yet a bullet went through her shoulder. The pain was sharp. Though she heard the honking of a car, she was unable to get to her feet. Later, crying, the driver told Otto that the car brakes were malfunctioning and he could not stop the car from mounting the curb and pinning the fallen victim against a wall.

It must have been a hallucination. It couldn't have been her husband's voice. Otto moved in his seat. Through the loudspeaker, Otto heard that dinner was being served. He glanced at Charlotte and Mazal, his friends and neighbors for more than twenty years.

Charlotte had already tied a napkin around her neck, neat as ever, even in that narrow space. Mazal's earrings dangled, while her hands gestured to him. He could not hear what she was saying, but the O formed by her thumb and forefinger meant everything was under control.

47

It was Lotte's first visit to New York, her first visit to America. When Otto asked Shlomi's "adoptive mothers" to join him, she had misgivings.

"Shlomi is a grownup," Lotte told her husband, "he doesn't need us to wipe his nose."

"He didn't need you to wipe his nose since he was seven years old," answered Hugo Gruber. "But I'll bet his eyes will light up when he sees you two." He was addressing Mazal, too, who had just entered their apartment. "Especially if Lotte bakes some of his favorite pastries and brings them along."

"He wanted to come back last year when the Six-Day War broke out. He said he was going to fight like his father and die for his country, but I stopped him. I said, 'Stay where you are and make our country proud.' I know he got upset." Charlotte, already baking treats for Shlomi, wiped the flour off her hands onto the apron.

"I am going," Mazal declared. "How can we miss his New York debut? He is our boy. Besides, I've never been out of the country. Otto is treating us. He'll feel hurt if you refuse."

"But what do you think about Otto's crazy idea? Now, after so many years! Why contact Shifra's family, twenty years after her death? Let sleeping dogs lie, that's what I think."

"Maybe he feels guilty. His lies were enough to dry the Mediterranean Sea. It's time to tell Shlomi the truth," Charlotte's husband said.

"And what if Shlomi has a breakdown? For so many years he has asked us about his parents and we've been mum. Why now? He's happy, has a girlfriend, a career. Why wake up ghosts?"

"After Gretchen's death I observed a change in Otto," Mazal said. "He was withdrawn, a tortured soul. He never told Gretchen that on that fateful night in Berlin, he saw the S.S. dragging Ruthie out of the house and didn't try to save his daughter from their hands. He's an old man now. The time has come to make peace with his ghosts. And Shifra is one of them."

It was Mazal who contacted Chana. The only thing Mazal knew was what Shifra told her about the chance encounter on Jaffa's beach with her childhood friend, a friend whom she refused to acknowledge. It was very little to go on, Charlotte said at the time, but Mazal wasn't the type to give up. She went to Jerusalem to look into the registry of Geula, the neighborhood where the girls had lived. She found Shifra's name in the records, but there were more than a few Chana born the same year. Disappointed, she was ready to leave, when the clerk asked, "Maybe I could help you. Who are you looking for? I was born one year ahead of the year you look at, and except for one girl, Shifra, who died, I know everybody else."

"You are right," Mazal answered, "Shifra is dead. I'm looking for her best friend, a girl named Chana, whose father came from Germany and who sometimes played the violin."

Mazal continued, "I could see red blotches appearing on her face. Her eyes blinked like she was trying to hold back tears.

"Chana is my younger sister," the clerk finally said. "My father played the violin and I remember Shifra coming to our house and listening to him enraptured." The clerk remained silent for an instant, before she suspiciously asked, "What do you want from my sister?"

"I couldn't convince her to lead me to her sister," Mazal told Charlotte and Otto. "She didn't want to have anything to do with it. One can't bring back the past, she said. But I read her hyphenated name-tag and immediately got an idea. I was sure that I'd find Chana if I asked the grocers in Geula, now that I knew her maiden name. Grocers, and especially grocers' wives, are always happy to gossip. Not only did I find out where she lived, but I was told when she got married, how many children she had, that her boys had fought during the Six-Day War, and the year Chana's father died!"

Charlotte was fond of Mazal, whose enthusiasm was infectious. Gone were the times when she looked with superiority at Bruno's *concubine*. "Finally, you made an honest woman out of her," Charlotte told Bruno at their wedding, as she embraced the newlyweds.

Now, in the airplane, Charlotte looked at the picture Chana brought, a snapshot of the three girlfriends, taken by her father, when they were twelve years old. Like the other two, Shifra, the sun shining on her blond tresses, wore a dark skirt and a long-sleeved blouse. "She was so beautiful. She was the prettiest of us all," Chana sighed.

If Mazal wouldn't have been embarrassed she would have prayed *Tfilat Haderech*, as Chana did, when the airplane took off.

Next to her Chana and Charlotte snored but Mazal couldn't sleep. Anxious, she thought about Shlomi's reaction when meeting Chana. The movie *Salach Shabati* played on the large screen. She had enjoyed this movie many times, but not now. She closed her eyes and like so many times in the past twenty years, she heard Shifra's quick steps following her and whispering, "*G'veret, G'veret* Mazal, did *Adon* Otto send you to find me?"

"You can't wait any longer," Mazal had answered. "There is no time to wait."

Mazal opened her eyes. Charlotte was awake. She signaled Mazal to follow her to the alcove in the back of the airplane. Mazal's legs skipped over Chana without waking her. *A mother of six needs her sleep.*

"What's your opinion?" Charlotte asked. "Will Shlomi be happy to meet Chana, or will he curse us for the rest of his life?"

"We have to stay positive. It's too late to have doubts," Mazal answered. "We are on a mission, like the one when we rescued Shifra."

Charlotte looked ready to cry, and Mazal thought that with age she was becoming more and more emotional. "Do you remember?" Charlotte whispered.

Mazal hugged her, "How could I forget?"

The two returned to their seats and saw Chana, already up, looking again at the photograph she had brought with her.

"You told me that Shifra loved her husband," Chana said, bewildered.

"I can see her, like it was yesterday. She cried, 'He saved me, I owe him my life,' answered Charlotte.

"But convert?" Chana asked with distaste. "Did she have to go that far?"

Charlotte looked to Mazal for help. "That is the only way a Muslim could marry a woman of another faith. Though she took the *Al-Shahada*, Shifra said that in her heart, she remained Jewish."

"The day before we rescued her, Shifra came to see Otto. She kept wringing her hands. She was told nothing, she said; every decision had always been between her mother-in-law and her husband. Shifra knew that it was only a matter of days before they would be leaving the country. She looked so young, so unprotected, and afraid. "My mother-in-law doesn't talk to me," she said. "In her heart I am the *Yahudia* who brought the *nackba* upon her family"

Mazal took over, "Otto said, 'I am wondering about your talented son; I hope somebody will discover his talent, wherever he'll be.'

"When Shifra clung to Otto's hands, I thought about the *conversos* in Spain, hundreds of years ago, who never gained the trust of their new co-religionists," added Charlotte. "But I couldn't bring myself to tell the poor girl."

"Gretchen stood up. She looked formidable, her eyes sparkled," Mazal said. "That scene still brings shivers down my spine when I think of it. I couldn't understand because she spoke German, but Otto, Charlotte and Shifra did, and I could read on their faces that what she said was frightening.

"She screamed, 'Heinz, Heinz, stop! Ruthie is as German as you and I. Heinz, my little brother, I beg of you. You laugh? Yes, she is German, she is not a *mischling*. I kneel in front of you. Have pity on us. Let me have my little girl. Heinz, Heinz, what are you doing? Your boots are breaking my hands. Why, why Heinz? Because I married a Jew, you say. You want to punish me! Go ahead! Break my hands, but don't take Ruthie.'

"I saw Gretchen falling on her knees, crawling, her shaking hands trying to reach up. It was like watching a horror movie." Mazal's hands covered her eyes.

"Otto was as shaken as the rest of us," Charlotte whispered. "We made her lie down. When Otto tried to give Gretchen a sedative, she refused. With so much turmoil, we forgot Shifra."

"Not I," Mazal said. "Shifra was as pale as the moon, and trembling. I took her in my arms. The silence was overwhelming. We didn't notice, but Bruno and Hugo, alarmed by Gretchen's screams, rushed into the apartment."

"We were still dumbfounded by what we'd witnessed when Gretchen opened her blue eyes, which in spite of everything she went through, had remained clear and beautiful, looked at Otto and said, '*Sweetheart,* I'm sorry. You don't deserve this pain.' Weeping, Otto kissed her hands."

"With a voice as gentle as a sea murmur," Mazal said, "Gretchen turned to Shifra and said in a mixture of German and Hebrew, 'Young girl who remind me so much of the daughter I lost, think of the future of your child while there is still time. My own brother took my daughter to the slaughterhouse. Yes, yes,' Gretchen dismissed Otto's denying gesture. "He did. That's what happens when hatred seeps into people."

"As Shifra returned our glances we saw a new determination in her eyes. 'I'll be ready,' she said. Mazal held her tight. After she left, our husbands discussed plans for rescuing Shifra and her child," concluded Charlotte.

Chana's eyes were moist. "You saved her," she said.

"Unfortunately, for a short time only. That untimely accident," Mazal shook her head in disbelief. "Her life cut so short, so—"

"We are starting our descent to New York. Please return to your seats and buckle your seatbelts."

Chana turned to Mazal, "You two saved Shifra's child. Who saves one soul, saves the entire world." She took Mazal's and Charlotte's hands in her own. "I feel privileged to know you, and I am looking forward to meeting Shifra's son—your son."

Shlomi felt better after his run. Back in the apartment he made himself a cup of coffee. "No more than one cup on the day of a concert, you don't want to have jitters," Otto always warned.

He shaved and turned on the shower. The water warmed up slowly and Shlomi lost patience. He loved a hot shower, and his girlfriend B.D. as their Juilliard colleagues had nicknamed her— short for Beatrice D'vora—frequently kidded him that one day he might get burned.

The rehearsal was scheduled for 10 a.m., and Shlomi wanted to arrive earlier to warm up. "Scales played slowly and with full tone will do it," Otto's words rang in his ears.

Otto, why can't I stop hearing his words? He glanced at his watch. No wonder, Shlomi thought, by now he is probably resting at the hotel, he and my childhood's protective angels. Shlomi smiled, remembering that in a phone conversation, he squeezed out of Otto the surprise he was bringing with him.

Dear Charlotte, loaded down with the pastries she had baked the night before leaving Israel, would raise a scolding finger and say, "You are too skinny, you have to come back home and let me feed you properly," while Mazal, smiling, would ask if he lost weight running the New York Marathon. Always sly, that Mazal, but he was fond of both of them.

After a while Shlomi realized that lost in thought he was headed for Carnegie Hall on foot. Any other day he wouldn't mind walking the almost forty blocks, but not today! "Carnegie Hall," he said as he opened the door to a yellow cab.

"Wow," the cab driver said with respect. "Have you practiced enough, young man?"

Both laughed. Everybody knew the jokes about Carnegie Hall, the *Sancta Sanctorum* of all concert halls. *The great violinists who graced Carnegie Hall, Jascha Heifetz, Isaac Stern, Nathan Milstein, make one feel humble,* thought Shlomi. He felt a thrill of pleasure thinking of Isaac Stern. He and his wife Vera would surely be at the concert tonight. Vera was the director of the Israel-America Cultural Foundation, and it was Isaac who insisted that Shlomi should study in the United States. "How long do you want to hide him in Israel?" Isaac chided Otto. "It's time for Shlomi to spread his wings."

It was still early when he arrived at Carnegie Hall. People swept the aisles. It was cold and dark. He'd better warm up. Carefully, Shlomi took the violin from his case. It was Otto's violin, made by *Vuillaume*, a famous 18th century French violin-maker, which he had presented to Shlomi on his eighteenth birthday. "You deserve it," Otto had said. "My teacher gave it to me. I hope you get as much pleasure from it as I did."

Shlomi never changed the interior of the case. On the silk, behind the two bows, was Gretchen's smiling photo together with her daughter Ruthie, playing flute. Otto and Gretchen told him that his mother, Shifra, resembled their daughter, *dieselben blauen Augen*, was Gretchen's continuous refrain. Shlomi loved to look at Ruthie's photograph and imagine his mother. He had so few memories of her, a woman in a long dress running after him on the beach, her hair waving in the wind. He wasn't sure if it was real or if he made it up. Shlomi felt too self-conscious to add D'vora's picture to the case, so he kept it in his wallet.

In half an hour the members of the orchestra would appear. After warming up, Shlomi started the opening theme of the Mendelssohn, his favorite concerto, the concerto Otto didn't allow him to play at age twelve, saying that he was too young to express its passion and emotions. At the time he didn't dare stand up to Otto, who was the ultimate decision-maker.

But Shlomi felt that the Mendelssohn concerto was his homage to the mother he lost at such a young age. From the first notes of the soaring melody, he would pray as he did when he was young calling his mother, with his own lyrics for the melody, "Mother, can you hear me? I play for you. My music should tell you how much I miss you."

Every time he fingered the first phrase of the concerto, like now, so many years later, the words were there, ready to explode in his head. He felt a kinship with Mendelssohn, and though he played most of the violin concertos; Bach, Mozart, Beethoven, Sibelius, he always returned to his favorite—as tonight, when he chose to play it at the Leventrittt Gala.

The applause of the orchestra members interrupted his thoughts. Shlomi blushed. He had asked Otto not to come to the rehearsal, yet there was an unexpected guest in the hall. It was Isaac Stern! When Shlomi was about fourteen years old, Isaac Stern in one of his many concert tours in Israel heard him play. "The boy should come to the United States," he said. "In Israel he swims in a small pond; outside Israel he'd have no barriers. Look at Itzhak Perlman who came at fifteen or Pinky Zuckerman at sixteen."

But Otto was stubborn, "Shlomi has a lot to learn in this small pond." After a few months of training in the Israeli army he was offered a chance to become the first violinist of the Israeli Defense Force string quartet. Shlomi, disappointed that he was not going to be a fighter like his father, completed the application for the Israel-America Cultural Foundation and obtained the coveted scholarship to study at Juilliard.

Before he left for the United States, Otto took Shlomi aside. In his hand he held a checkbook from the Deutsche Bank issued in Shlomi's name. "A long time ago, Gretchen and I decided that we were not going to accept German reparations. What we suffered and what we lost couldn't be repaid. After you became part of our life, we reconsidered it. This money will serve Shlomi's future, we said."

Though moved by Otto's offer, Shlomi refused to accept it. "Grandpa Otto, you are getting old, you'll need it for yourself. I can't take it."

"Tz, tz, you talk too much! End of discussion."

Shlomi never used his Deutsche Marks. He started performing concerts at Jewish communities from Miami to Duluth, from San Diego to Martha's Vineyard. The audiences welcomed him with enthusiasm, especially after the Six-Day War, when people wanted to touch and kiss him. Shlomi, embarrassed, told them he was only a kleizmer, not a war hero.

"Gentlemen, let's begin. You are familiar with Shlomi Gal, our soloist." The conductor raised his baton and with everyone's eyes focused on him, he started the rehearsal.

340

4 8

Israel

1948-1953

W*hat time was it? Where were Suha and Selim?* It was the day Musa was due to return home. "Come on, everybody up," Samira yelled, waking with a jolt and a headache. "We have a lot of work to do!" But there was no answer.

Samira tried to recall what had happened. She remembered that Suha came home late, saying she went to see a *Yahudia* woman doctor who treated her when she was a child.

"Look," she opened her palm and showed Samira the pills the doctor gave her. "These are for headaches, the others to have more appetite. You don't have to worry about me anymore." She took Selim in her arms and started dancing, "Selim, you and I are going to cook supper. Tonight *Jedatha* Samira should rest." Then she tied an apron around her waist.

Who could have guessed then the curse she would bring upon us? Oh Yarab-el-Alameen-Harachman Al-Rahim, World G-d, forgiver and merciful, *why didn't I die that morning rather than face Musa when he arrived from Jerusalem?*

Samira's wails, as she searched the empty house brought over Fatima, who after Musa's marriage had never entered his house. Samira didn't have to tell her what had happened. The table was covered with dirty dishes, and on the shelf she saw the half-empty bottle of *arrack*.

"You miserable scum," Fatima screamed. "You got drunk like a sailor, and let her run away. That thief took my grandson with her, my Selim!"

"In my entire life I have never put a drop in my mouth," Samira said, but Fatima pushed the tea glass under her nose to smell.

"Oh, *Allah Harachaman*! Suha—a curse on her—prepared the tea. She planned to get me drunk and then run away!" Samira cried

"*Nackba*, the *Yahudia* brought us only disaster," Fatima cried. "You trusted her; you encouraged Musa's foolish love. Now you'll have to answer to my son. What can you say to him? That you betrayed him and all of us?"

Fatima picked up a knife and came closer. Samira knelt. "Kill me," she said, "I don't want to live anymore." Through her tears, Samira saw big chunks of her hair falling.

Suddenly they heard Musa's voice. "Eumi, stop, stop immediately. What are you doing? What has happened? Have you gone mad?" He pulled the knife from his mother's hand.

"Ask her what happened!" Fatima said before storming out of the house.

"Why didn't your mother kill me? It would have been better than to see the pain I inflict on you with every word I utter," Samira sobbed.

Musa stood frozen, numb, as if he didn't understand Samira's words. "Selim," he called, "Selim, my son, Abu Selim is home. I know you are hiding." He ran from one room to another, unable to accept the reality. "My son, my son," he moaned, calling Selim. Musa fell to his knees, banging his chest with his fists, "Selim, Selim."

When he rose, his eyes blazed. "I'll find her, even if I have to comb each house. No one plays games with Musa Ibn Faud." Samira could hear Faud's voice in Musa's words, and recognized the pride of the Masri family speaking through him. "If she's left me, she's nothing now but a *sharmoota*, a prostitute, and she'll be punished for it, but first I want my son back."

When Fatima reentered the house, Musa told her, "I am going to find my son. I'll never leave the country without him."

Musa did not find Selim. While Samira cried, abandoned by all, she heard Fatima accusing Musa, "It's your fault. You warmed an enemy, a serpent, at your breast." When Musa didn't respond, she took another tactic, "You jeopardize the lives of your sisters and brother. Have you forgotten your responsibilities? Where is your pride? Are you an Arab man, a Muslim, or a bag of rags?"

Musa became angry only when his mother said, "You are young. Think. Allah will bless you with many sons and help you forget the pain of today."

"Never, do you hear me!" Musa yelled. "Never will I trust a woman again."

What made Musa decide to leave immediately, the Deir Yassin massacre or the arrival of Amina's husband? Samira wondered on April 8, 1948, the day of that catastrophe, a day forever imprinted in her memory. She had arrived home exhausted after walking from farm to farm to beg for eggs, flour and vegetables. Jaffa's *souk* was empty. Even before she opened the gate she heard Fatima's wails. Samira froze. *Somebody died. Who?*

Fatima, whose radio was on from morning till night, heard it first. From Ramalla to Cairo, from Damascus to Beirut, every Arab radio station blasted the news, making each broadcast more frightening than the previous one: *The Yahudim have attacked Deir Yassin, assassinated all men and children, raped the women, and burned the village to the ground.*

"Na'ima, my dear daughter, Mahmood, my grandchildren, where are you? Oh, Allah Ackbar, who decides upon life and death, why did you let me live to mourn the death of my children?" Terrified, Rama, Nur and Ahmed surrounded their howling mother.

Samira's bones shook so hard she thought she could hear them rattle. Musa showed up, his face the pallor of death. He brandished a rifle. "I swear on the holy Koran, before I'm killed, I'll shoot all of them." He went into the courtyard where the two armed Iraqi soldiers waited for him.

Fatima, suddenly awakened from her stupor, screamed, "Ibni, my son, in the name of Allah, don't go!" Rama and Nur tried to hold him back, while nine-year-old Ahmed yelled, "Brother Musa, take me along. I too want to kill the *Yahudim*."

That afternoon, the stretched silence, like the silence of eternity, was broken only by Fatima's sobs. No one moved. It must have been past midnight when they heard the noise of a car brakes jamming.

"*Eumi, Eumi*," a voice cried. Fatima ran out. From the armored military car a disheveled Na'ima descended, holding two sleeping boys in her arms. Behind her, a red-haired British officer saluted, taking off his cap.

"Na'ima!" screamed Fatima. She kept repeating her daughter's name, as if doubting a vision. "Eumi, this is George, Amina's husband. He came immediately after he heard what happened. He found us buried underneath the rubble of our house. He saved us, *Eumi*! We owe him our lives."

All wept and embraced again and again. Nobody asked about Mahmood. Only at dawn, when Na'ima and the children were asleep and a fatigued Musa had arrived home, did George tell them that Mahmood, who was the fighters' leader, had been one of the first victims.

"I have borrowed the car from our headquarters for twenty-four hours," George said. "Amina's orders, and my ardent wishes, are to drive you to safety. Ramalla will be our first stop."

Fatima watched Musa. He was the head of the family. Her eyes told him clearly what he should do.

Samira had to make her bed in the shed, since Na'ima used her room for her sleeping boys. When they left, Fatima locked up both houses. *In their hurry to leave, nobody remembered to say good-bye to me*, Samira thought with bitterness.

She couldn't continue to live in the shed. She was cold and hungry. But it was a good place to hide. As the news about Fatima's leaving spread, the Iraqi soldiers, together with their peers, got drunk every night and in their stupor broke Fatima's golden edged dishes and the crystal glasses she used only on holidays. In the mornings after their orgies, Samira collected the broken pieces they had hurled through the windows and hid them in the shed.

Samira saw them carry out the precious Shiraz carpet, which Fatima's father had brought from Iran. After that, the thefts never stopped. Samira cried; it was so hard for her to witness. She had to leave. But where would she go? She would ask Uhm Zaide for shelter in her hut, but was the old woman still alive? All Samira knew was that outside a war was raging.

"Battalions of Brits have taken Jaffa," she heard one of the Iraqi soldiers say. "They are planning something big pretty soon."

"They're concentrated around the Hassan Bek Mosque in the Manshieh Quarter. They know that our snipers and raiders have shot thousands of Yahudim from there," the other Iraqi added.

A few nights later bombs fell on Jaffa. From the shed, Samira saw the flames illuminate the sky like big patches of bright blood. She heard the shouts of the fighters mixed with the screams of the wounded. Samira opened her Koran to find the prayer for the dead, sure she was going to die, but her hands trembled and her eyes were full of smoke and tears. She couldn't read the prayer, the prayer which would have delivered her from her sinful life.

Suddenly she heard a terrible explosion. *Was it the end of the world?* In that moment Samira was happy for Fatima and the children, who were in a safe place. Much, much later, when she had the courage to climb out of her hole, she learned that the explosion wiped out the Manshieh Police Station, where most of the Syrian Liberation Army was stationed.

The streets were quiet, like the calm after a storm. *What should I do? Where can I go? I am ready to work for a piece of bread, but who would hire me?* When she started walking, her legs carried her to the English Convent. The gate was open wide, but there was nobody there, not a soul. A woman beggar approached. Samira gave her one of her last piasters.

"Are you looking for work?" the beggar asked.

Samira nodded.

"Go to the French Convent. The French nuns didn't run away. I heard they are looking for a washerwoman," and she left. *A washerwoman!* Samira sighed. Any work is decent work, she said to herself, climbing the steps to Notre Dame de Sion.

Samira rang the bell. A young nun in a black habit and a huge wide hat, its sides waving like the wings of a big bird, smiled and spoke in French. Samira did not understand. She said in Arabic, "Work, any kind, bread."

When the French nun opened the gate and took her hand, Samira entered a new world. The nuns moved quietly, and spoke with gestures. They even helped her hang the laundry in the huge courtyard.

And how beautifully they sang! Their marvelous blending of voices comforted her soul. One sang like an angel. Her voice reminded Samira of music she had heard but couldn't recall where. In her mind's eye, she saw herself walking with Suha on a quiet street, when Suha suddenly stopped and said, "Listen!" and Samira heard the strains of a violin, playing with the same heavenly effect as the nun's voice. It was the violin teacher! Oh, a curse on him!

That night Samira couldn't sleep. Maybe the violinist knew where Suha was hiding. The thought racked her brain. *Would it be safe to go and look for him?* Maybe she could go on Friday, her free day, the nuns' day of fast. *But was it safe to leave their sanctuary?* Maybe she should forget about it altogether.

. The Mother Superior had observed that in her free time Samira liked to help in the kitchen. The cook, an old nun with swollen hands, could barely chop the vegetables. Even worse, she had lost her sense of smell. Many times Samira saved food that would have burned otherwise. A few weeks later Mother Superior decided the nun should supervise the vegetable garden and Samira should cook. In her new job, Samira's time passed faster than she expected.

When the nuns reopened their school, there was a flurry of girls, Arabs and Jews together. To Samira's wonder the nuns didn't treat them differently. There was a little *Yahudia*, with big blue eyes just like Suha's. Samira's heart ached. *Where were Suha and Selim now?*

On one of their outings to the market, where Samira went with the nun who kept the money purse, they passed Fatima's house. In the courtyard Samira saw a young woman nursing a baby. She stopped transfixed. The woman was dark-skinned, yet she didn't look Arab. Samira wanted to ask her who she was, but the words died in her mouth. "Are you looking for somebody?" the woman called out in Hebrew.

Samira answered in Arabic, "I am looking for the owner of the house."

"The house belongs to the Israeli government and it was allocated to us," the woman responded in Arabic in which Samira detected a twinge of French. "We are immigrants from Tunis."

For the first time, Samira learned that she was living in a country called Israel. It was not Palestine anymore. In that moment, she understood that there was no hope of seeing Fatima and her children again. They would not return to a country that was no longer theirs. She was ready to die.

A cloud passed over the young woman's face. "Is your name Samira?" she asked. Samira nodded.

"Somebody left an envelope for you. He said he'd had it for more than a year but didn't know where to find you." She went inside the house to get it. A wave of warmth penetrated Samira's heart, when she recognized Musa's writing, but she didn't want to open the letter in front of the unknown woman.

The short note from Musa said, "I'm sorry. What happened wasn't your fault." Inside the envelope was money and Amina's address written in English. The letter was addressed to Habib, the apprentice in Mr. Nathan's shop. Samira hid the letter. *Allah, in His great compassion, has decided to give new meaning to my life. For Musa's sake, I have to find Suha and Selim!*

But where should she start? The first Friday, her only free day, she went to search for the neighbors she remembered had lived next door to the violin teacher. She had not walked on that street for almost two years. Those neighbors, whose servants she had befriended, had abandoned their homes, and the newcomers, Jews who spoke Arabic well, looked at her with narrowed eyes when she asked about the *Yahud* violin teacher. Samira could read their thoughts. *Why does an old Arab woman seek a violin teacher?*

Her first attempt ended in failure. Another, when she went to look for Mr. Nathan or Habib at the reopened bazaar, ended the same way. The shop was closed; wooden bars crossed each other on its window and door. There was only a sign, "Moved," in Arabic.

Samira racked her brains. She couldn't think of anybody who could help. Then, during one of her sleepless nights, she dreamed of Nabiha. *Of course, Nabiha! She had worked for the violin teacher and his handicapped wife. Why didn't she think of her sooner?* Samira felt that she was onto something. *Where can I find her?* Samira didn't know where Nabiha lived. She used to see her at the *souk* when she shopped there, and they would exchange a few words, but that was all.

Samira had been Fatima Masri's housekeeper in the days when Nabiha crouched on the dirty floor of the fish-seller's stand, was cleaning and packing the fish for customers. "*Mrs. Samira,*" she used to address her with respect. Those days were long gone. Finally, Samira remembered that there was a *chaikhana* where maids used to meet, drink nana tea, smoke a *nargilea,* and gossip about their masters. Samira never went there, feeling it was below her position, but now she had to go. To her disappointment, Nabiha wasn't there.

A toothless old woman asked who she was looking for. Everyone raised their heads when she mentioned Nabiha's name. "She used to come here, but it must be at least two years since we last saw her."

"If she comes by," Samira said, "please tell her that Samira is looking for her. She can find me at the French Convent." The women nodded, and again Samira left empty-handed.

The *hamsin* in the fall was followed by the winter rains. Samira was waiting for spring to restart her search. Musa had not answered her letter, and she was torn between the desire to find Suha and Selim and the impulse to leave everything to Allah's will. She was in the convent's kitchen decorating cookies for the children when a little girl came running in, almost out of breath, "Samira, Samira, somebody's at the gate asking for you."

"You should be in class, instead of watching every passer-by. Do you want me to report you to Mother Superior?" Samira reprimanded her. The girl had tears in her eyes, "I did nothing wrong."

Samira hugged her; the girl was one of her little helpers. "Then go, go quick, before someone sees you."

Reluctantly, Samira headed for the gate. A woman dressed in black was peering through the iron bars. "Salaam Aleikum," she said timidly.

Samira did not recognize her. "Aleikum Salaam," she replied, staring at the holes in the woman's slippers. A beggar, she thought.

"It's me, Nabiha," the woman spoke up. "I was told that you were looking for me." Samira threw open the gate. They embraced and cried. Samira felt as if she had found an old relative.

The school bell rang for recess.

"Come with me," Samira took Nabiha's arm. "Wait for me in my cell, until I finish serving the midmorning snack. We have so much to talk about." Nabiha bent to kiss Samira's hand.

She looks so skinny and old, though she must be at least fifteen years younger than me. Samira could barely wait to hear where Nabiha had been the last few years. After that, she would ask the questions burning in her mind. *Does Nabiha know where the violin teacher lives now? Has she seen him lately?*

What if Nabiha becomes suspicious and starts asking me questions? Should I tell her what happened? With so many thoughts turning in her head Samira burned her hand pulling the trays of cookies from the hot oven.

Samira, you are getting old, she said to herself; *you are fifty-five years old and want to play detective. At your age! But now, with Nabiha here, isn't it a sign that Allah has heard my prayers?*

In the late afternoon, Samira, carrying a tray of food, entered the unadorned cell that served as her bedroom and found Nabiha asleep. As she set the tray on the small iron table by the bed, Nabihah woke up.

"I was so tired," she excused herself, quickly rising.

"Sit, eat, you must be famished," Samira said, gratified to see Nabiha attacking the food with a wolf's appetite. After Nabiha wiped her mouth with the back of her palm, stifling a hiccup, Samira said, "Now, tell me where you've been, what happened to you. It's been a long time since we last saw each other. I remember you worked for a *Yahud* violin teacher."

"Those were the good times," sighed Nabiha, 'but that was long ago. When my employers moved to Tel-Aviv, my life spiraled downward. I couldn't find a better place to work so I went back to the fish store. When the first wave of our people left Jaffa, we lost many customers. The fish-seller felt that it was dangerous to remain, especially after his wife gave birth."

Nabihah stopped and took a sip of the nana tea. Samira waited patiently for her to continue. "They had relatives living in Sassa, a village north of Tiberias, and he thought it would be safer there. 'Come with us,' he said, 'you'll help my wife take care of the baby and my older children.' I went. How was I to know that it would be worse than remaining here?"

Nabiha wiped her eyes. "The war caught up with us. It didn't take long to be driven away by the Syrian soldiers who camped there. We went to Tuba Zangria, another village close by, but not for long. We were chased from village to village by the Yahudim army. No food, no water, no shelter. The baby boy died. At the end, I had to part from them. My employer said, 'Nabiha, I have to save the lives of my other children. We are Mennonites and many of our co-religionists live in southern Lebanon. We are going there. You decide what you want to do.'"

Nabiha took another sip from the tea, now cold. "I wanted to return here, to Jaffa, the city I have known all my life. I have no family, I am alone, but if I have to die, better to die among my own people."

Samira took Nabiha's hands in hers. She felt the hard calluses in her palms, "I'm sorry. We all went through difficult times."

"What happened to Sit Masri and her family?" asked Nabiha, "Why aren't you with them?"

"That's a long story," Samira said. "I'll tell you another time. First I want to hear what happened to you."

"I wandered from place to place, mostly by foot, begging, many times sleeping in the burning fields, every dwelling ravaged by the war. Sometimes I was lucky to sleep in a shed not entirely burned, and where there was still a little food stashed aside. When I got to Nazareth, the monks at St. Paul gave me bread and water in return for cleaning their stalls. I don't remember how I arrived in Haifa barefoot, my slippers had given up long before. I heard somebody say that there were still a few Arabs living in the city. I went to the port. I missed the sea so much. What a better place to die than on the seashore?"

Nabiha stopped. Samira didn't urge her to continue. She was deeply touched by her friend's story. After a long pause, Nabiha said, "I saw a lonely old Arab fishing. He looked sad. After he watched me for some time, he said, 'I'm alone. My wife died, my children ran away. I was too old for them to take me. I have no money, but I need a woman to clean, wash and cook for me. If you are that woman, you'll have a bed and fresh fish to eat every day.' I went with him. He lived in Wadi Nisnas, in downtown Haifa."

Nabiha wiped her nose with a sleeve. "Until the day he died, about a month ago, he kept his promise. The money he left was enough for his burial, and a little for me to return to Jaffa. At the women's *chaikhana* I was told that you were looking for me." Her eyes looked hopeful.

"You can stay with me here," Samira said. Nabiha took her hand and kissed it again. "It's late and we are both exhausted," Samira continued. "You need a good night's sleep to gain your strength."

The next morning, a Friday, Samira's free day, she woke up to see Nabiha already dressed and waiting. "Why did you wake up so early?" Samira asked. A serious Nabiha looked her straight in the eye. "Yesterday you said that you'd tell me why you were looking for me," she said. "I think it's time."

"First, let me bring two cups of Turkish coffee. Friday is the nuns' fast day so I'm not on duty." Samira needed to think. A few minutes later she brought the steaming coffee with pita and leben on a tray.

"Do you know where the violin teacher lives now?" Samira asked, going straight to the point.

Nabiha looked surprised, "His address? Why? Before they moved away, he wrote it on a piece of paper and put it in an envelope together with a month's pay, which he said would tide me over until I found another job. Such a good man! I probably lost the paper. Anyway, it was written in a foreign language." Nabiha repeated, "Why do you need his address? What do you want from him?"

"It was him," Samira said with bitterness. "He was the one who turned Suha's head. I am sure of it. He and his accursed violin! I have to find her and Musa's child."

"What are you talking about? I was there the last time she visited. We planted flowers together in the garden. The boy played the violin, like he was born with it. Otto *Effendi* and his wife cried. They loved Selim. His name is Selim, isn't it? You must be mistaken, Samira. Those people couldn't hurt a fly."

"They are wicked," Samira screamed. "They and their music destroyed Suha's marriage. And it's my fault. I should have seen it coming."

"I don't understand. Start from the beginning. Tell me what happened."

When she ended her story, Samira said, "I have to find them, for Musa's sake, for my own redemption."

After a long silence, Nabiha said slowly, "I remember a number, a house number, fifty-four, or maybe forty-five. It was on the map Otto *Effendi* drew for me. He said they didn't move far from Jaffa, and to come to them if I needed help."

Samira sighed. Nabiha was her last hope, but what she knew led nowhere.

"I do remember something," Nabiha exclaimed. "On that design with streets crossing each other, he made two signs. He said, 'This mark is a hospital, if you get there, then you are close to our place, which is the second mark, three houses down the street, across from the hospital.'"

Samira repeated, "A hospital, not far from Jaffa! When Suha returned home the evening before she ran away, she said she went to see a woman doctor at a Jewish hospital. I thought that she lied to me but what if it wasn't a lie?"

Pacing the cell, she said. "Nabiha, we might be onto something. Tomorrow I'll ask the Mother Superior about hospitals in Tel-Aviv and which one is the closest to Jaffa." She clasped Nabiha's hands. "Something tells me," she said in a tremulous voice, "that we can find them."

"Samira, think, it's been two years or more since you last saw them. So many things have changed. It's time for you to wake up. This is not our country anymore. Open your eyes to the real world."

Samira embraced Nabiha, "You are a brave woman. I'm glad we found each other. Like you, I have nobody else. Be my sister. From now on we'll share everything."

The next day, Mother Superior looked worried when Samira asked her about the location of hospitals in Tel-Aviv.

"Are you sick?" she asked, "We have medicine sent to us from France. One of our nuns is a nurse. She could take care of you." Samira quickly told her she wasn't ill, that her question wasn't important, and that Mother Superior should forget about it.

During the weeks while she enjoyed Samira's hospitality, Nabiha searched for work. One day she returned, excited. "I was hired to take care of an old Yahud. His grandchildren arrived with him from Yemen. He is a frail man. While they are at work, they need somebody to watch over him."

Memories of *Adon* Grunwald, the sweet old man who was her first employer, returned. "How did they find you? How did you find them?" Samira asked.

"They stapled notices in Arabic on the walls of the *souk*. People who knew I was looking for work told me. They even helped me make the telephone call. The old man was so happy to hear me speak his mother tongue. I am going to start tomorrow." Nabiha collected her meager things. "But I'll come visit you as often as I can. And, Samira..." she hesitated. "Forget about finding Suha. It's been so long. You are looking for a needle in a haystack. You live in a convent protected by tall walls and have no idea what's happening outside. It's a new world. Yahudim have poured in from all corners of the world, thousands, maybe millions. Take my word. They work, they build high-rise houses. You wouldn't recognize old Jaffa, much less Tel-Aviv."

With Nabiha gone, Samira felt empty. Nabiha was right; she was a dreamer. She still dreamed of her life in Fatima's house; brushing Fatima's hair during their long talks, Na'ima's festive wedding, and of Musa, her favorite, and the laughter of the children.

Life in the convent became oppressive, the silence in the afternoons after the schoolchildren left, overwhelming. Samira wondered if she should look for work elsewhere. *Who'd hire me at my age, with swollen knees wobbling when I move? Am I strong enough to hold a baby in my arms?*

Since the nuns took their *repast* at midday, they didn't need her to serve the evening meal, so Samira was free to go see the changes that Nabiha had described. She developed a new routine, walking. She must have been longing for Fatima's house, because her feet led her there. She admired the garden, where the owners had planted new roses and cypress trees. The newly painted house looked clean. The gate was open, but the house was locked. Disappointed, Samira was ready to turn back, when a cheerful voice speaking

Arabic stopped her. It was the same young woman she had once seen nursing a baby, holding now the hand of a kindergarten-age child.

"God must've brought you," she answered Samira's *Salaam Aleikum*. "I recognized you immediately. You came by years ago."

"I used to live here," whispered Samira.

"I remember you saying so. As the last time, I have a letter addressed to you, or anybody who knows you. It came only a few days ago. Roni," she addressed the child, "there is a letter on top of the dresser. Bring it out."

A letter from Amina! Samira opened it feverishly. Many thin pages fell out. Her eyes scanned over the traditional greetings.

My heart is full of sadness as I'm writing to you. Our dear mother, Fatima, passed away last week....

Samira did not recall how she got back to the convent.

Clutching Amina's letter in her hand, Samira sat on her narrow bed. Fatima dead! She couldn't fathom the news. A chill went down her spine. She felt old, very old. Quivering, she dragged her feet to the kitchen to boil a cup of strong Turkish coffee for the long sleepless night ahead of her. The sadness that she couldn't properly mourn Fatima overwhelmed her.

Samira sat in the dark, her head empty, tears washing her face. She turned on the only bulb, and read, mouthing each word.

Bath, England 1953

Dear Samira,

You can't imagine how much we miss you, all of us. When my family arrived in England five years ago, everybody thought it would be a short holiday. My mother even refused to unpack, except for necessities. But soon we realized that Israel, the new Jewish state, would not welcome the return of Palestinians.

Was this the reason for my mother's illness? Her melancholy was aggravated by the fact that Musa wouldn't hear of remarrying." When I married, it was for life," he said, every time our mother broached the subject.

Maybe that's why he lived with us for a short time only. Musa was hired by the British International Bank. He lives in London and travels a lot, hoping that one day he'll enter the country where his wife hides his son.

Samira stopped. Her body trembled. *How could I forget the promises I made to myself to find Suha and Selim? I owe it to Musa, poor soul, now more than ever.* She continued to read.

But we have joys also. Nur is so pretty that Eumi wanted her to wear the hijab, which she refused." At least let me dispel the evil eye," my mother said.

"This is England, not a backwards place like Palestine" Nur answered. She studied nursing also, and now she is an assistant nurse at my hospital.

With my mother and Na'ima living with us, I decided to work again. The Mineral Water Hospital in Bath is one of the most sought-after hospitals. Its waters have healing powers, and people come from all over the world to be cured.

A young Pakistani doctor, a resident, began to visit Nur's ward assiduously. His name is Rafik Malek, a Muslim. I invited him home to meet our mother. My mother liked Rafik, who had been brought up in the best Muslim tradition. He sympathizes with the fight of the Palestinians to return to their homeland.

He is a Shiite, and sometimes his fanaticism scares me. For their wedding, he brought a mullah from

London to recite their marriage vows. Shortly after, they moved to London. Three years after their marriage, Nur still has no children, to Rafik's greatest chagrin. He invited our brother Ahmed to live with them. They pray together at London's Central Mosque. Nur is happy to have Ahmed with her, she said, but worries that the boy has become extremely religious.

I'm sure that thoughts of Musa, Nur and Ahmed, living far from her, aggravated my mother's illness. One day she said to me, "I miss your father and I don't feel needed anymore." Na'ima worried her too, because she wouldn't remarry, "One husband was plenty," she said.

Our bright Rama has adopted England! Rama's tales about her school, teachers and students amused our mother, who in the afternoons sat by the window, impatient for Rama's return. She never got used to the chilly English rainy season. I knew that she longed for our beautiful Jaffa, with its sun shining brightly.

Dear Samira, I hope that somehow this letter will find you.

Take care of yourself. Everybody sends their love,
Amina

A few days after she received Amina's letter, Samira went to the bazaar. She found it swarming with people. She had heard that many Yahudim, store owners who ran away from Jaffa during 1948 fights, had returned and reopened their shops. Maybe Adon Nathan was one of them! How come she didn't think of him sooner? Samira remembered how, in the bazaar, Suha always stopped to exchange a few words with him. "All I need is a bit of luck," thought Samira.

It wasn't difficult to find the shop, but to her dismay it was no longer the watchmaker's shop. In the window were displayed beautifully ornate silver candlesticks, tea sets, *Kiddush* cups, necklaces with silver Stars of David, others with silver crosses, prayer books with elaborate silver covers. It was a silversmith shop.

She stood in front of the window for a long time, until a young man, the image of a younger Mr. Nathan, appeared in the door frame and asked, "Jedati, how can I help you? Are you looking for something special?"

"Oh, young man," Samira answered, "I was looking for Nathan *Effendi*, who once owned this shop."

"He is my uncle," exclaimed the young man. "When we arrived from Morocco, on the magic carpet, as my Yemenite wife called the airplane, my uncle, knowing I was a silversmith, helped me start the shop. And as you can see, with G-d's help, the shop prospers."

A young man who likes to talk, thought Samira. *Should I ask him about what really interests me?*

"What did you want from my uncle, maybe I can be of help," the solicitous young man said.

"I wanted to greet him, *Shalom, Ahlan Wa-Sahlan Beek,* welcome back. But I'm glad I've met you. You seem to be as nice as he." Gathering her courage, Samira raised her eyes to the young man. "I need to find the name and address of a Jewish hospital in Tel-Aviv, the one closest to Jaffa."

"Are you talking about a maternity hospital?" he asked. Guessing that she didn't understand the word, he said, "Where women give birth, a women's hospital?"

Samira hesitated. "I think so."

"Then I can help you. My wife gave birth to our son there. An old hospital, maybe demolished already. Freud Hospital on Yehuda Halevi Street," he said aloud as he wrote on a slip of paper. "Here," he handed the paper to her. Then he saw his uncle standing behind the old woman signaling to keep his mouth shut.

"*Salaam Aleikum*, Samira," Adon Nathan said aloud. Samira turned, her heart throbbing.

"Did you bring news from Fatima Masri?"

49

New York

November 1968

The artists' room at Carnegie Hall filled up with people. Exhilaration was in the air. It was not every night that a new star, recipient of the Leventrittt Award, was introduced to the public. In the middle of the room, tired and smiling, Shlomi looked at the long queue of well-wishers waiting to congratulate him. He was happy, he knew he had played well, but he would have felt more at ease if he had been able to change into a pair of jeans and a T-shirt. The heat in the room was overwhelming. Sweat trickled down his spine.

"When I grow up I hope to play like you," a little boy, holding a half-size violin, said shyly. The boy reminded Shlomi of himself, addressing Isaac Stern, after one of his concerts in Israel. But where was Isaac? Shlomi's eyes searched the noisy room. He saw him in a corner, a glass of champagne in his hand, chatting with Otto, both smiling back at him.

Otto had not talked to him yet, except for the hug before the concert, and to say *merde*, the French word musicians use to wish good luck to one another before a concert. Sol Hurok, the famous impresario, approached Shlomi.

"Young man," he said, "I have watched you play for some time. You have grown into a mature artist. Congratulations. Here is my card. Call me."

Hurok was a man of few words but great deeds. To be represented by Sol Hurok meant an open door to an international career. Why didn't he feel more excited about the opportunity? His eyes searched the crowd again. Where was D'vorale his roommate, his love? Why wasn't she by his side?

Oh, there she was, animatedly talking to Mazal and Lotte, his adoptive mothers, her arm around the waist of a middle-aged woman, a stranger. All were looking at what seemed to be a photograph, then to him, again to the photo and back to him.

While he signed the souvenir program for his admirers his mind went back to D'vora. Tonight she'd have to cajole him into making love!

The group including Otto, wearing his perennial bowtie (*he seems so much shorter now*), Mazal, smiling, her golden earrings dangling, and Lotte, puffing (*probably the girdle is too tight*), came toward him. Isaac walked behind his darling D'vora, his eyes fastened on the movement of her slim body; alongside her walked the unknown woman.

"This is my cousin Chana, actually my father's cousin," D'vora introduced her. It was clear that the woman wore a *shaitel*. "My grandfather and Chana's father immigrated to Eretz Israel from Germany. Each one followed a different path, but we remained close and share in all of our family *Simchas*."

"In the airplane we sat next to Chana," Mazal followed D'vora's words, "and as we told her the reason for our traveling to New York, she said she was a music lover also, so Lotte and I consulted with Otto, and decided to invite her to your concert."

"A happy encounter," D'vora declared. "Now Chana is here and shares in your success," D'vora stopped in mid-sentence to kiss Shlomi, "I haven't congratulated you properly yet." With a glint in her eye she murmured in his ear, "But we have the entire night to celebrate."

"This is such a happy and unexpected event that I have invited my cousin to spend the weekend with us," D'vora continued, looking straight into Shlomi's eyes.

Is she talking about the surprise we've prepared for our visitors? Shlomi and D'vora had rented rooms at a bed and breakfast in Dobbs Ferry, not far from New York City, where an elderly widow hosted musicians, tired from life's fast tempo in the big city. She catered to them, happy to listen to their relaxed music-making.

D'vora had asked the hostess to let them have the entire house. *Now she wants to bring her cousin, too. Why?* Seeing all eyes riveted on him, Shlomi acquiesced.

"It's getting late, and we are tired," Otto said, "the travel, the emotions of the concert, the memories it evoked. It is hard to describe what I felt during your performance. Our life together seemed to unfold in front of my eyes. I am so proud of you."

Mazal and Lotte nodded in agreement.

"I'll accompany you to find a taxi. We'll see each other tomorrow morning at breakfast at your hotel," D'vora, who seemed to have taken control of the plan, said.

"I saw Sol Hurok speak with you," Isaac Stern said. "That's a good sign, my boy, a good sign," and he chuckled.

Dobbs Ferry, N.Y.

They had taken the train to Dobbs Ferry, a short distance from New York City. Shlomi was too tired to drive the morning after his concert. He had looked forward to taking long walks with Otto on the banks of the Hudson River, where they would replay the games of his childhood, competing in their knowledge of flowers and trees.

Besides playing violin duets with Otto, Shlomi's biggest pleasure had been their hikes together with their regular group of *Shmurot Hateva*, every Saturday morning, from Eilat to Metula, to discover Israel's beauties. The instructor, seeing Shlomi's enthusiasm, took him aside, "Are you sure you want to be a violinist?" Shlomi must have been thirteen or fourteen at the time, "With your love for nature and your fabulous memory, you could definitely become a botanist or a horticulturist."

Otto had smiled. "He takes after his mother. Like Shlomi, she loved music and flowers." Anytime Otto talked about his mother, Shlomi's heart listened.

Now, seated next to him on the train, Otto seemed smaller and thinner. Shlomi looked at the four women, D'vora, Lotte, Mazal and Chana, D'vora's cousin, the woman who had appeared from nowhere. They had turned one of the train benches to face one another and were talking with animation. Shlomi was pleased by Lotte and Mazal's arrival, he considered them family, but he felt uneasy about the newcomer. D'vora must have guessed the reason he wanted her and his loved ones to be together. He had planned to propose again. "It's about time to make you an honest woman," he'd said the first time, but she laughed and brushed away his words.

Why did D'vora invite this orthodox woman to share our vacation? Shlomi had not alerted the owner of the B&B that there was going to be an extra person, and now he wondered if there would be an extra bedroom.

"Dobbs Ferry, next stop!" the train conductor announced.

"Avanti," Shlomi said, taking Otto's arm. From the corner of his eye, he saw D'vora helping Chana, while Charlotte and Mazal buttoned up their jackets.

On the station platform, Shlomi turned to the group, "Are you ready for adventure? First take a deep breath, ozone, clean air, so different from New York, *is nicht war?* Lots of surprises await you here."

D'vora shuddered. *Surprises are in store for you, too, my darling. Soon you'll have to face them, and I am scared, scared for you!*

"The B&B is not far." Shlomi said.

"In that case, let's walk," Otto proposed. "After sitting in the train it would feel good to walk."

On the way Shlomi introduced the town, "We discovered Dobbs Ferry by chance. D'vora calls it an enchanting village."

"The spring is glorious here," D'vora took over, "Daffodils and daisies, irises and forget-me-nots, a real symphony of colors. Even now, in the fall, you can see coquette geranium pots in the windows along Main Street."

"We hiked on the Croton Aqueduct, which was the original water supply for New York City. You can still walk the trail today. The view of the Hudson River from the hills is spectacular. We actually plan to—"

"Stop, stop," Charlotte interrupted Shlomi's enthusiasm. "You forget our age, *langsam*, slower, my dear child, I am tired already."

Shlomi heard Chana whispering, "It's so quiet here, it must be a nice place to raise children," and saw D'vora's response in her luminous smile.

"We have arrived," D'vora said, after turning the corner onto Oak Street. She opened the gate in front of a white two-story house, surrounded by a luxuriant garden.

"Ach," exclaimed Otto, "what breathtaking colors. The trees are already dressed for the holidays."

"All maple trees, Scarlet Red maple and Autumn Purple Ash. Behind the patio you'll see the Autumn Blaze, my favorite," Shlomi said.

"C'mon friends," Mazal called out impatiently. "You'll have time to admire the trees later. Let's get settled first."

Inside the spacious living room, the women admired the low beams and the fireplace in which a friendly fire sang quietly. With a sigh of relief, Charlotte threw herself onto one of the large chairs covered with floral chintz.

"Welcome to Dobbs Ferry." The owner of the B&B, a woman in her mid-sixties with gray curls escaping from a tight chignon, greeted them, her hands still drying on a kitchen towel. Shlomi introduced his guests. A frown passed over the owner's forehead, "I thought you mention five people? Of course I can ask my neighbor if she would...."

"Don't trouble yourself," D'vora hurriedly said, "we are all going to share the rooms, my cousin and I, Shlomi and Mr. Schroeder, and Charlotte and Mazal told me that they'd like to be together."

She turned to Shlomi, whose eyebrows formed an angry line. "I thought it would be best, since you and Otto have so much to tell one another." She looked innocently at him, while Shlomi frowned. *Why doesn't she want to sleep with me—does the others' presence make her shy?*

"In a minute I'll serve coffee and tea. My petit-fours are about ready. And for Shlomi, his favorite, cranberry jam," said the hostess. "Please, make yourselves comfortable and think of this house as your own home," she ended graciously.

"We'd better unpack, even though we brought the minimum," said Charlotte, ready to mount the staircase. She addressed the hostess, "Please show us our rooms first." Mazal, Otto Chana and Charlotte followed the hostess, while Shlomi gripped D'vora's arm.

"What's all this?" he whispered. "Since last night I've had a nagging feeling that this holiday, which I so much looked forward to, is not going to turn out the way I expected."

"Ouch, it hurts," D'vora cried, freeing her arm. Shlomi thought he saw a cloud passing over her face. "I love you," she said. "I want you to always remember, I love you with all my heart. You are, as my mother would say, my *basherte*. But," she said coquettishly, "that's on condition that you love me just as much."

She kissed him on his lips, "Now I have to run upstairs and see if everything is in order."

Shlomi headed for the porch, where he could see the maple tree basking in the sun. If he had remained longer at the bottom of the staircase he would have heard a worried D'vora say to Mazal, "He's suspicious. He doesn't feel at ease. The sooner he's told, the better."

At lunch, the guests delighted in the homemade bread, the Caesar salad and a spinach quiche. By the time the coffee was served, an exuberant Shlomi pushed his cup aside and opened a wide map of Dobbs Ferry and its surroundings.

"It's a shame to lose time. It's so pretty outside, almost an Indian summer day. I propose we go exploring. Whoever wants to walk at leisure could visit the galleries and the boutiques on Main Street. Or we could take a trail up into the hills from where one can see almost as far as New York."

After a few seconds of silence, Otto said, "Shlomi, we came to celebrate your big event, but also to talk to you about matters that have weighed on me for a long time, for which I never found the right opportunity. I hoped to talk to you after your service in the Israeli army, but six months later you left to study in the United States."

Shlomi frowned. *What was this?*

"Did I do well by waiting?" Otto continued. "After your mother's premature death, you, not even four years old, became so sick from the shock that we thought we'd lose you, too." Charlotte and Mazal nodded. "You were such a sensitive child."

Shlomi observed that Otto's intertwined fingers were blanched from tension. "We respected your mother's will. She wanted us to raise you. Watching you grow was our biggest joy."

A bell of alarm rang in Shlomi's head. *What is he talking about?*
Why now? That chapter is closed.

"Your mother wasn't an orphan; she wasn't a child refugee in
the Teheran train, as we told you. Shifra was born in Jerusalem in
an orthodox family."

Otto stopped and looked at Chana for help, but Charlotte was
faster. "Thanks to Mazal, our detective, we discovered Shifra's old
friend. Mazal had a real adventure."

Shlomi felt his head cracking. "Mazal's adventures don't interest
me. Can any of you tell me what's happening?" He raised his voice.
"At twenty-three years old, I still don't know who I am. My mother
is dead, though now I doubt even this, and the grave of my father,
according to your words 'the hero of '48,' was never found."

Chana pushed Shifra's picture toward Shlomi, "Your mother is
in the middle." How many times he would have jumped for joy to
see a picture of his mother, but now he pushed it away.

"Lies, I grew up with lies," Shlomi closed his eyes.

He did get a glimpse of the picture: a girl with blond braids and
eyes opened to mirror the entire world. In a flash, he recognized in
her the woman with clear eyes and blond hair waving in the wind,
who ran calling him desperately when he got lost on the beach.
How old was he then?

Around him everybody was talking at once. He heard fragments.

Chana said, "He was a strong father. All the neighbors knew
that he promised Shifra's hand to an old widower, a father of three
girls close to her own age. When Shifra disappeared, her mother
accused her husband of driving her away. She stopped coming to
shul. But Shifra was never found."

She must have been raped or became a prostitute, thought
Shlomi. He ached all over. "I am a *mamzer*, that's what you've come
to tell me, the offspring of a one-night stand with a thief or worse;
a criminal father and a prostitute mother!" Shlomi screamed. He
wondered if the pain and the shame would kill him on the spot.

He heard a chorus of voices, "No, that's not true." "You are mistaken." But he had heard enough. Holding the table for support, he tried to get up. Barely breathing, he said, "I have to go, I need...."

"Shlomi, where are you going?" Scared, D'vora ran after him.

"Leave me alone. You are on their side. You knew what awaited me; you must have heard it from your cousin. I am a prostitute's son! Next I suppose I might find out she's alive in a mental hospital or in jail."

"Stop! I know you are hurting. But it's not true. Turn back, Shlomi. Please calm down, for my sake. I love you! Your mother was a fine person who suffered the circumstances of her upbringing. It revolted her...."

D'vora breathed heavily; she could not keep in step with Shlomi. "Listen," she tried again, "according to Chana, your mother was very talented, she loved music, she sang beautifully. Her father took her out of school, to stay home and help her mother raise her brother and sisters."

D'vora stopped. "Shlomi, please, I have no more strength. Come back, come..." She hoped the wind would carry her words to him.

It was almost evening when an exhausted Shlomi returned. He found them in the same position as when he left, silently sitting around the table, their faces, masks of sorrow. Mazal saw him first, and a sob burst from her throat. Everybody looked up. D'vora ran to him. Shlomi's clothes were wrinkled, his shoes dirty, dead leaves hung in his hair. He fell into a chair,

"I am ready," he whispered. "Start from the beginning."

Watching Otto intensely, he asked, "You haven't told me about my father. What do you know about him? Have the two of you ever met?"

Otto remained silent. "Who was he? Surely my mother must have told you about him," Shlomi's voice went crescendo.

"Your mother loved your father very much," Otto started, his voice sounding uncertain, "and he loved her...."

Shlomi cut him short, "You didn't answer my question! Who was my father?" Shlomi stubbornly repeated. "What else are you hiding from me?"

Mazal placed a soothing hand on his shoulder, "You know, Shlomi, this was an exhausting day for all of us. We are drained emotionally. Please, let's continue tomorrow."

Shlomi felt his anger mounting, "Why do you want to postpone telling me what you know about my father? To lessen what could be another blow? Why do you still treat me like a child?" he screamed.

D'vora embraced Shlomi, whose heart wanted to scream, *you are the only reality in my life.*

"Do you remember, Shlomi," Mazal started, "that, for years, the two of us went to the beach on Friday afternoons after you came home from school? Friday was a short day, and we always hurried because there was little time left before Shabbat."

Shlomi remained silent. "One day," Mazal continued, "about four or five years after your mother died - you must have been about eight at the time - I saw an old woman, a gypsy I thought, crouched across the street, in front of Levy's pharmacy, her eyes riveted on our house. Something about her attracted my attention. "*Yala, yala*, move!" a policeman screamed at her. The woman got up with difficulty. A few days later I saw her back at her post. Again a Friday, around the time Otto used to bring you home from school. You only had to put your books away before we headed for the beach."

"I remember," Shlomi said, "that Otto taught violin until late in the evening. Gretchen couldn't take me to the beach. You were my protective angel. But what has this to do with...."

"It has, believe me. That woman followed us. She waited patiently during the two hours we spent at the beach and then followed us back. Early one morning, again on a Friday, as I was returning from the *souk*, she crossed the street and asked me in broken Hebrew mixed with Arabic, "Have you adopted the boy?"

"*Yo-seida*, old woman," I answered in Arabic, "why in the world do you ask me that?"

"I know his parents," she said. "I raised his father. I was the boy's nanny. But the boy's mother ran away with him. Since then nothing could console my Musa." Tears fell from her tired eyes. "She destroyed him. It was my fault," she kept repeating, "my fault alone, because I trusted her."

Mazal stopped. The colors in Shlomi's face changed from pale to dark red and pale again. In a voice in which the others could hear his despair, Shlomi whispered, "My father was an Arab." He got up from his chair. "An Arab who raped my mother, Oh, God," he repeated, while his shaking hands covered his face. "What a shame, what a shame."

With his bloodshot eyes fixed on Otto, Shlomi started to laugh, an unnatural laugh that ended with a sound like broken glass. "You waited until I was on my way to a big career in order to tell me that I am a bastard. *Is nicht war*, Grandpa Otto?"

The flame in Shlomi's eyes scared D'vora. "Shlomi, please," she pleaded.

"That's not true," Mazal screamed, while Otto sat crumpled in his chair. "You are mistaken, Shlomi. Your parents were married. Please let me finish. I am just at the beginning—"

"I don't need to hear anything more. Enough, I've heard enough from you, all lies. I'll never forgive you," Shlomi looked at his guests with hatred, "Never!"

"Shlomi," D'vora knelt in front of him, "I know that nobody can take away your pain, but for my sake, please listen to Mazal." D'vora's head dropped on Shlomi's knees, her arms encircling him.

"You're in tandem with them. Your cousin must've told you. Otto needed to bring a full delegation. What a masquerade!" Shlomi pushed D'vora's arms away.

But D'vora wouldn't relent. "You forget that each one gathered here loves you and cares for you."

"I am Arab! I am Arab! I placed my father on a pedestal, a hero of the Independence War, as he told me," Shlomi pointed an accusing finger at Otto, "A hero, really! My only hope is that a good Jewish fighter took care of him," he said bitterly.

. "Your father is alive," Mazal said softly.

"Little wonder Shifra never told you about her family. She knew that her parents wouldn't care for her Arab bastard," Shlomi continued, deaf to Mazal's words.

His eyes looked like spears when he addressed Otto, "You wanted to appease your conscience, no matter the price." Otto wept silently.

Three women spoke. D'vora said, "Shlomi this is not the way to talk to the man who raised you." Mazal and Lotte took over, "And for whom you became the center of his universe."

Otto raised his hand, "Shlomi is right. I failed him as I failed Ruthie."

"Your father is alive," Mazal repeated.

Shlomi raised his eyes. He had heard her, but he didn't care. Whoever and wherever his father was, for him he was dead.

"Samira told me…" Mazal started. At the name Samira, Shlomi's body shuddered. He saw eyes that smiled at him, heard guttural laughter. His lips shaped the word, Samira. He said it, like tasting a word long forgotten, "Jedati Samira."

"She was the old woman," Mazal said. "For years, she said, she had searched for you and your mother. She didn't want to tell me how she discovered us. I told her your mother was dead. She cried 'I loved her, as I would have loved my own daughter if Allah had blessed me with one. Yet she betrayed me.'

"I saw Samira many times after that, and little by little she told me about the beginning of your parents' budding romance which she encouraged, against all odds."

Shlomi's eyes were closed. Mazal wasn't even sure that he was listening.

"A love story! Please continue, Mazal," D'vora said, "I love romances."

The rain had started, drops beating furiously on the windows.

"Musa, Shlomi's father, saved Shifra from drowning. Samira called her Suha, the Arabic name the Masri family gave her. Musa fell in love with her and against his mother's wishes, they got married. Not long after, Selim, the name they called you, Shlomi, was born."

The telephone rang, startling them. It was almost midnight. The hostess called out, "Shlomi, it's for you." Shlomi got up, and D'vora, who still held his hand, went with him. From the living room they heard Shlomi's voice. "Thanks for calling. No, I am not hiding." And after a while, "I'll think about it and let you know. Soon, I promise."

"It was Mr. Hurok," D'vora reported back. "He already has two contracts for Shlomi."

"I wonder how he knew where to find me," Shlomi said, watching Otto.

D'vora said, "Mazal, please continue."

"Samira blamed Otto. She said, 'It was the violin teacher who put ideas in Suha's head.'

"How," I asked her, 'Because of the music,' she said. Though she told Suha that the violin was the devil's instrument, she never realized that Suha continued her visits and took Selim with her, too.

"There was much tension, with the war almost at their gate. Fatima, Musa's mother, pressed him to leave the country. If Suha had acted like a devoted Muslim wife, she would have followed her husband, but she disappeared, taking the child with her. Suha's death was Allah's punishment, Samira said."

"Abu Selim, Abu Selim" Shlomi whispered suddenly, his eyes closed. "Was there ever a time when I called my father's name?"

Mazal answered, "One night during your illness, when it was my turn to watch you, you hallucinated and called his name, like now."

Shlomi shrugged, as if wanting to get rid of a bad dream. "For years I wanted to learn about my parents, hoping to discover who I am. Now, I know."

He left the room.

5 0

Tel Aviv

August 1969

In the spacious guest house of the Israeli Philharmonic Orchestra, D'vora browsed through recent newspapers, eager to read the musical reviews. It was early in the morning. She sat on the bed, one leg curled beneath her, the other one hanging bare, while her diaphanous nightgown sculpted her supple body.

She sighed with satisfaction after running her eyes over most of the reviews. "Shlomi," she called, "Come read. Maariv, Jerusalem Post, Yediot Aharonot's critics compete in their praises for you. Hear a few of the headlines: **Shlomi Gal's playing is of international caliber, Shlomi is following in Itzhak Perlman and Pinchas Zuckerman's footsteps, Shlomi's Beethoven radiated enthusiasm and assurance.** And there is much more."

The bathroom door opened and Shlomi appeared, shaving cream spread over his face. In one leap he was at her side, his arms circled around her body, "Mmm, you smell good." He hid his face in her hair.

"Shlomi, stop it. Look what you did. Now I'll have to take another shower. I want you to read the reviews, not to jump on me like a wild animal," she was laughing.

"I can't refrain being wild when I am near you," Shlomi said. "Let's make love. We'll read the reviews later. Just looking at you I get hungry." He wiped his face on her nightgown before sliding it off her body.

"Shlomi," she protested mildly, "be serious, we have a rehearsal in a couple of hours, this is not the time." He closed her mouth with a kiss. Their bodies knew each other so well, their rhythms and frissons identical to the rhythm and emotions of their making music together.

"Marry me," Shlomi said. "Let's get married today." Picking her up in his arms, he sang Mendelssohn's Nuptial March, matching words to the music, twirling her naked body around the room.

"My darling, I want it as much as you do, but today doesn't seem to be the right time. Please read your reviews. I've started collecting them since the Leventrittt Award opened the gates of the international music world for you. From London, Rome, Copenhagen to Helsinki and Vienna, only accolades for your performances. I am so proud of you."

With their heads, one blond, one dark, close together, they started to read aloud. Shlomi was invited to play a concert for the Israeli Festival with the Israeli Philharmonic Orchestra in Tel-Aviv and Jerusalem, and both he and D'vora were asked to coach students at the Rubin Academy.

"Before a large audience of music lovers and students, Shlomi and D'vora proved that their teaching was as professional as their performances. The students were thrilled with the way they were taught." D'vora read aloud the critique in The Jerusalem Post.

"Look at this one," Shlomi exclaimed, picking another newspaper. "It really warms my heart to see Otto mentioned. When he told me that after twenty-seven years with the Philharmonic it was time for him to retire, I felt that he was saying good-bye to the most important part of his life. 'My hands have arthritis,' he told me when I stopped in Israel between my European concerts, 'It's time to leave. I know that many talented youngsters are waiting for an opening. It's not right to hold a chair which, by now, belongs to others.'"

"He and his *yeke* upbringing, you said then," D'vora reminisced. "You were impressed by Otto's modesty. He was completely unaware of the surprise you'd prepared for him. You knew that if you suggested that you would perform a concert dedicated to Otto, the management of the Israeli Philharmonic, eager to have you perform for free, would agree immediately."

Shlomi read, **On the podium Shlomi Gal addressed the bewildered man seated in the second violin section of the Israeli Philharmonic Orchestra; 'Dear Otto, please allow me the honor of performing together the Bach Concerto for Two Violins.' Then Gal turned to the sold-out captive audience. "This concerto," he said, "is dear to both of us. We played it many times, my teacher, who is also my adoptive grandfather, and I. I wouldn't be playing violin if not for him. The piece hasn't been announced in the program. It's the surprise the Israeli Philharmonic and I want to offer Otto on the eve of his retirement."**

"Otto had tears in his eyes. He was visibly moved," D'vora recalled, "and of course he knew the music by heart."

She continued to read: **"Their phrasing, tone, and perfect give-and-take reminded me of the performance I heard with David Oistrakh and his son, Igor. I thought at the time that only blood-related artists could arrive at this level of unity and musical understanding.'**

"That's only the Davar's critic," D'vora said, "but I'm sure there will be others too."

"I am happy," Shlomi said, "I'm going to call Otto."

D'vora was pleased. Though Shlomi didn't tell her, she knew that since that evening in Dobbs Ferry when Shlomi was told the truth about his parents, he had not had any contact with Otto. He was nervous and agitated whenever she mentioned Otto. She had pleaded with Shlomi, "It's time to make peace. Otto is an old man." Shlomi only returned a cold stare. But the recent concert proved that he had listened to her.

"Let's get married right now. We can be at City Hall in half an hour," Shlomi said interrupting her reverie.

"And how about a rehearsal that starts in half an hour?" retorted D'vora. "I have to shower and get dressed, all in ten minutes." She took his face in her hands. "Ask me again when there is no concert to perform on the same evening."

D'vora suspected Shlomi kept secrets from her. One day, as she was cleaning his tuxedo, she saw an empty envelope falling from one of its pockets. No letter. It was addressed to Shlomi c/o Hurok Agency. The return address was Bath, England, written in a beautiful handwriting, careful penmanship, definitely a woman, she thought.

D'vora didn't ask Shlomi about the letter. And she did not dare ask Mr. Hurok's secretary; probably an admirer. D'vora knew that Shlomi's profession and his long tours could present dangers. But each time he returned home from a concert tour, he was more passionate than ever.

51

News travels fast in the music world. Yehudi Menuhin's invitation to have Shlomi perform at his annual Bath Music Festival in England in June 1969 was proof. During the months following the Dobbs Ferry revelations, D'vora had asked him numerous times if he was planning to meet any of his relatives while he was there.

"Leave me alone," he answered. "I am not interested."

But he was. He thought of Samira, the only witness of his early childhood, and longed to see her. Her image was clearer in his mind than his mother's. Before flying to England, Shlomi called Mazal. He hadn't spoken to her—or Charlotte or Otto—in seven months. "Shalom Aleichem," Mazal answered to his, "Shalom."

"I am going to play a concert in England, and I want to swing by Israel first."

"Otto will be happy to see you."

"Mazal, you said that you know Samira. I'd like to meet her. She's the only person from my childhood I can recall clearly. In my ears I hear the tinkling of her many bracelets. Can you help me find her?"

"I probably can. She lives in an old people's home in Jaffa. But Shlomi, Otto will be disappointed if he learns you were in Israel and didn't visit him."

"He doesn't have to know," Shlomi said sharply.

"Then there is no point in finding Samira's address," retorted Mazal. "Good day, Shlomi."

"Mazal, wait..."

"Call me again if you change your mind." Mazal sounded upset.

The next day he called, apologetic. Yes, he was wrong, he told Mazal. All three of them, Otto, Charlotte and herself, his adoptive family, they deserved better. "I am stressed, my mind tells me to do one thing, my heart another. And my concerts! I have to be on top of my performances, even on days when I'd prefer to crawl into a dark place."

Shlomi stopped for two days in Israel. After a short visit with Otto and Charlotte, he accompanied Mazal to the old folks' home in Jaffa. He was dismayed to see the decrepit building where Samira shared a room with three other women.

Samira knew from Mazal that Shlomi was coming. If Mazal had not pointed her out, Shlomi wouldn't have recognized her. Samira had watched for his arrival, close to the entrance. When she saw him, she screamed, "My boy, my young master, Selim Ibn Musa Ibn Faud Masri, Salaam Aleikum. Allah Ackbar has sent you to shine upon my old eyes."

Shaking, she started to kneel, but Mazal and Shlomi wouldn't let her.

"Talk to me, please," she said in Arabic, kissing his hands and touching him shyly, as if wanting to make sure it was not a dream.

Mazal was the translator. Shlomi kept repeating, "Jedati Samira," caressing Samira's calloused hands, bare of bracelets. *Did he only dream her bracelets?*

Samira pressed into his hands a few yellowish papers written in Arabic, "From England, from your Aunt Amina, your father's sister," she said. "Amina, Na'ima, twins, Nur, Rama and Ahmed," she counted on her fingers, "Your aunts and uncle. I sent Amina your pictures which Sit Mazal, Allah bless her, gave me, though I kept a few for myself, too. Look!"

She showed him a few old black and white photographs taken with Mazal's amateur camera at each one of his high-school end of the year concerts.

Shlomi looked at Mazal, who said apologetically, "She missed you so much. I gave her your pictures." Stains left by tears blurred his image.

He looked at the letters in his hand. "Samira probably wants me to read these, but I don't know Arabic."

Mazal fired a few words. Samira nodded. "Samira wants you to have them. I can try to translate, of course only if you so desire."

Samira's fingers were still intertwined with Shlomi's when he signaled that they had to part. "I'll come back," Shlomi promised, kissing Samira's forehead and arranging the fallen *hijab* around her face. "I am happy I found you," He looked at her bare arms, "Next time I am going to bring you the most beautiful bracelets," and he embraced her again.

"I know a coffee house close by, where nobody will disturb us," Mazal suggested after they left Samira, "You can have a cup of coffee while I try to decipher your aunt's handwriting."

Shlomi was overwhelmed. He wasn't sure he wanted to hear what his aunt wrote. What for? He was not interested in his father's family. He'd had a childish desire to see Samira. Now that he had seen her, he had to stop this nonsense. *Return to reality.*

"Mazal, those letters," he mumbled, "I don't want to know their contents. They were meant for Samira, not for me. Probably full of hatred for my mother, I prefer not to hear. Let bygones be bygones. Please return them to her."

Shlomi took the letters from his pocket and as he handed them to Mazal, he saw the return address on the envelope, Bath, England.

"Oh, my God, what a coincidence," Shlomi fell silent for a few seconds, "Bath is the city where I am going to perform in three days."

"Now you have an opportunity to meet your aunt through her writing," Mazal said. "What you'll discover might help you make a decision; whether to look for her or not."

Shlomi looked bewildered. "Samira is not stupid," Mazal continued. "Did she have an ulterior motive when she insisted you take the letters? I say, let's find out."

In the Jaffa coffee house Mazal translated Amina's letters while Shlomi took notes from time to time. *I'll read my scribbles on the airplane.*

Peering at his watch, he said, "Mazal, let's go, otherwise we'll be late for Charlotte's lunch. You know that for her, like for all *yekes*, punctuality is the most important attribute."

They returned in silence to the house where Shlomi grew up. As Shlomi and Mazal approached it, his nose distinguished the unmistakable aroma of Charlotte's cooking.

"Hmm" Shlomi said, as he entered. "If I'm not mistaken, it smells of sauerbraten and Wiener schnitzel. *Nicht wahr?*" he asked, kissing Charlotte's flushed face.

"Your favorites," Charlotte answered, "also a potato salad, 'a la Russe,' to complement the meal. Nothing is too good for the return of our prodigal son."

"Let's not exaggerate," said Hugo Gruber, Charlotte's husband. He, Otto and Bruno were seated at the table, wide napkins tucked into the collars of their shirts.

"First, wash your hands, you two," commanded Charlotte, "We don't need germs in here." Timidly, Otto asked, "How did the encounter go? Are you glad that you met Samira?"

Shlomi looked at Mazal. "I got more than I bargained for. I went to visit a memory. That memory reminded me of a reality that I'm not sure I am ready or want to face."

Everyone looked puzzled.

Mazal intervened. "Samira gave Shlomi the letters she received during the last ten, fifteen years, from his aunt, his father's sister, who has lived in England since the end of the war in Europe. Her husband is British."

"Please sit down. The food is going to get cold. Food is meant to be enjoyed on its own, and not as garnish for discussion," Charlotte said sternly.

Shlomi smiled, "Charlotte, the universe can change, but you remain the same. That's why we all love you. *L'chaim.*" he raised his glass.

"*L'chaim, Atzlaha and Briut*," for life, success and health, replied the chorus of voices.

Shlomi's El-Al flight was leaving at dawn, and Otto insisted on seeing him off. In the limousine, on the way to the airport, Shlomi broke the silence. "Otto, I always wanted to ask you, but somehow never did. How come my last name is Gal? Chana said that my mother's last name was Lefkowitz, by marriage she became Masri, Shifra Lefkowitz, Suha Masri. Where does Gal, the name engraved on her headstone, come from?"

Otto did not reply.

Shlomi persisted, "Why don't we share your last name—Schroder?"

"We never adopted you officially," Otto answered.

Otto peered through the limousine window at the approaching lights of Ben-Gurion airport. "Your mother had artistic inclinations.

She loved music and loved the sea: she said that for her, each *gal*, each wave has its own special sound when it chases the next one. When the wind blows hard, she could hear a full orchestra." Otto wiped his eyes.

"In 1948 many immigrants arrived in this country. They were survivors of the Holocaust eager to start anew. Most of them decided to change their names to Hebrew ones, like Alon, Zohar or Mishori. They wanted to get rid of their Diaspora names, which were a remembrance of their suffering. It wasn't difficult to obtain a name change. That's what Shifra did too. 'Shlomi Gal,' she said, sounded like music to her ears. I didn't dissuade her. I knew that Shifra, like so many others, was ready to start a new life."

In the airplane Shlomi opened the notes he had taken while Mazal translated Amina's letters, especially what she wrote about his father, but Amina had only mentioned that Musa traveled a lot and changed residences often. Shlomi was disappointed. Why did he want to know if his father remarried and if there were other siblings?

Shlomi closed his eyes. He could not remember his father's face, his voice. He whispered Abu Selim, Musa, but it didn't help.

Bath enchanted him. A city of flowers, large avenues, unhurried people walking slowly and greeting their acquaintances, groups of mothers strolling with baby carriages, and above all the mild temperature that was like a call to be outdoors. Glass windows of shops and restaurants featured festival posters. A poster on an easel, including pictures of the performers, his among them, stood in front of Bath Abbey where the concerts took place.

"Good acoustics, the rehearsal went well," Shlomi reported to D'vora, when he called her at noon. "Now I have free time to explore the city."

"There is a lot to see," D'vora sounded excited. "I read about Bath's history. Since the Roman times its mineral springs have made the city famous. The Georgian style of architecture is also interesting. Memorize every detail so I can see the city through your eyes."

"Maybe you can smell the flowers on me also," teased Shlomi, "the nature here is intoxicating."

"Don't forget to take a Roman bath, it has healing power."

"I would if we'd bathe together. No fun just by myself."

Shlomi was still smiling, remembering the conversation. Lazily, he opened the pages of the Bath telephone book. He looked for George Gardner, Amina's husband. Wow, quite a lot of Gardners—of course in a city with so many gardens—at least five baptized George, which one could be Amina's husband? Why should he bother looking for her? Even if he finds her, what would he say? *Here is your long-lost nephew, the Jewish one, the target of your hatred, who can't even explain what urges him to look for you.* Oh, I am an idiot.

At the top of a page he saw A&G Gardner, 44 Brock Street. Could this stand for Amina and George? He dialed the number.

"Hello," a woman answered.

"Are you Mrs. Gardner, I mean Mrs. Amina Gardner?"

"Yes,"

"Greetings from Samira," Shlomi felt knots in his throat.

"Samira." A pause, "Do you speak Arabic?"

"No, Ma'am. I am a volunteer at the old folks' home where she lives. My name, sorry, I didn't introduce myself, is Al, Al Sand. *Lie, go ahead, lie, why would the son be different from his mother?*

Silence.

"Well, good day, Ma'am. I fulfilled my promise."

"Wait, wait, please, Mister, ahh...."

"Sand, Mrs. Gardner, Al Sand."

"Mr. Sand, you took me by surprise. Samira, oh, I miss her so, she was like a mother to all of us. It's hard to believe that I haven't seen her in twenty-five years."

"She talks a lot about you and your family."

"How do you know, does she speak Hebrew?"

"Our volunteers include people who speak Arabic. We encourage the old people to tell their life stories. It keeps them alert."

"What else do the volunteers do?"

"We entertain, some of us sing, some play instruments. *What a fool I'm making of myself.* Others help with physical exercises, for people like Samira, who has arthritis in her hands and can't...."

"I've got an idea, Mr., Mr., excuse me I didn't retain your name.

"Al Sand."

"Mr. Sand, I'd like to invite you for a cup of coffee with some delicious Bath pastries."

"Oh, I couldn't," Shlomi got spooked. *What started as a joke...*

"I insist," Amina said. "I know you are Jewish." *She didn't say Israeli.* "Yet I think it's beautiful that you care for our Arab brethren. Once I had a Jewish sister-in-law," she sighed, "whom I loved like a sister."

"Sorry, I have to go now."

"Please, let's meet someplace. Do me a favor. I want to send Samira a woolen shawl. You know how cold and rainy Jaffa's winters are."

"I am here for only a short time."

"Four o'clock this afternoon, at Sally Lunn Refreshment House. It's a tourist attraction, one of Bath's landmarks. I'll wear a green raincoat and have a green umbrella. See you, Mr. Sand."

Four in the afternoon and my concert starts at seven. What drives me to get involved with her, except my yetzer hara, my evil instinct.

Shlomi contemplated himself in the bathroom mirror. The moustache had been D'vora's idea. She said, laughing, "You look so young, nobody will take you seriously."

"I think a moustache would emphasize my Arab origins," he answered, but he listened to her suggestion.

At quarter to four, dressed in jeans, sneakers and a sweat shirt, Shlomi sat waiting at a small table in the back of Sally Lunn pastry shop. He wore dark glasses. Posters of his concert covered the walls. He wanted to be there early, to observe her first. When the Abbey clock chimed four times, Amina entered. Shlomi recognized her from her description, a woman in her forties, tall and good-looking. He walked toward her. "I have only fifteen minutes," he said when they shook hands, "The guide is meeting our group very soon."

Amina took a long look at him, which made Shlomi fidget.

"I can't tell you why, but you remind me of somebody," she said, "your complexion, your hair. Maybe somebody I knew when I was young."

Maybe my father, Shlomi was relieved that she couldn't see his eyes.

"Since your call this morning," Amina said, "I haven't done anything but let the memories fill my heart. I've seen myself surrounded by my family, my mother, my three sisters, my two brothers, Samira, such a lovely clan. Then my brother fell in love with a Jewish girl he saved from drowning and married her."

A waiter came to the table to take their order.

"You are my guest," Amina said quickly. "While in Bath you must try Sally Lunn buns. They are famous."

"Thanks, you really shouldn't, I feel embarrassed."

"I didn't picture you so young, but your voice told me that you were a good and compassionate person...please eat," Amina said as their order appeared on the table. "It's Sally Lunn's own recipe."

Seeing her motherly look, Shlomi forced himself to eat, though he had no appetite.

"Until her death my mother thought that Suha, my brother's Jewish wife, brought the *nackba* upon us. But that wasn't true. Powers outside our little world decided our fate. We were like pawns in a chess game."

Amina started crumbling her bun. "When we were reunited I hoped that we'd live close to one another, but before long our family dispersed. My older brother travels continuously. My twin sister lives now with her two sons who opened a car repair shop. Another sister lives in London. Rama, our younger sister, is a student of history and world affairs. She hopes to bring peace to the world. Peace," she sighed. "I don't even know where my younger brother is."

Amina lowered her head, "Please excuse me. My prattle must tire you."

"Not at all," protested Shlomi. He was afraid that saying more would show how much her words touched him.

Amina sipped her coffee, her eyes distant, "Today after my reminiscences, I started wondering if we'd ever grow roots in this country."

"I understand you," Shlomi said. "My grandparents emigrated from Germany, to escape the greatest tragedy in human history. Yet it was difficult for them to erase the old country; they spoke German at home and with their friends, a little colony of German Jews living in Israel."

"My only wish, "Amina said, "is for my brother Musa, to be able to reunite with his son. I think he dashes around the world, like the Flying Dutchman, only to forget his sorrow."

Shlomi became restless. *One more minute I'll lose my composure.* "I'm sorry, but I can't stay longer." He took her hands in his. "I hope that one day you'll decide to visit Samira." Shlomi felt a lump forming in his throat. "I'm glad we've met."

Amina stood up, "Do you allow me to hug you?"

Shlomi nodded. He couldn't speak.

As they left the coffee shop he impulsively asked, "Do you enjoy concerts? The Bath Music Festival is on right now."

"Music is my husband's domain," she answered. "Unfortunately it wasn't part of my education. My husband says that I don't realize how much I miss."

"I happen to have two free tickets for the concert tonight. Maybe your husband would like to go." Shlomi took an envelope out of his pocket.

"Will you be there?" Amina asked.

"Perhaps," Shlomi answered, and hurried to leave.

Amina's Letter

July 15, 1969

Dear Mr. Shlomi Gal,

Or should I address you " also known as Mr. Al Sand," since I have little doubt you are one and the same person. This letter has been waiting more than a month to be sent. Not because I didn't know where to send it. The Bath Music Festival gave my husband the address of your management in New York, though George, my husband, opposed my writing you.

Dear Mr. Gal, on the day of your concert in Bath, which my husband and I enjoyed tremendously, Mr. Sand, an Israeli, called and said he brought me greetings from my old nanny. I was born in Palestine and though I left the country twenty-five years ago, talking to Mr. Sand opened a flood of nostalgic memories for things past.

Mr. Sand and I met that afternoon and as we bade good-bye, he gave me two tickets for your concert. My husband, a music lover, convinced me to go. The delightful Mozart overture with which the concert started made me feel at ease, although I'm not a music aficionado.

Imagine my shock when you appeared on stage. Maybe I screamed when I recognized you, but thankfully the thunder of applause with which you were greeted covered my outburst. I gripped my husband's arm. "It's him," I whispered in one breath, "it's the fellow I met this afternoon, the one who gave me the tickets."

"You must be mistaken," my husband whispered back. "At supper you didn't stop talking about him, Samira, your reminiscences. Now let's enjoy the concert."

People started shush-shushing around us. I had never heard the Mendelssohn concerto before, but as the music soared, I felt lifted into new realms. The slow movement, so human in its sadness, spoke directly to my heart, the heart of a childless sorrowful woman.

And your encore! The conductor announced that the piece, the J.S. Bach chorale "Jesu, Joy of Man's Desire," was your own transcription for violin and orchestral accompaniment. It so suited our stately Abbey and the audience's sentiments.

"Let's go to congratulate him," I urged my husband at the end, though I knew he was a shy person. But you were already gone! And to my disappointment I couldn't find out if you were who I thought." Forget it," my husband said. But I couldn't.

A week ago, I received a letter written in English by the manager of the old folk's home in Jaffa. Samira, whose eyes are failing, had begged her to write me a thank you note for the shawl I sent her.

Samira dictated also the following words: "Now I feel that I can die in peace. Allah in his great wisdom had granted my wish to see our young master. What I hoped for, with Allah's will, is going to be accomplished."

Who are you? Why do I continue to feel there is a connection between your call, the concert, and the latest letter from Samira? Please help resolve this riddle.

Your faithful admirer, Amina Gardner

P.S. I kept the program from your concert. I reread your bio and found another coincidence between Mr. Sand's and your upbringing. You were both raised by a German-born grandfather. It's hard to believe that it is just a coincidence.

5 2

January 1970

"I'm at the Tokyo airport. We'll take off in half an hour," Shlomi's hoarse voice startled D'vora.

"What happened?" she asked, turning on the light. "Do you realize that it's four in the morning in New York?" When he didn't answer, she continued. "Didn't you promise Otto that at the end of your tour you'd join him in Germany? He was so looking forward to being with you on his first visit back to the old country. You were the one who encouraged him to take this trip, Shlomi."

"I've already spoken with Otto. He understands. I'm tired, D'vora. One month in Japan, playing each day in another city, I feel exhausted. I wonder if I'm cut out for this life."

"My darling, D'vora's special recipe for chicken soup will heal you in less than twenty-four hours. Her soup and her love," she blew him kisses and hung up.

D'vora was worried, Shlomi, usually so joyous after returning from his tours, sounded tired. Maybe he had a cold. *Do the Japanese heat their houses in winter?* She knew so little about Japan.

At Kennedy airport a pale, frail Shlomi embraced her. "I'm looking forward to sleeping in my own bed," he said.

"Not before drinking a cup of hot tea and some chicken soup," D'vora answered, her maternal instinct awakened.

"I bought you the most beautiful kimono in Kyoto," Shlomi whispered as he was falling asleep. "Cherry blossoms embroidered on white silk. For the mistress of my heart, I told the seller."

D'vora tucked him in bed. Men are like children when they don't feel well, she mused, smiling, before unpacking his bags. *A month is a long time to travel without a woman at one's side.* The shirts and tuxedo had to go to the cleaners, but wait! *What was hidden under his music?* She saw an English-Arabic dictionary, another one, Hebrew-Arabic, and a book, "The Thousand Words Most Used in the Arab Language."

D'vora frowned. *Should I ask him what this means? To learn Arabic, what an idea! He never ceases to amaze me.*

Finally, there was the kimono, delicately wrapped in rice paper. With a childish delight, she held it against her body. She admired herself in the mirror. It's so beautiful, she sighed, as beautiful as a wedding dress. Suddenly Shlomi was standing behind her, "How would you like to get married in your kimono, mistress of my heart?"

They ended up in bed.

Much later D'vora said playfully, "I thought you'd be interested in learning Japanese or Chinese, what are you doing with Arabic dictionaries? Do you want to translate Omar Khayyam's poetry into Hebrew?"

"It's related to an encounter in Bath, a few months ago, when I performed there. Something I haven't told you yet," his playful mood disappeared.

"Should I be jealous?" D'vora asked, remembering the envelope she found. "You're making me curious."

"I met my father's sister, Amina, under a false identity. I can't explain why. But she's suspicious. Here..." and he took a letter from the inner pocket of his jacket. "I haven't answered yet." Shlomi took hold of D'vora's hands. "Read it and tell me what you'd do in my place?"

Shlomi watched D'vora as she read Amina's letter, her eyebrows united in a thin straight line. He could not guess her thoughts. When D'vora raised her eyes, they had an unusual gleam. "I'm trying to understand," she said. "You told me that you stopped in Israel to see Otto. Was there another reason you didn't tell me?"

Shlomi blushed like a child caught lying. "I asked Mazal to accompany me to the old folks' home where Samira lives. I didn't think it was important to tell you. Samira showed us letters she had received from Amina through the years, letters which of course I didn't understand. Mazal translated a few, but the fact that Amina lived in Bath aroused my curiosity because I was booked to perform there a few days later."

"And then you decided to play a little game, didn't you?" Shlomi heard the harshness in her voice.

"I didn't know what I wanted at that moment," Shlomi felt miserable under D'vora's cold stare. *She's judging me, not a good sign.*

"What do you feel now? I don't understand your doubts. You should've known that when you play with fire, somebody's going to get burned. It's hard for me to believe that the man I'm going to trust my life with, is an impostor."

"Please, D'vora," begged Shlomi.

"You played with your aunt's feelings. I'm sure it must be hard to resolve the misgivings of your heart, but you must try. Wake up, Shlomi. I can't decide for you."

"I didn't know what to expect. That's the reason I used a fictitious name. It wasn't exactly a game, though I suppose looking back, you are probably right. It was foolish of me. The Amina I discovered is a nice, warm-hearted person."

"But you still have doubts. What are the Arabic dictionaries for?"

Shlomi blushed, "I wanted to see if I can remember some words. Samira said that when I was three years old I spoke the language fairly well."

D'vora glanced at her watch. "My God, I'm already late. I forgot about our rehearsal. The management of Alice Tully Hall has engaged our quartet for four concerts, starting next month. We'll play quartets by contemporary American composers. I asked to perform music by women composers as well, and it was approved," she said with pride.

"Why didn't you tell me right away? You know how pleased I am to hear about your success."

"You were caught up in your own problems." As she reached the door, D'vora added, "By the way, my parents are arriving in March to hear our second concert."

She blew him a kiss. "See you tonight. Maybe you should see Dr. Singer. Remember, indecision can affect your playing," and she was gone.

Dr. Singer was a psychologist treating mostly musicians. D'vora had seen him several times and told Shlomi she found him helpful, but Shlomi was doubtful. He told D'vora at the time, "Nobody can do for you what you alone can do for yourself." *Was it true, or was he an arrogant jerk?*

Shlomi thought about D'vora's parents' impending visit. A quiet couple, they had lived all their lives in Binyamina, a sleepy town between Tel-Aviv and Haifa. D'vora used to joke that only the *ma'asef* stopped at Binyamina' station, never the express.

Her father was a shy optometrist, who blew into his eyeglasses and wiped them with a large handkerchief before saying something.

The vocal one was D'vora's mother, a kindergarten teacher, with an ample bosom which pressed hard on Shlomi every time she hugged him. She never called D'vora or Shlomi by their given names, for her they were always "the children."

Now D'vora's parents' arrival was going to disturb the rhythm of his life. *Oh, well, stop thinking, Shlomi. Take a shower and go buy flowers to celebrate D'vora's success tonight.*

"January is such a miserable month; my fingers are icicles," D'vora complained on her return. "It took me a long time to thaw them before touching the new Elliot Carter quartet, which by the way is a real killer." Shlomi placed her hands under his armpits to warm them up. Her face glowed, a sign that she had enjoyed the music-making.

"What else is on the program?" Shlomi asked, as he opened two bottles of beer.

"We are working on a big project. Some of the pieces we'll play next at the Ciompi Quartet's invitation."

"Super," Shlomi said. "Your quartet is going to create waves."

"I hope so, but today I couldn't stop thinking of you," she said. "It was difficult to concentrate on the music. I am sorry. I came on too strong this morning."

Shlomi took her in his arms. "I can never be upset with you. You are my conscience."

D'vora turned to face him. "I believe the world is moving ahead in quick steps. Less prejudice; no more gossip in the small provincial towns like the one I grew up in. I remember that our neighbors' son married the daughter of his father's orange grove Arab gatekeeper. At the time the townspeople pointed at them, shaking their heads."

"Why are you telling me this?"

"I think that what torments you is the decision whether or not to connect with your father."

Shlomi's mouth felt dry. He was amazed. *How well she could see into him, better than he could himself.*

"To build a relationship between a father and son who haven't seen each other for twenty years will take time and good will from both sides. It can't be done overnight." D'vora's tone changed, "I think I've bored you enough with my female instincts. Let's have dinner. I'm starved." She looked appreciatively at the table. "You bought a lot of goodies."

For the dinner of falafel, humus, pita, and Baba-Ganoush, Shlomi had added a vegetable salad cut very small, Israeli-style, the way D'vora liked it. He asked her in a casual tone, "How long will your parents stay?"

D'vora laughed, "That's what bothers you, isn't it? Don't worry. After my concert they are going to visit a cousin of my father's in Florida whom he hasn't seen in more than twenty years."

"You misunderstood me," Shlomi was hurt. "This morning you said that it's time for me to take responsibility for my actions, your perennial leitmotif. And that's what I want to do." He got up and stood behind her chair, stroking her hair and whispering in her ear, "I want us to get married. Isn't this proof that I am ready to take on a big responsibility? I think this is a good time, my love, especially during your parents' visit. Think how happy it will make them."

He put a finger on D'vora's lips to keep her from replying. "I know that you didn't allude to our getting married when you said I need to take responsibility for my acts."

D'vora awoke in the middle of the night. Shlomi's side of the bed was empty. The light on the living room desk was on. He was writing. She tiptoed behind his back and read the beginning of a letter.

Dear Mrs. Gardner,
You were right. I lied to you. Al Sand doesn't exist. At birth my name was Selim Ibn Musa Ibn Faud. I didn't dare tell you I am Suha's son. In 1948

after my mother's death, I was adopted. Only recently I learned who my father is. You are a lovely person. Forgive me.

Shlomi closed his eyes while D'vora left as quietly as she had come in.

He continued to write in Arabic, *Salaam Aleikum, aunt Amina,*

"Arnold Schonberg likes us," D'vora screamed as she unlocked the door. The morning after the quartet's concert, she stole away from bed to look for *The New York Times*. She threw the newspaper at him, "Read it!"

Shlomi wiped his sleepy eyes, **A Young Quartet Shows Potential.** "Nice headline," he said.

"Go ahead, read the whole review," D'vora urged him.

Good programming, pairing the Amy Beach quartet with Elliot Carter's. Shlomi's eyes ran through the review. **The quartet successfully included Benjamin Britten's Dover Beach for baritone and string quartet in their program. This is a young, promising group. We should watch it in the future.**

D'vora snatched the paper from his hand and started dancing with it.

"Schonberg doesn't say anything about the baritone eyeing you during the performance," Shlomi pointed out. "When all of you came on stage to take your final bow, he held his arm around your waist."

"Oh, my God, you are jealous!" D'vora exclaimed.

"I want to warn you about singers, for them life is opera, and opera is life, they don't distinguish between the two."

"Jealous. Shlomi's jealous. It's hard to believe."

"Why didn't he embrace the violist, that mousy girl who couldn't choose between music and math? When she plays she looks like a math teacher, her head bobbing up and down like a metronome."

"She's the nicest person and you are intolerable," D'vora slammed the door.

What's wrong with me? Shlomi had wanted only to warn D'vora that one good review doesn't guarantee that Schonberg will always give praise. One pianist didn't dare to appear in New York for ten years after one bad review from Schonberg, and he was an excellent pianist.

Maybe D'vora's parents' impending arrival, or the fact that five weeks had passed since he wrote Amina, without receiving an answer, made him so prickly.

The baritone annoyed him. He would have to appease D'vora soon, especially since she'd been so good to him. She even succeeded in subletting the apartment of a bassoonist living in their building, who was going on tour with "Fiddler on the Roof."

"My parents' visit will disturb neither our practice nor our life during their stay in New York," she said, "Just the opposite, my mother is going to spoil you and cook your favorite dishes. You'll be pampered, and I'll have a difficult time to wean you after they leave."

At that, Shlomi smiled. In his mind's eye he could already see D'vora's waist as well as his gaining a few inches from her mother's sauces and her habit of adding sour cream and sugar to the vegetable salads. Oh, well, what doesn't one do for *shalom bait*. Shlomi laughed to himself—he was already thinking like a married man.

As always, D'vora was right. He had nothing to fear from her parents' visit. He felt surrounded by love. At home after D'vora's quartet's second concert, Shlomi opened a bottle of champagne. "For D'vora's continued success, and to you," he toasted her parents, "I wish to always have *naches* from her."

"Amen," her parents said in one voice. "To have *naches* from you both!" and they raised their glasses.

"As we are here together, tonight, to celebrate D'vora's successful concert, I want to ask your consent for our marriage." Surprised, D'vora opened her mouth but Shlomi was quicker, "D'vora is the most important person in my life; we have known each other as teenagers, and have lived together for the last four years. Nothing would make me happier," Shlomi said, opening a small box, "than to put this ring on her finger, of course if you have no objection to her marrying me."

D'vora's mother had tears in her eyes. "My boy," she said, "now I can really call you my son." D'vora's father shook his hand. D'vora remained mute. She looked at the diamond circling her finger. "You never stop astonishing me," she whispered. Shlomi heard the reproach in her voice.

"*L'chaim*, for a good life together," wished D'vora's parents. "We hope that you plan to have the wedding in Israel."

Taking D'vora's arm, Shlomi said, "I think my sweetheart would want us to wait. Her career is on the rise, and I have obligations to fulfill."

D'vora echoed his words, "Shlomi is right." For the first time that evening, she kissed him and looked straight into his eyes, "I am happy to be your life partner."

"Children, children, don't be so formal with each other; you've been life partners for quite some time. As a matter of fact we thought, as we were getting older, that it's about time to enjoy a few grandchildren." D'vora smiled, embarrassed.

Shlomi paled. "We might not have children," he said. Three pairs of eyes focused on him. "I doubt you'd like to have one-quarter Arab grandchildren."

"What did you say?" D'vora's mother asked, alarmed.

"Shlomi, I don't believe you said that," D'vora whispered, her face red, "Why do you want to spoil an evening that started so beautifully?"

"Because your parents should know who fathered me." Shlomi said in a tortured voice.

The next morning, D'vora's parents left for Florida as planned. They called the same afternoon, "There's something we have left unfinished last evening," D'vora's father said, "We love you. Shlomi, we consider you our son and you'll always be. Last night we were all too excited, but this is what we wanted you to hear. You are our son, and if G-d blesses your and D'vora's house with children, you'll make us the happiest grandparents."

5 3

Shlomi was on his way home from a harrowing recording session of the Walton violin concerto, so tired he did not even stop at a take-out to shop for his dinner. D'vora was in Israel, summoned there at the last minute by her former cello teacher who had fallen ill, to replace him in a concert honoring Odeon Partos, the rector of the Tel-Aviv Music Conservatory.

"You can't refuse," Shlomi said when D'vora told him. "You've been his favorite student. And while in New York it is still winter, you'll bask in the Israeli April sun."

D'vora looked at him quizzically. "Is there an ulterior motive in your wanting to see me gone?"

"You'll benefit from it, while I'll be madly practicing for the Walton recording. I'd rather be in your place."

From the beginning Shlomi had not been enthusiastic about the recording, but he'd signed the contract and had to honor his commitment. He complained to D'vora, "This piece sounds like a rainy day in England, small drops on perfectly manicured lawns. No lightning, no thunder."

D'vora laughed, "It's his country's character. Stop searching for the romantic in every composer."

D'vora was right. Trying to emphasize a romantic line brought the first incident with the English conductor.

"No *rubato*. Please, Mr. Gal, respect what's written."

"What's written is a matter of interpretation," answered Shlomi. He was upset and became even more so during the next interruptions.

Ten hours, Shlomi muttered to himself, ten hours to record one movement! What a dog's life! He almost failed to notice that he was in front of his building. He checked his mail. Two letters, one from Otto in Germany. Aha, Shlomi thought, Otto got tired of waiting for me to travel with him.

But who is Rama? The second letter came from England; on the back of the envelope there was only one name, Rama, POB 4670 London, UK. He opened the door of his apartment and heard the telephone. He ran, but the rings stopped. Maybe it was D'vora. What time is it? Nine p.m. Her concert was tonight, but she wouldn't call at this hour, four a.m. in Israel.

He sat down, trying to catch his breath. He looked at the two letters in his hand. Rama… why did this name ring a bell? Three months after he wrote to Amina, he gave up hoping to receive a letter from her. Rama! When he opened the letter thin papers fell out along with the picture of a small boy holding the hand of a girl in a long embroidered dress. They were both smiling. On the back of the picture the names *Selim and Rama 1946*, were written in Arabic.

March 25, 1970

Dear Selim,

I am Rama, your father's younger sister. I can't describe my joy when my sister Amina called to tell me about your letter.

Oh, my dear Selim, my nephew. When Samira let me hold you a few minutes after your birth, I kissed your eyebrows, my heart trembling with happiness. Your mother, Suha, looked peaceful and more beautiful than ever. And Musa, my brother—no one was prouder than him. He opened the front door and invited every passer-by to come in and drink a glass of arrack in your honor.

I remember you started to sing even before you started to speak. Your mother taught you songs and it was lovely to hear the two of you singing together. I couldn't wait to come home from school and play with you. You were my favorite doll.

I am so excited, dear Selim Ibn Musa Ibn Faud, our youngest Masri. Amina told me that you have a great gift, that when people listen to you playing the violin they forget the vicissitudes of everyday life.

The phone rang. It took Shlomi a few seconds to hear it, engrossed as he was in the letter.

"Hello, this is the third time I've tried to reach you. The minute I leave home, you become a vagabond," D'vora said, but her voice sounded full of joy.

"How was the concert?"

"A triumph! I want to tell you that everybody already knows about our engagement."

"Well, it didn't take long for your parents to spread the—"

"Listen," D'vora interrupted him, "there is a good chance that Haifa Symphony will ask us to play the Brahms Double concerto next season. Wouldn't that be fabulous?"

"Indeed! I am just reading a letter. You couldn't guess from whom,"

"From Amina?"

"No, from Rama, her younger sister. Come home, my love. I am lost without you."

Suddenly, the contact was lost. Though he was tired and hungry, Shlomi couldn't put Rama's letter down.

Your father is away on business in the Arab Emirates and we have no way to reach him, but we barely can wait to tell him the great news.

I was the first to teach your mother Arabic, and proud of her progress. The dress I wore in the photo and the embroidery were made by your mother. She had hands of gold.

Dear nephew, I pinch myself to make sure it's you I'm writing to. Please come to London soon.

Your aunt who longs to meet you,

Rama

Shlomi read the letter twice. He tried to recognize himself in the plump little child. What a wonder to see himself as a child for the first time. In the mirror he compared the picture with his adult face. He gave up. Maybe D'vora would see a likeness. He smiled thinking of her excitement on the phone.

Before he went to sleep he put the picture next to the photo Chana had given him.

At breakfast the next morning, Shlomi opened Otto's letter.

Baden-Baden   March 23, 1970

My Dear Shlomi,

I am sorry I didn't consult with you before leaving for Germany, but when you know the reason you'll understand my haste. Our dear friend Heinrich Schultz, the cellist of our old trio, lives now in a musicians' retirement home in Baden-Baden. I started corresponding with him after he inquired about my whereabouts at the Israeli Philharmonic. I told you that Heinrich's brother was crucial to our escape from Nazi Germany.

Heinrich discovered that the Berlin radio station had acquired the tapes of our trio's concerts. Two of the three performers were needed to sign the release of the tapes. Imagine how much I am looking forward to hearing again my beautiful Gretchen's piano-playing. Her performance was so full of life. Meanwhile there is a lot of bureaucracy, as some of East Germany's radio stations continue to create problems and delays.

Heinrich and I cried reminiscing about old times, mostly talking about Gretchen. I always suspected that he was a little in love with her, but I couldn't hold it against him.

It's strange to walk on these same streets, see the same coffee houses, and smell the flowers, which continue to bloom every year from that blood-stained soil.

Grandpa Otto

How much he had loved her, Shlomi thought, shivering. Fifteen years had passed since Gretchen's death. Her last years were a source of suffering for everyone around her, but not for Otto. She remained forever his angel.

Otto's letter made him realize how much D'vora meant to him, how much livelier he felt when she was with him and how much he missed her.

Amina told him that Musa never considered remarrying. Although Rama wrote how proud his father was at his birth,

Shlomi wondered if Musa would not resent that his son was alive while the wife he loved so much was dead.

A glance at his watch reminded Shlomi that D'vora's plane was due shortly. At a nearby kiosk he bought flowers; then signaled a taxi, "To Kennedy airport, please."

It seemed to Shlomi that not a week, but a month, had passed since he saw her last. D'vora waved her arms while she called his name. A new light radiated from her. He noticed that people around them smiled when they embraced.

"Tonight calls for a celebration. I made reservations for Tavern on the Green."

Shlomi knew it was D'vora's favorite restaurant. She once said, "One of my pleasures living in New-York is to smell the fragrance of the pine trees and feel part of nature as we walk through Central Park."

When Shlomi ordered champagne that night, D'vora said. "You're spoiling me."

Shlomi took her hand and kissed it. "That's what I'd like to do for the rest of my life."

"It's good to be back, though I feel that when I'm here I miss Israel and when I am in Israel, I miss America."

"Now you are here with me. It's all that counts."

D'vora woke up in the middle of the night. Shlomi's head resting on her shoulder made her feel uncomfortable, but she didn't move. She looked at him, her lover and best friend. She thought of the conversation they'd had a few hours ago and how happy Rama's letter made him, He seemed distracted that Amina didn't share her news with his father. *Shlomi is so vulnerable*, D'vora thought. She knew how important it was for him to be accepted by her family, not only for himself, but for his parents, too.

He reminded her of school friends, children of Holocaust survivors, who for years felt ashamed that their parents had lacked the courage to fight the Nazis. Years passed before her friends made peace with their parents' past.

Poor Shlomi, though different, is burdened by a similar problem. D'vora's heart throbbed, "I love you for who you are," she whispered, "and I'll help you win over your demons."

May, 1970

"I just got a call from Marlboro," Shlomi said. D'vora stopped practicing, lifted her eyes toward him and waited. The echo of the cello sounds still reverberated in the room.

"Mr. Serkin invited me to participate in this summer's Festival."

D'vora rose and placed the cello in its case. "Doesn't it seem kind of late?" she asked. "I thought the programs had been established already."

"I didn't ask for details," Shlomi felt embarrassed. "I don't have to go, D'vora. Five weeks is a long time. I haven't answered yet."

"Sweetheart, this is an honor. It took me by surprise. My best memories date from the summer we spent there as students. Not only because of the music-making or the beauty of the nature," D'vora took his hands into hers, "but because our romance started there."

At Marlboro, an oasis of music nestled in the rolling hills of Vermont, they found paradise. Marlboro, a commune of musicians, well-known artists and young aspiring ones, were all united by the same desire, to make music of the highest quality at an unhurried pace.

"If you don't want me to, I won't go," Shlomi said.

"Just the opposite, as I said already, I was surprised. I think it will be good for you, and not only musically. You'll be able to rest. The Vermont air will bring back your color. Lately you look pale and tense." Shlomi's lips touched her hands.

"I have to go. I'll be late for our rehearsal," D'vora said brightly. "Don't worry about me. Giorgio Ciompi of the Ciompi Quartet, resident at Duke University, has invited us for a performance of the Mendelssohn Octet during their summer season. I'll ask to be scheduled while you are at Marlboro. Will this make you happier?"

"I don't know," Shlomi joked. "Those Italians scare me. They see a skirt and start to run after it. I hear Giorgio has a reputation of—"

"Oh, stop it," D'vora closed his mouth with a kiss. "You know you can trust me."

D'vora was right, he thought. He needed to relax. He was stressed and not only because of his heavy schedule. After he received Rama's letter, he had asked his London manager to find her phone number.

"Selim," she cried, after he identified himself. "My dear, I'm so happy to hear your voice."

"I want to thank you for your letter and picture. It was a nice surprise, especially since I haven't heard from Amina."

"Oh, she's going to write you. I long to see you, Selim, when are you coming to London?"

"Not in the near future, I'm afraid, but I'm working on it."

There was silence on the other end. "Rama," Shlomi hurried, "Did Amina tell my father, I mean, about my letter?"

"Amina is our oldest sister and the closest to Musa. In the past, anytime she mentioned Samira's letters in which she wrote she found you, he claimed that those were the fantasies of an old woman and asked Amina not to bother him anymore."

"I shouldn't have asked."

"Musa is a bitter man. But, trust us. Now everything is going to be different.

Bye, my dear."

"Another reason for you to have a vacation, to meet old friends and make new ones," D'vora said after Shlomi told her about the phone conversation with Rama. "At Marlboro there are no phones, no contacts with the world outside, complete relaxation."

He didn't tell her that he had asked to have his mail forwarded.

He drove the four hours from New York to Marlboro in a rented car. A few years earlier the two of them had car-pooled with other Juilliard students. A letter from Otto, from Germany, which the mailman had brought just as he was leaving, was tucked unopened in his pocket. I'll read it when I stop for gas, Shlomi thought. *Strange that he's still in Germany. He's been there three months already.*

Shlomi thought about his father. How childish it had been to think the two of them would meet, embrace and live happily ever after. Shlomi could not bring himself to blame Musa. Life had treated him harshly and no doubt he was protecting himself from other disappointments.

Shlomi didn't realize how fast he was driving until he saw himself facing the entrance to Marlboro. The yellowish poster, *Caution, Musicians at Play*, made him smile. After the first time they made love, D'vora said jokingly that at Marlboro there were more ways for musicians to be *at play*.

He received a room as Spartan as the one he had a few years before, no TV, no radio, and, of course, no telephone. He was told that an oboist expected to arrive the next day would share his room. Shlomi unpacked and was ready to practice, when he remembered Otto's letter.

July 30, 1970

My Dear Shlomi,

You probably wonder why I'm still in Germany. For years I have wanted but lacked the courage to search for what happened to our daughter Ruthie, after she was taken away. When our friend Heinrich, the cellist, showed me Ruthie's last picture playing flute with a youth orchestra, I wept. Heinrich let me cry.

He suggested I cut out Ruthie's picture and send it to Bildzeitung, with a caption asking that whoever recognizes her, or had seen this girl, to please call.

I was doubtful. What I knew was going to die with me, but Heinrich insisted. We placed the caption in other city newspapers, not only in Berlin. Then we waited.

Nothing happened. I was ready to leave Germany when a woman called. In a trembling voice, she said that she had seen this girl, who played flute in the camp prisoners' orchestra. She said her playing was so beautiful, sounds like tears dripping from the flute.

I asked her, which camp? What did you do there? Did you speak with her? What happened to Ruthie? I was losing my mind, my body was shaking. For almost thirty years I was hoping against hope to hear those words.

Heinrich took the receiver from me. Please could we meet with you, he asked. You'll receive compensation for your time.

Meine Herrn, she answered, I was this girl's age, but it was forbidden to get close to a prisoner, I would have lost my job, maybe my life. For years, I couldn't get her out of my mind. I waited two weeks before I decided to call you. Maybe now I can finally find peace.

I heard a click. She hung up. Heinrich wanted to call the phone company for her number. I didn't let him. We couldn't talk. This letter is mailed from the

*airport, before taking off. I am going back to Israel,
the only place I can call home.*

Grandpa Otto

Shlomi folded the letter and put it away. At long last Otto had
said good-bye to his daughter.

He picked up his violin and drew the bow across the strings. But
the violin wasn't responding the way he wanted. It had happened
at other times, when his mind was not quiet.

54

Bath, August 15, 1970

Dear Selim,

I started to write you a letter describing our family. I changed my mind thinking that you'd be more interested to learn about your mother's life in our midst.

In the spring of 1943 two months before I left home to join the British Army as a student nurse, something happened that changed the tranquil life of our house, and maybe all of us. Musa walked on the beach, and heard screams of, "A girl is drowning!" Without hesitation he threw himself into the sea. He saved and brought home a fragile girl with a faint heartbeat.

Who was she? Was she a runaway? We never found out. During her recovery Musa fell in love with the unknown girl. Suha, the Arabic name by which our mother called her, must have felt the same.

I was the one who discovered her talent for drawing and convinced my mother that Suha could replace me. Though pleased by Suha's work, my mother's eagle eyes had observed that Musa couldn't stay away from the beautiful blond girl with skin like fresh milk. She decided that Musa should leave for Jerusalem to learn the business of banking.

I was marching in a new direction also after George encouraged me to become a professional nurse. My mother's rage knew no bounds when I told her that I was going to marry George.

Musa, the only one I corresponded with, informed me about his marriage to Suha, another blow to my mother. I was delighted to read about your birth, Selim, our youngest Masri.

I didn't see my family again until 1948. Having no news from them I was desperate to get them out. George left for Palestine on an assignment, but mostly to find my family. He met Musa when he brought our sister Na'ima and her children to Jaffa after the catastrophe which befell her village, Deir yassin. There, another drama awaited, Musa's wife and son were missing.

"I have to find Selim" Musa said; he was going to search every house until he found you. Our mother reminded him of his responsibilities as the head of the family. She won at a terrible price!

And now there is a chance for Musa to meet you! Would it be possible for you to come to London in September? Musa will be there for the entire month. Rather than wait for him to visit me, Rama and Nur think that the three of us should meet him in London. Our ardent wish is for you to join us.

D'vora insisted on accompanying him to the airport. "You should have left the violin at home. It's insured, so you have nothing to worry about. Now it's only going to encumber you." Shlomi didn't answer.

"What do you expect to happen?" D'vora had asked him. He knew she worried for him. D'vora's recipe for important events was cautious optimism. "Don't get me wrong," she embraced him, "I wish I could be at your side, rather than go play the Schubert quintet in Puerto Rico."

"You agreed to play it," Shlomi held her tightly, "and it's going to advance your career tremendously. It's not every day that a young, still unknown cellist is asked to perform with the Schneider Quartet."

As the plane took off, Shlomi continued to see D'vora's smile and hear her whisper, "Be yourself—don't let anything change you."

"Would you like a pillow?" the flight attendant asked. It startled Shlomi. He didn't realize he had fallen asleep. He tossed and turned, but he could not sleep any longer. He read again the postscript in Amina's letter.

A few days before she died, my mother said that she never cared for Na'ima's boys. For the first time, I heard her crying and whispering, "Selim, Selim, my sweet grandson, where are you?"

Shlomi felt a chill. He, who couldn't remember his grandmother, had tears in his eyes. His throat was dry. He had to move about the cabin, stretch, drink a glass of water.

"Please, take your seats and fasten your seatbelts. We are descending toward Heathrow airport."

Shlomi felt tired. As he placed Amina's letter in the violin case, he read again Amina's last sentence, *Merciful God, I hope Selim will be the catalyst and help our family reunite. We need him as much or more than he needs us.*

London, September 5, 1970

A fine rain slid down the window as the plane made its way to the gate. Shlomi was glad that D'vora had forced him to take his raincoat. He made two phone calls before he left New York, one to Rama, to say that he would call her after his arrival, the second to Geoffrey, a former colleague from Juilliard, now assistant concertmaster at Covent Garden's orchestra and teacher at the Royal College of Music.

An exuberant Geoffrey offered to host Shlomi. "We'll play duets, as we did at Juilliard, old chap. I am kind of rusty and need you to make me work."

Though Shlomi told him that he had to take care of personal business, Geoffrey continued to insist. Shlomi promised to call from the airport.

When he took his small luggage from the overhead compartment, sheets of music fell out. To surprise Geoffrey, Shlomi had brought the Moszkowski duets, the most difficult pieces for two violins. *That will really make Geoffrey sweat!*

The big hall at Heathrow looked as gray as the sky outside. As he searched for a telephone booth, Shlomi saw three women holding a banner, WELCOME SELIM. Was this meant for him? At 7:35 in the morning, whoever they were, they must have been up since five o'clock.

Shlomi heard whispers, "That's him." He knew Amina; the tall lady; a younger copy of her was probably Nur, and the petite one running toward him, all smiles, was Rama.

"Salaam Aleikum," they greeted him,

"Aleikum Salaam," Shlomi answered, embarrassed. He didn't know whether to shake hands or to hug them.

Rama got hold of his hands, "I dreamed so much of this day," she said.

"I am your Aunt Nur," the tall one said. With her oval, luminous eyes, she was by far the prettiest. "You have to excuse Rama, she gets excited easily."

"Please," Rama said, taking Shlomi by the arm, "Selim must be tired from the long flight. He needs to rest."

I wish they wouldn't call me Selim. It makes me feel uncomfortable. Amina knows my name is Shlomi. She should have told the others.

"Selim, don't pay attention, the emotion makes them act like schoolgirls," Amina said. "We want you to have a nice visit. Everything is ready. Nur's car is waiting outside. She has offered to host both of us in her apartment near Green Park, a very quiet neighborhood. We invited your father for coffee tomorrow afternoon. He doesn't know yet that you are here."

Shlomi was overwhelmed by their solicitude—it was too much. How was he going to decline their offer without being rude?

"This is so unexpected," Shlomi said. "I'm touched that you came to meet me at the airport, but I have made arrangements to stay with a good friend, a violinist. I was just going to call him when I saw you."

The sisters exchanged glances.

"Please don't get me wrong," Shlomi said, "I didn't know about your plan, and it would be difficult to get out of my commitment." *I won't let them run my life.* "Be aware," D'vora had cautioned him, "women who seem protective can also be overpowering."

"Then when can we meet?" a disappointed Amina asked. "I know Rama and Nur would like to get to know you. It's important for us to talk, to be prepared for the meeting tomorrow."

"If I'm not mistaken that's the reason you are here," added Nur, coldly.

Rama came to his rescue, "Sisters, try to understand. We can't monopolize him. Selim," She squeezed Shlomi's hand, "I'm sure we'll have ample time to be together."

Shlomi smiled, "Any time, any place" he said.

"Call your friend," Nur commanded, "I'll drive you to his place. We'll decide later when to meet again."

What a whirlwind the last twenty-four hours had been, Shlomi thought, walking the short distance from Geoffrey's apartment to the Royal College of Music, where he had obtained permission to look over the manuscript of Elgar's violin concerto.

It was ten o'clock in the morning. At noon he was expected to have lunch with his aunts at Nur's apartment, four hours before Musa's visit. Shlomi smiled as he remembered that Amina, worried, had asked him if he would eat the Middle Eastern dishes they planned to serve.

"Humus, tahini, or baba-ganoush would be a real feast," Shlomi had answered.

"Oh, you are talking peasant food," said Rama, laughing. "A guest like you deserves the best, *kube* and *fattoush*, and, of course, baklava for desert."

Nur had dropped him in front of Geoffrey's apartment. Shlomi declined her offer to pick him up the next day. "I have an appointment at the archives of The Royal College of Music early in the morning. At noon sharp I'll ring your doorbell."

Geoffrey welcomed him with a hug and two bottles of cold beer. Shlomi barely had time to wash and change when Geoffrey said mysteriously, "I heard that Pollack has got his hands on an extraordinary bow. People say it plays by itself. Maybe you should try it."

Shlomi knew Pollack, the most famous violin dealer in London. Though he already had two bows, it was always exciting to try a new one.

"Afterward we'll play some music together," Geoffrey said. "And for the evening I'm taking you to my favorite pub."

Shlomi sighed. He had hoped for a quiet evening; to retire early to think about the next day's meeting, an encounter he wished for and feared at the same time…

"My apartment is on Maple Street, close to University College Hospital, where I work," Nur had told him.

As Shlomi mounted the exit steps of Euston Station, he faced an imposing mosque. He counted the minarets, knowing that the number of minarets indicates how rich or poor a mosque is. *This one seems to be well endowed.*

At noon he entered the elegant foyer at 254 Maple Street. The doorman followed him to the elevator. Arriving at Nur's floor, his nostrils were prickled by the smell of mid-eastern spice. He saw the apartment door set ajar.

"How did you guess that yellow roses are my favorite?" Nur asked as she buried her face in the bouquet.

Shlomi blinked to adjust his eyes to the heavy curtains, mahogany furniture, dark red upholstery and thick oriental carpets. A few hidden Moroccan lamps made it look like a place from "One Thousand and One Nights."

"You seem surprised," Rama laughed. "For the world outside, my sister Nur is as English as the natives, but at home she keeps our tradition."

Amina opened the door to the lighted dining room and Shlomi saw the feast awaiting them.

"This is what we think we'll do," after lunch, Amina said, as they sipped Turkish coffee served in beautifully hand-painted cups. "We want to make Musa feel at home, since we haven't seen him in quite some time. We don't want to startle him with the news that you are here."

"Assure him that our feelings toward him have not changed even though he hasn't participated in our lives lately," Nur said.

"There is an alcove, off the living room, which used to be Ahmed's room. Selim, please wait there. You can see and hear us," Amina said. "If everything goes as we hope, we'll call you. Is this agreeable with you?"

Three pairs of eyes watched Shlomi. Before he could answer, Rama said, "We are gathered here because we care for and love our brother—"

"And we love you, too," interrupted Amina.

"And we think it's time," Rama continued, "to make amends for the past, to forgive and...."

The doorbell rang. Silently, Nur signaled Shlomi to follow her, while, quickly, Rama took his cup and saucer to the kitchen and Amina stepped towards the door.

From his hiding place, Shlomi watched his father enter, a man about his own height, dressed in a dark three-piece suit, a raincoat on his arm. His sisters surrounded him, but as Amina bent to kiss his hand, Musa quickly lifted her head, hugged her and his younger sisters. Amina and Rama led him to an armchair.

They spoke Arabic, though Rama tried to throw in a few English words for Shlomi's benefit. Nur brought a fresh pot of coffee and a tray of pastries. "Turkish coffee, the way you like it piping hot and without sugar."

Musa laughed. He had taken off his jacket and Shlomi saw a white tailored shirt and an unobtrusive navy blue silk tie.

"It's good to be with you," Musa sighed. "The older I get, the more I feel the need to be with my family. My travels tire me, every few days in another city, each with its change of food and climate. I shouldn't complain, I make a good living and by not staying in one place, it helps me otherwise...." The phrase hung in the air.

Amina took his hands and spoke in a soft voice. Shlomi saw a cloud passing over Musa's face. Already accustomed to the dark, he could distinguish his father's features. Musa looked like Omar Sharif, tanned, dark eyes, the silvery hair at his temples giving him a distinguished look.

"Not Samira again," Shlomi heard his outburst. "That old rag finds Selim in every young man she sees. She's crazy. Don't tell me she was able to play detective in the Jewish country."

Musa got up and paced the room. "How many times I have told you to stop mentioning my foolish marriage and my son. I forbid you to talk about them. My past is dead," his voice cracked.

"Your wife is dead but your son is alive. We have the proof," Rama said, "Please calm down and listen to Amina."

Musa stopped pacing the room and stood in front of them.

"I don't understand why you want to open my wound again."

"Please sit down." Nur begged, "All we ask from you is to have a little patience and listen."

"You know how much we love you," added Rama.

The family conferred quietly. Suddenly Shlomi saw Musa jump up. "An impostor!" he said. "It was easy to fool Samira, but to fool you, too," he pointed an accusing finger at Amina.

"Everything I'm telling you is true."

"This individual must've heard of the Masri family's wealth. God only knows how much we left behind. Shrewd, as all Jews are, he could forge papers and demand an inheritance. Sisters," Musa said sarcastically, "your hearts are soft and innocent. You've seen too many romantic movies."

He took his coat.

"Stop," Shlomi opened the folds of the alcove's curtains. "I didn't know I was your son. When I found out I was devastated. My mother died in an accident when I was not yet four years old. Strangers, people who raised me, told me that my father was a hero of the War of Independence."

Shlomi, excited and fearful at the same time, felt his heart beat as strong as at the start of a concert. He faced Musa. "I am not an impostor. I don't want your money." He took off the chain hanging around his neck, and threw it toward his father.

"This should prove who I am." The sisters gathered around Musa who held two amulets in his hands.

"I remember," Rama screamed joyfully. "Suha wore them all the time!"

Musa fingered the *hamsa*. He couldn't take his eyes off it. "Probably stolen," he whispered.

"My adoptive grandfather gave them to me the first day I went to school. '*A mezuzah* and a *hamsa*, for good luck,' he said. 'They belonged to your mother.'"

Musa's face was cut in stone.

"I didn't want to meet you," Shlomi continued quietly. "I wrestled with myself. My future lay before my eyes; a clear-cut path. Long ago I stopped wondering who my parents were. Gone were the days when I dreamed about a father reading bedtime stories, taking me to soccer games or shooting baskets together. My adoptive grandfather, my violin teacher, was too tired, too old, and too worried about his wife's mental illness.

"Did my mother cuddle me when I had a bad dream or a cold? I never got a mother's kiss before going to or returning from school."

His throat was as dry as a piece of papyrus, but he could not stop. Words were hurtling out of his mouth as if they'd waited a lifetime to be heard.

"Only two years ago I heard that the stories I was told when I was a child were lies. The truth was that I had a Jewish mother who ran away from her orthodox home. And what about my father, I asked? Your father is Muslim."

"Enough," Musa screamed, as perspiration rolled down his cheeks. He rapped his fist on the table, "Enough."

"You don't believe me, do you?" Shlomi asked.

He opened his violin case and threw a photo on the table. "This is the only picture I have of my mother, at twelve years old. I received it not long ago, and I'm not even sure that this is she."

The three women stretched their necks to see.

"It's Suha," Rama whispered. "She wore similar clothes when Musa brought her to our home."

Amina and Nur nodded.

"Leave," Musa cried, pointing his finger to the door. He dropped to the nearest chair. "I can't take any more."

Pale, Shlomi closed the violin case.

Amina ran to him. "Please don't go. If you go now, everything is lost."

Shlomi didn't answer. He felt a lump in his throat. He kissed Amina's hand, and turned to the door.

"Wait," he heard a hoarse voice.

Shlomi stopped in his tracks. The figure who approached him wasn't the assured man he had seen entering Nur's home. With his shoulders drooping, his face ravaged, he extended his hand.

"If you are my son, or if you are not, you crossed an ocean to meet me. I owe both of us a chance to get to know each other better."

After he left Nur's apartment, Shlomi needed to call D'vora, the person closest to him. He wanted to tell her about meeting his father, and what had happened, but she was in Puerto Rico. What time was it there, same as in New York? Maybe she was just in the middle of a rehearsal or a concert. He called but there was no answer.

As in a slow-motion movie, his mind rekindled the entire afternoon, especially the scene after his father became a reality. Shlomi left, with the two of them deciding to meet the next day alone. Musa handed him his business card and asked Shlomi to call him in the morning.

Instantly, Shlomi responded with his own business card.

"Shlomi Gal," his father read. "Shlomi Gal," he repeated with a sarcastic smile. He turned to his sisters, "Does this sound Arabic to you?"

"It's a stage name," Amina said quickly. "It's what artists, movie stars do. They choose a name easy to remember."

"Sorry to disappoint you, but this is my name."

In the silence that followed his words Shlomi let himself out. *Am I going to call my father tomorrow? Maybe I should forget about it? Tomorrow's encounter could resemble two ships sliding toward one another, getting closer, but moving in different directions.* Musa said that Shlomi crossed an ocean to meet him. But the real ocean between them was an ocean of feelings and resentments, of memories and long years they did not share, different languages, cultures, religions.

No, he would not be a coward. He would call Musa. It might be possible, the thought warmed Shlomi's heart, that his father could leave aside for a moment his disappointment and hurt and share with him his memories of his young wife, memories their son was so eager to hear.

As other times when he thought about his mother his hand moved to touch his amulets. No amulets. Did he, in the emotion of those moments, forget them or did Musa surreptitiously take them?

He walked for hours, daydreaming. It was dark, and he found himself on streets he didn't recognize. From afar he heard the call of the muezzin. He looked for a taxi. None in sight. People streamed toward the mosque. What if somebody snatched his violin? With his heart in his mouth he ran until he saw the sign for the underground station. Only then did he start to breathe freely.

Musa could not fall asleep. The charms he set on a small pillow next to him brought memories he thought were buried long ago; embracing Suha and feeling the warmth of her body heat the amulets while his head was hidden between her two pigeon-size breasts, listening to her wild heartbeats. Earlier in the evening he made copies of the picture; she looked only a couple of years younger than the day he met her, the day his fate was sealed. Musa worked his camera and took a number of pictures, changing the exposure each time. He would return the amulets and the picture tomorrow.

Though Shlomi Gal said he'd call at nine in the morning, Musa was ready and waiting at eight. *Will he call?* Musa jumped when the telephone rang. After they exchanged salutations, Musa said, "I have a Greek friend who owns a luncheonette in the University district. Colleges are still on vacation so the place will be quiet. My friend would make sure nobody disturbs us." *Did I sound too anxious?*

Musa arrived early and sat at a table from which he could watch the door. His son entered at eleven o'clock sharp. Like Musa, Shlomi was casually dressed; slacks, an open shirt and a dark red sweater, similar to the one Musa had chosen for himself that morning. When Musa introduced Yanni, the Greek owner, Shlomi exclaimed, "Greek food is my favorite. I could eat spanakopita and tarama every day."

"A guest like you is what my heart desires," Yanni smiled happily.

In the ensuing silence, father and son watched one another, not knowing who would speak first. Yanni brought coffee. "It's strong, Mr. Gal," he said, "real Greek coffee, bitter, too."

"Yanni," Musa said, happy for the diversion, "my sister Amina told me that Mr. Gal is a well-known violinist."

"Would you play at my daughter's wedding, Mr. Gal? We Greeks love music!" Enthusiastically, Yanni raised his arms, snapped his fingers and started the first steps of a fiery Syrtaki.

"I'd do it with pleasure," Shlomi answered, "but I'm flying back to the United States tonight."

"So soon," Musa immediately regretted his rush of words.

"My fiancée is waiting for my return. Also, the concert season is about to start."

"This brings to mind a question I meant to ask you," Musa said. "How did you choose your profession? When did it occur to you that you had musical talent?" If the young man was indeed his son, he did not inherit this gift from him, Musa thought.

"It was chosen for me," Shlomi answered, "by my mother. She loved music. My adoptive grandfather said that she sang me lullabies long after I had fallen asleep."

Musa shuddered. Many times, coming home from the bank, he'd find Suha singing with her eyes closed, but she'd stop the instant she saw him. "What are you singing, my angel?" he would ask and close her mouth with a kiss. Blushing, she would answer, "Just old melodies."

After the baby was born, he heard her sing to him softly in a language he couldn't understand. He knew it wasn't Hebrew, because in dealing with his mother's associates he was able to understand a number of words, some quite close to Arabic.

Musa cleared his throat, "My wife sang songs in a foreign language. She said it was a song about almonds."

"I know the song. It is a famous Yiddish song, *Rojenkis mit mendlen*, raisins and almonds," Shlomi exclaimed. "My mother spoke Yiddish with Grandpa Otto, who never learned proper Hebrew."

Musa saw in the young man's eyes the blue azure of his mother's, eyes as clear as Jaffa's sky on a spring day. He wanted to ask more, but Yanni came with a great flourish holding up two steaming plates.

"Spanakopita for your pleasure," he announced with a booming voice, "and I added Yanni's famous Greek salad, which I make only for special guests."

"And what about your father?" asked Musa, "I mean," under Shlomi's inquisitive eyes he stumbled on the words, "Your mother surely remarried, didn't she?" He continued in the same breath without waiting for Shlomi to reply, "I imagine your last name, Gal, must be his name."

Musa saw a cloud passing over Shlomi's eyes. He didn't answer immediately.

"My mother died in a stupid accident in the fall of 1948. She never remarried."

Musa waited silently, while a storm was forming in his head.

"Her death was a shock. I was ill for a long time afterwards. For almost twenty years I was spared the details of her untimely death. Only two years ago I heard about it and I was told the truth about my father's family. My adoptive grandfather told me that my mother was on the way to the hospital where she worked as a nightshift nurse when she heard a man's voice calling 'Suha.' Grenades were falling around, but she, joyful and exalted, raised her head to see where the voice came from and didn't feel the bullet hitting her shoulder. She fell, unaware of the approaching car, whose lights were off because of the curfew. On her deathbed, barely able to speak, she told Otto what happened.

"Later, Mazal, one of Otto's neighbors found a letter among my mother's belongings. It was addressed to you. Here it is. I had never opened it."

Musa's shaking hands picked up the crumpled envelope. While he read, the quivering of the muscles on his face were enough for Shlomi, to know how he felt. When Musa raised his eyes, Shlomi saw in them an unusual glitter, "I wish I could bring back the past," Musa said. "I thought I created an environment in which she'd feel like a princess in an enchanted garden. I realized too late that I was mistaken not to share with her my worries or my plans for the future," he ended in a hoarse voice.

Without looking at Shlomi, Musa pushed the charms and the picture in his direction, "They're yours."

For the first time, Shlomi felt pity for the disturbed man sitting in front of him, his father. "I still didn't answer your question about my last name," he said, hoping to dispel the gloom. "Otto, my violin teacher, my grandfather, said it was my mother's idea. She loved the sea and she loved music. *Gal* means 'wave' in Hebrew. My mother said that the waves of the sea tell a story, they make music. Gal, she said, was a name befitting a musician; my mother had already chosen a stage name for me, at a time when I could barely hold a quarter-size violin in my hands."

"I want to hear you play," Musa said, suddenly animated. "I'm sorry that there wasn't music in my upbringing. I think it might be too late for me to understand it."

"Music is like poetry. You are not asked to understand it. Just let it speak to your senses. The love for beauty exists in all of us."

How enthusiastic young people are. "I'll catch up with you," Musa said. "I'll watch the papers, and I'll find a way to attend one of your concerts."

Shlomi smiled, "I'd be very pleased."

Later on, far from the current of emotions which passed between them during their meeting, Musa thought again of what divided them. *Would he ever be able to come to terms and accept that his son now belonged to the people who drove him and his family away from their native land?*

It was midday when Shlomi arrived home from Kennedy airport. He felt exhausted. The frequent concert tours had decreased his ability to fall asleep in an airplane; now, he was also reliving the emotions of meeting his father. A shower and a nap was all Shlomi wanted when he entered the apartment. D'vora's image floated before his closed eyes and he smiled. In less than eight hours, she would be back from Puerto Rico, and find a warm nest in his arms.

He woke up with a start. Glancing at the clock he realized that he slept six hours straight. Not a lot of time left. He went to pick-up Greek food and on the way home he bought blue irises, D'vora's favorite flowers. Fifteen minutes later, as Shlomi was setting the table, a flushed D'vora opened the door.

"So good to be back!" she exclaimed, while Shlomi helped her put away the cello before taking her into his arms.

"I missed you," they said in one voice, laughing.

"We were gone only four days, but it seemed longer." D'vora closed his mouth with a kiss.

"Aren't you hungry?" Shlomi said, eyeing the table. "Yesterday I had lunch with my father," he moved his tongue around the word, father, like tasting an unknown fruit. "in a Greek restaurant. The food was excellent. And now, here, for your pleasure," he mimicked Yanni's slapping fingers and dance, "you can delight in stuffed grape leaves and moussaka."

"Shlomi, stop it. I am not hungry for food. I am hungry to hear everything that happened in London—all the details." Her eyes sparkled with anticipation. "Start from the beginning."

"If you hope to hear that my father opened his arms and said, 'Come, my prodigal son, my long-awaited one, embrace your father and let bygones be bygones,' you will be disappointed."

"I am not a child and don't believe in fairy tales, but I thought—"

"Let's be realistic," Shlomi said, taking her in his arms. He saw a tear glitter in her eye. "As I told you on the phone, it was a first encounter, as touching for him, I suppose, as it was for me. Musa is not a person who wears his heart on his sleeve, though in one moment I saw him unable to mask his feelings."

"You talk only about him, as if you were in his place," D'vora said with impatience, "But what about you? How did you feel, what went through your mind?"

"I felt like a person who jumped into the sea without knowing how to swim. In the beginning, his lack of trust made me angry, and we both shouted at each other. He asked me to leave and I was ready to go. Then suddenly his attitude changed, and I saw a man overcome by doubts, but with maybe, also, a glimmer of hope." Shlomi paced the room, "After we met in the restaurant, he said he wanted to hear me play. I remember his words, 'I'll make sure to catch up with you.'"

D'vora hugged him, "I know that you did well by going, it was good for your peace of mind. The two of you are starting to walk on a new path together."

"Still a path full of rocks which might be hard to remove," said Shlomi.

"As long as you both want to clear this path, I emphasize *want*. To quote Herzl, "Where there is a will there is a way.""

"My D'vorale, the mind reader, can we finally have supper? I'm starved. Talking about rocks, the cold moussaka has probably become as hard as a rock now."

Shlomi went behind D'vora's chair and blew on the delicate hair on her nape, "Let's sip a little French liquor I bought at Heathrow, and have a ball. Say yes," he whispered in her ear. "

"Shlomi, please, can't you be serious for a minute?"

"Only one minute. I want to prove how much I missed you."

5 5

Israel

March 1972

D 'vora lay in bed, cradled by a feeling of unabashed happiness. The rays of sun intruded through the blinds and
played across her face. She smiled to herself. Everything
was going to be fine. She felt at peace. For an instant the noise of
her mother moving pots and pans in the kitchen interrupted her
thoughts. She didn't know what time it was, but she didn't care. In
Binyamina, in the little house surrounded by palm trees where she
grew up, she felt secure and loved. As her hand moved over the
empty space next to her, she felt the bed still warm from Shlomi's
body. *He must be running.* She stretched lazily.

March in Israel was one of the months blessed with perfect
weather. It was the beginning of spring, the renewal of nature, and
in a couple of days a new life waited for D'vora, the life of a married
woman. Hard to believe that for years she kept postponing it. She
never doubted that Shlomi was her *Basherte*, she knew it from
the moment she saw him again at Juilliard, but the institution of
marriage scared her.

The pregnancy changed everything. First the surprise, followed by the realization of the miracle happening to her body. She kept it a secret from Shlomi, but called her mother in Israel in the middle of the night with the news. After the emotion of the first minutes, her mother said with urgency, "It's time to get married. Don't worry. I will take care of everything. Oh, I can't wait to tell your father."

Shlomi's reaction, after asking her again and again if she was sure of it, was to buy all the books on pregnancy he could find and start reading with the same attention he devoted to his violin practice. He monitored her eating; out went the salty herrings and the wine she liked most. He bribed her to take long walks with him, "for the health of the baby." D'vora adored the novelty of being spoiled.

The long walks provided them with the opportunity to talk and rehash the events of the last eighteen months since Shlomi's father became a presence in their life. D'vora had met him when he attended one of Shlomi's concerts in Amsterdam. For two days they stayed in the same hotel and met for breakfast and again in the afternoons, after Shlomi's rehearsals with the Concertgebouw orchestra. D'vora was impressed by the concentration with which his father listened to the music.

"Growing up, classical music was not part of my education." Musa apologized. "At home my mother favored the ballads of Uhm Kultum, the famous Egyptian songstress. This new world of sound is fascinating. I hope it's not too late to learn what I missed as a youngster."

D'vora recognized the similarity between father and son, the willingness to take on new challenges. After the concert, Musa said, (did D'vora detect a whiff of nostalgia in it?) "I wish I had known that your mother loved music so much." He never called her Shifra or Suha, only "your mother."

"Musa is as cold as a fish," Shlomi complained.

"What do you want?" D'vora asked him. "You yourself said, after your return from London, that there are still barriers between the two of you. Give him time. Don't be impatient."

"He's already conquered you. I watched you falling prey to his European manners, his kissing your hand, his compliments. After twenty years of living in Europe, my Arab father knows how to please a woman."

D'vora laughed. "Don't tell me you are jealous of your father." Her face became serious. "I think he's behaving correctly. Look at how much time he spent with us."

"Correctly yes," Shlomi said bitterly. "He never calls me Shlomi or my son. He never mentions my mother's name, either."

"And you," D'vora answered him, "did you go out of your way to make him feel closer to you?"

D'vora's mother bustled into the room, with a filled breakfast tray. "Even pregnant women get out of bed when the sun is at its zenith. Shlomi has been gone for more than two hours. Where? God knows. The wedding is in two days, though both of you don't seem to care. Have you said since you arrived, *Ima, Aba*, can we help you? Not that God forbid we need your help. Everything is under control. You wanted a wedding in the Baron's vineyard, and that's fine with us. You asked for a reform Rabbi, we said O.K., though my parents must be turning in their graves. You were smart to bring your civil marriage license issued in New York. I wondered, how did you know that the Rabbanut would not recognize your marriage if officiated by a Reform Rabbi?

D'vora reached to embrace her. "You are the best of mothers. I have become a bit lazy since we arrived. Put me to work, tell me what to do."

"Be pretty," her mother had already forgotten her outburst. "Sit in the garden, where the sun will caress your face until it turns the golden color of our *sabras.*"

D'vora let the book fall on her knees. *Where could Shlomi be?* He was so mysterious lately. D'vora sighed. They had seen quite a bit of Musa, while D'vora was in London where her quartet performed a concert, and following that, when they visited with Amina and Rama. No one discussed politics, though D'vora was sure it was in everyone's mind. People couldn't escape reading or listening to the news of the guerilla war initiated by Egypt against Israel, about Fedayeen shelling kibbutzim during their almost daily border incursions and Israel's swift response to their attacks. Nasser's death in 1970 didn't calm things down.

Shlomi's aunts and his father seemed to retreat behind a screen, all of them polite but tense. D'vora wanted to ask if they had heard from their brother Ahmed, but was afraid to do so. *Did Ahmed belong to the PLO, attacking Israel from Lebanon?*

A few days after their arrival in Israel, both she and Shlomi stopped listening to the morning news. It was too depressing.

She knew that Shlomi had invited his father and aunts to the wedding. *But were they going to come?* Only Amina answered. A lovely letter filled with good wishes, but no confirmation. She wrote that George was busy with a new architectural project; it might be difficult for him to get away. "My sisters and I send you our good wishes. May you be blessed with a hundred sons; the old Arabic wish." The letter arrived a month ago. Since then, silence.

Where was Shlomi? Maybe I should call Otto, or Mazal. He always confides in her when he has a problem. D'vora closed her eyes. The sun felt so good, as if it was kissing her. But it was a real kiss, it was Shlomi.

"I have a surprise," he said, a new light in his eyes, "but you'll have to wait until tomorrow."

5 6

March 21, the day before the wedding. Walking early in the morning, Shlomi noticed the dewdrops on the flowers and trees on each side of the paths of Nahalat Yitzhak cemetery, where his mother had been buried more than twenty years ago. He felt his heart beat in his ears. How long had it been since he last visited her grave? He remembered how resentful he was when, as a child, Otto made him come along to "visit your mother" while Otto cried, a little farther away, prostrated on his wife's grave. For a long time Shlomi had been angry with his mother, who had left him, a child, to face the world alone.

For an entire week, since their arrival in Israel, he acted quickly, working on the plan he had made before leaving New York. He did not share with D'vora what he had in mind. Yet Shlomi couldn't totally keep his secret; he needed Mazal, who, at his call, agreed to help him. How otherwise could he find a stone carver and engraver, serious professionals, ready to deliver their work in the short time he needed?

On the old headstone, he saw the words he remembered:

SHIFRA GAL
MOTHER OF SHLOMI
PASSED AWAY ON DECEMBER 15, 1948
YOUR SON WILL ALWAYS REMEMBER YOU

That was all. No date of birth for her. Shlomi looked at his watch. The workers must arrive any moment now, he thought.

Last night he talked with his parents-in-law, while D'vora fell asleep in front of the TV. Since she became pregnant, she had these spells. "My need to sleep." she said, "is stronger than my will to stay awake."

Shlomi told them about the next day's event. "I don't know if this is a superstition, but I have heard that many Jews believe that if a person's parents are alive, this person is forbidden to enter a cemetery. I hope you won't object if D'vora, whom I love more than anything in the world, stands next to me tomorrow."

He continued, "Your daughter is smart and very sensitive. When I complained about my father's coldness, she said. 'What do you expect? What have _you_ done for him? Have you acknowledged him as your father? Does anybody know he is your father?"

The stone carver and his team showed up, carrying the new headstone, a simple black marble, the words engraved in gold, the way Shlomi specified. They worked in silence, only from time to time the stone carver gave guttural instructions. Shlomi mouthed the words on the new stone. He was satisfied. In his pockets he felt the candle, the matches and the little booklet.

Would they be finished in time? He became impatient. Shlomi caught the stone carver's glance and pointed to his watch. The stone carver made an assuring gesture. From afar he saw Mazal holding Otto's arm, both carrying flowers. Behind them Charlotte and her husband moved slowly to keep in step with Otto. More people were searching through graves, but too far away for Shlomi to recognize them.

When the workers left, Shlomi felt relieved.

He knew Amina intended to come, because she called Mazal for the address of the cemetery. *Was she alone?* He looked at his watch, ten minutes to eleven. *Why am I so nervous?*

Two women dressed in black who supported an old lady between them gave his heart a start. If he was not mistaken, they were Amina and Rama and between them, Samira. Yes, Jedati Samira, *his Morabia*, his old nurse, the nurse of his father and his aunts.

A large group was approaching including Chana, his mother's old friend. *Mazal must've called her. Who else was coming with her?* Protecting his eyes from the blinding sun, Shlomi saw his future in-laws, his bride walking in the middle.

He heard the whispers as they neared the grave. From a whisper, it grew, the way a sea wave swells closer to the shore. *What did they think? Were they surprised, upset, angry?* D'vora looked straight at him, a smile in her luminous gaze.

It was time to start. "We are here to honor the memory of my mother, Shifra. You read the headstone and probably wonder at the name Shifra Gal-Masri. My mother had been married to Musa Masri, my Palestinian father. This I was told only recently."

A sob interrupted Shlomi's speech. He raised his eyes and recognized Musa, who was standing back, behind everybody else, his eyes fixed on Shlomi, who went and gently pushed him forward. "I want to bring closure to two young people who loved each other very much, who were young, maybe too young, for the choices they had to make in critical times. It's not for me to judge them. As a sign of respect to both of them, I decided to change the words engraved on the old stone."

**HERE LIES SHIFRA GAL-MASRI, WHO DIED
ON DECEMBER 15, 1948
SHE WAS 20 YEARS OLD.
FOREVER MISSED BY HER HUSBAND, MUSA,
AND THEIR SON, SHLOMI.
AN ANGEL, MAY SHE REST IN PEACE IN THE
MIDST OF ANGELS.**

"I also want to tell those who knew my mother that it took more than twenty years for my father and me to find each other. I hope that the blood that runs through us will be stronger than our differences."

Shlomi lit the candle and carefully placed it in its niche. Nobody moved. It seemed to him that people even stopped breathing. Shlomi opened the booklet and started, "*El Maale Rachamim*, God full of compassion…"

To his surprise, Musa, his glasses on, took the booklet and in a wavering voice, uttered the next words, "*Shochen b'Meromim*, Dwelling in Heaven…." Together, they ended the ancient prayer for the dead. Musa shook Shlomi's hand, and after a slight hesitation, hugged him and held him as if he would never let him go. "Thank you," Musa whispered.

With tears in their eyes, people placed little stones on Shifra's grave, as is the custom for visitors. D'vora said, "I'm proud of you both. I am happy we'll all celebrate our wedding tomorrow—and Musa, promise me that you'll dance your wildest *Debka*."

Amina, Rama and Samira surrounded them. Samira was shaking, "Now I can die," she said. "Allah Ackbar granted my wish, to see you together. It was the dream which kept me alive the last twenty years."

D'vora embraced her. "You have to live for our little Shifra, who, in a few months will need you, a loving *morabia*, as every one of the Masri children had."

Over D'vora's and Samira's heads, Musa and Shlomi's eyes met. Shlomi hadn't told his father that D'vora was pregnant. He could read his father's thoughts now, his features reflecting the past and the present melting into one. Musa smiled at his son, the son who soon would become a father himself. It was the happy smile of a future grandfather.

Without words, yet with a song in his heart, Shlomi returned the smile.

LIST OF MAIN CHARACTERS

Shifra (Suha)
Chana: Shifra's friend
Fatima Masri: widow
Fatima's children: Musa, Amina & Na'ima - twins,
            Nur, Ahmed, Rama
Samira: The Masri's family housekeeper
Selim (Shlomi): Musa and Suha's child
Mahmood: Na'ima's husband
Abdullah: Fatima's cousin, banker
Uhm Zaide: a witch
George: English soldier wounded in the war, Amina's husband
Otto Schroder: Violin teacher, Holocaust survivor
Gretchen: Otto's wife, German pianist
Heinrich Schultz: German cellist
Schroders' neighbors in Tel-Aviv:
        Charlotte (Lotte) and Hugo Gruber
        Sigmund Hochmeister
        Bruno Herbst and Mazal (girlfriend)
Nabiha: Schroders' servant in Jaffa
Mr. Nathan: Watchmaker
Beatrice-D'vora Sonnenfeld: Shlomi's girlfriend

ACKNOWLEDGEMENTS

First and foremost I want to thank my husband, Avram, for believing in this book, for his dedication and continuous encouragement. I thank my daughter, Talya Kupin, and my son-in-law, Warren Kupin, for their thorough review of the manuscript. Thanks to my grandson, Aaron, who said, "You can do it, *Savta*," in response to my encouraging him during his piano lessons, "You can do it, Aaron."

Thanks to the people in my first writing group, Alice Levine, Joseph Weisberg, Joyce Cash, Howard Gleichenhaus, Martha Moffet, Judith Slater, Bilha Ron, who had been very attentive listeners and objective critics every step of the way.

My thanks go to Harry Haika who introduced me to Arab customs and helped with the Arabic translation; also to my friend Ruth Guttman Ben Zvi, Israeli music critic and historian for the information about the Palestine Philharmonic concerts during the Mandate.

I am grateful to my friends, Rabbi Bruce Warshal, his wife Lynne and to the poet and mentor, Janice Indeck for their enthusiasm and support.

Historical facts are authentic. All main characters in the story are fictional.

GLOSSARY

A: Arabic **G: German** **H: Hebrew** **Y: Yiddish**

Adon (H)	Mister
Al Kiddush Hashem (H)	For the Sanctification of God
Al Shahada (A)	Oath converting to Islam
Allah Ackbar (A)	Mighty God
Allah Harachaman (A)	Allah the compassionate
Arrack (A)	Arab alcoholic drink
Baladia (A)	City Hall
Bashert (Y)	Predestined
Beit kafe (H)	Coffee house
Beit Yaakov school (H)	Religious school for girls
Benti Al-Azeeza (A)	My dear daughter
Bubba meisses (Y)	Old wives' tales
Chaikhana (A)	Tea House
Chalas (A)	Out
Challah (H)	Braided Bread
Chametz (H)	Not kosher for Passover
Chasana (Y)	Wedding
Chussens (Y)	Grooms
Debka (A)	Arab patriotic dance
Dieselben blauen Augen (G)	The same blue eyes
Effendi (A)	Master

445

Epicorsim (Y)	Atheists
Eretz Israel (H)	The Land of Israel
Erev Shabbos (Y)	Shabbat eve
Etzel (H)	Right wing Jewish military organization during the British mandate
Eumi (A)	Mother
Fatma (A)	Destiny
Fedayeen (A)	Palestinian militant groups fighting Israel
Garin (H)	A young group settling in or creating a kibbutz
G'veret (H)	Lady
Hada (A)	Dear
Hamsin (A)	Hot dry wind
Hashem (Y)	G-d
Hashomer Hatzair (H)	Socialist Zionist youth movement during the British mandate
Heder (Y)	Religious kindergarten for boys
Hevra (H)	Friends
Hijab (A)	Traditional women headdress
Hob Rachmoones (Y)	Have pity!
Ialda (H)	Girl
Ibni (A)	My son
Idul Fitri (A)	The feast of breaking the Ramadan fast
Iftar (A)	The evening meal, the daily meal during Ramadan fast
Ima, Aba (H)	Mother, Father
Imam (A)	Prayer leader of a mosque
Inshallah (A)	God willing
Is nicht war? (G)	Isn't that so?
Jedatha (A)	Your grandmother

Jedati (A)	My grandmother
Jedi (A)	My grandfather
Jelebia (A)	Traditional woman's dress
Jugend Gruppe Kommandant (G)	Youth group commander
Kafia (A)	Man's head dress
Khan (A)	Hostel
Kipa (H)	Yarmulke
Klezmer (Y)	Popular musician
Kol Nidrei (H)	Holiest Prayer on the Eve of Yom Kippur
Kol Zion Halochemet (H)	Jewish Radio Station during the British Mandate
Koran (A)	Muslims' Holy Book
Kova tembel (H)	Pioneers' hat - (slang)
Lehi (H)	Freedom Fighters (the Stern Gang)
Leikeh (Y)	Cake
Ma'asef (H)	Local Bus
Mamzer (H)	Bastard
Mavrook Wa-barak Allah Fecum (A)	Congratulations and God Blessings
Mehitze (Y)	Division between men and women in orthodox synagogues
Meine Hern (G)	Gentlemen!
Mezuzah (H)	Encased prayer on door posts
Mikve (H)	Ritual bath
Mischling (G)	Crossbreed
Mitzvah (H)	Good deed
Morabia (A)	Nursemaid
Mukhtar (A)	Mayor
Mutter (G)	Mother
Naches (Y)	Satisfaction
Nackba (A)	Disaster

Nargilea (A)	Smoking water pipe
Neft (H)	Kerosene
Nishtvisendick (Y)	Making the impression of not being aware
Oud (A)	Bazooka
Palmach (H)	The elite fighting force of the Haganah, the Jewish Paramilitary during the British Mandate
Prosit (G)	Here is to you, cheers!
Rabbanut (H)	The Organization of Rabbis
Sabras (H)	Israeli-born children
Salaam Aleikum (A)	Peace be with you
Sayyid (A)	Mister
Shaitels (Y)	Wigs
Shalom Bait (H)	Peace at Home
Sharbat (A)	Sorbet
Sheinele (Y)	Pretty one
Shesh-besh (A)	Backgammon
Shiva (H)	Mourning
Shmurot Hateva (H)	Nature Reserves
Shmus (Y)	Gossip
Shtetl (Y)	Small town
Shukran (A)	Thank you
Shul (Y)	Temple
Simchas (Y)	Joyous events
Sit, Sitat (A)	Lady, Ladies
Souk *(A)*	Market
Tanur (H)	Stove
Thobe (A)	Ceremonial wedding dress
Tzitzis (Y)	Fringed garment worn by orthodox Jews
Yahud (A)	Jewish man

Yahudia (A)	Jewish woman
Yekim (H)	German Jews – nickname given by Israelis
Yetzer hara (H)	Evil instinct